P9-AFF-005

FACE BLIND

Also by

LANCE HAWVERMALE

The Discretionist

The Tongue Merchant

FACE BLIND

LANCE HAWVERMALE

Minotaur Books

A Thomas Dunne Book
New York

This is a work of fiction. All of the characters, organizations, and events portrayed in this novel are either products of the author's imagination or are used fictitiously.

A THOMAS DUNNE BOOK FOR MINOTAUR BOOKS.
An imprint of St. Martin's Publishing Group.

www.thomasdunnebooks.com
www.minotaurbooks.com

Library of Congress Cataloging-in-Publication Data

Names: Hawvermale, Lance, 1972– author.
Title: Face blind : a mystery / Lance Hawvermale.
Description: First edition. | New York : Minotaur Books, 2016. | "A Thomas Dunne book."
Identifiers: LCCN 2016001432| ISBN 9781250078339 (hardcover) | ISBN 9781466890572 (ebook)
Subjects: LCSH: Serial murder investigation—Fiction. | Interpersonal relations—Fiction. | Face perception—Fiction. | BISAC: FICTION / Suspense. | GSAFD: Suspense fiction. | Mystery fiction.
Classification: LCC PS3615.R585 F33 2016 | DDC 813/.6—dc23
LC record available at http://lccn.loc.gov/2016001432

First Edition: August 2016

10 9 8 7 6 5 4 3 2 1

To Mom. Go, fight, win.

ACKNOWLEDGMENTS

Thank you to Jonah Straus for taking a chance on this story, to Rob Mason for proofreading it, and to Jennifer Letwack and her editing team for making it shine.

CHAPTER ONE

No rain has fallen here in four hundred years.

Gabe knew this was true, knew it even though he stood on a stretch of ground where knowing anything for certain was iffy. The desert did that to you, especially this one, where there were no Gila monsters, no cacti, no Arabs gliding majestically on camels. You couldn't be sure about anything in a place that hated you. It fooled you every time.

Gabriel Traylin stared across the nighttime desert, smoking his way to some future, ghastly cancer and thinking about the improbable dryness around him. Four hundred years, not a single teardrop from the sky. The Atacama Desert of northern Chile made the Mojave of his homeland seem like a floodplain. Precipitation here was measured in millimeters, and even then it came only as an infrequent fog. The billion crystal stars overhead were no more mysterious than this desolation, this empty skull of earth. What happened here happened nowhere else: the complete and bleak denial of all life.

"Like a few women I've known," he said to himself, only half meaning it. Always the comedian, even when he was alone. He should've done stand-up at eighteen instead of Stanford. After all, there wasn't much difference in being a penniless comic and being a doctoral candidate free-falling through student loans. He knelt and crushed the remains of his cigarette on a stone that had never known the slickness of dew.

Behind him loomed the observatory, as huge and silent as a ghost ship.

The astronomers from the European Union had constructed the facility in 2008. The planet's arid edge provided their twenty-meter telescope a view of the heavens utterly unobstructed by even the thinnest ribbon of cloud. No radio waves muddied the sky. Few planes ever passed. Though the Atacama might be inimical to life, when you were talking about peering at ancient starlight, it was the most coveted seat in the house. Gabe was as bad as the rest of them, arrogant in their mapping of galaxies too damn far away to matter. At twenty-nine, he was also the youngest, which somehow bought him pardon for his sin.

The vainglory of Galileo, Rubat called it.

Oh, that Rubat. Spoke like a poet but had a panhandler's sense of hygiene. He'd promised to give Gabe a lift into town—Gabe was running low on comic books and smokes—but odds were strong that he'd forgotten. Gabe was just about to return to the observatory and track the man down when something flickered in the dark.

A hundred meters away in the wasteland, only vaguely revealed in the shower of starlight, something moved.

Not simply moved, but *glided.*

Gabe stood up, the cigarette butt between his fingers.

The figure traveled east to west, smoothly, with the fluid dexterity of a prowling cat or a gymnast. Of course, no mountain lions dwelled here, for there was nothing to hunt. And as for gymnasts or any other member of the human race . . . as far as Gabe knew, no one lived out there but the ghosts the Chilean natives claimed to see occasionally, spirits of the dehydrated dead.

So what is it?

He stepped away from the bulk of the observatory and advanced a dozen paces into the dust. Because there were no exterior lights that might interrupt the astronomers' work, Gabe knew he would be invisible to whoever was out there, so long as he held still. The chill in the air pricked at his arms, as he hadn't bothered to grab his denim jacket before stepping out for his smoke. The Atacama might be a desert, but it lay in the rain shadow of the secret-keeping Andes Mountains—the lee side, where the air was drained of all moisture by the mountaintops. At several thousand feet above sea level, the Atacama was not a sea of broiling Sahara sand but a bitter vacuum that scarred the planet like an acid burn.

Ignoring the cold, Gabe tracked the moving thing with his eyes, now certain this was no illusion, no phantasm cut from the black paper of night. It swept steadily but not swiftly, little more than a dark shape on a darker background and thus all but indistinguishable. It could have been anything. Or any*one.*

Stop.

Gabe heeded his own command. What the hell was he doing? In the six months he'd been stationed down here, stumbling along the tripwired road of his doctoral research, he had never once seen anything out there in the barrens. He knew what Rubat would say. The gliding figure was an outlaw of some kind, a Chilean thief out to swipe a few liters of gasoline from the observatory's garage. Rubat refused to trust the natives. He was a prejudiced Yemenese astrophysicist who assumed the locals would one day come for the foreign star-watchers, bearing torches and handmade rakes.

Gabe liked the curmudgeonly Muslim, even though—strangely—he'd never seen his face.

But there was no time to think about that now. The thing out there in the night cruised steadily west. Gabe had never considered himself exceptionally brave, and this was no time to win the Bronze Star. He wasn't about to go out there and tangle with whoever that might be—though he also had no intention of letting him break into the garage and make off with the gas. Without working vehicles, they'd be forced to call for an airlift, because walking in this waterless world was tantamount to traipsing to the gallows.

Whatever it was, it rippled like oil on dark water.

"Who are you?" Gabe spoke softly, the words barely leaving his lips. Hugging the building, he kept his eyes on the figure and moved with it. By now he was almost certain it was a man, though a man who moved without sound. The land was as quiet as outer space, and Gabe should have heard the interloper's footfalls. Yet there was nothing but the increasing rhythm of his own pulse.

Could be Bigfoot's cousin.

Gabe raised an eyebrow at this rogue notion. Last weekend one of the locals had told him the story of Gigante de Atacama, a giant who supposedly roamed this lifeless land. Just like Sasquatch of the American Northwest, Gigante was always a blur when captured on film.

A blur not unlike the one that moved tonight through the dark.

There were two reasons why he'd chosen astronomy as a profession. The first one was the chance for solitude; he'd never been gregarious, which he blamed on his condition. The second reason was because he loved the idea of Things being out there. Things not found on Earth. Things that built the universe.

Or, likewise, Things that roamed the desert night.

Shit. He had to go and he knew it.

Safe in the knowledge that the darkness would conceal him, Gabe paralleled the runner's course. A few seconds later it became apparent that Gigante wasn't headed for the garage but rather toward the power shed.

The pair of burly 500-kilowatt generators was the observatory's fail-safe. Those diesel-driven behemoths, resting on industrial-grade vibration isolators and weighing over eight thousand pounds each, provided the facility with full and uninterrupted power in the event of an outage, ensuring that the computer servers kept crunching data without a single binary morsel of the company's investment being lost. As nearly everything inside the observatory was computerized, right down to the shower cubicles, electricity was their patron saint, hallowed be thy name. Sabotaging the generators would—

"Why?" Gabe whispered. "Why would anyone care?"

He had no answer for that. Terrorists didn't need a reason. Or maybe that man running so smoothly through the night was not a terrorist but an anarchist. Or an eco-terrorist. Or a religious fundamentalist. Or some other kind of pissed-off *ist.* The list of suspects in the modern world was endless and probably known only to the CIA and certain staff members at the *National Enquirer.*

The figure kept moving. Gabe gave chase.

They closed in on the power shed.

The generators were housed in a corrugated steel outbuilding on a concrete foundation that had been poured by local workers but funded by Swiss taxpayers. Though the Quest-South Observatory was a public project jointly governed by twelve different European governments, it was no secret that the Geneva-based aerospace corp, Zubriggen Global, was the leading commercial financier. Gabe had never met anyone from the famously neutral Switzerland, but he figured they wouldn't be so impartial when it came to punishing those who threatened the operation of their South American Taj Mahal.

He considered turning tail and fetching reinforcements. What if the guy had a weapon?

Forget it. There wasn't a single warrior among the observatory's inhabitants who could lend any decent assistance. In fact, they all dwelled at the opposite end of the dial, pushing the needle toward maximum geekdom. Gabe himself was as close as they came to being cool, and that was only because he knew his Chuck Palahniuk as well as his Roger Penrose and didn't look like a total wannabe when wearing a leather jacket. Then again, he knew that the hallmark of the true geek was self-delusion.

He kept going. His footfalls sounded too loud to his own ears. He only hoped the intruder was so intent upon his task that he wouldn't hear his pursuer. Gabe named him the Midnight Messenger, like the name of a comic-book character, and then suddenly the Messenger wasn't running anymore, but slowed down as he approached the power shed.

Gabe was close enough now that he was certain this was not Gigante but rather a man, one who was lean and not exceptionally tall. His features were nothing but brushstrokes of shadow.

Where had he come from? He'd run from the direction of the desert's heart. As far as Gabe knew, there was nothing out there but ghost towns that had supported the nitrate mines before the tunnels were abandoned years ago. The mines were now closed up, the towns empty husks, like places in an old Western film, where doors banged in the wind and a slight weight of menace hung in the air. No one had lived out there since the forties, when synthetic nitrate squeezed out the last small demand for the natural stuff. Nothing remained of the old saltpeter families but their rubbed-out towns and cemeteries.

The Messenger slipped around the shed's corner and vanished.

Clinging to the hope that the night would conceal him if he kept low, Gabe advanced around the opposite side of the building, keeping about five meters from the metal wall. No overhead lines ran from the shed to the observatory; the cables were buried. The shed hummed faintly. Inside was a million euros' worth of hardware. Though the control mechanisms were in a secure room down the hall from Rubat's quarters, anyone inside the shed, standing between the generators and a full megawatt of juice, could shipwreck the project for weeks.

Gabe slowed as he neared the structure's far edge. He sank to his knees, then lower still.

He waited.

The stars roared silently. Their lion's call was a hundred million years old, and far older. Gabe knew the names of many of them. He was rotten with people and had perhaps only two real friends, but he was a blood brother with every silver light in the night sky. He lived for those moments when they spoke to him. And he always spoke back.

The darkness shifted.

The Messenger appeared from around the far corner, and then did something that made him entirely human.

He bent over, put his hands on his knees, and tried to catch his breath.

Why are you running? Gabe, who had theories for everything from the nature of God to quantum foam to the man on the grassy knoll, had no theories for this. There was simply no reason why a lone man would be running across the most desolate place on Earth in the middle of the night.

Just as the Messenger was straightening his back, something struck him in the head.

Gabe flinched.

The man's skull snapped sharply to the side. Though Gabe could see him only in silhouette, it was clear that the motion was unnatural. A second later, there was a sound as faint as a sigh, and then the Midnight Messenger collapsed.

Gabe turned, half expecting to see Gigante with a fistful of rocks, but there was nothing but the hovering dark.

When he looked back, biting down on his lip, the erstwhile runner was only a heap on the ground.

Gabe held his breath. Then he exhaled softly and waited. The figure remained crumpled and motionless. Though something had clearly hit the man in the head, the hand behind the projectile was nowhere to be seen. Considering how dark it was, the desert might have been full of assassins, and Gabe would never have known.

Assassins?

Get real, Lucille.

Still the Messenger didn't move. He might have been—

"Don't be dead," Gabe whispered. "Jesus, don't be dead." He wanted to turn around but instead got himself moving toward the prone figure. He advanced slowly, heartbeat wild in his wrists. His life was uneventful. He studied spectrometry readings and watched the Syfy Channel like a proper nerd. He rarely drank to excess. He'd been laid only once in his life. Her body had been as divine as that of a Vargas girl, and Gabe had stitched the memory of it forever in his mind, though he could not say the same for her face, which had made no impression on him. All in all, that wasn't the math of a life that added up to this kind of business, this pawing on all fours across a desert in Chile at one in the morning toward a stranger who was possibly dead.

Forget possibly. Gabe got close and saw the blood.

At this proximity, the rods in his eyes received just enough light to reveal the dark halo on the ground around the man's head.

Had there been any decent light, Gabe knew, he'd see that the man's body had become a desert shade. The Atacama was said to have such power. It transformed drifters into itself; it sapped the moisture from you; it turned you into a mummy.

The Midnight Messenger had died in a sweat. The odor of unwashed skin hung in the air. The man's pants were shapeless in the dark, but his shirt revealed a few dimensions: long sleeves, buttoned at the collar, formerly white. One of his wrists was clunky. Gabe leaned down and decided it was a watch, one of the big, rambunctious chronographs favored by sportsmen. Now that he had a better angle, Gabe saw the dial, the tritium hands glowing at the time of one minute past the man's death, and counting.

Not just dead, but murdered.

Expecting an attack, Gabe spun around. His eyes swept back and forth, but the night gave up no secrets.

Had the killer run away? Or was he still out there? And how the hell had he been able to see at such a distance in this thunderous dark?

Sweating despite the cold, Gabe returned his attention to the fallen runner. Maybe it wasn't too late. He found the man's wrist and clasped it too tightly to feel a pulse. He took a breath, forced it out, released some pressure, prayed for a pulse.

He felt nothing . . . or perhaps he did. Was that his own heartbeat in his fingertips, or was this man still alive?

His eyes, for no reason at all, went to the man's face.

You'd think by now he would've stopped trying. But no. Here he was again, scanning the facial features—nose, mouth, eyes and ears creating the usual symmetry—but coming up with only a meaningless haze.

Ever since he could remember, Gabe had been face blind.

The term the neurologists used was *prosopagnosia*—the inability to differentiate between faces. Gabe had grown up recognizing his mother by her clothing, her slender wedding band, and of course by her voice. But her face had appeared no different from that of his father, nor of his uncle, nor of Dan Rather when he'd read the nightly news. Friends encountered at random around town were strangers until they spoke. He could meet a man a dozen times and still not know him at the thirteenth handshake, unless his suit was cut a certain way, or his lip was pierced: Some damn thing had to stand out, or every face was literally and utterly the same. It wasn't that faces appeared as a blur. Gabe could see every detail. But a developmental aberrancy in his brain made it impossible to compare those details to other faces. He recognized his own face in a mirror only because he knew he was standing in front of it. But show him a photo of himself and a headshot of Ernest Borgnine, and Gabe's odds of pointing to himself on the first try were heads or tails.

He told hardly anyone about it because nobody ever believed it. Besides, he'd learned to compensate like a son of a bitch.

Little good that did him now. The Messenger could have been his brother and he wouldn't have been able to tell without checking for Ronny's birthmark on his inner elbow.

Who are you? he wondered. It was his most repetitive thought, sounded every time someone met his gaze.

Who are you?

Face blindness aside, what Gabe had here was a shitstorm of trouble. He ran both hands through his hair, trying not to freak out but feeling his body tilt that direction. Where was the rock? For some reason he had to find the missile that had done this, evidence that Gigante was truly out there, picking people off.

There was no rock.

Damn. If there was no rock, then that meant—

Gabe closed his eyes.

The Midnight Messenger had been shot. And because Gabe hadn't heard the whipcrack report of gunfire, it implied that the weapon had been outfitted with a sound suppressor.

A silencer.

Gabe bolted to his feet, aimed himself at the lightless observatory, and hurtled toward it. He would never recognize his mother's face, but he knew her laugh and gentle touch, and he recalled with sudden clarity how she'd whispered *Love you, Peekaboo* the day he'd left for Chile. He was still a kid, really, and had no business being down here, having grown up in the shelter of his room, away from the accidental social encounters that might cause his condition to bring him grief. Gabe thought of her as he ran, wondering how far he'd get before the next whispered gunshot sent him down, to slake the Atacama's endless thirst with his blood.

CHAPTER TWO

He made it.

No bullet carved the night and found him. No brother of Bigfoot hurled a rock with the force of a medieval catapult.

Gabe threw himself through the door and ran down the corridor, the darkness parted by red lamps that would not disrupt the night vision of those who worked here. The tiles squeaked beneath his shoes.

He passed offices, the rec room with its foosball table, the lounge with its TV that usually played those maddening British sitcoms or equally excruciating soccer matches. Gabe was nobody's patriot, but he always sided with the U.S. when it came to proper football. He turned right and found the two oldest men in the facility bent over a bank of computers with multiple monitors. On those screens, analogs of the universe turned and spiraled and flowed in the language of math. He could identify neither of them, but he shouted anyway.

"Rubat!"

He frightened them. Montero jolted and barely kept his coffee mug from toppling to the floor. Gabe knew it was Dr. Montero because he always wore house slippers inside the observatory. But his face looked absolutely no different from that of the man beside him.

The other man hissed an Arabic curse, which meant it had to be Rubat.

"Call the police," Gabe said, his lungs like sentient things, greedy for air.

Rubat yanked the glasses from his featureless face. "Police? What is this you say?"

"Someone's been shot."

Montero made the sign of the cross.

"Out there." Gabe pointed. "At the power shed. He's down, bleeding. I think he's dead, but I'm not sure."

"Who?"

"I don't know, just call the goddamn cops!"

And he was off again. He'd never been a runner. He was already short of breath, which was pitiful, really, because he was lean and young, and you never knew the night in your life when a nail would go missing and it would be up to you to keep the kingdom intact. For want of a treadmill, the astronomer was lost.

He flew into the night.

The openness struck him again, as it always did. You had a sense out here that Columbus was wrong. Go too far into the desert and you'd find that place where it snapped off and left you with nothing but deep space, where distance was reckoned by how long it took for light to get there.

A dozen suns suddenly burned behind him. Rubat and the staff were throwing switches inside, causing the powerful spots to flash to life. In moments the ground was illuminated as brightly as a prison yard, exposing Gabe as well as his destination.

Something was wrong.

Was he so unnerved by the event that he'd forgotten where the man had gone down? Had the stranger fallen on the other side of the shed?

Gabe circled the metal building, which was now fully revealed in the powerful klieg lights mounted on poles around the observatory's perimeter.

He saw nothing.

He stopped. Panted. Turned a complete circle.

No body lay on the ground, dead or otherwise. The Midnight Messenger was gone.

.

The cops down here used yellow tape, just like those in the States.

Gabe sat on the base of the Kepler statue, coffee between his hands. The uniformed officers, the Carabineros de Chile, had set up a cordon despite the fact there wasn't a body to protect.

Evidence, Gabe thought, remembering his television crime shows. *They're preserving possible evidence against contamination.*

They'd come by helicopter from Calama, the nearest major city. They were nuts about safeguarding foreigners. When they spoke to Rubat, you might have thought he was the pope. Gabe knew they would get to him eventually, and he let his coffee go cold and sat at the stone feet of the man who first correctly described the motion of the planets. That was a hell of a thing. Kepler's sculpted feet should have been big enough that everyone could have sat at them. Gabe thought of him as the one-eyed man in the land of the blind.

"Gabriel?"

He looked up and forgot Kepler when he saw two men who could have been anyone. On the left was Rubat, identified by his lab coat and the way he said Gabe's name. The other, in a suit, was as anonymous as unmolded clay.

"Are you well?" Rubat asked.

"Wolf."

Rubat crossed his arms. "I do not understand."

"The story about the boy who cried wolf. That's what you're thinking, right? I'm delusional or stoned or just making it up. I'm crying wolf. But they probably don't know that story in Yemen, I guess."

"Are you doing that? Crying the wolf?"

Gabe took a swallow of his coffee. It wasn't worth sipping; you either had to man up and swallow it or quit clutching it like a security blanket. "Maybe if I hadn't touched him I'd say it was just the desert. Some kind of night mirage. But I touched him. I *felt* him."

The figure in the suit said something in Spanish.

Gabe didn't have much of a handle on the local lexicon, and Rubat knew even less.

The man spoke again.

Gabe just looked at him, looked at that face that his brain saw the way it saw a white sheet, looked and waited, and then a voice from behind him said, "Kepler was the Earth-around-the-sun gentleman, was he not?"

Gabe turned. He saw only another suit. This one was a bit rougher at the seams, and the shoes were penny loafers, of all things. But those weren't pennies in the little slots. They looked like—

Peso loafers, he realized. He wished he had the heart to be amused by that.

"Kepler, yes?" the man asked, his voice accented only lightly by his native Spanish.

"Copernicus," Gabe said.

"Ah. Of course. I did not always sleep through science class. But on those days when Antonella Savedra took the seat in front of me, it was more difficult to concentrate." He extended his hand. "Braulio Fontecilla, Policía de Investigaciones."

Gabe clasped his hand. "Gabriel Traylin."

"You should have seen her."

"Who?"

"Antonella. She was seventeen. I was sixteen, the youngest in my class. My mother, she enrolled me a year early because I could read. Antonella had the blackest hair I had ever seen. Or ever will."

Gabe held the man's gaze not because it did him any good, as Fontecilla remained a voice and body without facial distinction, but because he knew that cops liked that from a guy, especially guys with shady stories.

"I know he was out there," Gabe said.

"I agree with you. Either that or you purposely stained the ground with blood to mislead us, which would not be the strangest thing I have seen in my days, but it would be—what is the word? Nonlikely?"

"Unlikely."

"Yes. Unlikely. As I said, we found blood."

"Yeah. Something . . . hit him in the head."

The other man, Fontecilla's partner, produced a notebook. He was one of those clever South Americans who apparently *habla*'ed *ingles* but preferred not to. He wrote as Gabe recounted what had happened.

By the time he finished, Rubat had also taken a seat on the statue's base, hands folded carefully in his lap. Fontecilla stood a short distance away, fists thrust in his pockets, looking up at the stars. Gabe realized, belatedly, that the man wore a hat. A trilby, he thought it was called. He hadn't noticed it before because he'd been too intent on holding the man's stare so as not to look suspicious. He had no intention of telling them about the prosopagnosia. Like everyone else, they would simply find it too goddamn bizarre to be true.

". . . and when I came back out," Gabe concluded, "there was nothing here."

Fontecilla made no comment for a while. Gabe grew tired of pretending to be interested in his face. He let his eyes trail back to the stars. He looked in the direction of Centaurus. There, a mere fifty light-years away, was a rock known as Lucy. As it turned out, Lucy was a planet-sized diamond, ten billion-trillion-trillion carats in size.

"You are certain he was dead?" Fontecilla asked.

"I thought so at the time, yeah."

"Then I must ask the obvious question."

"I don't know what happened to the body," Gabe said. "I was gone only for a few minutes. When I got back from the observatory, the only thing left was blood."

Fontecilla absorbed this. His partner shifted uneasily. Gabe had the growing sense that the two of them were telepaths, trash-talking him in their minds.

"Look," Gabe said, "I don't know what else to say. That's the way it happened."

"Do you own a gun, Señor Traylin?"

Though the desert night was cold, it couldn't account for the chill along his arms when he realized what Fontecilla was implying. Gabe was a nobody. He lived an uneventful life. Flying here to South America was the boldest thing he'd ever done. He'd never even had a traffic ticket. And now this. This missing body. This cop thinking he was suspect.

"You do not need to answer that," Fontecilla said, letting him off the hook—at least for now. "Sometimes these questions, they just come out of me. It is what we call a bad habit, yes? As far as we can see, no crime is here. We have a bit of drying blood, nothing more."

"Yeah. I guess so."

"And prints."

Gabe looked up. "You've got fingerprints?"

"Finger?" Fontecilla shook his head. "Foot." He pointed toward where the technicians were putting away their gear inside the yellow tape. "Tracks. Two pairs, one I would guess matches your expensive sneakers."

Gabe looked at his shoes. He'd bought the pricey cross-trainers before signing on for this gig. The left one chafed his heel. "You didn't find any others? Anything . . . bigger?"

"Why would you ask that?"

Gigante, he thought. *The creature killed the man and carried him away.*

"No," Fontecilla said, "we found only two sets. But the other pair, it was not shoes."

Gabe searched for and found the man's eyes again. "What do you mean?"

"This possibly dead stranger you say you found, he was not wearing shoes like yours or mine. He had boots on. Boots with a very distinctive sole. Boots like a soldier."

Gabe tightened his fingers around the coffee mug. "He's military?"

Fontecilla spread his hands as if to say he didn't know, while above them all, Kepler stared toward the heavens, searching for an answer in the cosmic dust.

CHAPTER THREE

Luke looked earnestly at the flight attendant and said, "You have very large breasts."

Standing behind her brother, Mira winced.

Thank God, the stewardess didn't slap him. Like a veteran poker player, she read his face and understood something basic about him. She kept her own face rigid in a smile. "I hope you've had a pleasant flight, sir."

"I'm not *sir,*" Luke said, "I'm *Luke*!"

Mira intervened—she was always intervening. "I'm sorry, ma'am, he didn't mean it." She felt the heat in her cheeks. "Well, actually he *did* mean it, but not in the way it sounded."

"Quite all right." Still the smile held, as carefully balanced as a walker on a high wire.

"He just says what he sees."

"It's okay, really."

"What's okay?" Luke asked. "Sis, what's okay?"

"You," Mira said, nudging him in the back. "Now get the train moving before we derail for good."

"What train?"

"Never mind." She passed the flight attendant and tried to match the politeness level of the woman's smile. She almost got there. "Thank you."

"Thank *you*. And enjoy your stay in Santiago."

Mira ushered her brother from the jet, shrugging the blush from her face as she always did. The distractions helped. New airport. New city. New *continent*. This was it, her best shot, her Rocky Balboa moment, here in this foreign land. Mira had never been out of the country before, so she put on what Luke called her Danger Cap and tried to take in all the signs and sounds and not get them lost on their way to a taxi. Luke wore his Danger Cap when crossing the street and running the hot water for a bath. It was his way of focusing. More than once, the invisible Danger Cap had kept him from being hurt.

And more than once it had failed him.

"Wow, look at that!" Eyes wide, Luke pointed at something, maybe the man with the guitar on his back or the woman with the bright dolphin tattoo. "Wow, wow, and *wow*!"

"No time for sightseeing," Mira told him. "It's baggage claim or bust."

"Bust what?"

"I don't know. Bust somebody in the lip if they lost our luggage, I guess."

Luke stared transfixed at the black conveyor that summoned suitcases from a hole in the wall and drove them around like a weird carousel. Mira knew he was stationary for the moment—he was obsessive when it came to new visual stimuli—so she pardoned her way through the suits and skirts and wrestled their two bags into compliance.

"Let's go, Eskimo," she said.

The bags had wheels. Luke said it was like pulling a wagon, but not as fun. Still, he made the occasional *whoosh* noise as he dragged his things.

Beside him, Mira sent her eyes dashing here and there, thankful that her small arsenal of Spanish phrases would not be put unduly to the test: Most of the signs were also printed in English.

"Cool place," Luke decided. "Cool people, cool clothes, *coolcoolcool.*"

"As a cucumber," Mira agreed, listening with only one ear. From somewhere came the sound of a Chilean *tonada.* Mira had learned about such things when researching this trip, this last mad gambit to make sense of her brother's breakthrough. For nearly a year she'd been saving, planning, and secretly hoping. Maybe this was finally the place.

Maybe.

The taxi ride bombarded them.

The first bombs were the lights. Santiago was an architectural cluster of the old and the new, but in the neon signs, digital billboards, and constant headlights, it gave up its cultural contours and became a city like every other city, pulsing and loud.

"Pretty," Luke said, nodding and nodding, his wide head going up and down, up and down. "Pretty like Grandma's."

Their grandmother prided herself on the artfulness of her Christmas lights. Luke loved her house. Then again, Luke loved everything. He was a child of love, one of the blessed ones, they said, who never tasted the brine of hate or the week-old milk of jealousy.

Mira envied him as often as she wished things had been different.

He turned to her, his smile visible in the back of the dark taxi, revealed in the passing red and purple shades. "Sure is fine, ain't it, Gretel?"

"Yes, Hansel. It's fine. But we don't say ain't."

He grinned to say that he knew that and then stuck out his tongue. Despite his differences, sometimes he was just an ordinary, obnoxious brother. They were all alike.

"You are here for wine, yes?" the cabbie asked.

Mira leaned forward. "I'm sorry?"

"Wine. Colchagua Valley tour. Many popular wineries. Many tourists."

"Uh, no, that's not us. We're not tourists."

"Easter Island? It is Easter Island for you, then?"

"I'm afraid not."

Luke cocked his head. "Easter Island?" He blinked, the epicanthic skin folds of his eyelids one of the many characteristics of Down syndrome, a disorder about which Mira was as knowledgeable as all but a handful of specialists. Screw the PhD. She didn't need one in order to read and memorize and read some more. "An island of Easter?" Luke asked. "A whole *island of Easter candy*?"

The driver had barely given them a glance when they climbed in, so he hadn't noticed there was anything different about Luke. Either that or he was damn good at being polite. "No, no, it is the place of the big faces. The statues, you know? Tall rocks, tall eyes. They watch the sea, and they wait."

"Wait for what?" Luke asked. The question was sharp with curiosity. Luke's mild retardation was marked by instances of pure inquisitiveness, tiny spot-welds that made him into something more. He was Mosaic Down, which implied a hell of a lot but most importantly meant that his IQ was in the upper zone of the Down community. Yet he couldn't live safely on his own for several reasons, one of which was his come-and-go memory. He would forget to close the front door, to turn off the stove, to keep metal out of the microwave. Thus he had lived with Mira for all of his twenty-seven years.

"Wait. For. What?" He said it slowly, carefully shaping each word, followed by rapid-fire: "Waitforwhatwaitforwhat?"

The taxi driver lifted a hand and gestured vaguely. "Sometimes waiting for something is better than seeing it arrive. Do I make sense? My English, it comes mostly from television."

"Sadly," Mira said, "that's where Americans also get their English."

"You learn a lot from *Miami Vice.*"

"I didn't think that show was on anymore."

"I own the first four seasons on DVD." He smiled at her in the rearview mirror. "I wanted to be Don Johnson when I grew to adult, you know, and now I am driver for tourists."

"We're not tourists," Mira said again, but too softly for him to hear.

Luke stared out the window, his nose an inch from the glass.

Minutes later, the cab pulled to the curb outside the hotel. Even at well past midnight, the sidewalks boasted their share of humanity. Women in designer jeans hung on the arms of dark-eyed beaus in leather jackets. Strung-out drifters skulked in groups of two and three, the cherries of their cigarillos like extra eyes beneath their sweatshirt hoods. The hip-hop from the stereos of students clashed with the traditional radio stations and their *cueca* dance numbers. Brightly glowing signs made promises in Spanish that Mira didn't understand.

She got out, Luke bounding to the sidewalk behind her. He turned a complete circle, trying to see everything at once. He grabbed the camera he wore around his neck and began flashing off shots at a man beating a tambourine on the corner, chanting some kind of native song with a coffee can for money between his feet. Luke seemed content to fill up the camera's digital memory card right here beside the cab.

Mira handed the driver his fee, plus what she hoped was a fair tip in pesos. She hadn't studied the currency rates as closely as she'd planned, as there simply had been too much to do. *"Gracias,"* she said.

The cabbie accepted the fare and glanced at Luke, who was busy giving Jimmy Olsen a run for his snapshot money. "He is happy to be here, yes?"

"That is definitely true."

"You two, you are brother and sister? Siblings?"

"Not just siblings." Mira offered him a kind smile as she hoisted her bag and turned away. "We're twins."

CHAPTER FOUR

The sun detonated on the desert's eastern horizon. Dawn happened in the Atacama like the Big Bang; the world went from a tiny singularity at night to full-on daylight. Suddenly everything was orange and slate and the white of old bone.

Gabe hurried around the observatory. Since the police had departed, he'd done nothing but think about the dead man, the Midnight Messenger, the man without a face. He put himself in that man's place, running across the wasteland, running and sweating and running some more, finally pulling up for breath outside the observatory and dying without even knowing he'd been struck. Dying *alone.* That's what ate away at Gabe, who knew aloneness the way other men knew a lover.

"Vicente!" Gabe called, searching for the maintenance supervisor.

Rubat had already dismissed the incident. He thought Gabe was hallucinating, smoking pot he'd procured from the locals. He ascribed the spilled blood to a wounded animal, and though Gabe had argued that there *were no* animals in this place—no rattlesnakes, no coyotes, not even any goddamn earthworms—Rubat had only waved a hand and muttered epithets in Arabic. "You want to stay on this project," he'd said, "you stop crying the wolf."

"Vicente!" Gabe found three men tending the small solar array behind the observatory. All three wore coveralls and caps. Gabe looked helplessly from one to the other. "Vicente?"

The man on the left said, "Hear you had a wild night, *amigo.*"

Gabe knew him by his voice. "Yeah. You could say that."

"Something about a body?"

"Maybe. I don't know. But there's blood."

"*Sí,* I saw where the cops had dug it up." He put down his socket wrench and wiped his hands on a rag. "Hey, you want to hear a good cop joke?"

"On any other day, Vic, yeah, but I need to use one of the four-wheelers."

Vicente didn't seem to hear him. "One day, everyone gets to arguing about who is the better police force. Our *carabineros* say they can catch a rabbit faster than the army and the American FBI. So they have a contest and set a rabbit loose in the forest."

Gabe hardly heard him. He thought about the Messenger, the man he'd named for a comic-book character. What had he been running from? What the hell could possibly be out there? More importantly, what had happened to his body? Had someone dragged it away while Gabe was inside?

"The FBI goes into the woods," Vicente said. "They conduct surveillance with illegal wiretaps and pay off all kinds of animal informants. After two solid months of expensive investigating, they conclude that rabbits do not exist."

What about the boots and watch the man had been wearing? Did that imply he was a member of the military? And if he was, how did that change things?

"After that," Vicente continued, "our steadfast Chilean army embarks on a rabbit-finding campaign. After a week with no luck, they burn half the forest down, killing God knows how many animals, and they consider the mission a success. They have a parade."

Gabe swung his attention back to his friend. And Vicente *was* his friend, a rare and dubious honor. Gabe owed him more than just feigned interest.

"Finally, the *carabineros* take a crack at it. They go into what's left of the forest. After only two hours, they come out, dragging a bear with bruises over most of its body, a bloody nose, and one broken leg. The bear is yelling, 'Okay, okay! I'm a rabbit! I'm a rabbit!' "

Gabe smiled. "Not bad."

Vicente laughed, a spirited sound that carried across the desert. "Not bad? You, my friend, should be chuckling your white ass off. I guess getting interrogated by the *carabineros* really wore you down, eh? You know what we call them here? *Tortugas ninjas.*"

"The Ninja Turtles?"

Vicente seemed to find it very funny.

"Well, it wasn't an interrogation, and it wasn't them. I had the honor of speaking with plainclothes detectives."

"Oh, investigators, very impressive."

Gabe touched the man on the arm. "I need one of the four-wheelers."

"Isn't this about the time of day you should be in bed? I heard that astronomers are like vampires."

"In more ways than one. Is borrowing one of the quads going to be a problem?"

Vicente considered him. "This is serious?"

"Feels that way."

"You really saw somebody get shot?"

"I need to get moving, okay? The tracks may already be gone."

"Who shot him?"

"I don't know. Gigante, maybe."

"Why is it even any of your concern?"

"I can't turn away from this. It's . . . hard to explain. Call it accidental empathy."

Vicente drew in a breath, held it, then exhaled loudly. "You going alone?"

"Not if you're volunteering."

"Say I am, if only to keep you from getting lost. What is it that we're hoping to find?"

Gabe gazed in the direction of the desert's heart. "Whatever was chasing him."

They started at the blood.

The cops had taken it. Where last night there had been a Rorschach splotch of dried blood, today there was only a shallow hole. The crime-scene techs had carefully cut away that section of the ground, bagged it, and trucked it off to the lab in Calama. Though Fontecilla's group had arrived by chopper, the blue-collar cops had driven six hours in a van full of forensic equipment, then turned around and hauled it all back.

Astride a green Arctic Cat 400 ATV, Vicente said, "Platypus."

Sitting on an identical vehicle, Gabe looked up from his inspection of the ground. "Come again?"

"My son, Sergio, he loves the zoo. Everywhere we go, we visit the zoos. Buenos Aires, Mexico City, San Diego . . . The strangest thing I've ever seen is a platypus. Do you know this creature?"

"I've seen pictures."

"The platypus is a mammal, like a fox, but it hatches from an egg like a turtle."

"And why is this important?"

"Had you told me there was a venomous mammal that laid eggs, I would probably not believe you until I saw one for myself."

Gabe knew where this was going. "And if I told you that I saw a man get shot, that I had his wrist in my hand to feel for a pulse, and that his body vanished when I wasn't looking . . ."

Vicente held his gaze, wanting to believe.

He ran and died alone.

Gabe didn't try to express what he felt, this weird kinship with a murdered man, this connection that pulled him along, farther into the unknown. "Come on." He twisted the throttle and followed the boot tracks in reverse, wondering if he was going crazy.

They kept the ATVs on either side of the prints, moving at no more than fifteen kilometers an hour. They'd brought along more water than was necessary and both a digital and an analog compass; getting stranded out there in the open was a mistake you made only once. The tracks revealed the ripple pattern of the boots' soles, a pattern that Fontecilla had rightly called distinctive. Though the impressions were faint, Gabe was able to keep his eyes on them without needing to look up. He wasn't going to crash into anything out here, so he could afford to drive with his attention fixed on the ground between them. Though he was usually crawling into bed by this hour, he tested the edges of himself but found no weariness. Too much stirred within him, a nebula of emotions. Fontecilla and the police didn't believe him. Rubat had warned him not to pursue it. Yet here he was, trundling out in his faded boonie hat and sunglasses, for no other reason than to follow the strange pity he felt for a man he didn't even know.

"If there was no body," Vicente said, "then shouldn't there be another set of prints?"

"What do you mean?"

"Well, somebody had to come carry the body away, yes? There should be signs."

"Maybe. The ground here is fairly hard. My tennis shoes hardly even make an impression. The only reason we're able to see these boot tracks is because of their rigid soles. If someone was wearing moccasins or something, they'd probably leave almost no print at all."

"They're getting fainter," Vicente observed.

It was true. The desert was eating the tracks, stiff soles notwithstanding. The ground had nearly erased all traces of the man's passing. In a matter of hours, perhaps less, he would be nothing but a phantom running through the dark of Gabe's mind.

"Let's pick it up a little," he suggested.

Vicente looked back. The observatory was already a kilometer behind them. "Is it safe?"

"I have a good sense of direction," Gabe said. "We won't get lost."

"Famous last words." Vicente gave his vehicle some gas, and in seconds the two of them had tripled their speed.

For a few moments Gabe did nothing but enjoy the breeze produced by the moving ATV. Around him lay a field of coarse soil and scattered rock. As the sun pushed higher into the sky, it unlaced the shadows to reveal weird contours and oddly buckled hills. Earth's driest place was seemingly put together with spare parts, each of them alien and as arid as rust.

"Did he have a bota?" Vicente shouted over the growl of the engines.

"A what?"

"A bota! A wineskin, canteen, something like that."

"Not that I saw."

"So . . . how did he survive out here?"

He didn't, Gabe wanted to say. *He died right in front of me.*

"Maybe he prayed to Illapa," Vicente said, answering his own question. "He's the old Incan weather god. They say he kept the Milky Way in a jug and sometimes poured out rain. What do you think?"

Gabe looked down and saw no more tracks.

Applying the brakes, he slowed the four-wheeler and searched the ground. Finding nothing but the patterns of swirled soil made by the wind, he turned a circle and inspected the area on either side of him. Maybe he'd veered from his original course, or perhaps the Messenger had approached from a different direction.

After ten minutes of searching in ever-widening swaths, he pulled up beside Vicente and hoped the man didn't try another joke. Vicente was half Canadian, half Aymara Indian, a citizen of Chile but a patriot of American sitcoms. He had a way of timing his wit as if waiting for the laugh track. But he must have sensed Gabe's mood, because he said nothing, only took a swig from a water bottle and belched dramatically.

"I know what I saw," Gabe said quietly, eyes on the distant, angular hills.

"It happens out here."

"That was no hallucination."

"Of course not. The police have the bloody dirt clods to prove it."

"And those tracks."

"*Sí*. The tracks. But the desert has smothered them."

"I'm not sure I can leave it at that."

"You're saying you want to keep this up, piss off Rubat, and get yourself sent home?"

"I'm saying it's a shitty way to die." He shook his head, wondering what Vicente looked like. Even as they sat beside each other on their matching ATVs, he felt separated from him by a chasm that Vic could never comprehend. Vic looked exactly the same as Rubat, exactly the same as the Sultan of Brunei, exactly the same as everyone else. Gabriel Traylin lived on a planet of seven billion people, but not one of them did he know on sight. "I'm just saying it sucks that he spent his last moments on Earth without—"

A light flashed in the hills.

"What?" Vicente noticed Gabe's expression and turned in his seat. "What is it?"

Gabe squinted, trying to get a better look. There was nothing there. The desert was dealing wild cards again.

"I don't see anything," Vicente said, shielding his eyes with his hand. "Not surprising, though. Those UFOs, man, when they start moving, you really got to keep your eyes peeled. Know what I mean?"

Gabe saw it again. For a moment it was there, a mirror ricochet of sunlight, as mysterious as the pulsars that so often called to him from space.

"There's something out there."

Before Vicente could respond, Gabe goosed the throttle and charged after it.

CHAPTER FIVE

Mira and her brother finished breakfast and went in search of the miracle man.

Apparently Chileans didn't agree with that old saw about the first meal of the day being the most important, as the hotel's café offered only coffee, bread, and pastries. Nevertheless, Luke fell in love with a caramel-flavored topping called *manjar,* slathering it over his toast. He said *hola* to everyone in the café, proud of his command of this foreign tongue, and the passersby were kind enough to return the greeting.

Things were different on the street.

The war zone common to American cities was no different here, with horns and digital advertisements and everyone walking too quickly. Having grown up in a rural town on the Missouri River, Mira had never learned to soldier through these battlefields. When she'd visited New York after college, she'd loved the shows but hated the stress. This morning, though, with so much at stake, she would storm the beaches bravely and see what waited on the other side.

Armed with a single address and a Spanish phrase book, she boarded a green and white Volvo bus, part of the city's Transantiago system, and hoped she'd picked the right stop. Luke claimed a window seat, as always, and he spent the ride mesmerized, as always. Mira had converted eight hundred dollars before leaving the States, and if her spreadsheet was correct, she'd be forced to use her credit card only occasionally, which was good, since the thing was beginning to bend like an overloaded bridge.

"Gretel! Wow! Check it out!"

Outside the window stood a hundred-year-old statue of the Virgin Mary, arms held beneficently at her sides, tourists idling around her feet. The look on her face was neither kind nor aloof; Mira thought the mother of Jesus looked rather bored.

"She's as pretty as the Statue of Liberty," Luke said.

"Maybe a little shorter," Mira suggested.

Luke laughed. "Yeah. A little. A little shorter."

Mira glanced from the street to her phone and back again. She'd downloaded maps of the city. Currently she and Luke appeared to be about four blocks away from where X marked the spot. She felt the proximity in her stomach, where the nerves fluttered their wings. She'd been hoarding vacation days for the last fourteen months, and now that she was finally here, her most immediate concern was not what this visit might mean for her brother, but simply the fact that she might throw up all over the floor of this nice public-transit bus. A year and a half ago, some kind of magic had happened, and the man responsible was now only minutes away.

Luke turned to her. He looked very serious. His blond hair was the same color as Mira's, and so too were his brown eyes. They'd inherited these from their mother, Cathy the Carefree, Cathy the Leftover Hippie, Cathy the OD'd.

"This is a great, super trip," Luke said. "The super best!"

"We just got here."

"We just got here and it's the super best!"

She smiled. "Don't forget to take pictures."

His eyes widened. "Right!" He dug out his camera from his fanny pack and pressed the lens against the bus window.

Mira managed to keep her *manjar* down for the rest of the ride, and when she led Luke off the bus, he was still firing away with the camera.

"Don't fill up that memory card too quickly, Mr. Shutterbug. There's still plenty left to see."

"Mr. *who*-bug?"

"Mr. *you*-bug. Let's go. His place should be just down the street."

They passed a group of boys wearing shin guards and soccer shirts—*fútbol,* she reminded herself—and a woman steering a baby stroller with one hand and holding a cigarette in the other. The street was narrow, the flat-roofed buildings wedged tightly together in a way that was mildly claustrophobic. A delivery boy on a sputtering scooter wove through traffic and honked a horn that sounded like a wounded bird. He wore a yellow jersey, a replica of those enjoyed by the leaders of the Tour de France.

"Wait." Mira stopped, her brother bumping into her. "I think this is it."

Luke watched a jet leave a white exclamation point between the clouds.

"Yeah, this is the one." Mira dropped her phone into her handbag and glanced down at herself. She wore jeans, sandals, and her favorite scoop-necked top. The outfit made her look either sporty or as if she were trying to be nineteen again; she couldn't quite decide which. Then again, at twenty-seven, she wasn't far removed from that young age. She'd been an adult by the time she was in junior high. Being your twin's bodyguard did that to you.

"Hansel?"

"Yep?"

"Let's do it."

"Let's do what?"

Mira didn't elaborate. She jogged up the five steps and entered the apartment building, knowing that he would follow because that's how it always was. Just once, she would have liked to follow *him*.

Two flights of cracked tile later, they stood before a door that was buried in shadows, as the hallway lightbulb had apparently burned out.

Luke put away his camera. He didn't seem to sense what Mira felt on the skin of her arms, the anticipation of the unknown.

Mira knocked.

"It smells in here," Luke said. "Don't you think it smells in here?"

"Maybe a little."

"Maybe a lot."

She tried again. He had to be home. She hadn't waited so long and flown five thousand miles to face an unanswered door. She *willed* him to be home.

"Maybe a *lot* lot."

She banged harder this time, using the butt of her hand, and then the door pulled open abruptly, startling her.

"He's home!" Luke sang.

A middle-aged black man stood in the doorway. A flannel shirt clung to his bones.

Mira collected herself, swallowed, and said it: "I'm looking for Mr. Benjamin Cable."

"So am I." He closed the door softly in her face.

CHAPTER SIX

Gabe rode through a void.

He'd never been this deep before, not out here, not where things were parched so exquisitely dry that cacti didn't grow. They warned you about going out too far. Even Antarctica had microscopic little beasties flourishing in the glacial vaults. Parts of the Atacama were as lifeless as a realm carved from lead.

Over the wind and the engines, Vicente shouted, "What the hell is it?"

"I don't know!" The sun dappled it again with a few pulses of light.

"Take a guess!"

"I'm thinking maybe Gigante."

Vicente didn't reply, implying that he was taking the suggestion seriously. Gabe waited for some kind of quip, but the man said nothing, which only heightened Gabe's growing sense of unease.

When he was nine he'd gotten lost in a Los Angeles shopping mall. Standing in the middle of the promenade, gazing at thousands of faces that looked identically like nothing at all, he slipped into a panic so deep that it manifested as paralysis. He stood there for over two hours before his mother and a pair of relieved security guards finally swept him up.

He ate a mouthful of hot air and eased up on the throttle.

It lay only a few hundred meters away. Still it was indistinct, an irregular shape on the ground, partially concealed by the shadow of a car-sized rock. As Gabe watched, sunlight again blinked from some metallic part of the object, a senseless Morse code he couldn't translate.

"I don't suppose you brought your binoculars," he said.

"Negative." Vicente spit the dust from his mouth. "How about if you stay here and I go back and fetch them?"

Gabe narrowed his eyes, trying to guess what was lying beside the stone. "Sorry, but something tells me you wouldn't come back."

"Why would you think that? I *love* tracking the ghost of a dead man across the desert."

Gabe dropped his speed and closed in on the object. "Hey, Vic."

"Yeah?"

"Is that a pinwheel?"

As the ATVs rolled closer, the spinning toy defined itself. Its shaft was thrust into the soil, its foil blades turning sluggishly, like the hands of a clock in a Dalí landscape.

Vicente leaned forward on the handlebars. "I don't get it. *Why?*"

Gabe had no answer. He licked the sweat from his upper lip and drove until he was nearly on top of it, but still it made no sense. Then he saw the backpack. He killed the engine, and when Vicente followed suit, only the sound of a soft wind remained.

A head and an arm protruded from the faded canvas backpack. The boy's eyes were closed, his hair buzzed close to his sunburned scalp. The hand on the end of that skinny arm rested near the pinwheel's stem, as if reaching for it. A patina of dust covered the boy and the backpack in which he rode.

Gabe dismounted, unable to look away.

Vicente whispered a prayer as Gabe knelt nearby. Before last night, he'd never seen a corpse, and now here was his second in less than twelve hours, a crash course in forensic science, but this was so much worse: The boy's mouth was open, his tongue and lips like things of wax. The backpack itself wasn't unusually large, which meant the boy had to be crammed in there, his limbs folded around him so he'd fit. Someone had been transporting him.

"The Messenger was carrying him."

"Jesus, Gabe. I mean . . . *Jesus.*"

Gabe wanted to look away, but his curiosity had a target lock and wasn't letting go. Though the small body had been here for hours, no bugs had gathered. This stretch of the desert, like the shores of hell, was the bane of all life, even down to the scale of maggots and flies.

Vicente's voice came from far away. "Who is he?"

Prosopagnosia had no answer for that. Though Gabe saw the open mouth and the pale tongue, and though he knew there'd be a nose and ears, none of it developed on the film of his mind. Who was this boy? He was as much a cipher as the Messenger himself.

"Gabe?" Vicente cleared his throat. "Gabriel Traylin, do you hear me?"

Gabe forced himself to nod. "Yeah."

"Let's go. We have to tell somebody. We have to . . . to *report* this."

The pinwheel turned again as a breeze as light as a sigh touched its blades. Then the wind faded. The toy had no business being out here. It was as senseless in these surroundings as a fire hydrant or a Wurlitzer jukebox.

He looked back at the boy. Since he couldn't unpuzzle the riddle of his face, he tried the bag in which the body was mostly enclosed. It was a standard external-frame model, the kind with the aluminum poles providing its support.

Gabe moved a bit closer.

"What are you *doing*?"

"Does this bag look small to you?"

"Are you insane?" Vicente ripped off a long invective in Spanish. "Let's get the hell back to the observatory, *now.*"

But Gabe was certain that something wasn't right. Judging by the size of the backpack, he didn't know how this kid fit inside it. The boy would have to be a contortionist.

He pinched the corner of the canvas.

"Don't do this, Gabe."

Was this the quest that the Messenger had failed? Had this child died on his back?

He got a better grip and tugged. The pack barely moved.

"Shit, here we go." Vicente got off the quad and sank to his knees beside Gabe. He looked down at the boy. "He looks the same age as my son."

Gabe took hold with his other hand. He squared himself so that one sudden pull would skin the pack from the boy's body.

Vicente took off his hat. "I don't think I want you to do this."

"Can't help it."

"The hell you can't. I don't want to see."

"Me neither." Gabe yanked the pack free.

Vicente reacted first, recoiling, pitching backward and landing on his ass. Gabe spent that first moment unable to make sense of what he saw. His system lag ended a second later, and he covered his mouth and blinked against the sudden tears.

The boy's left arm and both of his legs had been removed. The stub of his left arm was bound in duct tape. That of his right leg was smooth and healed, while the other one was a jagged mess, recently sawed away, the flaps of skin sewn hastily together with thick stitches.

Vicente gave an inarticulate cry and turned away. Gabe wanted nothing more than to follow his friend's lead, but he was horribly transfixed, trapped in the awful undertow of the boy's mutilated body. The child had fit in the backpack because he'd been truncated. For whatever reason, someone had removed vast hunks of him, so that he was nothing more than a torso, an arm, and a face that Gabe couldn't see.

"Gabriel!" Vicente grabbed a handful of his shirt.

The boy lay on the desert floor, clutching the pinwheel that was staked into the earth like a banner claiming this land for a foreign power. He had died of infection or dehydration or the simple lack of a will to live. Gigante didn't do this. That mythic monster hadn't torn the muscle and bone from the boy's body. The black thread that laced his leg meat together was the work of a human hand.

"Gabriel, please."

He allowed Vicente to drag him to his feet. As repulsed as he was by what he saw, he was afraid to leave. What if the boy's body, like that of the Messenger, evaporated into the empty sky? What if they brought the cops back to this very spot and found only a pinwheel turning somberly in the breeze?

Vicente started one of the quads, the sudden noise at last pulling Gabe free of the vision that held him in place. A greasy fluid surged in his stomach. He fell toward the handlebars and leaned against the machine, waiting either to be sick or to wake up sweating in his bed. Surely this couldn't be real.

But when he glanced back, the boy remained, his secrets as impenetrable as the desert's guarded heart.

CHAPTER SEVEN

"Grumpy guy," Luke said to the closed door.

Mira took a step back. She'd never shut the door on anyone before, and to have it happen in reverse was so startling that she didn't have a ready response. Though rudeness abounded everywhere, it still surprised her.

"Like Scrooge McDuck," Luke decided. He looked at his sister. "You lied."

"I what? When? What are you talking about?"

"You said he wrote the book, Ben Cable, he wrote the book, and you said he's here."

"He *is* here."

"Ben Cable is Scrooge McDuck?"

"Looks that way."

"But he said he's *looking* for Ben Cable. That's what he said. I heard him, and I have good ears. He can't be *looking* for Ben Cable if he's *being* Ben Cable." He frowned. "Can he?"

"Just hold on a sec, okay?" She stepped toward the door and tried the knob.

It was unlocked. The door opened.

"Oops," Luke said, "we are *breaking and entering*."

"Mr. Cable? Please, my name is Mira Westbrook, and I need just a few minutes of your time."

The knob jerked out of her hand, and the man again filled the doorway. His black hair was shot full of gray arrows. "Westbrook? I don't know anyone by that name."

"We haven't met. I tried to e-mail you, but the address I found online kept bouncing back, and your Web site's been down for—"

"Two years. Yes, I know."

"My brother and I have come a long way, sir, and I've spent way too much money to turn around and go home. I'm not some kind of crazy stalker person who chases their favorite writer around the world."

"That's comforting."

"And to tell you the truth, I'm actually not a huge science-fiction fan. I'm more of a mushy-melodrama woman myself, so this has nothing at all to do with me." She glanced at Luke. "It has to do with him."

Slowly, as if he doubted everything she'd told him, Cable swung his eyes from Mira to her brother.

Mira wondered what he was thinking. She resisted the urge to say more, afraid that she'd only ramble and further indict herself as the nutcase she surely appeared to be. She studied his face while he studied Luke's. The lines around his mouth indicated vintage laughter, and his teeth were the remarkable white attained only by dental procedure. His skin was a deep, lustrous brown.

"I'm Luke." He smiled and extended his hand.

Cable stood very still.

Luke possessed an insouciant patience that disarmed everyone, eventually. He just kept grinning and offering his hand until Cable reached out and accepted it.

They shook.

"I'm Luke."

"So I heard."

"And you are *not* Scrooge McDuck."

Cable paused only for a second before saying, "No, but I *have* been mistaken for Wile E. Coyote. Both of us have a tendency to blow ourselves to bits on most days of the week."

Though he might not have understood that Cable spoke figuratively, Luke laughed with spirit. "He buys dynamite from Acme."

"So he does. Some fools never learn." Cable looked at Mira. "Assuming I believe that you're *not* a crazy stalker person, Mrs. Westbrook, what is it that I can do for you?"

"It's *Miss,* and you can let me come in and talk to you about my brother's ability to read your book."

"Glad he enjoyed it. You two come all this way for an autograph?"

"Luke doesn't read, Mr. Cable. In addition to Down syndrome, he's severely dyslexic. Except when it comes to *your* writing."

"Forgive a middle-aged man his lapses, but I'm not sure I'm following you."

Mira backed up and tried again. "My brother not only has a serious reading impairment, but he doesn't really even want to learn to overcome it. Books just aren't his thing. But for some reason, he can read your novel perfectly, quickly, and flawlessly. Your novel, and nothing else."

Mira accepted the coffee and summoned to mind the speech she'd been rehearsing for fourteen months. Cable's apartment had the look of something temporary parlayed into something permanent. Suitcases served as dresser drawers. The pots and skillets in the tiny kitchenette were stored in a cardboard box covered in international mailing labels. A lone window provided a stunning view of the brick wall of the adjacent building. A small geranium stood defiantly on the sill.

"I don't usually entertain," Cable said.

"That's okay. I'm sorry we just burst in on you like this—"

"You're unlisted," Luke said. He nodded twice. "Unlisted means the phone-book people don't write your name down."

"I contacted your publisher," Mira explained, "but all they said was that they'd be happy to forward written correspondence to you, but they couldn't give out your contact information."

Cable blew the steam from his cup and took a long drink. Mira sensed his unease. In his eyes she saw guarded curiosity and a good helping of suspicion. She was ready for suspicion; she'd been planning this monologue for over a year.

"Do you mind if I start at the beginning?" she asked. "It's kind of a long story."

"She's a good storyteller," Luke assured him. "Gretel's the A-one, best-there-is-and-ever-*was* storyteller. That's how I fall asleep sometimes when I can't."

"That would be fine," Cable said. "God knows I've got nothing else to do but that damned Sudoku all day."

"Okay, well . . ." She slid forward an inch in her chair. Her own pulse surprised her. Was she really here, after all this time? Had all the planning and all the saving actually gotten her here? "Luke and I are—"

"Dizygotic!"

Mira smiled at her brother. "Yes." She looked back at Cable. "He likes that word. It's a fancy way of saying fraternal."

Cable slowly cranked up an eyebrow and studied them with renewed interest. "Twins?"

"He's one minute older."

Luke shot up a hand. "Big brother!"

"Our mother was a little surprised by the challenges Luke presented. She was one of those people who got trapped in cycles, and when you're in one of those bad places, it's hard to make time for anyone but yourself." Mira was impressed by her own distance when she said this. Normally she kept those feelings close, and though Cathy Westbrook had been gone for over a decade, sometimes the tears sprang from ambush. "Needless to say, I had to grow up pretty quickly and do what needed doing."

"Like tell stories," Luke said. "And clean the fish tank. It gets gross."

"I'm sure it does." Cable seemed to have lost interest in his coffee. "For what it's worth, you two certainly have my attention. Normally at this hour I'm napping with the morning's *Diario Oficial* on my chest."

"I'm sorry. We had to come."

"Don't be sorry, sugar. I had to come down here myself."

Mira intended to ask him that—why on earth had he written one book and then secluded himself in a South American city?—but she wasn't ready yet. First: dyslexia. "Luke actually did pretty well in school, all things considered, except when it came to reading."

At this, Luke made a choking sound and grabbed his throat. "Going . . . to . . . barf."

"Yeah, yeah." Mira rolled her eyes. "Anyway, as you can see, he wasn't a big fan of school in general and reading in particular. We saw a lot of literacy specialists, but between his severe dyslexia and his overall dislike of the act of sitting on his caboose and trying to read, he never got very far. Both phonological and surface dyslexics can overcome their disabilities, but it takes work. Sometimes hard work, especially when they're already faced with other, more serious challenges. To tell you the truth, Mr. Cable, we had enough hard work on our plates already."

"We choose our battles," Cable said.

"Exactly."

Luke glanced back and forth, first at her and then at Cable. Mira wondered what he was thinking. Usually she could guess—call it a twin's telepathy or a sister's intuition. At the moment, though, she was too anxious. Maybe she wasn't the storyteller that Luke made her out to be, but she had a tale waiting to be told, and the time for the telling was finally here. "I work as a credit analysis manager at a bank in Omaha. It's a good, stable, boring job. Luke works three blocks away—"

"I roll tires."

Cable looked at him. "Come again?"

"Tire shop. I roll tires. Showroom needs new rubber."

"He also keeps the shop picked up," Mira added.

"And wash with Lava soap!" He held up his hands, both of which were very clean.

"We live together in the same house we grew up in." She didn't bother telling him that the house almost caught fire one night when their mother dropped her Betty Boop Zippo while trying to put a flame to the underside of a spoon. "A year and a half ago I was a dating a guy who turned out to be more interested in *Star Wars* conventions than he was in remembering my birthday. It didn't last."

"Nerdy bird," her brother chimed.

"One day I found a book of his under the bed. I left it on the kitchen counter, debating whether I should donate it to the library or send it down the garbage disposal in a kind of modern-day voodoo. When I walked back into the room half an hour later, Luke was standing in the middle of the room, reading the book."

There. It was out. The single most astounding thing that had ever happened to her, finally given wings. She waited to see if it flew.

Cable turned to Luke. "I thought she said you weren't very good at reading."

"Reading sucks."

"And the words look all funny to you when you try?"

"They're scrambled eggs."

Mira saw the skepticism in the man's eyes when he returned his attention to her. "So let me see if I have this straight. Someone who can hardly read a lick, someone with dyslexia, someone who says reading sucks was apparently contradicting all of that and reading nonetheless."

"There's no *apparent* about it. He can do it. He can read only one book. I've tried others. Believe me. From children's books to the Bible to Web sites to a hundred things pulled randomly from the bookstore shelves. The only thing he can read is one book. Your book. Like magic."

"*Magic*," Luke repeated, the wisp of wonder on his face.

Cable put his cooling coffee on the floor beside his chair and folded his fingers in his lap. "Show me."

Mira was ready. From her oversized, zebra-print handbag she produced a road-weary paperback copy of the Nebula Award finalist *This Mayflower Mars*.

The cover depicted a tortured orange landscape crisscrossed with tire tracks. Thrust partially up from the ground was a human hand. The fingers were frozen as if grasping for something that would remain forever out of reach.

"Third printing of the mass-market edition," she said.

"Too bad it didn't see a fourth. Maybe I could have afforded a better place."

"You wrote it five years ago."

"No, actually I wrote it about *eight* years ago. It took a while to see the light of day. Nature of the business. Or so they say. It's not my business anymore."

"Why not?"

"I thought we were going to have ourselves a reading?"

Mira wanted to press him, but again she curbed her eagerness. She'd waited for this meeting so long that she couldn't afford to screw it up now.

She tossed the book to Luke.

He was ready, and he caught it like his summer softball coach had taught him, looking it all the way into his hands. As he had done so many times before, he licked the tip of his finger and slowly turned through the copyright and title pages, none of which he could read without the usual nagging difficulty. He reached the story's prologue, settled back in his seat—

"Wait," Cable said.

Mira was so intent on her brother's pending display that she started at the sudden sound of Cable's voice.

"Not the first page," he said. "Open it up to somewhere in the middle. Somewhere random."

Luke's thick eyebrows met in the middle of his forehead. "Random?"

"I realize that you probably won't find anything in there but purple prose and an overuse of adverbs, but humor me. Just flip to a page and start from there. Any page. You pick."

Luke shrugged. "Okeydokey." He used his thumb to produce a satisfying fan of pages, and then stopped dramatically somewhere in the thicket that was the novel's midpoint plot. Mira had read the book three times herself, hoping to find some kind of clue, some key that would unlock the box of this riddle. Though she'd admitted she wasn't into sci-fi, she knew this particular work as well as anyone. It involved the second human expedition to the Red Planet. The team's flight engineer was a clone of the man who'd served the first crew, all of whom had lost their lives twenty-four years before the second ship touched down. Though on the outside *This Mayflower Mars* was an adventure story—the reviewer from *Kirkus* had referred to it as "Isaac Asimov meets *The African Queen*"—on a deeper level it was the story of someone trying to find his own identity in the shadow of a man who'd come before, a man who looked exactly like him. In a way, Benjamin Cable's book was a tale of twins.

Luke leaned toward the pages, cleared his throat, and read. " 'The sun when seen from this series of Valles Marineris cliffs always reminded him of frail things. It was so distant that it was nothing more than a dandelion head, yellow but pale, waiting, or perhaps hoping, to be blown by the breath of a passing boy so as to seed more interesting places.' "

Goosebumps rose on Mira's arms. No matter how many times she heard him read like this, she still felt its sheer incredibleness in her spirit.

" 'Lieutenant Dycar clung to the cliff face and stared at the sun, its luminescence dulled by the vast gulfs of space. The ancient civilizations of Earth had worshipped it. But he couldn't help but wonder what they would have thought of its far less impressive persona had they built their ziggurats here on this volcanic plateau where the sun played little more than a supporting role. Dycar asked himself if something so fragile was worthy of sacrifice and beating drums.' "

Luke looked up. "More?"

Cable scrutinized him. But he said nothing.

Luke tried his sister. "Gretel?"

"Mr. Cable?" She saw the puzzlement on his face. It was not unlike that on the faces of the doctors and specialists who had ultimately written off Luke's feat as a developmental and neurological anomaly without medical explanation. There were autistic savants who could play classical piano with the mastery of a Juilliard graduate and wards of psychiatric facilities who could recite the Chicago phone book from memory.

Suddenly Cable applauded. "*That,* my young friend, was a hell of a reading."

"That's what *everybody* says!" Luke exclaimed. "But they don't say hell."

"My apologies." His dark eyes jumped to Mira. "He can't read anything else?"

"We could show you, if you'd like."

"I think I would. But if all this is true, then why me? Why my book?"

"I don't know. No one does. But that's why we came here. We want you to help us find out."

CHAPTER EIGHT

The body bag was too big.

Gabe watched them transfer it from the back of the off-road Toyota to the ambulance. They'd rolled the bag's excess plastic like a toothpaste tube.

"Jesus." He fumbled for his cigarettes and vowed to quit after the pack was empty.

Though he'd dreaded making the call to the *carabineros* and requesting an encore of their performance of hours earlier, he had no choice. They'd followed him through the desert, the pinwheel like a road sign in a land with no roads. When they saw the boy, their reactions were not those of trained professionals but those of fathers, brothers, human beings.

Someone approached him from behind. He heard the footsteps long before anyone else would have, having trained himself to make up for his disability. By the slight shuffle in the gait, he guessed it was Rubat.

"What is happening here with you?"

Gabe turned toward him. Though he could see nothing in Rubat's features, he knew the observatory's elder statesman was glaring at him. The man's gray hair had parted, revealing a bald valley along the center of his scalp.

"They told me to wait here," Gabe said, glad to hear that his voice no longer quavered like an old telegraph wire. "So I'm waiting."

"Waiting?"

"Following orders. I figure they'll be along with their rubber hoses pretty soon and beat the truth out of me." He wanted to add *So can you cut me some slack?* But Rubat was in full administrator mode and had forgotten he'd once gotten drunk and cried on the shoulder of the man he now confronted.

"You need please to stop this."

"Stop what? I haven't done anything."

"Having the police authorities here once is an unfortunate occurrence, but twice *within twenty-four hours* is unacceptable. The company already is close to shutting us down. No money, they say. Now they just look for a reason, and I will not give them one. Do you realize how this will look in the newspapers?"

"The newspapers?" Gabe gave a sharp bark of laughter. "I found two bodies today, *dead people,* so pardon me for having to involve the cops. I suppose I should've considered all the bad press and just buried them myself."

Rubat crossed his arms. "I enjoy you, Gabriel. You make good sense of humor, and you will be fine astronomer. But we answer to higher powers, you and I. If the agency in Europe says cut you loose, I will of course follow instructions."

Though Gabe had anticipated an ass-chewing, he hadn't considered that somehow this could cost him his residency and thus his doctorate. "You called them?"

"It is part of my job. They should hear it from me instead of read about it online." He sighed. "Gabriel, let us not get our claws out over this. Do not make any trouble for us, for me. The policemen will find out what this is all about. And you will do your work, and that will be it. This too shall pass, yes?"

Gabe wasn't so sure. But he didn't know what to say.

"I plan one day to speak well on your behalf and see that you are called Dr. Traylin. But that is not today. You will not make further inquiry into this . . . this matter of the corpses. You will not give interviews, and you will stay out of the desert. These are my conditions for you to remain as a student."

"I've done my part for king and country. I'll gladly let the cops take it from here."

"Very good. Best of luck to you, because here comes one of them now."

The man's hat gave him away. Fontecilla snapped the cover shut on his tablet computer. "Walk with me, please."

Gabe fell into step beside him. He was out of his depth and in increasing need of a shower.

"Do you mind," Fontecilla said, "if I burden you with the usual questions?"

"I'm not sure if I know what the usual questions are."

"I believe you do. They are the same questions the TV policemen would ask, yes? For example, did you know this boy?"

"I answered this already. I've never seen him before. I was trying to figure out where that guy had come from. I think he was carrying the boy on his back, and when the boy died, he went on alone."

"Have you traveled here before, in this Atacama?"

"Only as a sightseer. On a bus. One of those weekend things for tourists."

"Do you know what could account for the condition of the deceased?"

It took Gabe a moment to figure out what he was being asked. "You mean, do I know why he was cut up like that?"

"Yes."

"I'll have to leave that up to you. All I know is that he didn't lose all three limbs at once, or at least that's how it looked. They were removed at intervals."

"Why?"

"You tell me. Or do you already know?"

"I wish I did. Matters would be so much easier if I had learned the art of augury. My grandmother, she claimed to see things from afar. Clairvoyance, they call it, yes? Apparently it is not a genetic trait. To be quite frank with you, Señor Traylin, I am presently as confused as I have ever been as a professional. I believe the proper English term is *baffled.*"

"Join the club."

Fontecilla stopped, removed his hat, and used a blue handkerchief to dab his brow. "I am going to instruct an officer to take down more details from you as part of our report. From your friend, as well. Here is my card so you may contact me directly, for whatever reason. We will also issue to the media a statement. But I would ask as a personal favor that you refer the journalists to me."

"Sure."

"Are you going to be well?"

"Maybe after I throw up."

"I could arrange for a physician."

Instead of declining the offer outright, Gabe let it linger in the air between them. He wasn't opposed to the idea, if only because he could take the opportunity to ask the doctor about the amputations.

"¿Señor?"

"Sorry." He gave Fontecilla the best eye contact he could. "There's something going on out there, isn't there?"

"Perhaps. But perhaps not. I know that a boy died in the desert. Only that. No more."

"Then maybe we should call your grandma."

"I am afraid the Lord has done so already. He called her home last winter." Fontecilla fixed his hat on his head. "Please try to go the rest of the day without requiring my assistance. What do those TV policemen say? The paperwork is starting to pile up."

Gabe didn't watch him walk away, but instead looked in the direction of where the pinwheel had stood before being stowed in an evidence bag. It had been the boy's last banner. He'd stabbed it into the ground, proclaiming himself, and then he died.

"Who were you?" Gabe whispered.

The boy's spirit, lost somewhere in the desert, made no reply.

Though his body needed the rest, Gabe's imagination would not relent. In his mind he'd linked himself to the dead boy and the Messenger by way of his prosopagnosia because he knew that one day he'd die as they had, without seeing the face of someone he loved. And when the dead dragged you on a mission, you could seldom resist the pull of their chains. At some point in the middle of the afternoon, when he was usually snoozing with a book on his pillow, he took a seat beside the foosball table and opened his laptop. He logged on to one of the facility's shared hard drives and accessed the seldom-used folder labeled TOPOGRAPHY.

Gigante won't be found on any map.

True enough. But he had to see what, if anything, was out there.

The maps revealed nothing. They were strong on geological features but lacked the detail he sought. The observatory itself wasn't even marked on them, so Gabe didn't know where to place himself on the map. Without the benefit of the stars, he was a shoddy navigator.

Okay, Magellan, now what?

He knew how the nightmares would play out if he slept. The boy would crawl across the sand, dragging himself with one arm, trying to reach safety. Gabe would be unable to see the anguish on his face, but he'd damn sure hear his lamentations.

To fend off those images, he went online and tried to read the news.

That lasted only fourteen seconds, and then he pinched his bottom lip between his teeth, opened a mapping program, and zoomed in on the observatory. Using satellite imagery, he panned across the Atacama in broad strokes, then tightened his field of vision to the smallest degree of detail possible. He located the general area where he thought the boy had died. Tracking outward from there, he looked for anything that stood out in the wasteland.

The word *nothing* seemed inadequate. The virtual map revealed extinct volcanoes, fluted escarpments, and long tongues of russet-colored stone. The Midnight Messenger and his pinwheel-bearing passenger had a point of origin unobserved by satellites.

Gabe closed the laptop and tipped his head back. The tiny canals in the ceiling tiles offered him as much information as the Atacama atlas.

"What about the autopsy?"

Gabe looked at the man in the doorway. It was Mick Jagger. Or Prince Charles. Or the soccer star Jorge Valdivia.

"Vicente?"

"Do you think they will find anything?"

"Anything like what? They'll learn the cause of death, if that's what you mean."

"What are you doing in here?"

"Things I shouldn't be doing."

"Playing with yourself?" Vicente laughed, though Gabe could tell it was forced.

"He was trying to save him," Gabe said. "He was trying to get that kid out of the desert."

"Yeah, maybe."

"And they shot him for it."

"They who?"

"Spacemen, cannibals, the Israeli secret police. I don't know."

Vicente leaned in the doorway. "The detectives asked a lot of questions. I told them everything I know, which is nothing, really."

"They think I'm a suspect."

“Huh? Why do you say that?”

“I look suspicious. Just ask Rubat.”

“One, you don’t look suspicious, and two, Rubat is overreacting. He’s not going to fire you, because you’re not going to give him a reason.”

Gabe sat up and put the laptop aside so he could rest his elbows on his knees. It was a better position if he wanted to resist the weariness that tugged at his bones. “What I don’t understand is *where* they were coming from. That’s the craziest thing. Assuming they didn’t cross the whole damn desert, all the way from Bolivia, they had to have *something* as a starting point. And there’s nothing out there.”

“Well . . . that’s not entirely true.”

Gabe had no luck trying to deduce the man’s sincerity through his body language. Was Vicente just playing him again? Was he about to expound upon the alien landing pad the government was concealing in the desert? Or the taco stand operated by the ghost of Elvis?

“Speak,” Gabe said.

“You’re new here, so maybe you don’t know. But this used to be prime saltpeter country. Hundreds of millions of pesos were made around here. Trains and trucks went back and forth twenty-four hours a day from the mines.”

“I’ve heard. But then it went bust.”

“True. Synthetic nitrate took over. Everybody left.”

“So?”

“So . . . there are ghost towns out there, *amigo*. And graveyards.”

CHAPTER NINE

Ben Cable stared at himself in the bathroom mirror and wondered if the Westbrook twins were trying to scam him.

"You ain't worth scamming."

Maybe that was true. His reflection remained unconvinced.

Santiago had been his home for the last year. Outside the tiny bathroom were the sounds of his neighborhood and a partial glimpse of his new life. On the corner stood the cluttered cigarette shop where he liked to visit just to smell the pipe smoke, the little Mapuche Indian woman behind the counter wearing her turquoise bracelets and hand-woven straw hats. The fishmonger two doors down with his baskets full of salmon heads, the kids on skateboards listening to their weird fusion of folk music and American rap—these were his people now, even though they were not really his at all. He'd come seeking inspiration on the suggestion of none other than a NASA field scientist. Ben had taken the man's advice not only because he'd served as technical adviser when Ben was crafting *This Mayflower Mars* but because he was, as it turned out, Ben's older brother.

But this time, Jonah Cable was wrong. There was no sequel. Ben had spent that year as he had spent the previous four: drifting, false-starting half a dozen novels, and shooting pool with old-timers in local bars. Jonah worked six hundred miles northeast of the city on a NASA-sponsored project that should have been cutting-edge enough to provide even the dullest hack with piles of usable story material. Grist for the literary mill.

"Yet here we are."

He flushed the toilet and washed his hands, drying them slowly. Though his nine-ball skills had appreciably improved here in southern Chile, he'd been unable to provide New York with a follow-up manuscript. His agent had simply stopped calling.

But now this. Here, at last, was something.

Damned if he knew what to make of them. Mira Westbrook was a good-looking young professional with more determination in her eyes than Ben had in his entire beleaguered bod. Her brother, her *twin,* was likable as hell and seemed to handle himself just fine despite the monkey wrench that genetics had tossed into his double-helix machine. But after that, everything fogged up. Until he could wipe himself a clear light of sight, Ben would have to take it on faith that they were legit.

"No more hiding in the head," he told the man in the glass.

As he left the bathroom, he asked himself if he was becoming more than just antisocial. At what point did a one-hit wonder go from media-shy celebrity to grade-A, pasteurized recluse?

He returned to his small living room to find the two of them waiting expectantly.

"So . . ." He rubbed his hands together and then felt foolish for it. What did they want him to say?

"Do you . . . have any ideas?" Mira asked. She was blond, her hair pulled back in a practical way, her face nearly free of makeup. "Any suggestions?"

"Not a one. You're telling me he can't read anything else? No magazine, blog, e-mail, article, nothing at all?"

"Not easily. We have some middle-reader books that he works with, but they're not high on his list of favorite things."

Ben looked at the young man. He had little experience with Down. It was a chromosomal problem, if he recalled. Something about too many copies of the such-and-such gene or not enough protein in the so-and-so enzyme. "What about comic books? You like those? Superman, Wolverine, that sort of thing?"

"I like the movies. *Batman! Iron Man!* Front-row tickets!"

"I see." He didn't see at all; it was simply too strange. Luke had read those passages not only fluently but also with a certain amount of eloquence. It was as if he were channeling someone else's voice, not to mention someone else's command of vocabulary and inflection.

"I tried finding more of your work," Mira said, "a short story in an anthology or a letter on an op-ed page, but—"

Ben laughed.

Startled by his own outburst, he clamped his mouth shut. How many weeks had it been since he'd made a sound like that? When was the last time he'd had an actual conversation? Recluse, nothing. He was heading toward full-blown hermitage. "Sorry," he said. "But you just hit my personal nail on the head. I'm not exactly what you'd call prolific. I laugh on behalf of my agent. Though I suspect he's moved on to tears by now."

In response to that, the poor girl plainly had nothing to say.

Ben scowled at himself. He was coming off as a freak. "Maybe if I could hear something else . . ." He looked at Luke. "Would you mind?"

"Mind what?"

Ben looked around, grabbed a copy of *Pool & Billiard,* and flashed through a few pages. Finding an ad with large, easy-to-read words, he handed the open magazine to Luke. "Here you go, son. Give this one a try."

"It's okay," Mira told him. "Just do your best."

Luke brought the magazine close to his face, holding it in both hands. Then he pulled back, his eyes going through a series of squints.

"You're stalling," Mira said.

Luke stuck his tongue out at her, then went back to his assignment.

Ben waited. He didn't know what was happening. He'd entertained no guests since Jonah had visited him two months ago. And now he had the single oddest pair of twins he'd ever met, one of them sitting literally on the edge of her seat, the other sounding out the word *ball* with the prowess of a six-year-old.

Luke struggled. He made it past the first two words but, like a climber coming upon a cliff face devoid of handholds, jabbed at the next word forcefully, as if he were driving pitons into rock.

Ben saw the devotion in Mira's eyes. In a rare moment of insight, he saw deeper than that, into the layers of patience and the slim stratum of her consternation.

"Bray . . . key," Luke read. Then, a moment later: "Break!"

"Good job." Ben offered him a smile. "Breaking is a very important part of pool, you know, and it has nothing to do with getting mad and splintering your cue stick."

"I like the eight ball," Luke said.

"You do, huh?"

"Yep. I shake it and it tells me the future."

"Ah, of course. Too bad we don't have one of those right now. I could truly use one from time to time." His eyes settled on his receipt from the market. He made one visit a week, stocking up on fresh fruit. He might be a hermit, but at least he hadn't fallen so far that he gave up mango and cantaloupe salad. For ripe strawberries, on certain mornings, he would have charged the guns of Navarone.

He grabbed the receipt and a pen, and then spent a minute jotting down the first thing that came to mind.

"I know it's weird," Mira said, "our coming here. I would have called ahead, or sent an e-mail or something, but . . . Anyway, if it seems like this was kind of brash, just getting on a plane and flying down here, it wasn't actually like that at all. I've been planning this for a while."

"You don't have to justify it to me," Ben assured her. "Lord knows I'm not in any position to go pointing out eye-specks when I've got a veritable redwood sticking out of mine." He gave the paper to Luke. "Humor me for a moment. See if you can make out what I've written here. My handwriting is more along the lines of Egyptian hieroglyphs, but hopefully you can—"

"'I have a dream that my four little children will one day live in a nation where they are not judged by the color of their skin, but by the content of their character.'"

Luke handed the paper back. "'I have a dream.'"

Ben stared at him. He knew then, finally, what his father had meant when he talked of how it felt when a ghost walked over his grave.

"Easy-smeasy," Luke said. He batted an errant hair from his face.

Ben opened his mouth, but he had nothing to say that seemed adequate.

"It's not the book, Mr. Cable," Mira said, her amazement evident in her whispered voice. "It's *you*."

One hour passed.

Ben had no whisky. He could not remember a time when a slosh of Johnnie Walker over three perfectly square cubes of ice was more appropriate than it was now. In its place he worked his way through a third cup of coffee. He'd heard somewhere that decaffeinated varieties existed, but he figured that would be like selling bullets without the gunpowder, so he put no faith in the rumor.

"No more!" Luke said, pushing the papers away from him.

"One last time." Ben banged away on his laptop. The three of them, like kids, sat on the floor. Within easy reach were pretzels and half a bag of chocolate chips. "Here, I'm printing it now."

The ink-jet spit out another page. This one contained a trick. Ben had copied a block of random text from the Internet, pasted it into a blank document, and mingled it with his own sentences.

Mira grabbed it, scanned it, and handed it to her brother. She'd barely stopped smiling.

Ben knew love when he saw it. Her eyes glittered with it. There was an excitement fused to that love, making the moment so keen with possibilities that Ben, for the first time in the bluest of blue moons, grinned for no reason other than that it felt so damn *cool.*

Luke sighed with great drama and read. "'One of my favorite recording artists is Dr. Hook. Though I am dating myself by saying this, in . . . ta-he . . . *the* la-tee . . . *late* see-va . . . see-veen—'"

"Seventies," Ben supplied. "In the late seventies."

"*Seventies.*" Luke rubbed his eyes. "'. . . dah . . . dac-ta . . . *tor, doctor*!'" He pointed. "Hey, that says *doctor.* That's a *hard* word."

"It is," Mira agreed. "But you got it."

"It'll get a lot easier after that," Ben predicted.

He was right. Luke said, "'Dr. Hook impacted young people in America and crossed both genre and racial divisions.'" He lowered the page. "Is that enough, please?"

"Yeah, son. That's enough."

After the silence had spun out for a while, Mira said, "What are you thinking?"

"You want my most coherent thought?"

"Sure."

"My most coherent thought is *holy shit.*"

Luke giggled. "Shit isn't holy!"

Ben looked at Mira, and they both laughed.

Luke joined them. "You *guys.*"

Ben drained the last of his coffee and didn't even mind that it was cold. Something was upon him, something that had yet to expose its full dimensions but warmed him just the same. He didn't know what was happening or why he'd been chosen to play a role in Luke Westbrook's special talent, and perhaps that very *not knowing* was what so enthralled him. "If you want me to tell you why I think Luke here can read things

I write but can't read much else without difficulty, then I am sitting here on the floor in this gloomy apartment and telling you that I haven't the damnedest notion."

"I sense a *but,*" Mira said.

"*But* I am very interested in learning more. To say the least. And I haven't been interested in much other than Spanish-speaking snooker halls these last few months. I won't bore you with the details of my life and times as an underachieving adult, but suffice to say that I don't feel bored today. In fact"—even as he spoke, an idea came to him—"I have a rather radical proposal, if you want to hear it."

"That's why we came."

"Good. My proposal is in two parts." He glanced at Luke. "Listening?"

Luke cupped his hands behind his ears to show that he was.

"The first part is to extract a very serious promise from both of you, swearing that you will refrain from calling me *mister.* There are no misters among friends, and I would like to think that's what we suddenly are."

Mira smiled. "Done."

"Second, how about if the three of us were to visit that particular place that got all of this hullabaloo started?"

"I don't follow."

Now it was Ben's turn to smile. He let it slide across his lips, savoring it. "I'm talking about Mars."

Luke made a face. "Huh? Mars is too far. Mars is way, *way* out in space. We can't go there!" He leaned forward. "Can we?"

Ben thought that maybe they could. He sensed it was worth a try. For whatever reason, his writing made a connection with this young man, so instinct advised him to take that writing to the shores of its rust-colored heart.

Luke touched him on the knee. "Are we *really* going to Mars?"

"Well, son . . . it may not be exactly like the real McCoy, but it is positively the closest thing to Mars you'll find on Earth."

CHAPTER TEN

The setting sun blurred the Atacama's horizon like melting glass. Gabe stared into the glow. Eighteen hours had passed since the Midnight Messenger had swept across his field of vision and lured him into this puzzle where half-boys were smuggled in backpacks and head-shot bodies faded like the day giving way to night. Gabe was overdue for sleep and felt it in his eyes. As he watched the system's primary star irradiate the western hills, he spoke his thoughts aloud. "I'm still not ruling out Gigante."

"Stranger things have happened," Vicente agreed.

"Shouldn't you be getting home?"

"Sergio is staying at a friend's tonight."

"And your wife?"

"Artemis is in Rio, selling textbooks to teachers. Not a bad place for a business trip. You know, sometimes I think I'm too much for her."

"Sometimes you're too much for *me.*"

"Other way around today, *amigo.*"

"Point taken. Her name is really Artemis?"

"Goddess of hunting and fertility. That's my old lady, and then some.

Her father was . . . eccentric. He also happened to be a disgusting excuse for a human being, the devil take him."

"Sounds like we better change the subject."

"Yeah." Vicente spat into the dirt. "You sure you want to do this? Drive out there?"

"It was your idea."

"I've had bad ideas before. Rubat is going to come unglued."

"I don't have much of a choice."

"The hell you don't. You go out there, he'll kick your ass out of the program. And it's dangerous. People die out there. The desert eats them from the inside."

"I wouldn't have much luck convincing the cops to check it out based on a hunch."

"So you have to do it yourself?"

Gabe sighed. "That runner last night, he was trying to save that kid. And now there's not even a body left behind to prove that he existed. *I'm the only one who knows he was even alive.* So, yeah. I have to do it myself, and hopefully Rubat won't find out."

Vicente rubbed the black stubble on his cheeks and glanced at his friend. "I'll get the truck."

The truck turned out to be a 1986 Isuzu P'up with oversized tires and one headlight. Vicente called it Cyclops.

Gabe settled himself onto the tape-patched seat. The sun continued to flash-fire the distant hills. Though it looked red at this time of day, Gabe knew this perceived color was due to a photon effect known as preferential scattering. There wasn't anything romantic about a sunset. The peril of being a scientist was losing your myths.

"Cyclops," he said, liking the sound of the name, "let's get rolling."

The desert altered form at dusk. The shadows spilled from jagged rocks like running oil, tar pits in which the truck might get lodged like some prehistoric animal caught outside the cave after dark. They had packed well for the trip so that a breakdown wouldn't end up getting them killed. In a wilderness with neither shelter nor cell service, survival was always foremost on everyone's mind. During the daylight, the place was scarred and desolate. At night it would be a vacuum. But in the time between, the half-seen shapes took on menacing forms, like gargoyles dipped in wax.

"You're the navigator," Vicente said. "You better check the map."

Gabe handled the chart carefully, as it was old enough that the folds were soft and ready to tear. Dated 1955, it depicted the locations of what were once the desert's booming mine towns and rail lines. Over half a century had passed since then. Gabe had assumed that nothing remained of the nitrate towns but husks.

"Maybe I should have brought a gun," Vicente said.

"So you could shoot your foot off? Or mine? No, thanks."

"Think about it. You say you saw a man get shot. Are we driving out here looking for the shooter? Is that what we're doing? Because if that's the case, then maybe I'm about to come to my senses."

Gabe hadn't considered it. But perhaps the greatest danger wasn't Rubat's wrath.

Vicente shifted gears. "I don't hear you telling me to turn around."

"We'll just . . . take a look, okay? We'll start at the point where we found the boy, and from there we'll try the closest set of ruins and look around. If we see anything untoward . . ."

"Untoward? Who the hell says untoward?" Vicente, half Canadian, spoke English as well as any Canuck, but apparently he preferred to keep things simple.

"If we see anything *suspicious* we'll come back."

"Shouldn't the cops be doing this? They have planes, you know. They can scout the entire area."

"I'm not convinced that they really want to. Besides, they still have to do lab work on the blood and probably an autopsy on the boy. I don't know anything about the process except what I see on TV. But as far as they're concerned, they don't have a crime. They have a kid who likely died of exposure, and that's it."

"Yeah, one really *messed-up* kid. Damn, I've never seen *anything* like that."

Gabe fought the images, but they came back: arm and legs cut away, hand reaching for the pinwheel's stem . . .

He gladly dove back into the map, using a flashlight to find his way around it. After locating the general area where they discovered the boy, he traced his finger outward in concentric circles. He stopped when he encountered the word *Aceda.*

"Acid?"

"Huh?"

"There's something here called Aceda."

"Aceda? Not acid, exactly, but when something turns sour, that's *aceda.*"

"Doesn't sound like a very friendly place."

"How far?"

"Uh . . . maybe seven or eight kilometers." At some point in his graduate work he'd started defaulting to the metric system, as did 95 percent of Earth's population. "Try a heading that's more"—he pointed—"that way."

"Westward ho." Vicente turned the wheel, causing a peacock's tail of dust to rise and capture the setting sun in its motes.

The truck flew. This stretch of the Atacama offered no obstacles, only hardpan dusted with just enough soil to leave a quivering wake behind the speeding vehicle. Vicente pushed his foot closer to the floor.

They found nothing.

Even after circling back and widening the search area, they saw no indication that Aceda had ever existed. It had long since dissolved.

"There used to be roads out here," Vicente said. "Maybe this Aceda was one of the residential communities for the miners, or it could've been a way station or telegraph office. The only way we'd know for sure is to search the records. I'm sure they're on file somewhere, maybe at the university."

"Let's keep going west. About ten klicks away there's something called . . . no, scratch that. There's something closer." He lowered the flashlight beam to the map, leaning down to make out the faded letters. "Looks like . . . Mentiras."

"*Mentiras?* Are you sure?"

"Well, with all this bouncing around I can't be certain . . ."

"It means *lies.*"

"Pardon? Like the town is just . . . lying around? Or the other kind of lie?"

"The other kind."

"Weird name for a town."

"Not so much, really. My father was from eastern Canada. There's a place in Newfoundland called Blow Me Down."

"Seriously?"

"Could've been worse. Imagine it without the Down."

Gabe grinned in the vanishing daylight. "Your mind works in disturbing ways, my friend."

Vicente spent the next fifteen minutes talking about that very thing—his mind—and concluded that being the product of an interracial marriage gave him a mental advantage. He was plainly laying conversational bait, expecting Gabe to ask what type of advantage, specifically, but his monologue trailed away when the outline of buildings appeared in the gathering dark.

"Slow down."

Vicente complied without comment, letting Cyclops roll closer to the shapes that were mostly concealed by the night. The sun bled out, leaving only a pink vein in the west.

Gabe watched the shapes take on solid form. Perhaps two dozen structures stood silently on an otherwise featureless patch of ground. The road that once led here had been erased. A single telephone pole jutted up from the earth, leaning sideways. It looked like a wooden stake that Gigante might have plunged into the ground.

The truck stopped completely. It idled there, the lightless buildings seemingly unimpressed by the noise.

"Behold," Vicente said, "I give you Mentiras."

Gabe swung open his door and climbed out.

CHAPTER ELEVEN

"The Skyhawk has a range of over seven hundred and fifty miles," the pilot said.

Mira didn't know if this was an impressive figure for single-engine planes, but she affected the appropriate look and nodded as if she understood. She sat directly behind her brother, who rode beside the pilot and was nearly out of his wits with excitement.

"She can do about a hundred and twenty knots, but we probably won't push the little lady quite that hard. Everybody got your gear stowed?"

"Roger that!" Luke exclaimed.

Mira loved seeing him like this. When Cable had offered to fly them to his brother's research project, six hundred miles north of Santiago, Mira had assumed he was kidding. But the spark in his eye caught flame, and within ten minutes he'd convinced them to grab overnight bags from their hotel and meet him at the charter service.

Sitting beside her on the plane's rear seat, Cable said, "Thanks for trusting me with this. I know it's probably not your usual MO to fly away with a total stranger and spend the night in a Quonset hut in the middle of the desert."

She smiled in a way that she hoped was convincing. It was important that he realize how significant this was to her. And not simply significant but *vital.* "First of all, you're not a stranger. I've known you for a year and a half, at least in a manner of speaking. Second, I think I'd sleep just about anywhere if it meant getting closer to explaining Luke's . . ." She almost said *miracle* but then opted for something less religious; she wasn't quite ready to give the credit to God, not after all of His questionable calls as the umpire in her life. "His *breakthrough,*" she said. "He can read everything you write, and I want to know why."

"Me, too."

"You should've let me pay for this. I have the money."

Cable was hearing none of it, waving it away. "Steffen here always cuts me a good deal. Eh, Stef?"

The pilot gave a thumbs-up. "We expatriates have to stick together, and there ain't nobody more ex than I am. Except my last wife."

Mira didn't share Luke's fascination with being in the air. She wasn't so much afraid of heights as she was in love with the ground. Her career was nothing to shuck away; it paid well enough that she planned to retire by fifty-nine, if she was frugal. But she was certain that in a past life she'd been a gardener. She loved the elemental business of working the soil and partnering with it to make life in the form of flowers and fruit trees. Perhaps in her golden years she would raise corn. Of course, as she hadn't been on a date in six months, she might just wind up raising that corn solo.

Mira Westbrook, spinster of the maize.

She smiled to herself and admired the tapestry of the Chilean countryside as the night encroached.

"You don't need a paper bag, do you?"

She turned to Cable, whose eyebrows were raised in concern. "I think I'm fine."

"You think?"

"May I ask you a question?"

"My dear, considering the kind of day you've given me so far, I am completely in your debt. You may ask without reservation."

"Why haven't you written another book? A sequel, maybe."

"Sequel? Nah, a sequel means you've been forced to repeat yourself. But I've butted heads with other manuscripts, that's true enough, and in five years I've got nothing to show for it but a thicker skull."

"Writer's block?"

"We call it white-page fever. But no, I don't think that explains it. At least not *all* of it. Jonah suggested I come down and take a gander at the work the scientists are doing on the Mars issue these days, real cutting-edge simulations. You'll see. But no matter how many times I visit him at the site, no matter how many opening lines I jot down in my Big Chief notebook, nothing really puts itself into any kind of order you could rightfully call a plot."

"I didn't know anyone was doing Mars experiments in Chile."

"Only place they *can* do them, at least if they want a decent model for the real thing."

"Why is that?"

"Like I said"—he winked—"you'll see."

They spent the next six hours building bridges between them while Luke gazed dreamily from the window, whispering impossible things.

Gabe approached the ghost town of Mentiras.

Though the sun had set, enough gray light remained that he didn't require the flashlight, at least not yet. He let his eyes further adjust, probing the wells of shadow between the buildings. They were made of cinder blocks and wood. A few had roofs of corrugated steel. A plastic sack had snagged on a jagged metal lip and now turned slowly in a breeze too faint for Gabe to feel.

Vicente stepped up beside him. "Maybe we should have done this in daylight."

"You're probably right."

"So you think this is where he came from?"

Gabe pictured the Midnight Messenger with the boy bundled on his back. Tirelessly he ran across the desert. "Whether he was running toward something or away from something, he had to start somewhere."

"There are a lot of places like this out here."

"But he was being tracked, remember? No one would have followed him for fifty kilometers. They would have caught up a lot sooner than that, which means he had to start somewhere closer. The next location on the map is too far away."

"You sound pretty damn confident for a man too afraid to move."

Gabe realized he hadn't taken a step along the dusty lane that passed as Main Street. "Yeah, well, I don't see you knocking on any doors, either."

"Hey, I'm just the native guide."

Gabe switched on the light.

The beam bounced between the structures, revealing the rectangular voids of their glassless windows and open doorways. Nothing held any meaning. Was that an old tire lying there? Or something else? And was that a gas pump or an ancient obelisk?

Gabe walked.

"I guess that means we're tempting fate," Vicente said. "I hope it's true that fortune favors the bald."

"You should be safe, then."

"Receding hairlines are all the rage these days. My wife says it's a mark of maturity, and I'll take those wherever I can get them."

They came to a building where the porch was made of railroad timbers. Gabe relaxed his grip on the flashlight and made it a point to inhale, exhale. Ascending the makeshift steps, he fanned the light into the gaping doorway. Inside, the darkness parted in circles to reveal a metal bed frame and other household debris trapped in a coating of Pompeii dust.

The night deepened as they repeated this procedure at the next structure, and then the next. At some point, Gabe realized that Vicente had stopped speaking. He breathed audibly and rapidly.

They crossed what might have been the town's center point, which was little more than a widening of the track that connected the skeletal buildings. Gabe couldn't shake the feeling that he was trapped in an old Western. There was no smell of horseflesh and mesquite out here, but it had everything else going for it. Had Lee Van Cleef stepped around the corner, six-gun in hand, it would've scared the shit out of him but he wouldn't have been particularly surprised.

What's that?

His mind registered the hunched mass before his eyes focused on it. From this angle it could've been anything. He pointed the flashlight at it, slowed his steps even further, and approached.

If there had been a single sound in the air, something to remind him that he hadn't gone deaf, perhaps his nerves would have relented a bit. But the land was dead. There were no animals, no insects, no barn door lurching on its one remaining hinge. Why did Vicente have to choose right now to shut his mouth? It was like walking in a jar.

The bulk turned out to be what was left of a station wagon. The strips of rubber still clinging to the wheels were petrified to a state of stone. All four doors were missing, revealing an interior devoid of seats and dashboard. Gabe was just about to move on when the light fell on something hanging from the shattered rearview mirror.

He held the flashlight very still, watching the thing, nearly hypnotized by it.

Vicente leaned closer. "Is that what I think it is?"

"Looks like." Gabe reached into the car and snagged the yo-yo from the mirror.

Examining it, he saw that its green paint may have been faded, but its string looked relatively new. It bore a single word: O-BOY.

"Are we calling this a clue?" Vicente asked, his voice hushed.

"Check out the string. It's almost perfectly white."

"So?"

"So, yeah, we're calling this a clue."

"A clue to what?"

Gabe turned it over in his hands, studying it, letting it lead him where it wanted him to go. "Who would have a yo-yo out here in this place?"

"Things don't always make sense in the desert, my friend."

"A kid. A kid would have this out here. It's a child's toy."

"And?"

"A child's toy . . . like the pinwheel." He tossed it up and caught it. "That boy was here."

"Here *where*?"

Gabe didn't respond, just set out walking, his pace quickening. Vicente whispered a curse and followed him. They explored what might have once been a grocer's and an eviscerated filling station. Gabe used the flashlight to drive back every shadow, hoping he didn't miss the one thing that would explain the Messenger's intentions. He spotted a community drinking well and was heading toward it when a man climbed up from its depths, holding what looked in silhouette to be a human arm.

Vicente made a startled noise and grabbed Gabe's sleeve.

The figure stopped halfway out of the well when he saw them.

Gabe dropped the flashlight. It rolled a few feet across the sandy ground, revealing the man in pulses.

Whoever he was, he tipped back his head and screamed.

It was not a sound of fear but rather one of violated rage. Gabe staggered backward.

Vicente clawed at him. *"Come on!"*

The flashlight rolled away and pointed at the nothingness of the desert. The man seemed to vanish in the dark.

"Move, goddamn you!"

Had Gabe not gotten his balance, Vicente would have dragged him off his feet. He stumbled, caught himself, and tried to look over his shoulder as he picked up speed. His breath returned. Vicente ran beside him, his boots drumming the dry earth, a piccolo sound of fear issuing from him with every other stride.

Gabe glanced back again. The night was too thick.

They reached the truck and threw themselves against it, groping for the door handles. Gabe landed behind the wheel and cranked the key, willing it to start.

The engine caught. The truck came to life. Gabe hit the lights, and though only one responded, it nevertheless opened a blessed tunnel where the darkness couldn't reach.

Vicente pounded the dash. *"Come on, come on!"*

Gabe released the clutch as he crushed the accelerator. The tires spun a tornado of dust, bit hard, and sent them hurtling across the desert floor. Gabe didn't bother with directions. With few obstacles to impede them, he could send them howling east or west, north or south, it didn't matter so long as they got away, and this became his mantra. *Get away, just get as far and fast away as possible—*

A bullet blew through the back window and drilled a spidery hole in the windshield.

"Shit!" Vicente bent down, burying his face against his knees.

Though Gabe flinched hard when the shot passed through the cab, he should've expected it. Hadn't the Messenger died from such a wound, fired from a distance?

He didn't bother sliding down in his seat. Instead, he pushed the little knob and killed the truck's single light.

The bright tunnel disappeared. Gabe swung Cyclops to the right, then back to the left, hoping that an unlit, swerving target would prove a difficult one. He drove blindly, a creaking comet through space. It occurred to him that such tactics would be of little use against a skilled marksman equipped with night-vision optics, but he had no other play. He pushed the truck to its structural limit, until its engine wailed dangerously and the frame shook.

His heart would not stop pounding.

CHAPTER TWELVE

Clutching his duffel bag against his chest, Luke turned in a complete circle. "Wow, this is really, really *dark."*

Though Cable had called it a desert, Mira couldn't verify his claim. Midnight was upon them, its wings so heavy and so black that she saw nothing but the stars. The constellations were all wrong here in the southern hemisphere, giving her the impression that the Skyhawk had flown them through the looking glass. They'd landed at an airfield near a town called San Pedro de Atacama, nearly eight thousand feet above sea level. The night air was crisp and thin. Mira pulled it deep into her lungs.

"You get used to it," Cable assured her. "The atmospheric pressure, I mean. Or lack thereof. You brought some lip balm, right?"

"Uh, yes, I think so."

"You'll need it. This place'll suck the moisture right of out you. Let's get a car and head on out."

"Gretel, I can't see *anything.* Is Mars always black like this?"

"I don't think we're quite there yet. Maybe we should leave some breadcrumbs to find our way back again, huh?"

"Yeah! But I don't have any. How 'bout M&M's?"

"Only if you want to waste them. I imagine the buzzards will snatch them right up."

"Buzzards? Buzzards like vultures?"

"Hey, with Mars, you never can tell. You read the book. You know how it is."

Minutes later she took a seat in the Land Rover that Cable's brother had sent to meet them. A redheaded American named Donner drove them into the desert. Mira's improbable journey continued. Luke spent the trip asking questions about everything from the taste of astronaut food to the chances of flying a kite on other planets. With nothing to see around them but a wilderness of darkness and stars, he cured his boredom with frequent booster shots of Martian lore. Cable, for his part, seemed more than happy to speculate or in some cases sew his answers out of whole and fictional cloth. Mira studied him in profile. His rough face was a landscape that the years had sculpted just the way the constant wind shaped the surface of Mars. But his eyes defied time. Even in the dark they retained the glimmer of youth. Mira heard the storyteller in his voice, the one who'd once written of love and loss on a mountain slope called Olympus Mons. She recalled the novel's epigraph, borrowed from Elton John: *Mars ain't the kind of place to raise your kids.*

"This isn't a warm desert, is it?" she asked, interrupting their conversation.

"No ma'am, it isn't. Remember that this is summertime down here, even though it's February and freezing in some parts back home. Everything is backward below the equator. Temperatures might get up to eighty-five degrees during the day. And it may indeed be summer, but at this elevation, sometimes the nights can be a bit nippy."

"Colder than a witch's you-know-what," Luke said.

"You got it, my man. And darker than the inside of a cow's belly."

Luke chortled. "A cow! That would be *dark.*"

"And drier than a popcorn fart."

Luke roared.

Cable turned in Mira's direction. "Pardon the French."

She wished he could see her smile in the dark. "Don't mind me at all. I was just thinking that it was darker than midnight under a skillet and colder than a pocket full of penguin poop."

Now it was Cable's turn to laugh. He actually slapped his knee.

A white dome appeared.

Donner slowed the vehicle as the structure broke away from the gloom and gleamed to life in the headlights. He stopped a few feet away, the light reflecting off the smooth, rounded walls.

"Who's that?" Luke asked, all thoughts of cows and penguins forgotten.

Rolling toward them, defying the stirred-up dust, was a man who was half machine.

So quietly that Mira barely heard him, Cable said, "My brother."

Gabe hit the brakes.

The truck fishtailed. He released some of the pressure, let the rear end catch up with the front, and then eased down again on the pedal. He turned hard to the right, and Cyclops whipped to a full and dust-strewn stop.

Vicente, head resting against the seat, said nothing.

As the dust settled around them, so too did the silence. They'd driven for an hour, going nowhere and everywhere, *anywhere* so long as it was away from the town called Mentiras.

Gabe stumbled out of the truck. He slammed the door, snuffing out the dome light and leaving himself in the middle of the universe: The ocean of the night sky teemed with stars, but no light of civilization marked the way home.

Vicente climbed out and pushed his door softly shut. A few moments later, Gabe heard his voice. "Who was that man?"

They hadn't spoken during their flight through the desert. Gabe had his theories about the man in the well, the man with the *arm,* but each was more fantastical than the last. He wanted to hear his friend's opinion, hoping it would be solid enough that he could grasp it with both hands and say *Yes, this makes sense.*

"Are you even listening to me?" Vicente asked, a hint of belligerence between his words.

"I hear you. I just don't have an answer."

"You didn't happen to bring the satellite phone?"

"And explain to Rubat why I needed it?"

Vicente rested his elbows on the truck. "What have you gotten me into, Gabriel?"

"I'm sorry. I didn't know."

"You knew *something* was out there. That's why you wanted to go."

"And you volunteered to come along. Nobody drafted you."

Vicente laughed humorlessly.

Gabe knelt and pinched some dust between his fingers. His pulse had finally settled, though it didn't seem to do him any good. In the absence of adrenaline, weariness laid siege to him. How long had it been since he'd slept? Thirty-six hours? Forty? "Assuming we can find our way back, we'll just . . . forget about all of it."

"That easy, huh?"

"Maybe."

"What about the police?"

"And make myself even more of a suspect than I already am? Give Rubat the excuse he needs to cut me from the program? I don't think so."

"You're saying we should just let the son of a bitch get away with it?"

"Get away with what?"

"Don't play *estupido* with me." His voice carried across the vastness. "You saw what I saw. He was holding . . . He had something in his hand. And we can identify him."

Gabe said nothing.

"Yo, asshole. We need to tell the cops about him."

"I can't."

"The hell you can't!"

Gabe stood up. "I can't identify him, okay? I don't know what he looks like."

"You saw him as well as I did. Narrow face, eyes kind of sagging like a wino's—"

"I'll take your word for it."

"Fine. Then take my word that I'm calling the *carabineros* as soon as we get to a landline. I'll shake those Ninja Turtles out of bed and give them some goddamn police work to do. Now get back in the truck."

Gabe felt it all tumbling out of his grasp. In an effort to avenge the Midnight Messenger, he'd tracked the man's assassin but was unable to do more than run away. A hero would've tackled the bastard. And now, because he'd retreated, Fontecilla and the investigative police would have no choice but to take him in for questioning, and then, upon hearing of the figure at the well, they'd launch a manhunt that might spell the end of Gabe's job here in Chile. Rubat was already under too much pressure from the men with the purse strings. He'd opt to cut his losses, forcing Gabe to reboot his doctoral research elsewhere. If anyone would have him.

Vicente got behind the wheel, started the engine, and hung his arm from the open window. "We've got less than a quarter tank left, so you better hope we don't get stranded out here. Might as well sign our death warrants, 'cause it sure the hell ain't going to rain, and I'm already halfway out of water."

Gabe gazed up, getting his bearings the way men had been doing since they realized, thousands of years ago, that the heavens were a map of mortal paths. Though he couldn't pinpoint his location without the proper tools, at least he knew which way was north.

"Meter's running," Vicente said.

Gabe climbed into the truck. "Do you have any idea where you're going?"

"We're lost. What's your best guess?"

Gabe suggested southwest, hoping they'd eventually encounter the road used by the service trucks for the rare delivery. The scattering of encampments out here—those of soil scientists, geologists, racing teams, and a few radical stargazers—required occasional supplies. That road was the only true link to civilization, the only passage from the wastes.

Vicente drove.

Gabe lost track of time. He wasn't wearing his watch. This thought reminded him of the watch he'd discovered on the Messenger's wrist, an expensive chronograph out of place with the man's environment. That kind of hardware didn't sync with the surroundings. Then again, neither did his military-style boots.

Gabe drifted. It must have been nearly two days since he'd slept. How had the Messenger come into contact with the boy? What was their connection? If Gabe could just get his fingers around that, if he could just come to know its shape . . .

He awoke when Cyclops slid to a stop. He sat up quickly, disoriented, and blinked against the sudden lights. There were dozens of them, mounted on poles and fixed to racks along the ground. In between were what seemed to be igloos.

He rubbed his eyes. "Where are we?"

"No idea. I just saw the light and drove to it. We're out of gas, by the way."

Faces appeared, faces without form . . .

"Gabe?"

"Yeah?"

"They have guns."

CHAPTER THIRTEEN

Mira stepped instinctively in front of her brother when the truck appeared.

She'd only just met the man in the wheelchair, Jonah Cable, when someone shouted a warning. She'd gotten no further than "Pleased to meet—" before a single headlight appeared, and seconds later, a pickup slid to a ragged stop in a fallout of dust.

The man in the wheelchair released her hand. "Eduardo!"

One of the other scientists—Cable had said there were only three men stationed here—swung a rifle off his back and braced it inexpertly against his shoulder.

"Donner!"

"I've got it!" From a nylon satchel, Donner produced a handgun of some kind.

Cable stepped away from this sudden weaponry, backing into his brother's chair. "What the hell's going on, Jonah?"

"We heard there'd been trouble, that's all I know." His voice was harder than Cable's, just as the years weighed more heavily on his face. "We got a call about one of the area's astronomical sites."

The truck's passenger-side door opened.

With the guns tracking him, the man got out, hands held away from his body. The profusion of lights fully revealed him: Caucasian, a bit disheveled, hair touching the collar of his denim jacket, and at least a day's worth of stubble on his well-defined cheeks.

"What kind of trouble?" Cable asked.

"Unknown. We were told only that the police were involved and that certain criminal elements might still be at large. Hence the hardware."

Mira could do little more than watch and wait. One moment she'd been intent on making a good impression on Jonah, and the next she was waving back the dust from a vehicle that might contain *criminal elements.*

"Don't shoot!" The man waved his hands and squinted against the light. "I work at Quest-South, the observatory."

At the touch of a toggle, Jonah's chair rolled forward six inches, its wheels coated in desert powder. "Your name, sir?"

"Traylin. Gabe Traylin."

Jonah checked a paper in his lap. From the style of its header, Mira recognized it as an e-mail printout. Apparently satisfied, Jonah said, "He's on the list."

Donner and Eduardo, visibly relieved, lowered their weapons.

Then, before Mira could stop him, Luke marched toward the pickup.

Mira called after him, but Luke paid no heed. He stopped in front of Traylin and boldly presented his hand. "My name's Luke. Welcome to Mars."

A second passed.

Traylin shook heartily. "Damn glad to be here."

Gabe accepted the water bottle and spent the next few moments doing nothing but rehydrating. Vicente sat beside him on a crate made of high-impact aluminum, beneath a half-tent full of what looked to be provisions for a lengthy stay. Drinking bought Gabe a bit of time, which he used in observation. He had no idea where he was or who these people might be. But as long as they weren't carrying human body parts or toting sniper rifles, he considered them allies.

"You're American?"

Gabe wiped his mouth. The man who addressed him was black; that much he could tell by his skin. There were other telltales about his age. Gabe had automatically conducted recon of the man's hands and placed him between thirty and fifty-five. It might not be an accurate estimate, but in the absence of tea leaves, guessing was the best he could ever do.

"Sounds like you are, too," Gabe said.

"Guilty as charged."

"Flagstaff."

"Newport Beach."

"California? I got my bachelor's at Stanford."

"Small world. I'm Ben Cable. My brother, Jonah"—he tipped his head toward the larger of the white domes—"is lead engineer here."

"Where's here?"

"The Auqakuh Carnegie Edaphology Field, or ACEF, courtesy of a joint effort between NASA and Carnegie Mellon University. Jonah's associates there are Donner and Eduardo. And these are my guests, Luke and Mira Westbrook."

Gabe hated meeting people. No matter how many times he suffered through the introductions, they never got easier. That was the hardest thing for those unfamiliar with prosopagnosia to fathom: *Everyone looked exactly the same.*

Still, he went through the motions. He said hi to the man called Luke, the one who'd first welcomed him to the camp or compound or whatever it was. Luke sounded young and full of spirit. His wife was a bit more reserved.

". . . how you got yourselves lost?" Cable asked.

Gabe had been drifting, still shaken from their flight across the sand.

He tethered himself to the ground and said, "I guess you could say we were putting our noses where they don't belong." He looked back at the building. Where *was* that guy who'd gone to fetch the phone? Cell phones were no good out here. If you didn't let the satellites play intermediary, you might as well have been in the Stone Age.

"We came for Mars," Luke said.

"Yeah? So you guys are . . . planetary scientists?"

"*I'm* not a scientist."

"That would be my dear elder sibling," Cable explained. "He oversees various soil experiments. Edaphology is the study of—"

"How soil types affect other living organisms," Gabe finished.

"Actually, yes. I'm impressed."

"What can I say? I know my ologies."

Careful, your geek is hanging out.

"Is somebody bringing that phone?" He didn't want to tip his nervous hand, but he knew it was evident that he was anxious. *Anxious,* though, didn't quite do justice to the bullet hole in the Isuzu's window. "It's imperative that I get in touch with the observatory."

"Did you see any Martians out there?" Luke asked.

Gabe traded glances with Vicente. "Maybe so."

"What color?"

"It was too dark to tell."

"Did they have ray guns?"

"In a matter of speaking."

"What's that mean?"

"Luke." His wife intervened with that single word.

"It's all right," Gabe assured her, though personally he'd never felt less assured. "We're sorry for barging in on you like this. I'm sure it's not how you planned on spending your night."

"Not at all," Cable said. "As it happens, we've experienced sort of a strange day ourselves. Isn't that right, Luke?"

"And how!"

Cable took it upon himself to explain more about the ACEF project, but Gabe didn't catch most of it. Supposedly *Auqakuh* was the word for Mars in the old Quechuan tongue of the Incas. After that, nothing interested him. The Midnight Messenger had died without a name or history, without a story, without seeing the face of anyone he loved. The last living person he saw was a boy who'd been pruned of his limbs. What had they talked about during their humpback trip across the sand? What promises had they made?

Eventually the man in the chair returned. Gabe had already forgotten his name, but he accepted the phone gladly, excused himself, and left the perimeter of lights so as not to alarm the others with what he was about to say.

He punched in the number of Rubat's office—

Wait.

He paused with one digit unpressed. The conversation would be brutal, like the local street-side chefs chopping the heads from fish. Rubat would hear about the stranger with the rifle and then start hacking away, lopping off a few more pieces of Gabe's future as an astronomer. Some of Rubat's superiors back in Europe were already talking about putting the operation on hiatus; Rubat would not want them to see a reckless doctoral student as one more reason to shut it all down. Maybe it would be best to bypass the observatory's chief altogether.

He raked Fontecilla's card from his jeans.

Though it was well after midnight, the detective picked up on the second ring.

"Hey, it's me, Gabe Traylin, from the—"

"Observatory. One moment, please."

Gabe waited. Maybe Fontecilla was putting on his glasses or slipping out of his room so as not to wake his lover. No, on second thought, Fontecilla wasn't a mistress kind of guy. He'd either been married for a hundred years or was an eternal bachelor.

"Señor Traylin, are you still there?"

"You bet."

"What is the matter?"

Gabe turned a complete circle. He ran his hand through his hair. Now that he finally had one of the good guys on the line, he didn't know what to tell him. *Hey, Font, old buddy, I hope you don't mind, but a friend and I pretty much took the law into our own hands and went out on the trail of a dead man, and guess what? Yep, we ran face-first into a freakshow climbing up from a well, and get this: The bastard owes us a new windshield.*

"Traylin? Can you hear me?"

So if you thought I was crying wolf the first time, just wait till you take a posse out to Mentiras and find not a single quantum particle of evidence.

Would it go down like that? Would the police arrive to find that the man from the well had erased all signs of his existence and fled into the Atacama's endless corridors? Gabe would then be considered not only a potential suspect in the case of the dead boy but a nuisance, an official antagonizer of the Policía de Investigaciones.

"Traylin? Have I lost you?"

Gabe terminated the call.

Now what? While he stood here tapping the sat phone's antenna against his chin, the shooter from Mentiras was . . . what? Breaking camp? Tossing his butcher knives into the back of an RV? Gabe wanted to laugh at the image that came to him, an old Winnebago with a Parrothead license plate, but he found no humor in it. He kept thinking about that damned pinwheel and the boy.

He went to the truck, grabbed the map off the seat, and returned to the tent, where the man in the wheelchair was promising to give everyone the full ACEF tour at daybreak.

Vicente seemed far more interested in the phone. "Did you get ahold of Rubat? What did he say?"

Gabe ignored him. "Can anyone show me where we are on this map?"

"Are we driving back tonight? We'll need some fuel. Cyclops is down to a drizzle."

"We're driving," Gabe said, "but not to the observatory."

"I don't think I like the sound of that."

"And I'm not asking you to come along."

Cable touched a point on the map. "I think we're somewhere around here. That about right, Joe?" He handed the map to his brother.

"You can't go back there," Vicente said. By his posture, Gabe could tell Vicente was glaring at him. For once he was thankful he couldn't see anything more distinct. "There's no way you're going to confront that guy by yourself."

"Confront whom?" Mira asked.

"Martians?" Luke wondered.

The wheelchair shifted a bit closer. "I'll mark our position in pen, if I may, though I must say that this map of yours looks like it hails from the Truman era."

"Pen's fine," Gabe told him. He turned to Mira. She had blond hair and, he had to admit, a body that knew how to wear a pair of khakis. "And I don't know who, exactly. Somebody who may have done some bad things, I guess."

"What kind of bad things?"

Silence followed her words. The others looked up from the map. Gabe felt their eyes on him as certainly as if he could see their faces.

They waited.

"I won't know for sure until I get to Mentiras," he said. "But first I'm going to need to buy some gas."

CHAPTER FOURTEEN

Mira no longer heard the men arguing. The younger one, Traylin, seemed intent on a course of action that plainly didn't jive with his friend. They'd still been bickering when they returned, and apparently Traylin had won. He arranged to buy fuel from Jonah Cable and asked if anyone could drive his companion back to the observatory. When that was settled, he wrestled with the heavy twenty-liter gas cans until Luke, noble and selfless Luke, ran over to help.

"Sorry about the circus around here," Cable said, appearing behind her and wiping his hands on a rag. "As soon as these fellas vamoose, we'll see that you get the most comfortable guest cot available."

"That's okay. Honestly I'm not very tired."

"Know what you mean. For the last few months my old EKG machine has been running flatline, but then you showed up this morning. Result? Serious spikes."

"I hope that's a good thing."

"You kidding? What I saw your brother do today . . . It's weird, that's for sure. But it's also . . . scintillating."

"Nice word."

"Hey, I'm a writer. Or at least I was."

"You still are."

"That, little lady, remains to be seen."

Though she couldn't see much of them in the darkness, Mira heard the muffled sounds of the men as they refueled the truck. Something about their tone made her uneasy. Jonah's colleague Donner brought the Land Rover around in order to give Traylin's friend a lift.

"What about you?" Cable asked her.

Even in the angled lighting, Mira saw the true concern in his eyes. Those were eyes that had witnessed more than the rest of him was letting on. "What about me? I spent the entire plane ride talking your ear off."

"I know, you're here for Luke."

"That's right."

"Is it? Believe me when I say that I know, really *know* how it is to feel responsible for someone who . . . who isn't always capable of taking care of things for themselves."

"Your brother seems entirely self-sufficient to me."

"Oh, that's a fact. He's a one-man juggernaut and a royal, arrogant pain in the keister at times. He's Ahab without the whale. But it wasn't always like that. For a few years after the accident, yours truly was the only thing standing between Joe and a razor blade. But keep that under your hat."

Red taillights appeared, two animal eyes in the dark. The pickup drove away.

"And so the mystery man departs," Cable observed. "Hope he finds whatever it is he's looking for. They say this desert is full of secrets just waiting to be dug up."

"I guess that's why we came."

"You think?"

"Sure." Though naturally reluctant to give away too much of herself, she knew this trip was all-or-nothing. There was no longer any reason to be semihuman; it was time to unload everything she had. "Out of all the people in all the world, you're the one that can connect with Luke on that level. You're the key. I don't know how or why. But he not only reads what you've written, he *understands* it. His mind works differently when he reads that damn Mars book. I know this because I *feel* it. This isn't going to make any sense to you at all, but when *he* becomes freer, so do I. He's one wing and I'm the other. We're both just trying to get off the ground."

Cable chewed on this for a while, then looked at her in such a way that Mira suspected that he, too, had decided to lay it all on the proverbial line. "Before a rich man's son drove his car into us when we were kids, we had no prospects. Then, with our daddy dead and Joe a paraplegic, the lawyers told us we were wealthy. Joe had the money to go to college and the time on his hands to study. He's earned two master's degrees, for God's sake, he's under contract with NASA, and for some reason I'm still hanging around, trying to decide what I want to be when I grow up."

"So you came down here to find out?"

"Just like you, huh?"

"Looks like." She glanced around, but Luke had yet to return after helping haul the heavy gas can. Hands on her hips, Mira called his name.

He didn't respond.

"We best go track him down," Cable suggested. "Out beyond the lights, this place can disorient an Eagle Scout."

"Luke?" She and Cable left the sanctuary of the lighting racks and approached the storage container where Traylin had replenished his tank. "Luke, we need to get some sleep."

Though he still offered no reply, Mira wasn't worried. This wasn't the Byzantine congestion of Santiago. Outside the ACEF perimeter, there was literally nowhere to go.

Cable lent his voice to the effort. "Young master Luke! Return to base!"

"Luke, stop messing around." She found one of Jonah's associates, Eduardo, snapping a padlock on the storage container. "Wasn't my brother here helping with the gas?"

"Sure. He helped me roll the barrel out."

"So where is he?"

"Don't know." Eduardo looked around. "He was just here a second ago. I've been putting the siphon pump away. He couldn't have gotten too far, right?"

Now Mira let the worry sink its talons into her. "Luke, this is not funny!"

"You take this neck of the woods," Cable suggested. "I'll try the other side." He jogged away, calling Luke's name.

Mira stood there with the lights at her back and untold acres of stars overhead. Other than Cable's voice and the retreating footsteps of the scientist, she heard nothing. Luke had a tendency to talk to himself when he was alone, telling stories based on the latest movies he'd watched, but he offered none of them now, no breadcrumbs to lead this fretting Gretel back to her other half.

"Dammit, Luke, this isn't the way I want to spend my first night on Mars!"

He never played this trick on her. Though he was as pleased as any brother to pull a variety of pranks on his sister, he never went in for hiding. Experience had taught him that people assumed he was hurt or in trouble when he was out of sight too long. So to make them happy—and probably to keep them off his back—he made a point of sending out periodic vocal indicators, like a submarine's ping.

Mira realized then, in the absence of such a signal flare, that her brother was gone. Panic, that old dragon that had always dwelled best in darkness, breathed fire down her neck.

"Luke!"

Gabe was trying to convince himself he wasn't driving to his own funeral when a face appeared in the rearview mirror.

He cried out and almost lost control. Planting one foot on the brake and the other on the clutch, he rammed the truck to a stop, his shoulder harness locking against his chest. Throwing the gearshift into neutral, he hit the seat belt release and looked back—

The face was gone.

After ramming down the parking brake, Gabe shoved open the door and managed to keep himself upright as he stumbled out. The meager dome light revealed nothing.

Someone laughed.

Gabe backed up, trusting the darkness to envelop him. "Who are you?"

"I'm sorry!" A figure moved, causing Gabe to take several more steps away. "I didn't want to *scare* you."

Whoever he was, he jumped out of the truck bed.

Gabe almost turned and ran. Though he was tired, the muscles in his legs were Tesla coils, waiting to give him the voltage needed to sprint and survive. He'd spent his life bent over books and photometry results, but since seeing the blood on the Messenger's head, he'd convinced himself that he was something more.

"Mr. Gabe, it's *me.* Luke Westbrook. You met me. We shook."

Gabe let this work its way past his pulse and reach the rational parts of himself. "Westbrook?"

"Yep, yep, and more yep!"

"What the hell are you doing?"

"I am H-E-double-hockey-sticks coming with you!"

"Why? You don't even know me."

"Because. I want. To meet. The Martian."

Westbrook moved toward the open driver's door, permitting Gabe to get a decent look at him, at least as decent a look as he ever got at anyone. He wore baggy cargo pants and what looked like a football jersey. He was several inches shorter than Gabe, but wider through the shoulder and hips. Facially he might have been anyone from Adonis to Arafat.

"Mr. Gabe?"

Gabe realized he was wrong. Luke Westbrook sounded much younger than he'd first assumed. The cadence of his words, his style of speech—he was probably no more than fourteen. The woman, whatever her name was, must have been his mother. "It's not mister. Just Gabe. And you scared the shit out of me, by the way."

"Ben says shit is holy."

"Yeah? I guess sometimes it is." He returned to the truck, a few of his nerves relaxing. "Get in and I'll give you a ride back."

"But I'm here for the *Martian.*"

"It's not a real Martian, okay? I don't know *what* he is, exactly, but he's not from Mars."

"Then why do you want to see him?"

"Because he . . . he hurt some people."

"He's *bad*?"

"More than you know."

"He's bad and you're going to *stop* him?"

Gabe patted his pockets but found no crumpled pack, no last cigarette for the condemned.

"Stop him like a *hero*?"

Hero? In that single word, Gabe understood that he had no business here, tilting at this windmill that would only get him killed. This kid, Luke, pointed that out without even knowing it. "Yeah, you're right. Fat lot of good I'm going to do out there. End up with my arms and legs pulled off, most likely." He tried to smile at his own folly but didn't quite make it. "Just get in. Your mom's probably freaking out by now."

"My mom's dead."

"Then who—" He waved it away. "Forget it. Let me just put my tail between my legs and call it a night, okay?"

He started to climb into the truck, but he stopped when it was obvious that Luke had no intention of following his lead. Instead, the kid fumbled with the button of the big pocket on his pantleg. Tugging it free, he produced a bent paperback. In the light from the cab, he fanned through the pages with his thumb.

Gabe could only watch and wait.

Finding the correct page, Luke held the book close to his face and read: " 'Casting his shadow over the stalwart plants that had drilled their roots into rock, Lieutenant Dycar realized what had until then eluded him. If he were to survive the coming fray, he would have to make his heart like this soil, the stuff of ancient iron.' "

Luke looked up, searching Gabe's face over the top of the pages, then dove back into the scene. " 'This planet may have formed too far from Sol and thus missed its shot at water and white-tailed deer, but its story was no less worthy of being told, and the men who traveled it no less determined to defend it.' "

Luke quietly put the book away.

Gabe stared at him. He remembered, long ago, when he'd spent five bucks to have his fortune told at a Renaissance fair. The woman on the other side of the sequin-scattered table was likely a charlatan. Luke Westbrook seemed far more authentic. Then again, Gabe was subconsciously looking for a reason to avenge the fallen, a reason that was greater than his fear, so maybe it wasn't Luke's soothsaying that turned the final screw in his resolve but his own foolish desire to see that the Messenger's story was told and his ghost defended.

"Ancient iron, huh?"

Luke nodded. "That's what Ben Cable says. He wrote the book."

"Well, let's hope he knows what he's talking about." Though bringing the kid along probably wasn't wise, Gabe was running on instinct now rather than wisdom; letting Luke accompany him didn't sound like the right thing to do, but it *felt* right. "Get in."

"All *right*!" Luke clapped twice and raced around the truck.

Gabe slid behind the wheel, released the brake, and resumed his journey. Luke said nothing during the ride, just sat on his hands and evaluated the worth of the stars. Gabe could've been a proper tour guide, explaining the juxtaposition of constellations as seen from the southern hemisphere, but he couldn't muster the nonchalance. He forced his grip to relax so that blood returned to his fingers. Maybe his iron wasn't so ancient after all.

Well, he would know soon enough. As he rolled to an easy stop, tiny bits of silica crunched under the truck's wide tires. He estimated that Mentiras lay about two kilometers ahead.

"I don't see anything," Luke said.

"You will."

They got out and walked toward the unknown.

CHAPTER FIFTEEN

"Mira, calm down. We'll find him."

"I *am* calm, Ben. This is my I-am-a-rock-I-am-an-island face. But we need to get a car and go after them."

"You're assuming he left with that guy."

"Where else could he have gone?"

Ben knew she was right. Luke couldn't have accidentally hurt himself out beyond the limit of the camp lights, because there was nothing around but miles of empty ground. He wasn't lying somewhere snakebitten; there were no rattlers, no pitfalls, no predators or ankle-twisting terrain. Why the young man had chosen to hitch a ride into the desert was a question that only Luke himself could answer.

Jonah rolled back into the tent. "We scanned the area with infrared optics. I'm afraid there's no sign of him."

"We're thinking he left with the astronomer," Ben said. "You have a vehicle we can use?"

"Only the Land Rover. Donner is giving that man a ride back to his observatory, so until he returns—"

"That's all you've got?" Mira asked. "One stupid car?"

"There are only three of us stationed here, Ms. Westbrook." Jonah used what Ben thought of as his Hannibal tone, the one used to drive elephants over the Alps. "We have absolutely no need for a used-car lot. Forgive me if we're not equipped to serve as a taxi service for whatever strangers drop by in the night."

"Go easy, brother. She's worried, that's all."

Jonah flashed him a look.

Normally Ben relented in the face of that glare. It had been cowing him since they were boys, back in a time when white movie stars were their idols and their biggest challenge was getting up early enough on Saturday morning to help their old man mow somebody's lawn. Since then, Ben had heard the singing of many an "Auld Lang Syne" as the years turned to scrapbook pages. Still, he probably would've acquiesced had it not been for the woman standing beside him.

"You met Luke," he said. "You know it's probably not safe for him to be driving out to parts unknown with a total stranger. Your people are packing guns, for the love of God, so you understand that it might be more dangerous out here than usual. It's not safe for *any* of us, much less him."

"Since when were you afraid of guns?"

"I'm not, but you know damn well what I mean. Luke could get himself hurt out there, and I'm not standing around here scratching my crotch while that happens."

"So what would you have me do? Pull a Cadillac out of my—" He caught himself and simply folded his hands in his lap. "We'll have to wait until Donner returns with the Land Rover. There's nothing else we can do."

Ben had no choice but to relent. His brother, as always, was right. He turned to Mira. "I'm sorry. I was hoping this trip would be fun and maybe even a little bit enlightening. I didn't count on anything happening to Luke, not to mention the guns and the rest of the chaos. I apologize."

Mira might not have even heard him. As soon as it had become apparent that they couldn't set out after Traylin, she'd sent her eyes once more to the darkness, hoping to see a familiar figure emerge from the gloom.

Ben scraped together some courage and touched her shoulder. "Mira? It's going to be okay."

She crossed her arms. "Is it?"

Before Ben could launch into his manifesto about rose-colored glasses, peace on Earth, and how all things worked together for good, Jonah intervened. "You must forgive my brother, Ms. Westbrook. He is often sloppy with his optimism, flinging it around like paint. Through the years he's ruined more than one of my suits."

"Yeah, and I keep hoping you'll stop taking them to Glass Half Empty Cleaners."

Jonah ignored him. With a gentle touch he turned his chair so that he faced Mira. "I stopped believing in that paint in 1979, which means ever since then I've left nothing to chance." He sighed. "I suppose if you want to ensure that everything is indeed going to *be okay,* then we have no choice but to follow that truck."

"I don't understand," she said. "If you don't have any other vehicles . . ."

"We have *one,* but it's not exactly what you would call street legal. Fortunately for us, we won't be driving on any streets."

Ben grinned. "You have to be shitting me."

Jonah never looked away from Mira. "You'd think by now he'd know that I never shit anyone, at least not when it comes to ninety-thousand-dollar unpressurized prototype rovers."

Mira still seemed perplexed. "You mean . . . some kind of space car?"

"It's not half so grand as you might imagine, but yes, ACEF has a glorified dune buggy that provides an analog for what might one day be driven by planetary explorers."

"And we can use it?"

"We use it quite often, actually. I considered mentioning it earlier, though I'm sure you understand my reluctance to volunteer an expensive piece of government-owned equipment. But I suppose I can't see much difference in driving it to check on genetically modified barley and driving it to retrieve a lost visitor. I don't imagine it will take long to fetch him and bring him back."

"My man," Ben said, putting his hand on his brother's shoulder, "there may be hope for you yet."

"Perhaps," Jonah said, deftly spinning his chair away. "For now, let's just worry about getting through the rest of this night. Then we'll talk about hope."

The ghost town materialized.

Gabe didn't see it coming. One moment he and Luke were walking through the endless dark like swimmers in a sea without horizons. The next moment Mentiras appeared, its silent houses blacker even than the night.

Leaning toward Luke, Gabe whispered, "I'm betting the guy is long gone, but we need to be quiet just in case. Cool?"

Luke pantomimed the act of zipping his lips shut and elaborately stowing the key in his pocket.

Gabe would have to be satisfied with that. He hadn't intended to bring anyone else into what might be a dangerous situation, least of all a kid; still, he wasn't too proud to admit that he relished the company. Though he'd never feared the dark, this was darkness on a different level. But he didn't expect to find anyone here this time. Whoever that man had been at the well, he'd likely gone elsewhere now that he'd been discovered, as these empty homes and wooden shells offered no real place to hide. Gabe believed this was true, but on the off chance that someone was still here, he didn't want to be alone when he encountered them.

With a nudge he pointed Luke straight ahead. Though he'd initially planned to circle the town, he switched gears at the last moment and opted for the smart-bomb mentality of going right for the source. They passed through the narrow space between two walls, the angled rooftops occluding the stars. The wood still possessed a strong scent despite the years. Without rain to leech their essence, the boards hadn't rotted with time. Captured in the amber of the Atacama, the town remained much as it had when nitrate miners had caroused here half a century before.

Gabe stopped at the end of the narrow alley, Luke so close behind him that he felt the boy's heat. He checked the street in front of him, what was once the main thoroughfare. The well stood at its center point, the fulcrum that had once balanced the town.

Nothing moved.

Turn around. Drive away.

Gabe fought against the impulse to return to the truck. His desire to make sense of recent events battled with his heartbeat, now throbbing so forcefully that he felt it along the entire length of his body. What had Luke's book said about Mars? Something about how its story was worth telling and its travelers determined to defend it. Whatever. Gabe damn sure wasn't doing this out of loyalty for the Chilean desert, but rather absurdly for a dead man and a pinwheel.

Turn around. Drive—

"Shhh." He bent at the waist and advanced on the well.

He made little sound as he moved, though Luke's footfalls were somewhat heavier. There was something odd about the kid, which in fact served to draw Gabe to him, as Gabe himself had been a boy likely to have a sci-fi novel shoved in a pocket, ready to be whipped out like a blaster as needed. He'd spent his time not at high school football games or clandestine keg parties but instead at home with *Doctor Who*.

He reached the well and breathed through his mouth, listening, listening . . .

Convinced that he and Luke were alone, he dared to touch the well's mortared bricks. Had he really seen a man climb out of this thing? Or had the man simply been crouched nearby and, upon standing up, given the impression of rising up from below? Either way, the well was certainly dry. Finding water here meant digging to absurd depths, and even then the reservoirs never lasted for long. Any divining rod used in this desert was merely wishful thinking.

"Gabe?"

Even though Luke whispered that single syllable, the word as light as a moth's wing, Gabe touched him on the knee and transmitted a message of silence. Though Gabe might have merely imagined the man's hiding place, he knew that the rifle was real. Even that moth's wing would make them a target.

Gabe glanced over his shoulder. The light from the stars reached him after traveling for thousands of years and revealed nothing but the hollow husks of buildings.

He looked back at the well. It had no awning, no bucket, no capstan that might be cranked to deliver water from below. There was a time when it had been the town's nucleus, but now it was nothing more than a ring of stone and probably bottle-dry at the bottom.

Gabe leaned toward it and peered over the edge.

Event horizon.

That phrase came to him as he stared down the well's black throat. According to theory, the gravity of a black hole was so intense that nothing could escape its grasp, not even light, not even time itself. Though no one had ever observed a black hole directly, scientists assumed that its reach was defined by a special boundary, a galactic point of no return. They called it the event horizon. Run that particular stop sign and you were lost. Even God couldn't get you out.

"Gabe?"

The shaft's depth was anybody's guess. Maybe it really *was* a black hole, a conduit to some other, more interesting part of the universe. Bolted to the bricks on the inside of the well was a ladder made of pipes and chain.

"Gabe."

Gabe put his mouth next to the boy's ear. "You're going to have to be very quiet. I see something down there, a ladder, but I'm not sure what to do yet, okay?"

Luke nodded emphatically.

Gabe returned to his inspection of the well. The ladder wasn't corroded with rust; in the total absence of moisture, nothing rusted. The individual rungs were made of steel pipes, through which passed lengths of chain. The apparatus looked homemade and descended into the unknown.

Nothing good is down there.

Gabe agreed. He would not discover a lost cache of bandits' gold nor hidden Incan artifacts. The wise thing to do would be to get in the truck, drive like hell to Calama, and wake Fontecilla from his well-deserved rest. Let the Ninja Turtles play Journey to the Center of the Earth. They were the ones with the machine guns.

Luke grasped the well's edge and peered down.

Still Gabe heard nothing from below, and he suspected that sounds would carry easily up the stone-lined shaft. He supposed he was right about the man with the rifle. The bastard was too smart to hole up in his lair now that he'd been seen. He was far away by now.

Luke whispered, "What do we do?"

Gabe had a flashlight shoved into the pocket of his jean jacket, but he had no desire to use it, as its light would only reveal his position. Still, if he decided to brave the ladder, at least he wouldn't be completely blind at the bottom.

Trusting that he was right and the Midnight Messenger's killer had fled the scene, he gripped the rough lip of the well with both hands. "Luke?"

"Yeah?"

"Stay right here. I'm going in."

Before Luke could respond, Gabe swung his leg over the well, found the top rung with his foot, and crossed the event horizon.

CHAPTER SIXTEEN

Mira's hair trailed behind her in the rover's wind.

Jonah Cable sat behind the controls of a vehicle that was little more than chassis, batteries, and tires. After locking his chair into position and running a hasty diagnostic, he'd gotten them moving across the desert floor. The craft hummed as its electric motors turned the wheels. For quite some time, they'd ridden in silence, each of them armed with three water bottles that Eduardo had supplied. With the nitrate gone, the most valuable thing in this desert was what you kept in your canteen. Every time you ventured out, a chance existed that some random element of the wilderness would cause you to lose your way. And once lost, you rarely came back.

Having been warned of this, Mira hoped that Luke was wearing his Danger Cap.

Her brother hurt himself from time to time. He forgot things. He got too caught up in his imagination. The Danger Cap helped him pay attention. It kept him safe. As long as he concentrated on wearing it—figuratively, anyway—he wouldn't miss the warning signs.

"Looks like we've got about ten more miles," Ben observed, indicating the GPS unit that glowed from the rover's control panel. Before departing, they'd programmed the coordinates of something called Mentiras, the place Traylin had mentioned. Jonah had located it in ACEF's extensive map archive, though he admitted he wasn't aware of any towns or settlements in the area. "Shouldn't be much longer," Ben continued, "even if this here Martian dragster isn't really breaking any land speed records. You hanging in there?"

"I'm an overprotective sister," she said. "Hanging in there is what I do."

Ben seemed to understand. Mira realized that at some point she'd stopped thinking of him by his last name. Friends happened suddenly sometimes. Mira was thankful for it, especially now when she was having to deal with what her mother would've called a Lipstick Smear. Lifelong waitress and junkie to the manner born, Cathy Westbrook scaled every problem to the same size, so that a spilled cup of coffee and an eviction notice were of equal consequence. Just another Lipstick Smear, baby, so dig the compact out of your purse and deal with it.

". . . but it's primarily used out here to test its utility in the field," Jonah said, waving a hand at the rover's skeleton of roll bars and supports.

Caught up in the tangles of her own worry, Mira heard little of this tour-guide spiel, her thoughts only on her brother and where he'd gone. But even as she anticipated their arrival at Mentiras, she remembered what the cabbie had said in Santiago. *Sometimes waiting for something is better than seeing it arrive.*

"Just be okay," Mira said to the wind.

The wind, promising nothing, did not respond.

Gabe stepped from the ladder and touched down on the unknown. What had passed for darkness in the world above was only an amateur. Here was where the grown-up darkness dwelled, the stuff without stars.

He heard nothing. If the rifleman was hiding nearby, he was holding his breath.

Gabe switched on his flashlight.

A tunnel appeared, boring through the wall of the shaft and leading to what appeared to be a subterranean chamber. Whatever aquifer had once provided water to the people of this long-ago town had given up its final drop; the bottom of the well was covered in sand. When Gabe turned toward the passage, his feet made no sound.

He trained the light on the ground. Someone had walked a path in the sediment, going back and forth between the shaft and whatever waited in the cavern beyond. Had the Messenger been here, making some of those tracks? Had he visited this place and plumbed its secrets?

The ladder chains jingled.

Gabe looked up, the flashlight beam revealing the soles of Luke's shoes as he descended.

So much for telling him to stay behind.

Luke's movements were somewhat awkward as he cleared the last few rungs and reached the bottom. Before Gabe could warn him not to say anything, he whispered, "You can't explore Mars without a *partner.*"

Gabe put a finger on the boy's lips.

Luke nodded twice.

Gabe waited, listening for a hint that they'd been heard, but it seemed his prediction was correct. Realizing he'd been discovered, the rifleman had fled. He was likely on a motorcycle and halfway to Argentina by now.

Gabe proceeded along the tunnel. The low ceiling forced his head down. The walls were carefully shored up with boards that had probably been pilfered from the surrounding shacks. It was not the work of an afternoon or even a week. Someone had been down here for a while.

The crude hall opened onto what must have been the basement of a building that no longer existed in the stripped-down town above. Gabe surmised that the tunnel had been carved out to provide an escape route via the well shaft. Though Mentiras was mostly gone, its cellars and crawlspaces were intact and currently in use.

The narrow cone of light partially revealed the chamber's contents. On Gabe's immediate right was a control box of some kind, full of wires and fuses, and on the left was a bookshelf layered with the strata of stacked newspapers. Tables, benches, obscure tools—it was too much to take in at once. The strangest thing was the smell. Gabe swore it was freshly baked bread.

Luke poked him in the back. Gabe moved aside to let the boy step out of the tunnel. Together their eyes followed the light.

A headless mannequin stood sentry near an opening in the far wall. A piñata in the shape of a guitar hung from a coat hanger. None of it made sense. The room defied explanation. Was it a workshop? A hideout? A mad scientist's lab?

Gabe went to the bookshelf and slid one of the papers free.

With Luke looking over his shoulder, Gabe focused the light on the headline but had no luck reading it. "Spanish," he said into Luke's ear. The paper was dated 13 May 1978.

He returned it to the shelf and walked deeper into the room.

On a trestle table lay an array of blades.

Gabe stopped so suddenly that Luke bumped into him. Like a spotlight highlighting props on a stage, the beam revealed the instruments one at a time: a crosscut wood saw, scalpels scattered like jackstraws, an army survival knife, half a dozen hacksaws, and a machete with a blade shaped like a boomerang.

They cut off his arm and legs.

Gabe closed his eyes, trying to fight off the image of the torn-up boy. But the more he pushed against it, just like the Buddhists said, the more the thought refused to leave his mind.

They chopped off his limbs like he was something for the goddamn stew pot.

Before his stomach could capsize, Gabe hurried away from the table, not bothering to keep Luke in tow, wanting only to distract himself from what he feared was the truth. His knee encountered a low bench that turned out to bear no horrors other than a tangle of frayed rope. Gabe brushed his fingers against it, noting its texture, its thickness, and most of all its solidity. He waited for that to anchor him.

The bread would not leave him alone. Nothing else could lay claim to that particular olfactory experience. As he was wondering about the scent, guessing at its source, a sudden light filled the room, startling him, blinding him.

He stumbled against the bench and turned around, a whistle of air hissing between his teeth. He brought the flashlight to bear, a meager club, a child's toy, ready to strike at whatever target presented itself.

Luke stood near the tunnel, hand on the switch. "I don't really like the dark."

Gabe dropped the flashlight, bent over, and put his hands on his knees. He felt like crying out in relief, but his lungs were too intent on their work. He hung there with his mouth open. A single pellet of sweat dripped from his cheek.

"You sick?"

He looked up through his hair. His pulse beat in his jawbone.

"Gabe?"

With effort, Gabe wet his lips. "Pardon me while I change my underwear."

"Huh?"

"You scared the shit out of me."

"Shit is holy."

"Yeah, I'm starting to believe it." He straightened his back and looked around. "I guess that means we're alone."

"Yep. All the Martians flew the coop."

Gabe examined the wires that ran across the ceiling and connected the mismatched bulbs. "These must be powered by batteries, because I don't hear a generator running, do you?"

"Nope." Luke shook his head. "What's a generator?"

As his eyes continued to adjust to the sudden brightness, Gabe took a better inventory of the cavern. The ceiling was smooth, rounded where it met the walls, and supported by a pair of wooden beams encircled by a crawling ivy of Christmas lights. Tables occupied every inch of real estate save the aisle that ran from the tunnel to the exit hole in the opposite wall. Most of the clutter looked scavenged from Mentiras itself, the jetsam of a town that had been abandoned for fifty years.

Gabe inspected a stack of documents. Typewritten and numerically coded, they looked official, but official *what* Gabe couldn't say. Only a few of the Spanish words made sense to him. Printed across the upper margin in all caps was DIRECCIÓN DE INTELIGENCIA NACIONAL.

"Are these real?"

Gabe looked over to find Luke holding one of the knives.

"You better put that down."

"But are they *real*?"

"Looks like. Don't cut yourself, okay? I'm going to have a hard enough time explaining why I brought you along. Let's not make it any worse by bleeding."

"Gotcha. Roger that."

Gabe debated taking the papers or leaving them, then decided that he'd need some evidence to show Fontecilla. The documents weren't proof enough to validate Gabe's story, but it was either these or the scalpel. He rolled half a dozen of them into a tube shape and shoved it in his back pocket.

As he headed for the circular opening that appeared to lead to a second chamber, he briefly considered how strange it all was, to be exploring a bunker hidden beneath a dead town in the middle of the most barren place on the globe. The word they liked to use in horror novels was *surreal,* though Gabe didn't think that was exactly right. Surreal meant fantastical and dreamlike. This was too grim for that. And too full of knives.

He peered into the room beyond.

At first he saw nothing to give him pause. A bare cot. A white plastic tub. Hoses running across the floor. A desk was made from sawhorses and an old door. The source of the smell was clearly the cast-iron stove in the corner. A potholder with a floral design hung from the oven's L-shaped handle.

Then his eyes settled on the wagon.

The Radio Flyer was straight from the 1950s, purloined from the upper world and smuggled here to the nether region. Positioned near an exit across the room, the red wagon looked ready to be rolled away by a child who might soon return to claim it. A towel covered the bulge of the wagon's cargo.

At the sight of the wagon and its hidden payload, the fear in Gabe's gut was replaced by something more comprehensive. He'd never really experienced dread, not the real kind, and so it went without a name as it crawled through him.

Having no desire to go near the Flyer, he turned toward the tub instead. As he passed by the desk, he saw the gun.

Though its grip was that of any semiautomatic he'd seen in the movies, its barrel was thicker and rectangular in shape, marked with a strange series of grooves. It seemed unlikely that the rifleman would have left such a weapon behind, yet here it was.

"Is that a ray gun?" Luke asked.

"I don't know. Don't mess with it."

"Phasers on stun."

"Always."

Mounted on the wall above the makeshift desk was a section of corkboard, though whatever was once pinned there had been removed. Only thumbtacks remained. Gabe assumed that the rifleman had stripped the board before hightailing it out of Dodge. A single newspaper clipping lay on the desk, each of its four corners pierced by a tiny hole. Unlike the yellowing papers on the bookshelf, this one looked much more recent, and it happened to be in English. The headline read: CIA ADMITS TIES TO PINOCHET REGIME.

Though Gabe was distantly familiar with the name Pinochet, he couldn't recall many details. He folded the clipping and tucked it away, knowing that Fontecilla would certainly not approve.

Expecting the worst, he peered into the tub.

It was surprisingly clean. Two wide drains were ringed with water, suggesting that the container had recently been washed out and wiped down. At five feet long and half as wide, the tub was large enough to accommodate a man, but now it held only steel tools, their metal gleaming from a recent bath. Gabe noted two pairs of handcuffs, a section of heavy-gauge chain, and a carving knife with a polished bone handle and serrated blade.

And was there something else?

Careful not to touch the tub itself, Gabe bent over until he was sure he was looking at a pair of military dog tags.

This stranger of yours, Fontecilla had said, *he had boots on. Boots with a very distinctive sole.*

"Boots like a soldier."

"What did you say?" Luke asked.

"These are his dog tags."

"Who?"

"The ghost I've been chasing." He reached down and carefully extracted the necklace. The time had come for him to put a name to the Midnight Messenger, since he would never put a face.

"Gabe?"

"Yeah?"

"Something in the wagon is breathing."

CHAPTER SEVENTEEN

"There it is," Ben said. They had reached Mentiras. The buildings appeared out of the darkness like sunken things floating to the surface of a swamp.

"What is this place?" Mira asked. "Who lives out here?"

"Nothing and nobody," Ben told her. "As far as I know, these towns were abandoned many moons ago, as the Indians in the movies say."

"That's correct," Jonah confirmed as he guided them closer. "At one point, settlements such as this supported a robust mining industry. Saloons, supply stores, and brothels thrived. But like the railroads of American history, the mines made a few men wealthy and then left the rest for dead."

Ben smiled secretly to himself, despite everything. He'd always enjoyed listening to his brother talk. There was a time when Jonah had told stories from the bottom bunk, so that Ben fell asleep in the sky, listening to tales of bootleggers and banditos, pirates and princes. When they were kids, a random Chevy Malibu had changed their lives moments after they'd watched John Wayne himself being put into the ground. Their father had worked as a groundskeeper for the Duke, and he'd brought his two sons to the great man's funeral in the summer of '79. The careening car killed him instantly. Jonah's spine cracked in two places. After the accident, the brothers had moved into their uncle's house, which was large enough for them each to have his own room. No more stories after that, no more nights of derring-do. Not until Ben himself had resurrected them in *This Mayflower Mars.* He'd dedicated the book to Jonah and pretended not to see when his big brother wiped away a quick tear upon reading the inscription.

Jonah slowed the vehicle. The knobby tires eased to a stop, their treads clogged with the Atacama's skin. The electric motors—one per wheel—hummed softly.

Ben saw no sign of human passing. The few structures still standing were as quiet as mausoleums. The fact that Luke had come here with a stranger wasn't so odd, really, as the excitement of Mars exploration was bound to get the better of someone of Luke's particular disposition. What worried Ben was the stranger himself. He claimed to be searching for someone who might have done *bad things.* Just how bad, however, Ben couldn't say.

"I don't see his truck," Mira said. "They came in a truck, right? Are you sure this is the town he was talking about?"

"They could've parked anywhere out here," Ben said, "and we'd never know it in the dark. We should drive around, check the perimeter, get a feel for things."

"I'm really trying to keep the faith here, Ben."

"I know you are. And you're doing fine."

"Tell that to my heart."

"I could try, but I suspect it would only ignore me."

"Let's just find him, okay?"

Jonah took that as his cue. Though he had no use of his legs, the rover's controls were mounted on the wheel, so he got them moving with only a light touch of his fingers. The big tires rolled.

Ben played a hunch and reached for Mira's hand. He was not surprised when she squeezed tight.

Gabe walked slowly toward the wagon. The iron stove filled this side of the room with heat. A pile of broken boards was evidence of the oven's fuel supply, while a single pipe pushed through the earthen ceiling to vent the smoke. The rifleman hadn't feared being discovered by this discharged vapor. He could've lit a bonfire out here and no one would have known.

The form hidden under the towel rose slightly, then subsided. Then rose again.

After his experience with the boy in the backpack, Gabe shrank back from the thought of removing that covering. He could not imagine what could be worse than what he'd already seen.

The exit near the wagon gave him an excuse to delay things a moment longer. He put his head through the low opening and found nothing but a closet-sized space similar to what he'd found at the bottom of the well. A wooden ladder climbed up to what he assumed was another of the rifleman's escape hatches, the wormhole through which he passed when he needed access to the world.

His reconnaissance complete, Gabe turned reluctantly back to the wagon.

Luke stared down at it. He seemed hypnotized by the gentle tidal movement of what lay beneath the towel.

"Back up a bit," Gabe suggested.

Luke took two steps in retreat, arms hanging at his sides. "Is that a person in there?"

Gabe crouched beside the wagon, which, like the backpack, wasn't large enough to contain anyone who hadn't been . . . modified.

He pinched the corner of the towel. Part of him became unwired and refused to function, and he lacked the willpower to override it and initiate manual control. He knew that he should tell Luke to turn away or cover his eyes, but he found it difficult to breathe, much less to frame an intelligible command. The kid was on his own. When dread came on you like this, throwing your breaker switches, it was every man for himself.

From beneath the towel came a small and very human sound.

That did it. Strength surged into his arm, and he tugged the covering away.

What had once been a woman lay in the wagon on her back. Her legs and arms had been sheared away, replaced by scarred stumps. She was naked. Both breasts were gone, cut off like warts. Her lips were sewn shut with black thread.

Luke didn't scream. He put both hands over his mouth and dropped to his knees.

The woman's eyes were open, and she stared at Gabe with a look that both revolted him and filled him with grief. Tears trailed down his cheeks.

She made another sound.

Gabe had heard nothing more terrible than that. It reached through his conscious self to the mud pits, a feral noise of such misery that it was no longer human but elemental.

He staggered to the tub and clutched at the bone-handled knife. It took him three times to get his hand to work, but finally he had it, and then he fell beside her while Luke looked on, hands held over his face in revulsion.

Gabe cut the stitches away.

Her mouth opened like a boil being lanced. Saliva and blood oozed over her lips. Her eyes swam wildly. *"Corra."*

Gabe knew what she wanted. She needed to die, perhaps more than any person had ever needed it. She needed mercy. But that wasn't what she said.

He leaned down, so that he was only centimeters from her. "I don't understand."

The woman coughed once. *"Run."*

A shadow fell across them.

Gabe looked up. The rifleman stood in the doorway.

He wore soiled dungarees and a belt festooned with pouches. Apparently he'd climbed down the ladder in the well, as his body blocked the opening that led to the chamber with the newspaper and waiting piñata. His feet were bare, the toenails orange with desert dust. His hands were protected by latex gloves, and his face, his goddamn face, was inscrutable as the moon.

Gabe was halfway to his feet when the man rushed him.

The woman in the wagon screamed, an animal sound of fear and despair.

Gabe brought the knife to bear as he stumbled backward. He lost the ability to think, his conscious mind eclipsed by the darkness of survival. He swung the knife twice in a frantic arc, but he overextended and paid for it. The rifleman pushed Luke out of the way and struck Gabe in the throat.

His air stopped flowing.

Gabe gagged, tripped, and fell down coughing, one hand clutching his neck as the other waved the blade stupidly in front of him. His oxygen was clogged, unable to go down to his lungs or up to his mouth; the feeling was like being hanged.

The woman's cry warbled on, changing pitch as she clawed for the world with her voice, the only thing she had left.

The rifleman kicked Gabe in the hand. A cherry bomb exploded in his fingers, the pain vibrating in his wrist. He lost control of the knife. It flew beyond his reach.

He was no warrior. Fifteen years had passed since his last fight, and that had been nothing but a couple of teenagers scrapping over a girl or a sports team or some other trivial Maginot line that had since been forgotten. The sudden brutality stunned him, so that he could only scramble across the dirt floor and paw for the knife that remained just out of reach.

The rifleman towered over him. From his belt he extracted a carpet cutter with a hooked blade.

Gabe knew he was going to be gutted. As the rifleman stepped in the direction of the fallen knife, Gabe rolled to the wall and flattened his back against it, intending to kick outward with both of his legs and perhaps buy himself a few seconds.

The rifleman swiped the knife from the floor and switched it from his left hand to his right.

Luke shot him in the back.

The man's arms jerked and the muscles in his neck pulled taut. The carpet cutter slipped from his strengthless fingers. Behind him, Luke held the gun in both hands. Extending from its barrel was a metal filament no thicker than a spider's strand, ending in a pair of electrodes that were lodged in the rifleman's shirt.

The man's arms leaped outward as the electricity bombarded him. He stood there in cruciform, the voltage clamping his teeth together with such force that Gabe clearly heard the snap. He rose onto his bare toes, his body undulating, and then he dropped. He landed on his knees and toppled, unable to break his fall. His limbs spasmed as the pulleys of his tendons jerked up and down inside him.

Gabe braced himself on the wall and got to his feet.

Luke released his weapon. It struck the floor, flipped, and landed near the convulsing man. "Ray gun," he said.

Gabe ran a hand over his sweaty face and swallowed. "Fuckin' A it is."

How long would the bastard be down? Ten minutes? Ten seconds? Gabe lurched across the room and bent over the tub, his chest aching from the intensity of his heartbeat. He grabbed a pair of handcuffs and then returned to the rifleman, who was drooling onto the floor, knees against his chest.

The woman in the wagon took a noisy breath but didn't exhale. Her chest no longer moved.

Gabe took that as a sign. He'd hoped to be able to save her—some small part of him had argued it was possible despite everything—but with her passing, nothing remained here worth fighting for. Though he was afraid the man might break free of his neuromuscular paralysis at any moment, he dared to grab an ankle. With a quick ratcheting sound, he locked the cuff in place.

"I think she died," Luke said.

"Yeah."

"We should leave."

"Working on it." He'd never handcuffed anybody. Maybe he'd been wrong earlier: This was surreal. Though his hands were nearly shaking too badly to function, he managed to take the man by the wrist and join it to his ankle. He expected the skin to be inhumanly hot or cold, or perhaps poisonous to touch or covered in scales, but he noticed nothing of the kind. The man was of average dimensions. He'd left no tracks in the desert because he'd worn no shoes. He opened his mouth to try to speak, but nothing came out save the static of someone with no control over his vocal cords.

"Look at him, Luke." Gabe pointed at the man's face. "Remember what he looks like, okay? Do you understand?"

"I think we should really, really leave."

"You need to remember him."

"Really, *really* leave!" Luke ran around the fallen man and attacked the ladder in the little cubicle beyond. "Leaving now! Leaving now!"

Gabe followed. Though his legs were unsteady, he had no choice but to trust them to get him to the surface. Already the rifleman was regaining some power, curling his fingers into fists. Gabe passed the wagon without another glance at the dead woman, though he couldn't help but wonder about her name and how she'd come to be here. Had her abduction been coincidental? Or had she played a role of significance in these events? He sensed the truth of the latter but spent no time in contemplation. He jumped onto the rungs and climbed with abandon, hoping the wood wouldn't crack beneath his weight.

As he passed through a square opening at the summit, the rifleman groaned.

The room at the top looked to be the interior of the one of Mentiras's few remaining buildings. A lantern burned in the corner, near a neat stack of what appeared to be getaway gear. Satchels and duffel bags awaited departure, along with a pair of small ten-liter fuel cans. Gabe figured that he and Luke had interrupted the man in the midst of packing up what evidence he could and setting fire to the rest. The structure itself was hollow, the components of its interior walls now structural supports in the lair below. Luke found the only door and pulled it open, still repeating, "Reallyreallyleave, reallyreallyleave."

Gabe thought it was a helluvan idea, the best he'd heard in ages, just reallyreallyleave as fast as he could goddamn run. He caught up with Luke as the boy cleared the doorway, and the two of them ran down what had once been the town's central street but was now only a serpent's tongue of dust.

A white light impaled them.

"Hansel!"

Gabe heard the woman's voice but saw nothing except the solar flare of headlights and the wall of dirt kicked up by the tires of an onrushing car.

Luke grabbed him by the shirtsleeve. "My sister!"

Gabe needed no further encouragement. He and Luke ran like detention-camp escapees, the dust stinging their eyes.

The rifleman's scream chased after them.

CHAPTER EIGHTEEN

Mira threw her arms around her brother.

"Gotta leave!" Luke said, trying to wiggle free. "Gotta leave *pronto, vamoose, skedaddle.*"

"Are you okay? Are you hurt?"

"Better listen to him," Traylin said, bounding into the rover as if he'd expected to find it here waiting. "The cuffs won't hold forever."

"What are you talking about?" Her joy at seeing Luke again was welded to her fear of what was spooking him. "What happened?"

"Ma'am, I swear on Kepler's soul to explain, but right now we need to put as much distance between us and him as possible."

Ben looked in the direction of the scream they'd heard. "Who's *him*?"

Luke cried. The tears came without warning. "Gretel, he cut her up, cut her up *really bad.*"

"What?" Mira pulled him against her. "Baby, what are you talking about?"

"Cut her up into a *rectangle.*"

Traylin leaned over the seat and grabbed Jonah's shoulder. "My man, we need to haul serious ass. *Now.*"

"Do it," Ben said, and suddenly they were moving. Though the rover was built for durability rather than speed, Jonah edged it to its limit.

"I left the truck over there," Traylin said, pointing into the night. "You happen to bring that satellite phone with you?"

Jonah shook his head as he guided the rover in the direction Traylin indicated. "I'm afraid not."

"No radio in this thing?"

"Not one of sufficient range, no."

Mira rocked Luke in her arms, pained by the sound of his tears. Sadness was generally a stranger to him. Mira could count on one hand the number of times she'd heard him cry since their mother died. Luke was the more buoyant of the Westbrook twins. What had happened to him? What had he seen?

Mira looked over her brother's shoulder at the man who shared the backseat with them. Though she could see little of Traylin in the dark, she could tell he was leaning forward, staring at that small section of desert illuminated by the rover's powerful headlamps. He was but one more spontaneous human combustion in a day so full of them that Mira could hardly imagine it was a real component of her life. First she'd met Ben, and then she'd realized that his writing somehow connected him to Luke. After that, she boarded a plane for a field trip to a simulated Mars, and now she was running from a man who'd apparently cut a woman into a rectangle.

"Hey," she said.

Traylin looked over. She guessed that he was about her age. His hair was a little long, his eyes intelligent and alert.

"Tell me what's going on."

"I wish I knew."

"You know more than I do."

"Then consider yourself fortunate you didn't have to see it."

Mira had no intention of letting him evade her. "I need to know what happened to my brother, Mr. Traylin."

"You want to know what happened? He saved my ass, that's what. If it weren't for Luke, we'd both be lying in pieces in a psychopath's living room."

"He . . . saved you?" She put her head against Luke's. "Is that true?"

Luke muttered something she didn't understand.

"Your kid brother's my hero," Traylin said.

Mira didn't correct him. Luke was the older of the two, albeit by only a minute. And now his younger sister sat here suffused with warmth at the thought of her brother being someone's hero. No one had ever said that of him before, at least not anyone who sounded so sincere.

She reached across him and touched Traylin on the arm.

He was scanning the darkness for his truck; he turned at her touch.

"Thank you," she said.

"For what?"

What she wanted to say was *For not treating him like a child* or *For taking him seriously.* There was a pattern that people adopted when they interacted with someone with Down, but Traylin seemed unaware of it.

"Luke did all the work," Traylin told her. "He's the one who's quick on the draw with a ray gun."

"What's that mean? What happened back there? Who is this man you're looking for?"

"Later. I think I see the truck."

The rover's powerful lamps revealed the vehicle. Jonah had not even gotten them fully braked before Traylin slung himself out. He ran for the truck but then doubled back. "Wait a minute. The observatory's twice as far away as your place, and I need to get somebody out here before he torches everything. Your phone is closer."

"I'll go with you," Ben said, already climbing from the rover's passenger seat, "if only to hear exactly what the hell is going on. Okay with you, Joe, if he uses your phone again?"

"I suppose, though all of this is highly irregular. We'll follow behind as quickly as we can."

Traylin gave Luke a quick salute. "You the man." Then he turned and ran to his truck, Ben hurrying after him.

Luke looked at Mira, his tears replaced by a tentative smile. "I'm the man."

"Apparently you are." She watched the two men slam their doors and tear away in a funnel of dust. Though it was hours past midnight, she wasn't tired. While part of her was worried that she and Luke had crossed into dangerous territory, another part rejoiced in it: Luke was the man, and no one had ever told him that and actually meant it. Whoever Gabe Traylin was, and whatever peril he was facing, he'd already earned a promotion in Mira's heart.

The rover pursued the truck taillights until the distance between them grew too great.

"Gretel?"

"Yes?"

"He cut her up *bad.*"

Ben squatted in the trench and scooped up a handful of Martian soil.

They called it Daedalia Planum, a land of frozen lava flows and impact craters. Ben remembered reading of Daedalus, inventor to the gods and creator of the Minotaur's prison. Ben had drawn upon that lore when writing of his fictional Lieutenant Dycar, setting his protagonist at odds with the Martian landscape just as Daedalus and his son had challenged the sky. In the end, the heat melted the wings from the younger man's arms, and the cold solidified the blood in Dycar's veins. Both died, but both had finally known freedom.

"Live free or die," he said to himself. The battle cry of Harley-Davidsons everywhere.

He stood up.

This was not Mars. This single acre marked with yellow flags was no extraterrestrial frontier, but make-believe. Men of towering bravado such as Dycar and Icarus had no business here, where mortals scooped soil samples into dishes and guessed at the probability of growing wheat. Ben wondered if his lack of literary inspiration was due to an equal lack of courage. Nobody had guts of mythic level anymore. Nobody went hunting for the big game.

"Cops are on their way."

Ben turned, letting the last of the dirt run through his fingers. "I'm sorry?"

The astronomer, Gabe Traylin, held the phone in both hands. "The police. I gave them the Mentiras coordinates. Which means I probably just lost my job."

"I don't follow."

"My boss said he'd fire me if I kept stirring the pot."

"And that's what you were doing out there? Stirring the pot?"

"Luke and I, yeah. With one big-ass spoon." He wiped his forehead. "I think I need to sit down." He lowered himself gingerly to the ground, careful to keep ACEF's expensive phone out of the sand.

Ben watched him with growing concern. "Anything I can get for you? Bottle of water, maybe?"

Gabe shook his head. "I'll be fine."

"If you say so." Personally, Ben thought the man looked like he was ready to lose his lunch, but saying so wouldn't help. "So . . . you going to tell me what's out there that's worth the unemployment line?"

Gabe didn't look at him but kept his gaze safely on the stars. "I guess we found a murderer."

"You *guess*?"

"Maybe a serial killer, I don't know. That sounds sort of dramatic."

"I take it that you initially made this discovery by accident."

"I blame the Marlboros."

"Come again?"

"I was having a smoke when I . . . when I found his first victim. So, yeah, it was an accident, unless you believe that there are no such things."

"What do *you* believe?"

"Me? I believe that the universe began as a point smaller than a pinhead and that it'll go out the same way. Everything else is for someone else to worry about."

Ben considered that. From his readings in the sci-fi field, he understood enough layman's cosmology to know that Gabe referred to a theory called the Big Crunch. In the Big Crunch model, all of creation would end as it began, a tiny speck into which had been crammed the sum of everything. Just as space expanded, so too would it contract. It had been called the breathing in and out of God.

"Not the most optimistic view of things," Ben allowed, taking a seat next to the younger man. "But one to which you're certainly entitled, given the circumstances. Sad, though, to think that the world is in such a state that you can't even escape the bad mojo in a place as remote as this."

"I'm just glad you guys were out here. Vic and I had gotten ourselves kind of lost."

"Thank my brother. Jonah oversees this operation. He's the egghead in the Cable family tree. Everything you see here is his responsibility, from the hydroponics bays to the waste-recycling unit. Me, I'm just a vagrant enjoying the view."

"I hear you there." Gabe finally looked away from the sky, pulling a crumpled scroll of papers from his back pocket. In the light from the nearest track-mounted bulb, he smoothed the pages on his knees and studied them.

Though Ben wouldn't normally be so intrusive as to ask about the documents, he figured that a night like this warranted a moratorium on social etiquette. Maybe it wasn't any of his business, but he wasn't letting that get in his way. "I take it that what you have there somehow pertains to recent events?"

"I'm not sure. I found them down there in the son of a bitch's hideout. I've got a newspaper clipping and then some kind of report. I don't suppose the name Pinochet means anything to you?"

"Pinochet? Seriously? All of that nasty business went down before you were born, but that man's name is bad medicine here in Chile. Take a dash of Hitler and sprinkle in a bit of Charlie Manson, and you're getting the idea. But even a charming guy like that still has his supporters. Go figure."

"What did he do?"

"Oh, the usual sinister dictator stuff. Augusto Pinochet was a strong-arm general who took over the Chilean government in the mid-seventies. You know how it goes after that. Human rights violations, political assassinations, all your basic civil liberties mailed parcel post to hell."

Gabe held up the piece of newsprint. "It says here that a couple of years ago, the CIA admitted to supporting this guy's regime. They financed some of his operations."

"Does that surprise you?"

"I guess not, but it's pretty damned screwed up."

"Such is the way of the world, my friend. We're nothing if not screwed up. If our men in black aren't funding the coup to put a tyrant in command, then they're sending weapons to the folks they want to overthrow him. Either way, they're involved up to their eyeballs in most of the world's blood. Hell, half the time both sides in a war are killing each other with weapons they bought from the same source, that being Uncle Sam. But that's not the question that really matters, now is it?"

Gabe thought about it only for a second. "Why would that bastard in Mentiras care about something like this, especially when it happened over thirty years ago?"

"Bingo. That's what you'd call the sixty-four-thousand-dollar question. What else do you have there?"

Gabe handed him the documents.

Though Ben's command of the Spanish language would never win him a contract to translate the native works of Octavio Paz, he could usually muddle through the basics. Angling the paper toward the light, he scanned the dense type that began with the rather ominous header of DIRECCIÓN DE INTELIGENCIA NACIONAL. "The National Intelligence Directorate. This just gets more interesting by the minute."

"What's it say?"

"Give me a second . . ."

The silence that followed his words was utter and complete. Perhaps no desert on Earth was a suitable simulacrum for the Red Planet, but this absence of sound went a long way to reinforcing the illusion. When the winds on Mars weren't blowing, its plains knew this same kind of empty peace.

"Let's see . . . looks like the directorate, or DINA, was officially reorganized and renamed in 1977. Most of this stuff is just legalese about transferring employees from one office to another. Nothing very exciting."

"This directorate was . . . what? Some kind of national security agency?"

"More like secret police."

"Like the Gestapo?"

"A fair analogy, I suspect. I'm not very steeped in Chilean history, but I bet a visit to your local library could explain a lot. Not that anything's local out here."

"And that's all it says?"

"Unless you're interested in how DINA was reorganized as a law-abiding organization after years of illegal activities, then yes, that's all it says. Wait, belay that." Ben leaned closer to the paper. "There *is* a name underlined here."

"Yeah? Who?"

"Micha Lepin. Mean anything to you?"

"No. Is that male or female?"

"It's a man's name, I believe. Not any chance he could be your

Mentiras suspect, is there? If this is from the late seventies, then Lepin would have to be *at least* in his midfifties by now, and probably a lot older than that. How old was the man you encountered?"

"I . . . I don't know."

"Take a guess. Was he under sixty?"

"Maybe."

"Maybe? Surely you can tell if the guy was closer to twenty than seventy."

Gabe looked away. "It happened really quickly."

Though Ben had never considered himself exceptionally savvy when it came to his fellow man, he sensed now that Gabe was holding something back. "What did you see out there, exactly?"

Gabe seemed absorbed in his examination of what the poets called the firmament. Ben didn't know much about the stars, other than what he read in his horoscope, and recently the seers in the daily paper hadn't been kind to him. Gabe, though, was different. An astronomer understood the distance between those stars and why it made interstellar travel impossible for the current human physiology. Ben wanted to ask him about all of that because it fascinated him, but right now he'd settle for a simple answer to his question.

Suddenly Gabe said, "What if there was a crime so horrible that, if you told anyone about it, they'd just think you were a freak for imagining things like that?"

"Then I reckon I'd keep it to myself."

And Gabe did.

CHAPTER NINETEEN

Minutes later, Gabe remembered the dog tags.

He'd been sitting here with the phone in his lap, using a whip and chair to hold off the flashbacks of that woman in the wagon. Where her breasts had been were two patches of bloody gauze taped to the skin. The stub of her left arm had healed cleanly. Her right was a bruised mess, indicating a much more recent procedure. Her legs were the same way, meaning that the man had kept her hostage for a considerable length of time and periodically removed a limb.

Had Gabe merely heard about such an atrocity, he would've recoiled and pushed it from his mind, happy to go on with his life. But having seen it, having touched the bodies of the boy with the pinwheel and the woman in Mentiras, he couldn't escape.

He dragged the chain from his pocket.

The dog tags turned in the light when he held them before his face. Gabe allowed them to settle onto his palm, while in his mind a soldier trekked across the desert with a devastated boy in his pack. That soldier, otherwise known as the Midnight Messenger, was anonymous no more.

OLIVARES, ALBAN

Gabe closed his eyes and wove that name on the loom of his mind. *Alban Olivares.* He bound the threads around the soldier's fallen body, making him into something more than just a runner in the night. By christening him, Gabe *created* him. When he opened his eyes, Olivares was a father, a brother, and somebody's son. He played cards with his buddies in the barracks and got his heart broken by American girls.

"Gabe?"

He blinked away his reverie to find Ben looking at him. "His name was Alban."

"The man at Mentiras?"

"One of his victims. Alban Olivares"—he held up the dog tags—"tried to rescue a boy who'd been kidnapped and . . . and tortured. He was shot and killed. I saw it happen. That's what started all of this for me."

"So how'd he find out about it? You could say that Mentiras epitomizes the term *middle of nowhere.* How did your man Alban discover it to begin with? Did he track the killer out there?"

"I don't know. Hopefully the police will figure it out."

Ben laughed.

"What? What did I say?"

"Apparently you've had better luck with the constabulary than I have. I'm sorry, but I've never had a very high opinion of the boys in blue, and I wouldn't figure the ones down here are any better."

"You're saying the Investigative Police are incompetent?"

"Not at all. But when I was young, Jonah and I were involved in a . . . what you would term a rather serious accident. A member of a wealthy family was responsible. A wealthy *white* family, as it turned out. No offense intended to present company. When it came time for them to pay the piper, both legally and financially, they found that a few of the police officers were more than willing to doubt our innocence in the matter. We were very nearly blamed for the event that put Jonah in his chair and our daddy in his grave."

"Damn."

"Damn indeed. But it worked out in the end, as it always seems to do, though ever since then I've given cops a wide berth. Of course, by the time they get all the way out here, their quarry will likely be long gone, and there are places here in South America still wild enough to hide a man who intends on being hidden."

"Yeah, I've been thinking the same thing."

"Which means you're the linchpin of their entire case. Lucky you. I hope you weren't planning on flying back to the States. You're what the media calls the prosecution's star witness."

Gabe had nothing to say about such an idea. Face blindness didn't lend itself to being any kind of witness, star or otherwise. Gabe would never be able to pick anyone out of a lineup. "Well, I don't know about that. I'm pretty sure Luke got a lot better look at the guy."

"That may be, but we both know that the judiciary system will consider you the more credible of the two. It's probably not very socially correct to assume that, but . . ."

"Why would I be any more credible than anyone else?"

"It's not *you* I'm talking about. It's him. The defense attorneys will make it clear to the court that Luke isn't always the most reliable fellow, as charming as he might be."

"He seemed pretty goddamn reliable when he Tasered that asshole."

"You know what I mean."

"Actually, I don't. Would you have climbed into a well with me, knowing that a murderer was possibly down there? I was a total stranger to Luke, but you know what? He backed my play. If you ask me, he has a third-degree black belt in the balls department. So just because he's a kid doesn't make him unreliable."

"He's no kid. I'd bet he's right around your age."

"Say what?" Gabe realized he was missing the point, as he'd so often missed it in the past. What was it about Luke that Ben so clearly recognized? "But I thought—"

"He has Down syndrome."

Gabe waited for the rest. There had to be more, some punch line that would make sense in a moment or two. But Ben said nothing more.

You can't be serious. Such a reaction might have once served John McEnroe, but it seemed inadequate to describe the depth of Gabe's surprise.

"I assumed you knew," Ben said.

Gabe ran a hand through his hair. "It was dark."

"Sure."

Down syndrome? Had Gabe known, he never would have . . . No, scratch that. Any disability that Luke might possess was fully canceled out by his courage. Put anyone else down that hole when the rifleman showed up, and Gabe might have found himself tied up in that plastic tub, watching as his own leg was amputated. "He can share a foxhole with me any day of the week."

"He'd be proud to hear it, and so would his sister." Ben stood up. "I better get this phone back on its charger. This isn't the kind of place you want to be without one."

Gabe watched him walk away until the darkness claimed him.

How long would it be before the police arrived? The city of Calama was several hours away, giving the rifleman ample time to abscond with the bulk of the evidence. Gabe could do nothing to thwart him. Fontecilla had asked him to wait where he was, so even a return to the observatory was off the table.

It's not over, is it?

Though Gabe had done his part for the cause, almost dying for people he'd never met, he suspected that extricating himself would not be easy. He was a witness who'd looked the killer in the face but hadn't seen a thing. Terrific.

Somehow they were all connected: Micha Lepin, the man mentioned in the DINA papers; the Midnight Messenger, aka Alban Oliveras; the boy with the pinwheel; the woman in the Radio Flyer.

Somehow, somehow . . .

At four in the morning, Mira chased three aspirin with the best cup of coffee on Mars.

For the last hour, her brother's new best friend had described what sounded like either a tall tale or a ghost story, depending on the amount of peyote you were enjoying. Having been high only once—the typical and not-even-worth-mentioning ritual of life as a college freshman—Mira couldn't file it away as myth. Especially not when Luke was interjecting his own commentary. They were like a pair of sportscasters in the booth, except what they were describing sounded more like Auschwitz than a playoff game.

Jonah's colleague Eduardo had just completed an inspection on the buggy they'd driven to Mentiras. Now the six of them stood around the Land Rover in the lights marking the ACEF living quarters, where Donner was getting some sleep after returning from the observatory.

"How long will it take the police to get here?" Mira asked. She posed the question because she teetered on the cusp of collapse. This had possibly been the most eventful day of her life, and she wanted it finally to be over so she could plunge into a rehabilitating sleep. "If you called them over an hour ago . . ."

"They'll likely bring a helicopter," Ben said, "but even as the crow flies, they've still got a good stretch of desert to cover. We're deep in the big empty, sugar."

"I guess I didn't realize how far we are from civilization." She looked at Gabe. He hadn't touched the coffee that Jonah provided. She wanted to ask him more about Luke simply because of how she'd felt when Gabe described events. Though the whole episode had scared her panties into a figure eight—to use her mother's phrase—pride had replaced her fear. But she thought again of the woman he'd described and lost her grip on sisterly conceit. "Mars really knows how to show a girl a good time."

"You do realize," Jonah said, "that a day on Mars is nearly forty minutes longer than an Earth day. Imagine the trouble our friends here might get into with such time on their hands."

"Troubletroubletrouble," Luke said. "If it's not one thing, it's another."

"How is the day longer?" Mira asked.

Eduardo, the project's young botanist, eagerly elaborated. "When a planet rotates, the stars and the sun appear to move, but they often do so at different rates. On Mars, the stars complete their cycle in thirty-seven minutes, while the sun requires thirty-nine. So a full day on Mars, or its synodic period, is technically thirty-nine minutes greater than Earth's. NASA has considered making the official Martian hour last for sixty-two minutes, which would help synchronize events on the two planets." He pushed his glasses higher on his nose and looked at Ben. "But if I remember my fiction correctly, your Martian settlers chose to keep the standard hour and use those extra minutes more . . . creatively."

Ben shrugged. "What can I say? When men and women are cooped up in atmosphere suits all day, they're looking forward to a little R and R that is literally off the clock."

Mira smiled to herself. She remembered that part of his novel. Lieutenant Dycar and the other colonists referred to those thirty-nine minutes after midnight as the Trysting Hour. One chapter in particular was rather risqué, with Dycar and his lover, Tilanna, knowing each other in the biblical sense, and Luke blushed every time he read it. But to Mira, veteran of many a bodice-ripper, Ben's romance scene was rated PG.

"I suppose you're right," Eduardo said. "No matter what planetary body we might be roaming, human nature always wins in the end. In fact—"

His head tipped sideways. Red mist dappled Mira's face.

Eduardo fell.

Confused, Mira touched the moisture on her cheek. Blood stained her fingertips.

"Get down!" Gabe snagged her arm and pulled her to the sand. "Everybody on the ground!"

Mira realized, then, that Eduardo had been shot, though she'd never heard a sound.

Luke dropped to his knees behind the Land Rover, and Ben did the same. With a touch, Jonah drove his chair into the fender.

"It's him!" Gabe shouted. "Stay behind the truck!"

Mira pressed her back against the door, Luke on one side of her, Gabe on the other. Ben stayed near his brother, who'd lowered himself in his chair so that his head nearly rested on his knees.

A few feet away, Eduardo lay dead, a bullet hole just above his eye.

Mira surprised herself by not screaming. The sight of a dead man only two feet away from her was so improbable that she couldn't even give voice to her surprise. The suddenness of it robbed her of breath.

Jonah, however, mumbled a rapid stream of words, stringing them together senselessly, saying Eduardo's name over and over, interspersed with garbled syllables of fear.

Glass shattered. A few inches above Mira's head, the driver-side window turned into a kaleidoscope.

"I think he's mad at us," Luke said.

The sound of her brother's voice jarred Mira from her trance. Her mouth was as dry as it had ever been. The proximity of death seemed to have sapped the moisture from her, so that now she was a proper desert beast. She knew only that she had to keep Luke safe. She defaulted to what had been her prime directive for over twenty years.

Staying close to the ground, she reached up and opened the vehicle's door. "Inside!"

Luke had covered his ears with his palms. He moved his head right to left and back again, though he otherwise didn't look particularly frightened.

Mira jerked one of his hands away. "Get in the truck, Hansel. *Now.*"

Though he normally enjoyed badgering his sister by resisting her suggestions, he also respected her Danger Cap. You didn't screw with her when she was wearing it. He squirmed through the gap provided by the partially open door and crawled over the gear stick.

"Stay down!"

Again Luke did as ordered, sliding downward in the seat.

A taillight exploded.

Ben shouted in mounting alarm.

"Everybody inside!" Mira said. Whether or not they listened to her was irrelevant. She was Athena, wisdom in one hand, war in the other, and she was damn sure getting her brother out of here alive. She pulled herself into the driver's seat.

Behind her, Gabe got the rear door open and yelled at Ben to get his ass in the truck, just get in the truck, *just get in.* Ben barked back about Jonah's chair.

But Jonah was having none of it. "Do as the man says, Benjamin! I'll worry about my goddamn self!"

Ben got in and then spun around, ready to assist his brother. Jonah tipped forward in his chair, clasped Ben's waiting hands, and, with Gabe providing a bit of lift, transferred himself into the SUV's backseat.

Mira panicked briefly: *Shit. Stick shift.* She'd driven one only a handful of times. One of her mother's boyfriends had owned a Camaro with self-applied window tinting and speakers that crackled when the bass was too heavy. He'd taken Mira out on a dirt road when she was twelve and gotten his father-figure fix by letting her drive.

She pushed the image from her mind and twisted the key in the ignition.

Once Jonah was inside, Gabe jumped in after him.

Something thudded against the vehicle's steel and ricocheted with a high-pitched whistle.

Mira shifted gears with a sound like a millstone grinding rocks. She kept her head down so that she could barely see over the dash. The others did the same, huddled as low as the seats allowed. She glanced at Luke.

He looked like a model of a schoolroom tornado drill, head between his knees, hands clasped behind his neck.

She released the clutch too quickly. The engine died.

A bullet skimmed the hood, blazing a trail of sparks and leaving a silver gouge in its wake.

Ben struck the back of the seat. "Mira, please!"

"Pedal to the metal," Luke whispered. "That's a big 10-4, good buddy."

Mira turned the key, let off the clutch, and pressed the accelerator as hard as she dared.

The big radials bit into the sand. The Land Rover bolted from a standing position to warp factor six, dispatching a smoke screen of dust to cover its retreat. Wind whistled through the hole in the glass.

Mira didn't bother to look where she was driving. She shifted gears as best she could. Then, head down and foot on the floor, she used her shirt to wipe her face, frantically scouring the blood from her cheeks.

"He'll follow us," Luke said softly. "Martians never, *ever* give up."

CHAPTER TWENTY

Dawn cracked the iron shell of night. Gabe was the first to notice. The eastern stars faded and pink daylight appeared, as if to remind him that, despite everything, the universe was still functioning as intended.

Body count: four.

The scientist named Eduardo was the fourth and most recent ghost to lend its voice to the chorus in Gabe's head. He was too weak to fight off their song. Other than the nap in Vicente's truck, he hadn't slept in over two days. He so wanted to let sleep drop a black sack over his head and drag him away like a victim.

"Everybody more or less okay back there?" Mira asked.

Gabe met her eyes in the rearview mirror, though he knew it wouldn't do any good. For a moment they stared at each other. He wondered if she was beautiful. "As good as can be expected."

"Ben? Jonah?"

The brothers shared the backseat with Gabe. Jonah rode in the middle, his hands resting on his useless legs. He'd said nothing over the last hour, only stared blankly from the window.

"We're hanging tough," Ben said.

Speak for yourself.

Gabe wasn't sure if he was hanging tough or not. The cops would arrive at Mentiras to find half the town burned down. The rifleman had surely turned his underground warren into a furnace by now. Perhaps he'd knocked out the supporting timbers and buried everything under tons of rock. Gabe had no way of knowing this—unlike Fontecilla's grandmother, he wasn't psychic—but he wagered it was true. The rifleman's objectives now were to obliterate all signs of his passing and to eliminate the witnesses.

How did he follow us?

Gabe's weary mind had no answer for this. Maybe the man had supernatural tracking skills or satellite imagery at his command. Hell, maybe *he* was the psychic. It didn't matter. He was coming.

But why?

The rifleman's motivation remained a galaxy beyond Gabe's grasp. It was the astronomer's eternal and most bitter lament. Looking was the best you could do. Touching would be for a generation farther down the line.

"I don't suppose you ever heard of Micha Lepin," he said.

Mira again looked at him in the mirror. "That's not anyone I know. Why?"

"I'm not sure." He twisted in his seat enough to liberate the dog tags from his hip pocket. Though the morning light wasn't strong enough to reveal what was embossed there, he felt the name when he ran his finger over the letters.

Alban Olivares, the Midnight Messenger's secret identity, the persona he assumed when he wasn't alone in the Atacama, rescuing chewed-up children from hell.

Gabe sucked down more water, afraid to give the desert air any opportunity to dehydrate him. Foolish hikers died out here every year, and he'd learned to be wary. As he drank, he thought about the two names as well as he could, given his fatigued state of mind, and it took him a moment to realize that Luke had spotted a town. He was tapping his thick index finger against the window.

"What is it?" Mira asked.

"Lights. Lights and lights and more lights."

Almost as soon as he said it, the Land Rover thudded across a strip of blacktop. The two-lane road drew a perfectly straight line across the desert. Mira corrected course to get them moving in the right direction down the highway, though she didn't bother staying in the proper lane. No traffic challenged her from either direction.

Gabe's eyes throbbed in their sockets, and the names started to blend together: Eduardo-Alban-Micha . . . these foreign-sounding monikers made no sense to his weary American ears. Why couldn't the ghosts take care of their own problems? Who among them had decided to draft an inexperienced astronomer for the task of settling their debts?

"We need to call somebody," Mira said. "The police or someone."

"Yeah, yeah, I know. My good buddy Fontecilla in his damn trilby."

As they neared the town and whatever waited there, Gabe slid closer to the edge of sleep, his head resting on the window. When he heard Jonah weeping softly beside him, he offered no commiseration. At least Eduardo hadn't died in pieces.

Sweet melon juice ran down Ben's unshaved chin.

The wrinkled woman behind the crates offered him a rag and explained in Spanish her secret for always knowing when a melon was ripe.

Ben listened as if she were explaining religion. Through the years, he'd tapped with his thumb, sniffed the rind, and shaken the things next to his ear. Everybody had a different method, just as everybody had a different path to God. Ben had spent his life wondering equally about those topics. Perhaps if he could unlock one he'd learn the secret to the other.

They'd discovered a town on the desert's edge, one apparently self-sustained by family farms that received water from the only spring around for miles in any direction. The people here were likely descendants of the nitrate miners who once ruled this place but now were only memories.

A few feet away, Mira and Luke were talking about shoelaces while the sun came up behind them.

"Just try to be more careful," Mira said. "If you hadn't gotten out of the car so quickly, you wouldn't have been tangled up in your laces, and if your laces had been tied—"

"IknowIknowIknow! Double knots!"

"Yes, double knots."

"Gretel?"

"Hmmm?"

"Why did the Martian kill that man?"

"I don't know."

"Was he aiming for *me*? I think he was aiming for me. I zapped him with the ray gun."

"I said I don't know. Let's just worry about being safe, okay?"

They'd been in town for twenty minutes. There was no sign marking the city limits, only a single wooden post that might once have borne the name of the place but was now a perch for a blue-hooded Sierra finch. It was the first wildlife Ben had seen since his arrival at Jonah's facility yesterday evening. The finch implied the existence of an ecosystem, which the area around ACEF entirely lacked.

He looked over his shoulder. The highway ran on forever.

Satisfied that they were still alone, he returned his attention to the woman and reluctantly interrupted her lesson on knowing a melon by the texture of its skin. "I better just pay for this one and be on my way."

His smile convinced her, pesos changed hands, and Ben returned to the SUV. It sat in a patch of *suspiro de campo,* purple wildflowers that bloomed in places where other plants would shrivel for want of water. Ben offered a melon half and a plastic fork to his brother, who sat silently in the backseat.

Jonah stared at him with reddened eyes. "Don't start, Benjamin."

"What the hell does that mean?"

"A man is dead. A friend of mine. He . . . he died *right in front of us.*"

"Lay off. I was there. You think I'm not upset? You think I'm immune somehow?"

"Immune? Sure, I'll buy that. It's always been that way. While I work my black paraplegic ass off and get hit with whatever God decides to blow off the fan, you just breeze on through, *immune.*"

"It's just a goddamn cantaloupe. I ain't forcing it down your throat."

"Everything all right?" Mira asked, making her way back to the car.

"Not in the least," Jonah said.

Ben felt the barbs of his brother's eyes as he turned to Mira. "The Cable siblings will be just jim-dandy. What about the Westbrooks?"

Mira had bound her hair behind her head and had used the corroded restroom behind the market to wash her face. "One of us is fine, more or less. The other is . . . well, she's kind of freaked out at the moment, if you want to know the truth."

Jonah clucked his tongue. "See there? One gets to be immune, and one gets bloody."

"Don't be a shitheel," Ben told him.

Jonah spread his hands. "I'm just saying . . ."

"Yeah? Well, quit just saying. We're all in this together."

"Nice cliché, but it's not so easy to swallow when you don't happen to be—"

"Don't say it, Joe."

"—bulletproof."

Ben bit his lip. He hadn't hit his brother since they were kids. But to everything there was a season, and all that. For the time being, he managed to keep himself in check.

"What's that mean?" Mira asked. "Bulletproof? I don't understand."

Ben's thoughts swirled. A man had been gunned down. The killer was chasing them. Gabe hadn't yet emerged from using the phone, maybe because there was no help on the way and he didn't want to break the bad news. And now Jonah was poking at the ground, once more exhuming the oldest and most troublesome secret between them.

"It means," Jonah said, "that some of us are blessed. Or lucky. Or whatever you want to call it. Some of us aren't even afraid of guns. And it's always the rest of us getting rattled. Why do you think Luke wasn't afraid to follow Traylin down that hole? He's probably like Benjo here, *immune.*"

"Last time I offer you any melon." Ben got out of range of his brother's intercontinental ballistic glare, veering around to the back of the vehicle and not at all surprised to find that he'd lost his appetite. The truth was clear enough: It *wasn't* the last time. He'd go on offering whatever he thought Jonah might enjoy, regardless of their occasional spat. That was part of the code.

Meanwhile, twenty feet away and oblivious to the conversation, Luke guzzled one of the bottles of soda Mira had bought. He held the thing in both hands, head tipped so far back he looked about to fall over.

Suddenly inspired, Ben approached him. "Excuse me, sailor."

Luke wiped his mouth. "I'm not a sailor. I don't even have a ship!"

"Good point. You got a minute?"

"You bet!"

"Great. Do me a favor and read that word right"—he pointed at the bottle with his fork—"there."

Luke looked at the label as instructed. He squinted. "That's a big word."

"Sort of."

"I don't think I do words that big."

"You have no idea what it says?"

"Um . . . *C*-something?"

Ben knelt and, using his fork, printed ten letters in the dirt. Then he stood up.

Luke gazed down at it. "Carbonated."

Ben shook his head, wanting to say so much but unsure where to begin. "How the hell do you *do* that?"

Luke grinned. "I don't do it, Ben. *You* do!"

"Then what is it that I'm doing that makes you able to read?"

"I dunno. Casting a spell. Making Martian magic."

"But *this*"—Ben tapped the bottle in Luke's hand—"has nothing to do with Mars."

Luke stopped smiling. He took a step closer and looked up at Ben. "It all has to do with Mars."

"What do you mean? Tell me what you mean. I need to know."

Gabe emerged from the little house connected to the market, the screen door slamming behind him.

Luke broke eye contact and waved. Whatever he might have said was lost.

Ben wanted answers, but there would be no finding them right now. He saw the trouble written on Gabe's face, even if Luke did not. "What's wrong? Phone broken?"

"Unfortunately, no." Gabe's eyes were heavy and red. "I couldn't talk to the investigator in charge because he's already en route to Mentiras, with a second team headed to ACEF to meet *us,* but of course all they're going to find is a body, assuming that it's still there when they arrive. A captain or somebody came on the line, and he wasn't happy, to say the least. He told me . . ."

"What? What did he say?"

"That I'm officially a person of interest."

"A suspect?"

"Not quite. Sort of like being the first runner-up to the suspect. He told me to stay put, and if I wasn't here when they arrived, he'd authorize my arrest."

"But you haven't *done* anything."

"Yeah? One, I call about a dead trespasser who vanishes by the time the cops arrive. Two, I find a dead boy with his arms and legs cut off. Three, I ring up again, this time with a story about a man who lives beneath a ghost town and dismembers living victims. And do I stop there? Am I content with the hat trick? Nope, because now I'm calling them *again,* saying there's *another* body, but oh, by the way, we're no longer at the scene because the five of us would rather take cover in a one-phone town and try to hide from a marksman murderer than hang out around the dead man waiting to get our heads blown off."

"I'd tell you to chill out, but I'm not very chill myself."

Luke looked from one of them to the other. "The policemen are coming?"

"Eventually," Gabe said. "We're pretty far off the beaten path. But I guess if there's a sheriff or something in this town, they'll probably contact him."

"What about the embassy?" Ben suggested. "Should we get in touch with someone there?"

"Couldn't hurt. But you know what? Right now I'm too tired to care. The guy inside says there's a church that lets hikers and hippies and people sleep upstairs. An off-road racing team was bunking there a few days ago. If I don't get there in the next ten minutes, the cops'll find me comatose on top of one of these vegetable crates."

"I could use a bit of shut-eye myself."

"I'm not tired at all!" Luke exclaimed.

"Like I told you," Gabe said with a companionable slap on the shoulder. "You the man."

Ben had no more taste for the melon. He stabbed his fork into its orange crater and left it for the flies. He returned to the car and listened as Gabe briefly updated Mira and Jonah, neither of whom appeared to take the news very well. They understood that they were becoming increasingly caught up in the wild tangles of Gabe's ordeal.

They drove to the opposite edge of town.

Just what this place had looked like in its heyday, Ben couldn't say. Most of the homes were abandoned, their windows devoid of glass. Like alien abductees, the people who lived there had left behind the detritus of their lives: a bent-up tricycle, an old Indian motorcycle with no engine, a single shoe hanging from a clothesline. Faces appeared in doorways, suspicion in their dark eyes. Ben couldn't blame them. An expensive and shot-up British SUV could mean only trouble.

The mission-style church was the only thing worthy of tourist attention. Ben didn't find it surprising at all to see that it was called Our Lady of the Desert. He would have been disappointed had it been otherwise.

"What are we doing here?" Luke asked as they swung open their doors.

"Waiting," Ben told him.

"Waiting for what?"

With a glance, Ben deferred to Gabe.

Gabe only waved a hand. "For whatever happens next."

CHAPTER TWENTY-ONE

Mira opened her eyes and saw Christ.

He reached down for her with fantastic compassion, though His feet were staked to a slab of wood and His skull bled from a barbed tiara. In her half-wakened state, Mira thought He looked a lot like the lead singer from Creedence Clearwater Revival. What was his name again?

"Mira?"

Damn, now the Son of Man was addressing her personally. What kind of oddball dream was this? Though she hadn't attended Sunday school as a girl—getting up early on the weekends wasn't Cathy Westbrook's idea of sane behavior—Mira had gotten to know good old Gentile religion on her own. Still, she didn't consider herself worthy of being on a first-name basis with the Prince of Peace. Then again, if He was in the mood for a little tête-à-tête, then Mira certainly had a few bones in need of picking.

"Mira, wake up."

She blinked several times. Jesus retreated to a state of sculpture, eyes nothing but dollops of flaking paint. "Gabe?"

"Hey."

She sat up. Hers was one of eight cots arrayed in neat rows in the church balcony. The congregation was too small to warrant the use of this upper area of worship, so the priest offered it to wayfarers as a means of supplementing the parish's meager coffers. The first thing she thought about was Eduardo. She hadn't known him, but he'd died with his blood on her face.

"Where's your brother?"

She rubbed her eyes. "What time is it?"

"About eleven a.m."

Eleven o'clock meant she'd been asleep for less than four hours. Somehow that was worse than not getting any sleep at all. Her mouth felt full of ash.

"Ben and Luke are gone," Gabe said.

"I know. They woke me up and said—" She yawned, only remembering to cover her mouth halfway through. "Sorry. I'm not always very ladylike in the morning."

He flashed a smile. "Ladylike is boring. Emily Post probably didn't get many dates."

"Sounds like a kindred spirit."

"You and Emily? Hardly. I don't think anyone would ever call you boring."

"I assure you that eluding men with guns isn't my normal routine."

"You drove like a pro."

"I'm sure you're confusing *pro* with *terrified ninny,* but thanks. How did he follow us that far, anyway?"

"He must have had a motorcycle or something stashed in one of the buildings. A getaway vehicle, you know? We drove with the lights off for the first few miles, but after that, I guess our taillights would've been visible. Besides, he could have trailed us by the sound of the engine. It's awfully quiet out there."

Mira supposed that made sense. "Have you checked on Jonah?"

"Downstairs staring out the window. He's pretty shaken up."

"That makes two of us. And the police?"

"Not here yet. We're way out in the boondocks. It's kind of like being in the middle of Siberia. Besides, between probing Mentiras and trying to locate the rifleman at ACEF, their personnel are probably spread too thin."

"They'll find him, won't they?"

"There's a lot of desert out there."

"You don't sound very hopeful."

"It depends on how many resources they're willing to commit. They'll need more than a single chopper or plane to cover that much territory."

"Something tells me that they're going to be taking it all very seriously after they see Eduardo and the . . . the woman you found."

"Yeah, that's what worries me. I wouldn't be surprised if I ended up in handcuffs the next time they see me."

"But you're not—"

"Without that guy in custody, I'm the best thing they've got. But I'm trying not to think about it. Tell me about Luke and Ben."

"They took a walk. My brother's never been much of a sleeper, and Ben suggested they do some experiments together, maybe learn a bit more about the reading."

"Reading?"

"Long story. Long and *bizarre* story, actually. Suffice it to say that Ben has a knack for bypassing my brother's learning disability. They woke me up and said they needed to get in touch with Mars or some kind of crazy talk like that. I told them to be safe, but other than that, I was too tired to worry about it."

Gabe was silent for a moment, and Mira wondered if he'd heard her at all. Though he needed some time with hot water and a razor, underneath the dust was a face that Mira had to admit was attractive. Or was it just the intensity of their situation that made his smile so inviting?

He turned his pale blue eyes toward her and said, "I need a computer."

"The Internet?"

"Yeah. There's a man, Micha Lepin, he used to be a member of something called DINA, part of the Chilean intelligence community. I think he's involved with what's going on here. That woman that Luke and I found . . ." He shook his head as if still trying to elude the memory. "She was a piece of the puzzle, too. She wasn't just a random victim."

"And you know this how?"

"I don't. I may be totally wrong."

"Fair enough. Next question. How do you plan on getting an Internet connection way out here? These people don't even have television."

"We're in a church. Maybe I'll pray."

"I wasn't aware that God answered requests for broadband."

"You should try it sometime."

"With my luck? He'd probably just stick me with dial-up."

"Are you always so irreverent when you wake up in the morning?"

"Hang around till noon. I upgrade from irreverent to sacrilegious."

Gabe laughed.

Mira permitted herself a smile, surprised by her sudden penchant for banter. She didn't normally have that effect on people.

Gabe sobered quickly. "Hey, listen. I'm sorry for getting you guys into this. That man, Eduardo, he's dead because of me."

"No, he's dead because a sociopath shot him. You don't get to take the blame for that."

"That sociopath wouldn't have been anywhere around if I hadn't provoked him."

"You and Luke both. But do you think my brother is blaming himself?"

Gabe looked away.

"No, he's not," Mira said, driving home her point. "It's amazing how much I've learned from him. And thanks, by the way, for not treating him like a child. Most people do."

"Most people do a lot of things I don't do. You want to know a secret?"

Mira, intrigued, nodded once. "Definitely."

"How we treat people is based on their faces. If a good-looking stranger comes up to you and asks you for a favor, you're more likely to say yes than if they're ugly or old or disfigured."

"Is that true?"

"You tell me."

"And you don't operate that way? You're not a sucker for a pretty face?"

He looked at her intently. Mira sensed that she'd found another layer of the secret. "I wish that I was. I really do." He turned away and jabbed a thumb at the narrow staircase leading from the balcony. "Come on. I think I have an idea where we can find that Internet connection without having to bother God about it."

Though Mira had been fatigued only minutes ago, a new energy passed through her, lightening her bones. And though she would've given her kingdom for a toothbrush, she figured this was no time to get hung up on little things like hygiene. "We should probably leave a note."

"We'll tell Jonah where we're going in case they come back while we're gone. Good enough?"

"Sure. It's just habit, you know, looking after him."

"Don't take this the wrong way," Gabe said, heading down the steps, "but from what I've seen, Luke is one dude who can take care of himself."

Mira had never heard anyone say such a thing. She slowed her steps, letting it fill her up.

Gabe looked back. "Something wrong?"

After a moment she shook her head, simply enjoying the feeling. "Nothing at all."

Ben carved prophecies in the sand.

> MARS IS HELL . . .
> ONLY WAITING FOR OUR ARRIVAL BEFORE IT BURSTS INTO BRIMSTONE AND FIRE

Luke walked among the foot-long letters and read the words aloud, concluding with "*Hell* is sort of a bad word, isn't it?"

"Depends on how you're using it." He pointed at the quotation with the stick he'd used to inscribe it. "You know who said that?"

"*You* said it."

"I mean originally. A man named Ray Bradbury wrote those words. Do you know who he is?"

"Nope."

"He's the king of Mars."

Luke made a face. "Mars has a *king*?"

"You bet. Mr. Bradbury thought maybe the rest of us would listen if he took us to Mars in order to show us how to solve our problems. You know what else he said? That the reason we're so fond of our red cousin is because we wonder about our own past and worry about our own future."

"I don't get it."

"He's saying we're connected."

"To Mars?"

"That's right. And to one another. We're just too caught up in ourselves to realize it." As the sun climbed higher, Ben went back to work with his stick, slicing letters into the ground. "This one isn't Bradbury. This one is pure Benjamin Langston Cable."

WE WILL BE TRULY SAVED ONLY WHEN _____ ON MARS

" 'We will be truly saved,' " Luke read, " 'only when *something* on Mars.' " He shrugged. "That doesn't make any sense."

"What's the missing word?"

"I don't know *that.*" He laughed. "*You* wrote it."

"Take a guess."

"But my guesser doesn't work with words. I *hate* Scrabble."

"You don't have any ideas? I think it's safe to say that you've read my hackneyed prose more times than anyone. And you can't fill in the blank? Give it another look. Try again."

Luke put his hands on his wide hips and bent over, reading with intentional slowness. "We. Will. Be. Truly. Saved. When." He wagged his finger at the ground. "You darn word! What *are* you?"

Ben sighed. He'd followed a half-baked hunch, though apparently it had misguided him. But there had to be an explanation for Luke's ability to read Ben's writing. If he could only—

"Baptized!" Luke blurted. "Is that the word, Ben, is that the right word?"

Ben would not have been more startled had Luke found a chunk of raw gold lying on the desert floor. He opened his mouth but had no words to express his sense of wonder. "That's right. Baptized. I . . . I don't know what to say."

"Shit is holy?"

A smile shook Ben's face with its force. "That's exactly right. Shit is *holy.*"

Luke clapped his hands. "What's next? More! More!"

Rolling now, Ben leaped to an unblemished section of ground and scrawled

CHAPTER ONE

"Behold, my young compadre, the two most powerful words in fiction."

"Chapter one?"

"You bet your mind-reading ass, chapter one. Now get that book out of your pocket."

Luke did as instructed, taking *This Mayflower Mars* from the leg of his cargo pants.

"Open it up to the last page."

Luke's thick fingers slowly located the proper place. "Now what?"

"Now what? Well, *read,* of course. The last paragraph will be enough."

Luke took a breath and dove into the final scene, what Ben's editor had called the *conclusion of the denouement* and what Ben had always thought of as the Obligatory Sappy Send-off. " 'At Dycar's grave they gathered, suits running hot to fight the cold, hands clasped to fight the isolation. That's what Dycar had died to save them from: being alone. Tilanna knew it wasn't the stygian temperatures or the plaintive winds that drove settlers mad on the escarpments of Hellas Basin. These things could be battled. But only Dycar—foolish, irritating, unstoppable Dycar—had owned a spirit capable of driving loneliness into a box canyon so that the others could pass. They knew this now, and until they died they would be both haunted and emboldened by it.' "

Luke closed the book. "The end."

Ben used the stick like a baton, tapping twice on the ground. "Is it?"

"Sure. That's the last page. Zip, zero, nothing after that."

"Imagine that there was."

"What do you mean?"

"If there *was* more, what would it say? Pretend there was another chapter." *Or a second book,* he thought, but was too afraid to say. "Just make believe that the story keeps going, and tell me, my squire, what happens next?"

Luke scrunched up his face, buried in thought.

"Well?"

"Um . . . once upon a time . . ."

"An excellent beginning!"

"Once upon a time . . . Tilanna got up in the morning and . . . and"—he brightened—"she was going to have a baby!"

Ben knew it was true the second he heard it. His hand shook as he reached for the book. "You better give me that. I need some paper." Taking the novel from Luke, he stopped at the first mostly empty page he saw. Then he took out the pen he'd brought with him from his flat in

Santiago. Maybe it was the most valuable thing he owned. Maybe he was a fool for not pawning it. Or maybe he kept it as a reminder of better days. In any event, the Montblanc fountain pen he'd bought for five hundred dollars upon receiving the advance on his one and only novel now served as a kind of rabbit's foot, a talisman against the ghosts that haunted him. He unscrewed its heavy cap and wrote.

Luke read over his shoulder. "'Tilanna woke up on a late-summer morning and realized she was pregnant on Mars.'" He hooted once in approval. "What's next?"

"You tell me. We're writing this together."

"We are?"

"You woke up Tilanna, now you better get her moving. She's impatient, you know. She won't be happy if she has to stand there too long."

Luke smiled. "She goes to the window and looks out, but . . . but the dust storm happened last night and . . . and she can't see!"

Ben wrote, following this madcap muse who'd somehow tapped into the circuitry of his soul.

Luke gobbled up the words in the wake of Ben's swiftly flowing pen. "'The window of her environmental cabin drew her as it always did, though she frowned when she saw the armor plating of dust. The sandstorm had encased her again, which meant at least an hour digging herself out.'" He looked at Ben. "Dycar used to do that."

"Not anymore." He kept writing.

Luke read over his shoulder. "'Things had been easier when Dycar was alive. It was not only easier to extricate yourself from sand-covered cabins, but it was also easier to breathe, not to mention to fight and to cry and to laugh until your stomach ached.'" He clapped. "That's really good!"

"Shut up and keep storytelling."

"Okay, um . . . Tilanna *never* likes being stuck inside. You remember when she had to hide in that cave for two days while Dycar was off getting the medicine?"

"Yes, yes."

"So she *can't* stay in the cabin. She'll go crazy!"

Ben found another partial page at a chapter end and kept writing.

Luke read, "'Though she'd never been diagnosed as claustrophobic, she'd damn sure wilt and fade without the meager Martian sun. And so, though a secret voice was telling her that her sickness was the result of Dycar's legacy kindling in her belly, she ignored it and stepped outside with a wide-bladed knife. It was Tilanna versus the dust once again, and by now the dust should've known who would win.'"

"Not too bad, eh?" Ben asked.

"But there's more!"

"Oh, I have no doubt about that. But if we keep moving at this breakneck rate, I'm going to need to find myself a fresh reservoir of paper. I can only fill up so many margins before there's nothing left. Not to mention the fact that my hand already hurts."

"Are we writing a whole book?"

"If they'd publish only half of one, I'd be thrilled, but I figure the readers are going to demand some sort of ending."

"But I thought you don't write anymore."

"The two things I've learned," Ben said, smacking the paperback against his palm, "are one, never spit in front of a lady, and two, you damn sure write when the urge is upon you. And my friend, the urge is beating me to death."

"Is it beating me, too?"

"That's for you to decide. Let me ask you this. Do you like talking about Tilanna and her unborn child?"

"You bet, sure! It's cool!"

"And are you curious to see what happens to her when she's all alone on Mars?"

"But she's not alone. Remember the Kanyri rebels? There're still some of them out there, and they *hate* Dycar's crew."

Ben nodded, never feeling more carried along by fate than he did now. "The rebels indeed. I think it's probably up to us to check in on them, see what they've been up to since Dycar's death. What do you say?"

Luke hoisted both hands skyward. "I say *shit is holy*!"

Ben joined him in celebration, the two of them exulting in the strange and unpredictable gift the desert had given them.

CHAPTER TWENTY-TWO

Gabe and Mira found the racers' camp a mile out of town.

"The dictionary defines *civilization* as a society capable of keeping written records," Gabe said as he turned off the Land Rover's ignition. "I tend to think of it as any place offering a satellite uplink."

The camp consisted of army tents, a stack of knobby tires, radio equipment, and a Texas state flag hanging from a ten-foot antenna.

"Check it out."

The truck stood tall on a chassis designed for maximum ground clearance. With a roll-cage, monstrous shock absorbers, and a wallpapering of sponsor decals, it reminded Gabe of a toy he'd had when he was seven. It looked expensive. He could almost hear his mother saying that line about boys being boys, and for some reason this made him miss her with sudden acuity. Splashed across the truck's nose was its creed: TREAD ON YOU.

Gabe and Mira got out to meet a man in a headset and a Firestone cap.

After Gabe introduced himself, he explained his problem. He and his friend were traveling South America's wilder places but found themselves in need of sending an e-mail back home. His lies surprised him by how natural they felt on his teeth.

Tony Brannon, crew chief of Redline Racing, noticed nothing. He subjected them to several minutes of tech-speak—Dynatrac steering knuckles, thirty-five-spline axle shafts, and selectable hubs—then caught himself and grinned like an old prospector. "Sorry about that. You folks just came to use the john, and here I'm giving you a tour of the living room."

"Not a problem," Gabe assured him.

Brannon showed them to the largest of the tents, where the Redline team housed their diagnostic gear and some of the more sensitive engine components. A card table supported a well-traveled laptop.

"Knock yourselves out," Brannon said. "All I ask is that you keep the porn video streams to a minimum." He winked and dropped the tent flap behind him as he left.

"So now what?" Mira asked.

Gabe sat down on the folding metal chair. "*Now* we find out just who's involved in all of this so we have something to show the police. If I don't want to go from being a person of interest to a full-fledged suspect, I have to give them a lead or two." He opened a search engine and typed in the true name of the Midnight Messenger. His death had passed the baton to Gabe, who was currently doing his best to run with it and avoid being caught from behind.

The term *Alban Olivares* generated a random sampling of Spanish-language pages, some featuring the first half of the name and others the surname. Gabe tried again, this time enclosing the name in quotation marks, but this produced only a single hit on a genealogical Web site; that particular Alban Olivares died in 1965 in Panama.

"So he's not on the Web," Mira said, leaning over Gabe's shoulder.

"I know how he feels. There's nothing more humbling than finding your name doesn't turn up any interesting results."

"Maybe it means you have more important things to do than get talked about online."

"Or it could just mean I'm lame."

"Well, if it makes any difference, I've known you for over twelve hours now, and the last thing you've been is lame."

"Under other circumstances I'd take that as a good thing." He entered "Chilean DINA" and found several articles detailing the war crimes and human-rights infractions perpetrated under the regime of dictator Augusto Pinochet.

"So DINA was kind of like a thug police squad?" Mira ventured.

"The same mentality, yeah. I mean, look at all of this. Kidnappings, execution squads, torturing of prisoners . . ."

"And they were funded by the CIA?"

"At least for certain operations. Of course, the U.S. claims it wasn't involved in the assassination of Pinochet's predecessor and some of the other nastier events, and that may or may not be true, but it says here that in 2000 the CIA released documents showing how they underwrote several DINA operations throughout the seventies."

"Okay, but that was a long time ago. Look, according to this, the DINA was disbanded in 1977. How could they possibly have anything to do with that woman you and Luke found?"

"Maybe Micha Lepin can tell us."

"Who?"

He typed the name into the search bar and hit ENTER.

That first link was enough. After reading only a few paragraphs, Gabe knew that Lepin was the pivot upon which the entire nightmare turned. "Here we go . . ."

Mira leaned closer and read out loud. " 'Biochemist Micha Lepin rose to prominence within the National Intelligence Directorate and became an integral member of Pinochet's covert development unit, Quetropilla. Though Quetropilla's foremost objective was the production of sarin nerve gas, Lepin was allegedly permitted to pursue experimental chemical toxins.' "

"A saint among men," Gabe said.

"It gets worse. 'Lepin subjected leftist detainees and other captive political dissidents to a diverse program of torture, primarily focusing on the introduction of neurochemical agents in doses small enough to produce effects without resulting in the victim's premature death.' "

"My God . . ."

" 'Known in the DINA by the alias Lantern, Micha Lepin was a key figure in the 1973 Caravana de la Muerte, or Caravan of Death, in which at least seventy people were murdered.' "

"Seventy?"

"That's what it says."

"So that's him out there?" Gabe wondered. "The rifleman is Micha Lepin?"

"Not according to this. 'Lepin fled the country upon the collapse of Pinochet's administration. He was extradited from Portugal in 1985 and is currently serving a life sentence at a detention facility in Chile.' "

Gabe drummed his fingers on the table.

"Any ideas?" Mira asked.

"It doesn't make sense. I'm assuming that those papers I found down there were somehow meaningful to the . . . the killer or rifleman or whatever you want to call him."

"I was thinking more along the lines of insane murdering dickhead."

"Yeah, that too."

"And if you're right and Lepin *is* important to him, for whatever reason, then we need to know *why.*"

"And how do we do that?"

"Run an image search, for starters, and let's get a look at this Micha Lepin just to make sure you don't recognize him as the same man you saw down below."

Gabe stopped drumming.

"What? What did I say?"

He'd often heard of people giving a rueful smile. He tried one on for size, though he wasn't sure if it was rue he was feeling. Hell, he wasn't even entirely sure what rue was. But there was irony on his lips, and not a small amount of regret. And that was enough.

"Uh, Gabe?"

"I'm not very good with faces."

"Oh. Well, it doesn't hurt to give it a try."

"It won't help."

"I know it's kind of grasping at straws, but what else do we have? We need to try anything that comes to mind. You're the one who roped me into this. I didn't ask to have you blow into my life, and I certainly didn't ask to have that man killed right in front of me."

"Trust me."

"How can I do that? I don't even know you. Let's just see the picture already."

Gabe almost made a fist. It wasn't a fist that intended to hit anyone, but a reflex of frustration and embarrassment. He got his Zen back together and kept his hands relaxed as he went through the motions of complying with her request, hoping that he wasn't blushing or transmitting any other sign of his unease.

Steady as she goes, Captain.

He took his own advice and stared straight ahead at the image of Micha Lepin that appeared on the screen. Lepin was either sixty years old or twenty-six; his cheeks were pockmarked or smooth; his nose was hawkish or as petite as a thimble.

"I take it you don't recognize him," Mira said.

"That is definitely, entirely true."

"No resemblance to the aforementioned insane murdering dickhead?"

"None that I can see."

"Okay, great, then we're still sitting here at square one. Where do we go from here? Do you have any more names?"

He wished that he did. But the boy with the pinwheel was as anonymous as the woman in the wagon . . . though he was certain they shared a common denominator.

"Let's go back to Olivares," Mira suggested. "What do we know?"

"Not much. I know that he found the boy and was trying to get him out of the desert."

"That means that Olivares visited the town of Mentiras."

"Right. He was out there, he was maybe even down in the rifleman's cellar."

"Did he find it by accident? Or was he out looking for the boy?" Her enthusiasm surprised him. She didn't think it was too strange or too horrific. She was more ready to accept the fantastic than Gabe would have expected. "If I were guessing, I'd say he was intentionally trying to find the boy. It's pretty unlikely that he could've found that underground place by chance."

"Agreed. He was in the military. Maybe we should contact them and—"

"Ask them if he's AWOL?"

"He *is* AWOL. I saw him . . . go down."

"Maybe we could talk to his friends or even find a family member."

"That's what I'm thinking, yeah."

"Can I ask you something?"

"Sure," he said.

"Do you do this kind of thing often? Solving homicides, I mean. Because this is pretty scary to me, and I haven't even done anything but flee a murder scene and watch you surf the Internet."

He put on a smile that he didn't feel. "First of all, I haven't solved anything. And secondly, no. I usually spend my time staring at a computer screen full of numbers that explain starlight from a million years in the past. It's not exactly as thrilling as running with the bulls in Pamplona."

"Good."

"Why good?"

"Because I wouldn't want to think I was the only one out of my element here."

Gabe stood up and slid his chair under the card table. "In my life, if there's an element, whatever it is, I'm usually out of it."

"You've seemed fairly sure of yourself so far."

"Glad it looks that way, but in the last two days I've managed to lose my job, derail my doctoral research, and become a person of police interest. I saw two men shot, I found a dead boy in the desert, and a woman with no arms and legs died while I watched. I promise that the last thing I am is sure of myself. But thanks for saying so."

He left the tent before she could respond, not wanting to explain that his real reason for pushing so hard was because Alban Olivares had died without seeing a friendly face. Gabe knew that whether he lived for five more decades or only five more days, he was destined to go out the same way.

"Someone's coming."

Mira turned from the passenger's window and saw the two Humvees rolling toward them, antennas bent in the wind. Returning from Brannon's camp, she and Gabe still had a mile to go before reaching the church, but now it appeared that they were about to be intercepted.

She looked at Gabe. "This is bad, isn't it?"

"Could be."

"Are they going to arrest us?"

"Me, maybe. Not you."

"But they'll question me. Because of Eduardo, right?"

"I reckon so."

"Is that safe? You know, you hear horror stories about American citizens in foreign custody and how they're treated . . ."

"You want me to head off into the desert and try to lose them?" He raised his eyebrows at her, and she wondered if he was serious. Then she realized how silly she was being. Her mother might have been strung-out and distracted, but she was as tough as something made on an anvil.

Cathy Westbrook wouldn't have squirmed at the thought of a little questioning from the cops, regardless of what language they spoke. "I suppose we can save the stunt driving for later."

"Go peacefully, huh?" He continued to slow down.

"This time, anyway."

"Yeah. This time."

Though Mira was only kidding, she detected a note of sincerity in Gabe's voice. He was close to spinning his tires and hurtling off into the hinterland, evading all comers. She couldn't blame him. If she'd seen those awful things that *he* had seen, she knew she'd be a little gun-shy herself.

They'd no sooner stopped than the Humvees boxed them in, one in front and the other sliding around to the rear. At that point, Mira knew that matters were worse than she'd predicted.

Doors swung open. The men who emerged were not plainclothes detectives but men in flak jackets and Kevlar kneepads.

"Gabe, what's happening?"

"Chile's version of the SWAT team."

"Why?"

"Hell if I know."

The men drew guns.

Mira automatically lifted her hands, but her instinct was to engage the door lock. Though she knew she'd done nothing wrong, and though these were supposedly the good guys, she panicked at the sight of the semiautomatic pistols. No one had ever pointed a weapon at her before.

In accented English, one of them said, *"Please exit the car."*

"They didn't catch him," Gabe said.

"How do you know that?"

"Because if they'd already bagged him, they wouldn't be acting like the two of us are Bonnie and Clyde." He pushed open his door. "Let's go, Bonnie. Leave the machine guns inside."

Had she possessed her mother's moxie, Mira would've returned the quip, but it was all she could do to work the handle and get her feet beneath her. If they arrested her, how would she get word to Luke?

"Turn around, put your hands on the car."

They moved swiftly, closing in on her. A female cop patted her down, and Mira realized with profound clarity that she'd never in all of her days been searched bodily, not even by the draconian TSA agents at the airport that day she accidentally left her nail clippers in her purse. Standing here now with her palms flattened against the hot steel was too improbable to be real.

The Spanish was like a stream flowing over smooth stones, too rapid for her to discern. But she caught the important word: *pasaporte.*

"My passport's at the church," she said, after they let her turn around. "It's in my bag. Everything's in my bag. My name is—"

"You will come with us."

"But my bag—"

"You will come with us."

Mira glanced at Gabe.

He shrugged. She read his thoughts: *You're the one who decided we shouldn't try to outrun them.*

The officers bundled them into the idling Humvees without shackling them, which Mira took as a good omen. The Old Testament Noah found his hope in the dove with the olive branch, and Mira found hers in the fact that she wasn't handcuffed and gagged. To each his own.

No one spoke during the short ride to the mission. The Atacama had given way to a bit of vegetation, and stunted trees whipped by them on either side. The driver spoke at length into the radio. Though Mira only recognized every sixth word, she detected the tension in his voice. Whatever was happening, it wasn't routine.

A helicopter had landed at the church.

The chopper was emblazoned with an emerald shield and crossed rifles. Standing in front of it was a man in uniform . . . along with Luke and Ben.

The winds of peace flowed through her at the sight of her brother. She didn't know what she'd do if they were separated. Of course any decent therapist would tell her that she was codependent as hell, but so what? No decent therapist had a twin like Luke.

Apparently these Chilean SWAT guys weren't going to permit a reunion. The man in uniform, while escorting Ben to Mira's vehicle, directed Luke to the Humvee where Gabe waited. She saw Gabe and Luke shake hands, and then Ben climbed in beside her. A cop in a helmet and dark glasses slammed the door behind him.

"Hey, sugar," Ben said. "Fancy meeting you here."

"What's going on? Where are they taking us?"

"What's going on is that our new friend Gabe Traylin has apparently not only stirred up a hornet's nest, he's put his whole damn hand inside and crushed a few of them to death. As for where we're going . . . I have no idea, but I suspect the chairs will be hard and the coffee a few hours old."

"Is Luke okay?"

"You mean my fellow author? Yes, he's just about as okay as anyone I've ever met."

"Author?"

"We're writing a book." Ben seemed ten years younger than when Mira had met him. "Maybe it won't be a bestseller, but it's damn sure the cure-all tonic."

Mira, mystified, put away the rest of her concerns, at least for now. Luke was safe, Ben was writing again. On the other hand, they were being driven to an interrogation room because her brother had seen the face of a madman. Mira forced herself into a placid state, despite the apparent size of this particular Lipstick Smear. For now, she had only one more question. "Did they catch him?"

Ben didn't have to ask who she was talking about. He shook his head.

Mira looked out the window and wondered if their convoy was being watched by someone out there in the sand.

CHAPTER TWENTY-THREE

"Mentiras is burning, Señor Traylin."

Gabe wasn't surprised. He'd spent the last forty-five minutes telling his story, and this was the first thing that Fontecilla dropped on him when he was through.

"You have no opinion on this matter?"

"I assume there's no way to put out the fire?"

"By the time our trucks arrived, there would be little left to see. So my officers, they could do nothing but watch it become smoke. As a matter of fact, they are doing this very thing as we speak."

Gabe imagined the destruction. The rifleman's underground chambers would be like ovens or, more apropos, crematoriums.

"You are lucky to be alive, yes?"

Gabe had no reply for that. He was tired. His few hours of sleep at the church had done nothing but fill him with the spiders of bad dreams. He was hungry. His last meal had consisted of a bag of chips from the vending machine just on the other side of the room's steel door. He was lost. They'd driven him to a city he didn't know and escorted him to a room full of lingering cigarette smoke and poor ventilation.

"You do not agree with that?" Fontecilla asked.

"It wasn't luck."

"No?"

"Luke was in the right place at the right time."

"And you do not consider that to be luck?"

"I consider it to be one guy saving another guy. Call it what you want."

"He is a remarkable young man."

"No more remarkable than the rest of us."

"I beg to differ." Fontecilla tipped his chair back so that the front legs rose an inch off the floor, then consulted his small tablet computer. "What concerns me is his description of the suspect. A young man with such a handicap is not always able to give the details in a way that is helpful. It is called being politically correct, yes? That is what I am trying to do when I tell you that Luke could not describe the man in any helpful manner because he is . . . challenged mentally."

Gabe didn't like where this was heading, though he knew it was inevitable. There was no way they'd let him leave this place unless he provided them with a description that he was unable to produce. He'd predicted as much, and so on a hunch he had withheld the names he'd learned. He had intentionally not mentioned the dog tags, hoping he could use them at just the right time to divert attention from the fact that he somehow hadn't seen the face of the man who'd stood a foot away and tried to kill him. It was a story they wouldn't believe.

"This is a very serious and very dangerous situation, Señor Traylin."

"No shit."

"As I said earlier, you are free to contact the U.S. embassy at any time."

"Do I have a reason to need an attorney?"

Fontecilla leaned forward, causing the chair legs to resound like gunshots. "I am going to make two requests of you, except neither is really a request. One, give us one more hour here so you can work with our artist, help us make a drawing of this man. Two, relinquish your passport to me and stay within the city limits for the next forty-eight hours."

"Stay? Stay *where*? I don't even know where the hell I am."

"We will assign a hotel to you. The Westbrooks and Señor Cable must also remain, as they were witnesses to the alleged shooting at the science facility."

"Alleged?"

"If any of this is going to be a problem," Fontecilla said, "I will again advise you to speak with the embassy in Santiago, though I would hope there would be no need to take matters to that level."

"Why don't you just tell me what's going on?"

"You assume that I know more than I do. What I have is a blood sample from the observatory but no body, a dismembered boy on the medical examiner's table, and a dead scientist on his way to the same place. *That* is what I know. What I *suspect* is that you are holding something back, and so I am going to keep your passport in my desk." He stood up. "I apologize in advance if this upsets you, but I am obligated to tell you nothing. The obligations here are yours, namely to obey the laws in my country."

"But I haven't done anything wrong."

"So it would appear." He took his hat from the table and made his way to the door.

"Wait."

Fontecilla turned around.

"At least tell me the boy's name. Were you able to ID him?"

Fontecilla chewed on that for a moment, plainly deliberating the wisdom of being candid.

Gabe knew he'd get nothing from this man. The victim was under age, a minor, and if things worked down here as they did in the States, the police would keep his identity a private matter.

"Nicky Lepin," Fontecilla said. "Does that mean anything to you?"

Gabe knew he was being scrutinized. Fontecilla's radar swept the room, searching for that one blip that would reveal a possible lead. And because the name *Lepin* struck Gabe like a physical blow, he did everything he could to hold himself peacefully in place.

Nicky Lepin? How is he related to the imprisoned DINA biochemist, Micha Lepin? And what does it mean?

"Traylin?"

Gabe looked at the man's empty face. "It doesn't sound familiar."

Fontecilla left, closing the door behind him.

As the air rushed out of him, Gabe lowered his forehead to the table. The metal was cold against his skin.

Tilanna squeezed her gloved hand into a fist when she saw the dust from their tires.

The sun was its usual pinhole in the sky, offering scant light. Nevertheless, Tilanna saw the shape of the tri-bikes as the pack of them rumbled over the undulating hills. She hurried back to the home that she and Dycar had constructed—"our geodesic love nest," he called it—and sealed the hermetic portal behind her.

Her hand went immediately to her stomach. Somewhere beneath her fingers was her dead lover's parting gift, the pollen of him left to float on the Martian breeze until it took root within her. It gave her strength.

She went to the locker and found his guns.

"Totally cool!" Luke shouted, his voice filling the room. "I forgot Dycar's guns!"

"So did the Kanyri bandits. And they'll pay for it."

Luke clapped his hands. "Keep going!"

"*You* keep going."

"Okay . . . um . . . I want to hear what the guns look like again. I liked that part."

"You did, huh? And here I thought I was too heavy-handed with the description. Let's see if we can do it a bit differently this time around." He wrote for a minute, gobbling up another page of hotel stationery, then handed it to his orator, this Cicero in Down's clothing.

" 'Tilanna lifted the bandoleer and withdrew one of the weapons.

What gleamed in the lantern's light was not the sleek titanium of modern automatics but rather the ageless steel of a bygone frontier. The revolver's rosewood handle was worn smooth from use. The barrel was as heavy as a lead pipe. Tilanna thought this thing less a firearm and more a steamroller. Other guns would kill you with surgical precision and Teflon-tipped bullets; this one would mangle your bones.'"

"Not too bad, eh?"

"Is Tilanna going to fight them *all*?"

"I was sort of hoping that we could find that out together. What do you think she's going to do?"

Luke rested his chin on his hand, unwittingly assuming the posture of Rodin's *The Thinker*. Ben just sat there, marveling at him, marveling at *himself*. Who was he to have a part in such a play? A bogeyman cutting people up, a dyslexic and mentally challenged savant . . . Ben Cable had no business among such extremes of humanity. He was a second-rate writer, a tinker, a tailor, a magic-bean buyer, but here he sat in the middle of something so large he couldn't yet see its final form.

Mira let herself into the room and interrupted whatever her brother was about to say. Gabe trailed after her, the usual look of wary curiosity on his face.

". . . and I don't even know what city this is," she was saying.

"Calama," Ben informed her, brandishing his stationery. "Says so right here. The Agua del Desierto Hotel, to be specific. The Water of the Desert. I like that."

Mira didn't seem impressed. She sat down on the bed and cradled one of the overstuffed pillows.

"I take it you two didn't experience any epiphanies during your walk," Ben said.

Gabe sank to the floor and leaned his back against the wall. "My only revelation is that I'm no fan of police sketch artists."

"I thought it was neat," Luke said.

"You were probably more helpful. The first time I ran into the rifleman,

I was with my friend Vicente. He described the guy as having a narrow face and saggy eyes, so I just went with that."

"Pardon me for pointing this out," Ben said, "but you don't look so swell."

"Goes with the territory."

"I'll buy that."

"How's Jonah?"

"I just spoke with him. He's on his way back to ACEF to run damage control with the higher-ups. He wasn't happy. In point of fact, he was as pissed as the devil, called me more than a few names I haven't heard since we were kids, and told me not to bother him until he rode out the storm with his supervisors. Eduardo was a member of a cooperating university and wasn't on the NASA payroll, but still, I imagine Joe's up to his afro in phone calls and long-winded explanations."

"Jonah doesn't have an afro!" Luke said.

"True enough. But he sure used to. Man, I have this picture of us in '76 . . ." Ben put on the brakes in midmemory. "Forget it. Styles change, and people do, too."

The room fell silent. Mira sat with her eyes shut. Luke reread the paragraph about Dycar's guns. Gabe stared at things only he could see. Ben recalled hearing a theory that said once every seven minutes there was a break in conversation. The four of them hadn't even made it that far.

After another thirty seconds, he knew that he had no choice but to jolt them from their respective trances. That old proverb about striking while the iron was hot . . . Well, Mars had never called to him as hotly as it was now. "I, uh . . . don't mean to be the lone voice of optimism here, but Luke and I . . . Well, we're onto something good here. I'd hate for us to stop. We sort of have this project going—"

"So do we," Gabe said, rising to his feet.

Mira looked at him skeptically. "We do?"

"The way I see it, we can either sit around waiting for the cops to grill us again or we can get out there like Alban Olivares and do something."

"What Olivares was doing got him killed."

"We're safe here."

"Are you sure?"

"We're in the middle of a city of nearly two hundred thousand people. We don't have to worry about that guy finding us."

"Martians never give up," Luke reminded him.

"So I've heard. Look"—he walked backward toward the door—"there are some things I need to know. What does Nicky Lepin the boy have to do with Micha Lepin the convicted torturer? And how did Olivares end up out there at Mentiras? How did he know where to look?"

"Sounds like something the police would be happy to investigate," Ben said.

"I'm not just going to sit around on my ass and hope there's a happy ending."

Mira stood up. "I'm coming with you. Don't ask why. Just give me a second." She stepped into the restroom.

While the water ran behind the closed door, Ben appraised the astronomer. He remembered that look, one part idealism and two parts stupidity. Ben had worn it himself not so long ago. These days, the most daring thing he did was to return to Dycar's literary grave and see him reborn in the womb of his true love.

Mira emerged, ponytail hanging through the back of a Kansas City Royals ball cap.

Luke gave her a wave. "Bring us back some *food.* Serious, *serious* food."

"Will do. You two going to be all right in the meantime?"

"The question is," Ben said, "whether or not *you two* will be all right. Luke and I here are kicking ass and taking names."

Luke made a fist. "Like Rambo!"

Mira smiled, but Ben knew it was only for Luke's benefit. He wondered how many of the smiles in her life had been for that very reason.

"Skedaddle," Ben said. "But stay on high alert. You never know." As soon as they were gone, he picked up his favorite fountain pen. Made of aircraft aluminum and inlaid with gold, it seemed a fitting device for those who sought the glittering mysteries of space. "So where were we?"

"With Tilanna."

"Right. And what was she doing?"

"Kicking ass and taking names!"

"Exactly. So tell me how it went down."

Luke told the story as it came to him, and Ben chased him across the dunes of Mars.

CHAPTER TWENTY-FOUR

Calama devoured them.

Mira fended off black-haired children looking for handouts—"*¡Señorita bonita! ¡Señorita bonita!*"—and dodged a flatbed truck stacked with chicken crates. Dirt streets intersected with modern thoroughfares lined with tourist shops, newsstands, and a corner bazaar selling what looked to be pirated DVDs. An elderly woman carried cloth sacks from the market, strings of garlic and onions around her neck. A dirty Volkswagen sat at the light, the vintage hip-hop of LL Cool J shaking its doors.

"Starting to feel overwhelmed?" Gabe asked her as they stepped aside to avoid a messenger on a bicycle with plastic ivy woven around the handlebars.

"I hope you know where you're going, because I have no idea where I am."

"I never get lost," Gabe assured her. "Famous last words, I know, but it's true. Mostly."

"Hopefully your sense of direction won't be totally canceled out by my remarkable ability to get lost at a moment's notice in any neighborhood I happen to be visiting."

"Do you know how to find north?"

"*With* my dashboard GPS or without it?"

"Funny. I mean with the sun."

"I know that it never sets on the British Empire, but other than that . . ."

"Remind me to show you how, assuming we ever get a moment to breathe."

"Better watch out," she said, feeling strangely playful. "You'll give away all of your top-secret astronomer's tricks."

"You're right. I better not divulge the instructions for making a telescope using only common kitchen supplies."

"And duct tape," she suggested.

"That goes without saying."

As they walked, Mira replayed those last few phrases in her head. Hold the phone, babe, but was she actually *flirting*? With a *man*? A real-live man and not the movie stars who wooed her in her daydreams? It had been so long that she wasn't quite sure.

"Micha Lepin is an old man in prison now," Gabe said, changing conversational tack without warning. "But that's too humane a fate for him, considering what he's done. He took people who had been kidnapped by the government and used them to test all the shit he cooked up in the lab, like they were rats or something."

"And Nicky Lepin?"

"That's what we need to find out. He was mutilated out there. Alban Olivares tried to save him, but Nicky didn't make it. If we can find out how the two Lepins are connected . . ."

"Maybe they're not. For all I now, the name Lepin is like Smith back home. There *are* such things as coincidences, you know."

"Could be. But I don't think so. It doesn't feel right."

They rounded a corner and walked into Los Angeles.

Though four thousand miles south of the border, Calama's commercial heart might have been that of any city in the States. Behind them were the rustic bones of the city, the barefoot children playing stickball, the old men in woven hats selling fish from the back of trucks. In front of them, the mannequins in the storefronts were streamlined mankillers in Parisian shoes. A popper on the corner made geometric dance moves for money, the stereo at his feet pushing out a bone-numbing bass. On each block was at least one shop that sold cell phones and protein bars.

"Every city is turning into the *same* city," Gabe observed.

"Is that a good thing or a bad thing?"

Gabe didn't offer an opinion either way, and Mira found a certain meaning in his ambivalence. They found a public console at an Internet café. While Gabe settled in, Mira went in search of java. She bought two cappuccinos, and by the time she returned to the table, Gabe was shaking his head.

"You found something?"

He accepted the cup with a nod and pointed at the screen. "That's Nicky's name right here, but the page is in Spanish."

"So?"

"So . . . I'm not much use beyond asking for the bathroom and bottled water."

"Isn't there some kind of translator thingamabob you can use?"

He took a sip and then hurriedly set the cup aside. "Duh. You're right. I totally blanked there for a minute. Pardon me while I reboot my brain."

"You're pardoned. You've had a rough couple of days."

"Let's hope they don't get any rougher." He banged away at the keyboard. "Thanks for the coffee, by the way."

Thanks for taking my brother down that hole, she almost said. She'd decided that Luke's foray into the murderer's cave had strangely been good for him. He wasn't traumatized by what he'd seen, and he'd proven himself when things got scary. It made Mira wonder about the other ways he'd stand tall if she didn't keep him always tethered to her side.

"Nicky Lepin was kidnapped," Gabe said.

Mira scanned the story, working her way around the awkward

phrasing of the online translation. Over a year ago, the boy went missing while visiting a Santiago museum with his classmates. His parents, Sachin and Carella, waited for a ransom demand that was never made. No body was ever found.

"Until now," Mira said softly.

The news story concluded by mentioning that Carella was the daughter of the notorious war criminal Micha Lepin, imprisoned indefinitely for crimes against humanity during the dictatorship of Augusto Pinochet.

Gabe crossed his arms over his chest. "Nicky was Micha Lepin's grandson."

"What does that mean? How does it fit?"

"I don't know."

"Then we need to find someone who does."

"The only person I know is the Midnight Messenger."

"Who?"

"Alban Olivares."

"But you said he was killed. He got shot, right?"

"Yeah, but when you've got no options left"—Gabe logged off and stood up—"you've got to find a way to speak with the dead."

Gabe was listening to the phone ring when he realized he was missing something important about the severed limbs. The rifleman had systematically amputated the arms and legs of at least two people, giving each sutured stump time to heal before sawing off something else. Though the primary question of *why* he was performing these surgeries remained, waiting in its shadow was the smaller question of *where*.

"Where did he put the cut-off pieces?"

"Hmmm?"

Standing on the corner next to a greengrocer's open-air market, Gabe had trouble hearing the faint rings. He pressed the phone tighter against his ear. "As sick as it sounds, I'd like to know what he was doing with them . . . the body parts."

Mira made a face. She didn't want to think about it.

Maybe he was eating them. Or stuffing them like taxidermy. Or feeding them to the demons from the Incan underworld. Gabe's imagination sped up as it chased the notion around in his head, one race car drafting behind another.

"Quest-South, Julio Montero speaking."

Gabe stepped away from the still-raw memory of the woman in the wagon. "Dr. Montero, hey, it's me."

"Traylin?"

"Is everybody doing okay there?"

"Traylin, the *police* have been here *multiple* times. What have you done to us?"

"I'd love to argue with you, Doc, but I don't have time. I need to talk to—"

"I'll get Professor Rubat."

"No! No, I'm not calling for him. Give me to Vicente, the maintenance chief."

"What?"

"Just please get him, okay?" He ran a hand through his hair. "Come on, Doc. I showed you the flaw in your King's Indian Defense. Do this one favor for me."

"I hardly think that a chess lesson is anywhere near as important as what's going on here." He sighed. "Fine. Hold on."

Gabe waited. He had a plan for tracking down Alban Olivares, but it would die a premature death without Vicente's help.

After thirty seconds, he stole a glance at Mira. She was inspecting a spinning rack of bottled spices but remained within earshot. Maybe she was a bombshell or maybe she was the bride of Frankenstein. Most likely she was somewhere in between. Gabe didn't care. She was cool. Far cooler than a geeky stargazer who'd memorized the Green Lantern's creed at the age of ten and visited gaming forums where people traded insults such as "My m4d skllz pwned j00 n00b!" Though astronomers and astrologers usually didn't view the universe through the same lens, this time, at least, Gabe counted himself lucky; his horoscope must have known he'd need a partner if he was going to survive this.

"So Luke and Ben are writing a book?" he asked as he waited.

Mira inspected a jar of dried epazote. "So they say."

"I take it by your tone that this isn't something they've done before."

"We just met. I've known Ben only a few more hours than I've known you."

"But you came down here to meet him, right? You and Luke flew all this way to . . . what? Talk to Ben about his book?"

"More or less. Luke can do things with Ben's writing."

"Things?"

"Magic things."

"Magic like pulling quarters from people's ears?"

"Except with words, yes. He'll have to show you."

"*Amigo,* that you?"

At the sound of Vicente's voice, Gabe disengaged from thoughts of Luke the magician. "Hey, Vic. Yeah, it's me. You all right?"

"For the love of Mary and the saints, Gabe, what the hell's happening?"

"I'm okay, at least for now."

"You confronted that guy? You found another body?"

"I need to know something about the lay of the land. Can you help me?"

"They're looking for you."

"I know. They found me."

"The consulate called."

"Who?"

"The bigshot ambassadors in Santiago. It's their job to butt in when a U.S. national is involved in criminal activity. And you, my friend, are involved."

"Criminal activity? Jesus, I . . ." He pinched the bridge of his nose and closed his eyes. "Forget it. I need to know about army bases."

"What? What the hell do I know about any of that?"

"Maybe more than you think you do. Is there a base anywhere near Calama or not? You're from this area. You live here. I need to know."

"Do I look like some kind of military installation expert to you?"

No, Gabe wanted to say, *you look like goddamn white wallpaper.*

"Gabe? You still there?"

"Please, Vic."

"Fine, fine, I, uh . . . I have some buddies in the military. Is that good enough?"

"It'll do. You got a name and number?"

"They hang out at a cantina called El Estribo. You're in Calama, right? El Estribo is one of those bars where the uniforms like to get together and talk shop. Really full of machismo, you know?"

"Yeah, I get you. When I was a kid there was a joint about two blocks from my house where all the firemen went."

"Same kind of thing, except without the Dalmatians. If you have army questions, I'd start there. Except there's one problem."

Gabe tightened his grip on the phone.

"Army types aren't the only ones who go there. It's also full of cops."

"Wonderful."

"I know I probably don't need to ask this, but you're watching your ass, right?"

"I'm doing my best."

"Good. Very good. I really don't want to hear secondhand that something happened to you. Something bad, I mean."

"Something bad has already happened. I'm just trying to keep it from getting any worse." He hung up.

Mira stopped pretending to be interested in the spices. "What's the verdict?"

He handed her phone back to her. "How does crashing a cop bar sound?"

"Dangerous."

"Well, I promise not to start any tavern brawls if you promise to limit yourself to four shots of tequila."

She dropped the phone in her purse. "You seem rather nonchalant about all of this."

"Actually I'm scared as hell. Glad to know it doesn't show."

"Not too much."

"I'll settle for that." He went in search of the grocer to get directions for El Estribo, but not before looking once more over his shoulder.

Not that it mattered. He wouldn't have recognized the rifleman had the man been standing right behind him.

CHAPTER TWENTY-FIVE

Mira planted herself on the stool and thought, Belly up to the bar!

She hadn't been in a place like this since college at the University of Nebraska. But the watering holes in Lincoln seemed carved from the same beer-stained wood as El Estribo, the neon signs promising the same distractions. Mounted above the door was a chrome-plated scorpion, gazing down on the patrons with lustrous animosity. The rest of the décor was a sparring match between soccer paraphernalia and yellowed snapshots of Chilean soldiers from bygone campaigns. Soccer, by virtue of the two flat-screens on the wall, appeared to be winning.

"Not so bad," Gabe decided, taking the stool beside her.

"The jury's still out." She glanced around. Apparently tourists were not the norm in this place, as several pairs of eyes stared at her from the semidarkness. They enjoyed the safety of familiar shadows, while Mira felt exposed. Perhaps the scorpion was not the only predator here.

Gabe kept his voice low. "You okay?"

"Not really. I can't stop thinking about the man who was shot."

"Eduardo?"

She nodded, then waited for Gabe to offer some words of commiseration. But he made no attempt. Mira had washed a murdered man's blood from her chin, and she'd have to deal with it. To distract herself, she checked out the other patrons. She counted only two other women in the bar, one of them with her hair screwed into an inflexible bun. She wore a police uniform, as did the two men sharing her table. None of them looked pleased to see her. "So what do we do from here?"

"I was hoping you'd have a brilliant idea."

"Not me. I'm just along for the ride."

The bartender addressed them gruffly in accented English and produced two bottles of something called Cristal when Gabe asked for beers. Just as Mira hadn't been bar-hopping in years, neither had she knocked back a brew anytime in recent memory. Was she so lacking in girlfriends these days that she hadn't even been properly hungover in ages? Did she hold so tightly to twindom that she'd forgotten what life was like on a Saturday night without Luke?

"Beer okay?" Gabe asked. "I just assumed . . ."

"It's perfect." She took a long swallow, the glass cold against her lips.

No jukebox interfered with the soccer commentators, and Mira found herself wishing for some music. It wasn't really a bar without half-drunk thirty-somethings slinging their arms around one another and belting out Patsy Cline or Journey. But instead she got play-by-play in a language she didn't understand, talking about a game that bored her. Far worse were the vibes she picked up from the regulars. She gave them another glance. She caught the lady cop looking at her. Though the woman turned away, she wasn't fast enough to conceal her suspicion.

"We should hurry," Mira suggested.

"Agreed." Gabe wasted no more time. For someone supposedly inexperienced at dealing with murderers and disappearing dead men, he acquitted himself well, asking the bartender about Alban Olivares and sticking an asterisk on the end of his question in the form of a fifty-dollar bill. Mira wondered about the wisdom of bribing someone with foreign currency, but evidently U.S. green was fluent in any tongue.

The bartender immediately went to one of the tables in the corner.

Mira watched him in the mirror. "What's he doing?"

"Probably laughing with his friends about how stupid Americans are with their money. Or plotting how to dispose of our bodies."

"I don't suppose it would do any good to ask you why it's not Officer Fontecilla here instead of us. I know things work differently down here, but I'm fairly sure that cops still get paid for investigating homicides."

"I guess Fontecilla isn't here because I didn't exactly tell him I knew the name of the man whose blood they found at the observatory."

"Okay, so you withheld information. Interesting. And you made this decision because you . . . feel responsible somehow?" Having just met him, Mira could only guess at his motives. But she sensed the idealist streak in him. It took one to know one, and all of that. "The amateur psychiatrist in me says that you're harboring some kind of guilt about it, but that doesn't make sense, because from what I understand, you had nothing to do with it."

"Maybe I just know how he feels."

"How could you know that? He never even said a word to you."

"Long story."

"Do I look like I'm on my way to a manicure? I have time."

Gabe took a lengthy pull on his bottle and stared straight ahead into the mirror behind the bar. He looked at his own anonymous reflection. "What if I told you that I have no idea who those two people are right there?"

Mira glanced at the mirror and saw the two of them sitting there with strangers forming silhouettes behind them. "Is this one of those philosophical questions about the meaning of life? Because if that's the case, then I'm afraid you're not going to get any answers from this particular chick, at least not on the first beer."

"What I'm saying is, why is it that we think we have to recognize a person to really know them? Isn't there a chance we could empathize with them without ever really seeing them?"

"Uh . . . sounds a little too esoteric for casual conversation, but we don't need to see somebody to feel a connection with them. I guess. We hear about people suffering in other countries and we feel sorry for them."

"I'm not talking about feeling sorry for anybody."

"Then I think you've officially lost me."

He didn't break eye contact with himself. "You know what I realized?"

"Lay it on me."

"The eyes aren't the windows to the soul."

"Okay, I'll bite. Then what *is* the window to the soul? And don't be predictable and say the heart."

"No, it's nothing as simple as that. It's our actions. It's what we do in the important moments that shows who we are. I don't know if that's the soul or just good old human guts, but there it is. Olivares died trying to carry a mangled boy across the driest place on Earth. I'll take that window any day."

Mira saw the truth in that. It wasn't such an earthshaking philosophy; Plato had nothing to worry about. But if every action was a kind of self-definition, then what was she saying about herself? She lived a compartmentalized life, working her daily routine like a Rubik's cube with all the sides the same color. She hadn't taken her little black dress out of the closet in God knows how long. And she'd certainly never cowritten a novel or Tasered anyone, so which of the Westbrook sibs was getting the most out of this deal?

Fortunately the bartender returned, saving her from admitting any of this out loud. "Sorry," he said. "No one here knows the man called Alban Olivares. You maybe come back tonight. Big crowd. Try again."

"That's it?" Mira asked him. "Nobody knows anything? This is a military bar, right? Olivares was in the army. Surely somebody recognizes the name."

Faces watched her from the shadowed tables. A chair leg scraped against the floor.

"Forget it," Gabe said. "Let's go."

"Show him the dog tags."

"It won't make any difference."

"It might."

"It *won't.*"

He was right. Trying to find a single man in a nation of sixteen million . . .

Gabe drained his bottle and led her under the silver scorpion and out the door.

She expected someone to follow them out, perhaps a gang of them. But her fear of being tailed was surpassed by her frustration. She'd been counting on El Estribo to produce results, and now she felt cheated. "What happens now?" she asked.

"More phone calls, I guess. Sooner or later we'll find something solid."

Having failed at the bar, they wove through the trestle tables of a sidewalk sale in front of a boot store, and then Gabe stopped abruptly.

"What is it?"

"Do you hear that?"

And then she did. Someone shouted behind them.

Even as Mira turned, thoughts tumbled through her mind: The murderer had found them, the police had issued a warrant for them, or the cop with her hair in a bun had decided she didn't like the look of these two Americans with trouble in their eyes. She saw instead a man jogging toward them. His hair was buzzed close to his scalp, a gold chain swinging at his chest. His polo shirt was tucked neatly into a pair of slacks with the sharpest creases Mira had ever seen. He didn't look like an assailant, but you never could tell.

"You know this guy?" she asked.

Gabe shook his head. "I don't think so. But honestly I'm not sure."

Whoever he was, he started talking even before he stopped in front of them, his long string of Spanish words like a strand of pearls, beautiful but of little practical use to Mira. He went on for twenty seconds, speaking so quickly that her pocket dictionary would've only sighed in defeat had she called it to arms. She understood only two words: *Sargento Olivares.*

"Sergeant Olivares," she said. "You know him?"

When it became apparent to the man that these gringos didn't understand him, he put his hand on his hips and—obviously irritated by their lack of lingua franca—said something that made no sense at all to Mira. *"Desaparecido."*

She looked at Gabe. "Any idea?"

"Yeah." He seemed suddenly distressed. "The Midnight Messenger is one of the disappeared."

"The disappeared what?"

"People. The kind who vanish one day and never come back."

Gabe found their interpreter at a coffee shop full of neo-hippies. His name was Andy, and as an itinerant guitar player, he was not about to turn down twenty bucks for five minutes of work.

". . . and he says you can call him Tadeo," Andy translated. "He's a *cabo primero.* I guess that's some kind of, you know, rank in the army or something. I ain't exactly sure. But he heard a guy asking around in the cantina, saying you wanted to find a certain someone."

Gabe introduced himself, not paying any attention to the bottle of water the waitress had placed in front of him. Olivares had known how all the pieces fit together. If Tadeo could somehow provide insight into the man's life . . .

Tadeo spoke at length, and Andy paralleled him as best he could in English. "Uh, he says the dude you're looking for, Alban, wasn't really a buddy of his, but like, uh . . . an acquaintance. They served together. Ol' Alban skipped town a week or so ago, which was, like, totally out of character for him. He was really on the level. Straight, you know?"

"I understand. So what happened?"

Andy relayed the question and then repeated Tadeo's response. "He says he thought Alban got kidnapped or something, like they used to do back in the day. I guess years ago there used to be some freaky shit going down around here."

"Freaky shit?"

"Yeah, like, uh . . . the feds putting bags over people's heads and kidnapping them."

"I didn't think that happened anymore."

"Doesn't, as far as anybody knows, but Tadeo here sort of panicked when Alban went missing, and he says the first thing he thought about was the old *desaparecidos,* the ones who get taken away and don't return."

"Why would he panic if he admits the two of them weren't even friends?"

"Hell, how should I know? I don't even know what you guys are talking about. I'm just the middle man. Alban was, like, the platoon leader or something. A sergeant. I ain't exactly an expert in army-speak, so maybe *platoon* isn't the right translation, but anyway, Alban was supposed to be somewhere and he never showed. And this was apparently a dude who *always* showed."

Gabe figured that was true. Any man who would go so far to save a child's life was a man who always showed up when duty required it. And even when it didn't. "Does he have any idea where the sergeant might have gone?"

Andy asked, then listened to the lengthy response. "Well . . . he says the last anybody heard, Alban was on weekend leave. They asked around at his usual hangouts and knocked on his apartment door, but he never turned up. Now Tadeo is asking what *you* know."

I know his sergeant was head-shot and killed.

"I don't have any answers."

"Why are you looking for him?"

"Is that Tadeo asking or you?"

"Both. Hey, man, you got me curious, that's all."

"Alban and I . . . we might have a mutual friend." He thought of the pinwheel, growing from the sand like a tinfoil flower. "But I suppose it's too late for any of that."

"Dude, it's never too late. Just remember what the Buddha said. 'Turn your tears into water, and your rage into rain.' "

"Did Buddha say that?"

"Yeah. Fat little guy, laughs a lot. You should give him a try."

Mira intervened, not distracted by Andy's wayward philosophizing. "You said that Olivares had an apartment?"

"I didn't say it. *He* did."

"Is it nearby?"

Andy asked, listened, nodded. "Says it's in a block of duplexes on the south end of town, just behind the school. Not the best neighborhood, but hey, what the hell, right?"

Mira stood up. "Then we're only wasting time sitting around."

Gabe agreed, though he was surprised by Mira's persistence. From what he'd learned about her, she'd come to Chile to introduce her brother to his favorite author. Luckily, Gabe's flight across the desert had led him straight to her. Half a kilometer in either direction, he wouldn't have her standing here now, pushing him closer to a dead man's motive.

"So what's this all got to do with the price of Mary Jane in Jamaica, anyway?" Andy asked. "What's going down?"

"I wish I knew." Gabe slid his chair under the table and realized that he hadn't even touched his overpriced water. He grabbed the bottle. "Tell him I really appreciate his help."

Andy did, then waited for Tadeo's response. "He says if you happen to find out anything, you can leave word for him at the bar. He'd appreciate it. He also says *vaya con Dios* and all that stuff." He used a napkin to print the address Tadeo had given him.

"Thanks." Gabe shook Andy's hand, then gave the two men an *hasta la vista* and fell into step beside Mira.

"Are we considering that a productive conversation?" Mira asked.

"In the last hour I've spent seventy bucks on information, so yeah, I'm hoping it was productive. I can't afford any more bribes, considering I'm probably unemployed."

"Probably?"

"I haven't gotten the official pink slip yet, but it's a lock. There's a bus stop. If our karma's in order, maybe the driver speaks English."

They crossed the street, picking their way through the traffic of compact cars and trucks with unregulated exhausts. A digital billboard advertised the very brand of bottled water that Gabe had just purchased, and then it melded into a promo for a concert by the rock outfit Lucybell.

"When we get to his apartment," Mira said, "what is it, specifically, that we're hoping to find?"

"Specifically? Nothing. Non-specifically? Anything."

"Anything like what?"

"Amend that. Not anything. *Everything.*"

The bus stopped in front of them and opened its doors with a hiss.

CHAPTER TWENTY-SIX

When the phone rang, Tilanna was breaking a man's finger with an ice ax.

. . . but the only way to set it properly was to rebreak it—a realization that turned her stomach into a paper airplane.

"Paper airplanes don't fly on Mars," Luke said.

"How do you know that?"

" 'Cause I remember from last time. When they tried to play baseball. It didn't work very good. Gravity's funny!"

"Yes, sir, it is." Ben scolded himself for doubting the young man's perceptive streak. There were many things too complex for Luke to grasp, but his antenna for all things Martian was uncanny. "You know, you're right about the airplane. But Tilanna isn't really trying to *fly* the plane. We're just using the plane as something called a metaphor."

"A meta for what?"

Ben smiled. "For describing things like queasy stomachs. As a matter of fact—"

His cell phone cut him off. Other than their own voices and the wild din of Mars, the last few hours had been quiet. If someone was calling, it was probably either Mira checking on her brother or the police bearing more bad news.

When Ben got up from the desk, he expected his lower back to issue a veto, one that he would be forced to override by mustering at least two-thirds of his will. But the old gods who governed Mars, the deities of Bradbury and Burroughs, must have dumped their healing waters on him. He rose without pain and answered the phone while Luke turned on the TV.

"Cable here."

"Benjamin, you have to get out of there."

The voice made no sense. For a moment Ben just stood there.

Then he knew. "Joe?"

"He was here, Benjo, Jesus God, he was here . . ."

It took no more than that to convince him. Ben knew by the sound of his brother's voice that things were bad. Maybe even worse than bad. Maybe *dire.* Jonah had used this same voice when lying in the street that afternoon in Newport Beach after the accident. Ben hadn't heard it since, but now he was struck by an echo from that moment, his brother lying on a broken spine: *Somethin' ain't right, Benjo. I think I'm hurt real bad.*

Ben held the phone in both hands. "I'm here, Joe. I'm always here. Just tell me what to do."

"That . . . that man showed up. He threatened to kill Donner . . ."

"Who? I don't understand. Who are you talking ab—"

"The one who murdered Eduardo."

It fell into place. Ben felt it physically, like a coin dropping through the slot and rattling home. Jonah was talking about the one Gabe called the rifleman. "Joe, please tell me that you're okay."

"He didn't hurt me."

"And Donner?"

"Alive. Scared shitless, but alive."

"Christ Almighty." Ben sank down to the bed, his legs suddenly unsteady. Luke shut off the Spanish soap opera and watched him.

"He said he would shoot Donner in the stomach. That's what he said.

That he would shoot Donner in the stomach so he would die slowly unless I told him."

Ben didn't want to know, but he had to ask. "Tell him what?"

"Where to find Traylin and Luke. I'm sorry, Benjo, I'm sorry, but I had to tell him. *He wasn't bluffing and I had to tell him.*"

"I gotcha. It's cool. You did what you had to do to keep yourself safe."

"You have to get out of there, do you hear me? I want you on the first plane back to the States. Do you understand what I'm saying here, Benjamin?"

"It's not that easy . . ."

"*The hell it's not.* This man is extremely serious about this. He came back after the police left with Eduardo's body. I don't know where he was hiding, but he came back. He wore a rag around most of his face like . . . like some kind of goddamn cowboy bank robber."

Luke got up, crossed the room, and sat down on the bed beside Ben.

"He had a gun," Jonah continued, each word chiseled sharp with fear. "A rifle. He knocked Donner down in front of me and pointed it at him. He . . . he asked me where the two of them went, and then he started . . . he started counting down from five. He made it to three before I told him."

"I'm sorry, Joe. I'm sorry you got involved in this."

"I don't give a damn if you're sorry. None of this is your fault. Just get out of there."

"But—"

"No buts. He told me that he was letting me live so I could warn you he was coming. *He wants you to know.* Do you understand what that means, what type of man you're dealing with here? He just left, so you have enough time if you hurry. He was driving one of those all-terrain things, an ATV. Calama's at least five hours from here. You have plenty of time to get to the airport. If there are no immediate flights to the States, just charter something to Santiago and go from there."

"Sounds perfectly reasonable, except it would mean leaving you behind. If this prick doesn't find us here like you said we'd be, he'll turn right around and pay you another visit, and this time he *will* kill you. No way I'm letting you face him alone."

"I already thought of that. I'll call the police as soon as we hang up and let them know that Donner and I will be heading their direction. We'll be there soon. Is that good enough for you?"

Was it good enough? Since that day when the Malibu had changed their lives in 1979, Ben had never been in a situation where death was a real presence rather than just an abstraction. For all these intervening years, he'd never had to act to ensure his own survival. His fight-or-flight instincts were collecting dust in his attic, but now the trapdoor rattled on its hinges.

"Do as I say, Benjamin. Get out."

"Keep the sat phone with you, brother. I'll be in touch." He ended the call.

Luke said nothing, only stared at him and waited.

"We better gather up our things," Ben said, staring at the carpeted floor.

"Why?"

"We've got to check out of the hotel a bit early."

"Why?"

"Because you were right about the Martian. He's not giving up."

"But I shot him with a ray gun."

"He's hard to kill."

"We need Dycar. He could beat him."

"Dycar's dead."

Luke didn't have a rejoinder for this, and as Ben began stuffing scribbled-on stationery into a pillowcase, he felt the sting of the young man's uncertainty. Lieutenant Dycar wouldn't run, but rather meet the rifleman in the hall and let fate take care of the rest. Heroes didn't need pillowcases as getaway bags.

Ben wondered, just for a moment, if he was doing the right thing.

Mira plundered a dead man's house.

Gabe had brazenly forced the back door. Mira, who'd never ventured into petty crime as a teenager, observed this forced entry with a kind of scientific awe. This was how the criminal half lived.

"We need to hurry," Gabe had said, leading her inside. A furrow of splinters marred the doorjamb, the exit wound of the kicked deadbolt.

Now, three minutes later, Mira stood in the living room smelling that unfamiliar scent of someone else's home. Eduardo died on a looped video in her mind. Every car that passed outside represented a threat. Had anyone seen them enter the house? Were the cops already on the way?

"Just hurry," she told herself. "Just go."

Though she never would've considered ransacking anyone's home, she'd convinced herself that Señor Olivares wouldn't mind. After all, wasn't she trying to avenge him, at least in a bumbling, amateur way? It wasn't as if she'd come to steal from the dead.

A noise from outside drew her attention.

She bit her lip, waited.

Silent seconds tumbled by.

When no one burst in on her and demanded an explanation for her trespass, she got back to the business of looking for answers. She remembered that old Bob Seger tune: she was working on mysteries without any clues.

There was little to see. When it came to interior design, Alban subscribed to the philosophy of the Benedictine monks. The carpet was worn but clean. A pair of bookends shaped like praying hands supported three novels and a Bible, all of which were written in Spanish. The only piece of furniture was a simple futon covered by a handmade afghan.

She heard Gabe moving around in the bedroom. Doors opened. Floorboards creaked.

How could she be expected to find any hints in such Spartan quarters? Damn you, Bob Seger.

She picked up the only photo in the room, a portrait in a gold plastic frame. Judging by the fashion, the hair, and the god-awful pull-down portrait screen, the picture was at least twenty years old. Man: smiling with teeth and toupee. Woman: primly perfect with husband's hand on her shoulder. Boys: curly-headed brothers with mischief crouched in the crooks of their elbows, waiting for release.

She carried the picture to the bedroom. "Anything?"

Gabe pulled his head out of the closet. "And I thought *I* had the worst fashion sense in this hemisphere."

"It's that bad?"

"Not if you're into beige. Guy's got eight pairs of pants in different shades of blah."

"That's it?"

"And a shoe box full of paper-clipped receipts and banking mumbo-jumbo, but other than a CD collection of people I've never heard of before, then yeah, that's it. What about you?"

She held up the photo. "Is this him?"

Gabe stared at it. "I don't know."

"It's not a very recent picture. The father here looks pretty young, so he might have been in his forties or even older when you saw him at the observatory. Any similarities?"

Gabe continued to stab his eyes at the portrait. Mira got the impression that it disturbed him somehow. He was looking at it as if trying to set it on fire, like Superman with his heat vision.

"Gabe?"

He resumed his search of the closet. "I don't know."

"It was dark that night, huh?"

"Yeah."

Mira wondered about his reaction, but there was no use making an issue of it. "Well, if this is Olivares, then I guess he and his wife must have split up, because there's no way a woman lives here, not unless they share all those pairs of brown pants."

"Definitely." He gave up on the closet and went to the chest of drawers.

Mira turned the picture over. Just for the sake of checking, she pried up the metal clasps and removed the cardboard easel. Her guesswork paid off. Printed on the back of the photo in faint blue ink were the names of the family members.

JESUS & RAINA OLIVARES

ALBAN & SACHIN

"Looks like I was wrong."

"What do you mean?"

"Alban isn't the father in the picture. He's one of the sons."

Gabe abandoned the drawers and studied the names. "Consider me impressed. That's some blue-ribbon sleuthing."

"I was Agatha Christie in a past life."

"Or Nancy Drew."

"Good enough for me. Should we try to track down Jesus and ask about Alban?"

"Tell a man that his son was murdered? I don't know if I'm built for that. But I *do* know that we need to get out of here. I don't want to wear out our welcome."

"Nancy Drew concurs." She returned the picture to its place in the living room, careful to wipe away her prints. This particular act—the cleaning of fingerprints—was so far beyond her usual element that she shook her head even as she was doing it. But that's the kind of life you led when you wore your Danger Cap.

They were rushing back through the kitchen to the back door when she saw the wedding announcement on the fridge.

"Hold on a sec." She crossed the small room and peered at the square of ivory cardstock held to the refrigerator with a magnet in the shape of a soccer ball. Though the text was faded and written in Spanish, she recognized the names.

"What's it say?"

"Sachin Olivares married a woman named Carella Lepin."

"Sachin and Carella. The ones we saw online? Nicky's parents?"

"Apparently."

Gabe pondered it for a moment. "The Midnight Messenger was the dead boy's uncle."

"So it would seem."

"Okay, then how does it add up? Nicky Lepin was the torturer's grandson. He was abducted, and his uncle, Sergeant Alban Olivares, went looking for him. But when Alban finally found him, butchered and sewn up, it was too late." Gabe didn't wait around for her opinion. He was through the back door before Mira realized it.

She hurried to catch up.

The lot behind the line of duplexes was a dug-up sand pit of cacti and derelict cars without wheels or doors. A dog with a rib cage like a xylophone excavated something that was apparently buried deep.

Mira looked around, but she saw no one watching them. "We should get back to the hotel. I need to check in on one of the great American novelists."

Gabe didn't reply but just kept walking, staring down at his feet.

"Hello?"

"Sorry. It's just . . . we've connected a lot of the dots, but you know there's only one man who can tell us everything."

Mira almost asked *Who?* before her ESP activated and downloaded at least a portion of his thoughts. She looked at him in profile as they walked. Was he really considering such a thing?

"It's the only way," Gabe said, showing her that two could play at telepathy.

"Is it? Then I think we may be out of luck. Though I don't know much about breaking and entering, I know even less about infiltrating Chilean prisons."

"We'll learn as we go," Gabe said.

Mira hoped he was right.

CHAPTER TWENTY-SEVEN

Someone grabbed Gabe's arm. A busy sidewalk in front of the hotel was the last place he expected an attack. Violence seemed impossible next to this corner ice-cream vendor surrounded by giggling children. Yet the fingers biting into his forearm hadn't chosen him at random. He knew this even as he turned to confront his assailant.

The man he saw was anyone and everyone.

Prosopagnosia was given its name in 1947, based on the Greek terms for *face* and *non-knowledge.* Over fifty years later, men and women with multiple initials behind their names had yet to explain its genesis, much less concoct a cure. Most of those who suffered from it were victims of head trauma. Others were born with it, a delightful little heirloom from somebody's cross-wired DNA. Growing up, Gabe hadn't realized he was different until he was nine years old, and he wasn't diagnosed until two years later.

"He's coming."

The face that spoke these words did nothing to calm Gabe's heart. He jerked his arm free and took an automatic step in retreat, the anonymous entity looming in front him. Things had been so easy at home, where he knew his parents and brother Ronny by countless little clues that had nothing to do with their faces. But out here, out in the wild . . .

"Take it easy, man!"

The voice made sense. Gabe had learned to compensate for his disability by developing his sense of hearing and a strong memory for the voices of those he met. "Ben?"

"No, the ghost of Jimmy Hoffa come back to kick some Mafia ass."

"Sorry, you just—"

"Scared you?" Luke asked. "Scared the *poop* out of you?"

"Something like that." He collected himself as he always did, then hoisted a smile to his face and hoped they believed it. "I'm just jumpy, that's all."

"Get ready to be jumpier. He's coming."

"Who?"

"The Martian," Luke said. "The Martian's on his way, and that ray gun didn't even stop him!"

"How do you know? Who told you this? The police?"

Ben scoffed. "The cops know exactly two things about your rifleman. One of those things is jack, and the other begins with an *S*."

"Salad?" Luke ventured.

"Jonah called," Ben continued. "The bastard was there. Nobody got hurt, but he threatened them and then lit out after us."

"He knows where we are?" Mira asked. Gabe couldn't see her face, but he heard the concern in her voice, amplifying her words. "He's coming after us?"

"Yes and yes."

Gabe wilted at this but pressed on; the meek would not inherit the rifleman's Earth. "So Jonah can identify him?"

"Not really. I'll tell you everything I know, which isn't much, but first I suggest we repair to less threatening environs, if you get my drift. Luke and I were hanging out at that bookstore on the corner. You two get your bags and meet us in the sci-fi section."

Gabe glanced that direction. The street seemed safe enough. A food truck sold cornhusk-wrapped *humitas* out front, doing heavy business. Immigrants mingled with locals on the sidewalk, speaking a fusion of Spanish and English that was probably a harbinger of some future universal tongue.

"Fontecilla told us to wait at the hotel," he said.

"The good inspector has my cell number, and Mira's, too. He can let his fingers do the walking. We won't be far away. Follow me, young squire."

"Sure!"

"Luke, be careful!" Mira called.

Luke waved as they crossed the street.

Mira watched them all the way into the bookstore. "I wish I had a dollar for every time I've ever said that."

"He seems solid enough to me."

"I guess so."

"I *know* so."

They headed into the hotel to retrieve their things.

"It makes me feel good to hear you say that and mean it," Mira said, "but the watchful sisterly eye never closes."

"Must get tiring after a while."

"You have no idea."

"How often are you two apart?"

She looked at him as they waited for the elevator. Gabe saw her eyes, but they might have belonged to any woman he met in the desert in South America, or anywhere else. "Let's just say I don't go out and party with the girls very often."

"You know what I think? Sometimes you just have to let go."

"And you're a good role model for letting go? I think Alban Olivares would have to call your bluff on that one."

"Yeah? Maybe you're right." He trailed her into the elevator, smelling her hair.

Mira met Tilanna over the body of a brigand who'd been shot through the mouth. The faceshield of his environmental helmet was shattered. With the sound of her brother's voice guiding her, Mira looked from the wound to the woman who had inflicted it, the barrel of her lover's gun cooling in the frigid Martian wind.

" '. . . but Tilanna had killed before,' " Luke read, " 'so the sight of the blood hardening to dark ice on the man's teeth did little to sway her. In fact, swaying was a luxury that had no place here, where the very biosphere was out to get you. Earth women could sway. But when you were terraforming a planet . . .' "

Mira blinked several times, the hotel across the street reappearing, the red landscape turning to fragments to be replaced by the Calama street at dusk. Her brother had been reading to her here in the bookstore for the last two hours. "And?"

Luke closed the Moleskine notebook Ben had bought upon their arrival at the store. "And what?"

" 'When you were terraforming a planet,' then what?"

"Don't know."

"Isn't that a sentence fragment?"

"A what?"

"Never mind." Through the same plate-glass window that looked out onto the street, Mira watched Gabe and Ben. The latter talked animatedly on his phone while the former paced and looked like a man in acute need of a cigarette. He'd told her he was trying to quit. Now didn't seem to be a very good time for that.

"She's having a baby," Luke said. "Tilanna is *preggers.*"

"It happens to the best of us."

"It hasn't happened to *you.*"

"No, there's not much chance of that, I guess. It takes two to tango." Though Mira was a strong believer in safe sex, the sad truth was that she was practicing the safest sex of all: lack of a love life. "Why did you and Ben decide to make her pregnant?"

"We didn't *decide.*"

"You're the writers, aren't you?"

"Tilanna *told* us."

"That so? What else did she tell you?"

Luke grinned. It was the grin that assured her he'd been a huckster in a past life, moving the shells too fast for the eye to see. "She told us she's having *twins.*"

"Ah, well, twins are certainly near and dear to my heart." She wasn't surprised he'd guided the story in this direction. Often in Luke's make-believe, the champions of his escapades were brother and sister. He and Mira had baked a thousand witches in the ovens of his imagination. "Looks like Tilanna's going to have her hands full. A single mom with twins? Poor woman's about to become an unwilling insomniac. She better get herself a nanny, and soon."

Luke just kept grinning. "Twins are cool."

"So how does this opus end, anyway?"

"We don't know the ending. We ain't there yet!"

"Aren't."

"We *aren't* there yet. And anyway, that's a *secret.*"

"Ah, of course." Mira didn't know how their story would evolve, but she'd never seen her brother quite this way, so whatever its conclusion, she gave it her approval. "You two can have your secrets, but if you're going to make me hang on till the last chapter, you better write faster. If I remember correctly, Tilanna's not a very patient woman."

Mira wondered briefly if she should take a hint from the fictional heroine. If they switched places, would Mira be able to tame the harsh frontier with such aplomb? Would Tilanna be content to—

"Shit is holy."

Mira was so unaccustomed to hearing her brother swear that her first instinct was to scold him in her usual sisterly way . . . but a second later she realized that his tone of voice wasn't frivolous this time.

Luke stared through the window, mouth sagging open.

The many streetlights resisted the coming nightfall, neons sharpening the haze. Tourists and locals blended into an Impressionist's swirl, their identities lost to twilight. A taxi idled in front of the hotel.

"I don't see anything," Mira admitted.

Luke clutched Ben's notebook like a shield. "It's him. It's the Martian."

"Where?"

He pointed.

A man stood on the far side of the street. Though not fully revealed in the dusk, he was clearly interested in the hotel, inspecting it from about thirty yards away. He wore boots and a shapeless coat, the sleeves too long for his arms. His face was narrow, but the rest of his features were hidden in the semidark.

"Are you sure it's him?"

"Absolutelypositivelyhundredpercent."

She stood up. "Don't move." She used that rare voice that would stand for no argument, then ran between the bookshelves to the door. Halfway there she stopped. What if her warning to Gabe prompted the man to take action? He'd murdered Eduardo and cut up Nicky Lepin. Mira couldn't risk setting him off like some kind of human bomb.

She returned to the table and grabbed her phone, nearly dropping it. She and Ben had exchanged numbers before Gabe had led her to El Estribo.

Luke hadn't taken his eyes off the man. He sat there whispering to himself at the reading table, his fingers held in the shape of a gun.

Through the window, Mira watched Ben as the phone rang in her ear. Ben paused in midconversation to check the cell's screen, then pressed a button.

"I'm still on the phone with the prison officials," he said. "Normal visitation hours are tomorrow . . ."

"Forget that. Don't turn around. Are you listening to me? *Don't turn around.*"

"Mira? I don't under—"

"Shut up. Just keep doing what you're doing, so he doesn't know we see him."

"What the devil are you talking about?"

"He's right across the street."

Mythical Medusa might have turned Ben to stone. Unmoving, he breathed into the phone.

"Do I have your attention now?" Mira asked.

Much quieter: "Are you sure it's him?"

"Luke ID'd him. He's . . . he's staring at the hotel."

"Where at?"

"In front of that ritzy shoe store on the other side of the street. There's a crosswalk there. He's standing beside the light."

"Is he armed?"

"Not that I can see."

"And Luke is *sure*?"

She glanced at her brother. His lips moved silently, and he pulled the trigger of his finger gun, over and over.

"Yeah, he's sure."

"Damn." Ben ran a hand over his face. "He's about an hour sooner than I predicted. Okay, listen. Hang up and call the cops. Gabe and I will mosey back into the store and hope he doesn't see us. Got it?"

Mira didn't bother saying *Be careful.* She ended the call and immediately dialed the emergency number she'd learned as part of her preparations to visit Chile: 133.

Outside the window, Ben put his phone away and motioned to Gabe. The two men convened, Ben discreetly grabbed Gabe's elbow, and they zeroed in on the bookstore's door.

The man from the desert turned and noticed them.

Mira saw it all. The next few moments, each lasting no more than two beats of her heart, unfolded before she could rock herself to action. Tilanna would not have wasted so much time. Emboldened by memories of her lost love, the first pregnant woman on Mars would've already opened fire.

The man in the too-big coat stepped off the curb without regard for traffic. Calama was one of those cities that gave every impression of driving itself into the internal-combustion future, hybrids and biofuels be damned, and the cars came in sudden surges. Tire rubber chirped on the asphalt as drivers avoided ramming the sudden pedestrian in their midst. Horns fired warning shots across his bow. He didn't slow or even acknowledge them.

Mira knew this would be more than a Lipstick Smear if she didn't get herself moving.

Ben and Gabe disappeared from her field of vision when they entered the bookstore. The store itself was sprawling and modern, a place where bestsellers were pimped by lavish cardboard displays and the classics relegated to a corner near the bargain bin. The numerous shelves blocked her field of vision.

The phone kept buzzing. Emergency services at 133 had yet to pick up.

The man in the street avoided the bumper of a brown UPS van and reached the near sidewalk. Mira made out more details, now that he was closer, even as she stepped away from the window so as not to be seen. The word that came to her was *craggy.* His gaunt skull was like a mountain face, something to be scaled, with a sharp overhanging nose and a curving handhold of flesh beneath each eye, revealing the redness within. Strings of hair hung down either side of his head.

"Let's go," she said to her brother, and then ran for the door.

Gabe stepped around a shelf and collided with her. He caught her and kept her from falling. The look on his face was absurd, as if he'd run into a random stranger and not someone who'd just aided and abetted him during a break-in.

"He spotted you," Mira said. "We've got to find a back door." She checked on Luke, then got a visual on Ben, who trailed Gabe by only a few feet. *And what the hell was taking 133 so long to pick up?*

Gabe needed no more prompting than that. "Everyone stay close!" He dashed between the shelves, heading for the rear of the store.

Out of habit, Mira turned to make sure Luke was near, but he was already racing by her, ambling after Gabe. Mira matched Ben's long strides, and when the emergency-services dispatcher finally answered, Mira was momentarily surprised to hear herself addressed in Spanish.

Her mental lag lasted only a second before she called herself a dummy and offered the phone to Ben. "Forgot that not everyone speaks English."

As Ben accepted the phone, weaving between the shelves in a jog, he said, "Did you know that China will soon become the number-one English-speaking country in the world?"

"And why does that matter now?"

"Just came to mind, that's all." He put the phone to his ear and was introducing himself when someone screamed.

Mira turned as she ran. Near the front of the store, a woman cried out. A man shouted something Mira didn't understand, and two voices responded to him.

"Go!" Ben yelled, planting a hand in the center of her back and shoving her forward. "Go, go, *go*!"

Mira ran.

Just ahead, her brother and Gabe vanished behind a display of cookbooks. Mira chased them, suddenly finding time to be afraid. Wearing the Danger Cap when you crossed the street was one thing, but wearing it when running from a murderer was another.

She turned the corner in time to see Luke disappear through a curtained doorway, above which was a sign that said something about *los empleados.* Assuming this was an employees-only area and hoping it led to a back door, she increased speed and burst through the curtain without bothering to see if Ben was keeping up. She hadn't run in ages. She'd done an aerobics class last year but hated it. Her lungs now collected back taxes.

Gabe had spotted the door: SALIDA. Luke ran toward it in his ungraceful way, arms pumping with exaggerated motions, cheeks puffing in and out.

Mira dodged a startled worker with an armful of magazines. Behind her, Ben yelled into the phone. Though his Spanish made little sense to Mira, his distress was unmistakable.

Gabe hit the steel door, blasting it wide. Once outside, he held it open for Luke, who shuttled through with Mira so close she could smell his deodorant. She couldn't help but wonder if Tilanna would've chosen an escape pod like this or if she would've turned and attacked. For a moment Mira wanted to do just that. After all, they outnumbered him four to one. But her fear outweighed her courage. For now.

She ran into a paved lot behind the store, the Dumpsters casting hulking shadows under the bug-swarmed lights.

"Over here!"

Mira followed Gabe's voice.

He led them around the side of the building. When Luke dropped off the pace, the others slowed to keep him in the formation. Mira swallowed mouthfuls of city-scented air.

She looked back.

A figure moved under the lights of the parking lot. It might have been anyone.

Mira returned her attention to the business of running, doing her part to maintain the pace that Gabe set for them. Together they fled along the sidewalk. Storefronts flashed by. People looked at them as they passed, stepping clear as they put a full block behind them. Tilanna might not have retreated like this, but her reason was a simple lack of anywhere to run. As Ben had written, Mars had no hideouts, and if it did, they were hidden well, indeed. Calama, on the other hand, had countless crannies and—more important—people.

Mira stalled out. Her muscles were molten. The others put on the brakes. Ben sucked air and didn't sound well. Gabe's hair was stuck to his face with hot sweat. Of all of them, Luke appeared the most ready to go another round, his eyes wide as he looked back and watched for their pursuer.

"Almost there," Gabe said.

They staggered under a restaurant awning, the patio full of outdoor diners and a roaming guitar player. Gabe found an empty table in the middle and fell into the chair.

The others did the same. They sat there breathing hard, eyes on the path behind them.

No one came.

Mira glanced around. Women in summer dresses and enviable shoes dined with husbands or lovers or girlfriends, somehow unable to hear the heartbeat that rang so loudly in Mira's ears. Lanterns burned on hooks around the patio. The guitarist played a salsa version of "The Way You Look Tonight."

"Where is he?" Luke whispered in between breaths.

Ben coughed. "Maybe he . . . went back to hell."

They waited and watched.

In the distance rose the sound of sirens.

CHAPTER TWENTY-EIGHT

"Buenas noches," *Ben said to the cop outside, then closed the motel door.*

"I've never been under police protection before," Mira said.

"That makes two of us."

Luke emerged from the restroom, drying his hands in his deliberate way. "Is Gabe in jail?"

Ben shook his head. "You don't worry yourself about our fair Mr. Traylin. We all took our turn with the police. They'll bring him back when they're done."

"*I* didn't get a turn. Why didn't *I* get to talk to them?"

"How about you and I just plop our fannies down here and see what's goin' down on the fourth rock from the sun?"

"Tilanna's having twins."

"So you say. But she only recently discovered she was pregnant. I reckon we have a lot of time to kill before the big event." He sat down on one of the room's two beds. The suite's adjoining room boasted the same configuration. The curtains were the color of a tea stain, and there was no continental breakfast, but Ben figured that it was upscale as far as safe houses were concerned. Officer Fontecilla, who seemed to be tiring of these blundering Americans, had relocated them to this Bates Motel on the edge of Calama. Ben had slept in worse. It was true.

Luke plopped down beside him. "Will there be explosions in the book?"

"Don't know. What is it you're wanting to explode?"

"The rebel hideout!"

"Ah. Well, those nasty Kanyri certainly deserve such a fate, but I'm not so sure how well things blow up on Mars."

"Huh?"

"Oxygen. Fire needs air to burn. For all I know, there's plenty of it in the Martian atmosphere to cause a king-sized detonation, but we'll have to consult somebody smarter than us to make sure. We don't want to get our science wrong and face angry e-mails from readers who know better. Assuming that we *have* any readers, which sometimes is a big assumption."

"Oh. Okay."

"But we can worry about that boring old research later. For now, let's assume that we *can* blow the holy living hell out of those bandits. What do you say?"

"I say *rock on*!"

"Great. The next question is . . . is Tilanna going to do this all by herself?"

"What do you mean?"

"Friends. She's going to need some companions to make this a proper adventure. Just look at us sitting right here. Is Gabe out there fighting the Martian all by himself? Am I writing this book alone?"

"No."

"That's right. We've got a *gang.* Every literary hero worth his quest has got to get himself a gang. Or in this case, get *her*self a gang."

"Like a band of heroes?"

"Precisely, dear Watson."

"Who's Watson?"

"A different tale altogether. Let's just concentrate on this gang. Who should she get first?"

"Um . . ." Luke flicked his chin with his finger as he considered it. "Maybe she meets one of Dycar's friends."

"Friends? From what I recall, the man made more enemies than compadres."

"What about the old man?"

"Vanchette? Yeah, I suppose he might still have a part to play, though I never really thought about it till now . . ."

Through all of this, Ben noted Mira on his periphery. She sat near the window, blond hair partially in her face, looking out at the detritus behind the motel, her thoughts certainly not on Mars but somewhere much closer to the big blue marble. "You okay over there?" he asked her.

She broke contact with her reflection in the window. "Okay? Are you serious?"

"Yes. At least I *think* I am."

"I've seen a man killed in front of me, I've been chased through a strange city by the murderer—who's still out there on the loose, by the way—I've been interviewed by the cops, and now I'm seriously considering contacting the embassy so I can get out of police protection and go home."

"Is that what you really want?"

"Not me," Luke said. "I'm writing a *book.*"

"This isn't why I came here, Ben. I came for *you,* because Luke can do something extraordinary with your writing, and I want to know what that means. But all the rest of this, everything else that's happened . . ."

"It sucks, I know. I was there when Eduardo went down, just the same as you."

"And yet you can sit there and write like nothing happened."

"On the contrary, I'm sitting here and writing *because* it happened." He closed his notebook and gave her every soldier of attention he could muster, considering most of them were marching off to war with Tilanna.

"You think any of this is coincidence? You think that the fact Luke can read my stuff is just happenstance? This may surprise you, Mira Westbrook, but there are still those of us out here in the post–Aquarius Age who believe that some things happen for a reason, that all of us are connected, and when we start pulling each other's strings, it brings us all a bit closer, for better or for worse."

"Sounds like metaphysics to me."

Ben gestured to Luke. "And this isn't? This . . . this *thing* your brother can do is normal?"

"I don't know."

"The hell you don't. You want to hear what I think?" He didn't wait for a response. "I think that you've spent so long believing in Luke here that you forgot how to believe in yourself."

Mira pushed her hair from her face and slid forward in her chair. "I hate to break this to you, Mr. Amateur Psychologist, but before we showed up on your shoddy doorstep, the only thing *you* believed in was shooting pool. So maybe what you think you see in me is just something you see in yourself. And now all three of us are in the middle of a major mess that isn't our fault at all, so I think I have a little license to show some concern."

Ben almost laughed at her. Not because she was funny. And not because he wasn't taking her seriously. He wanted to laugh just because, like Ben himself, she didn't know her own power when it was right in front of her. Ben had written a damn fine novel at one point in his life, its genre belying its themes. And Mira had a strength she didn't recognize. How else could she so easily do the things she'd done? Since he'd known her, she'd driven a Land Rover at high speed while under fire, broken into a dead man's house, and discovered clues about his connection to a savage murderer. She had no idea who she was. Goddamn Wonder Woman.

Ben gave her his most challenging look. "Whose doorstep are you calling shoddy?"

After an uncertain moment, she parted with a smile. "Sorry about that."

And now he *did* laugh, a chuckle from the depths of himself, rising up like something once lost at sea but shaken loose by the earth tremors happening around him. "You know what your problem is, my lass?"

"You're still analyzing my problems?"

"Your problem is that you insist on believing that the rabbit's in the hat."

"I think you've lost me."

"It's like this." He paused to consider what he was about to say. She would think he was insane. She would think that she'd hitched her brother's wagon to a mentally unstable star. But there was a thickness in his blood that hadn't been there in years, and it swelled his veins with the story. "On the day my father was killed and Jonah paralyzed, I was given a special ability."

Mira could not have been paying closer attention; she was fixed to him.

"What is it?" Luke asked. "What's your ability?"

Ben never looked away from Mira. Now that he'd started, there was no tugging on the reins. He might as well just say it, as farfetched as it sounded. "When a magician pulls a rabbit from the hat, sometimes you just need faith that there isn't a secret compartment, that there's nothing up the sleeve, that the hand isn't quicker than the eye. Sometimes you just have to accept the fact that maybe, just maybe, the magician pulled that rabbit out of nowhere, not with sleight of hand but with real and honest magic. At least as honest as magic can be."

"Ben, what's your *ability*?"

Ben wet his lips. "I can't be harmed by bullets."

Just what he expected to happen at this pronouncement, he couldn't say. He'd never stated it out loud. Maybe the walls should have trembled or a pipe organ should have played a few momentous notes. At the very least, he should've gotten goosebumps. And he did.

Luke scratched his head. "I don't get it."

"After we left ACEF," Ben continued, "when Jonah was complaining that I was bulletproof, he was speaking both figuratively and literally. He was there when it happened to me, in the summer of 1979, on the way home from the funeral of the noblest man I've ever known. One of the cops was talking to me, telling me I'd be all right. He did a magic trick with a bullet from his gun belt. Made it disappear from his hand. Jonah was right there beside me when that officer pushed a bullet into my heart and made me immune."

"You mean like Superman?" Luke asked.

"Yeah." Ben kept his eyes on Mira. "Just like Krypton's favorite son."

If he'd expected Mira to scoff at him, she proved again to be a woman of surprises. She appeared to be weighing it, or perhaps she was weighing her own faith. God knew that Ben had done the same thing himself.

"Do you believe that's true?" she asked after a while.

"Something's got to be true."

The door swung open, scaring all of them.

Gabe stood in the doorway. "They found the woman in the wagon, burned to a cinder in that motherfucker's cave. They can't identify her through dental records because he pulled out her teeth."

Ben closed his eyes.

"Tomorrow morning I'm going to the prison and talk to Lepin," Gabe said. "I'm going to make him tell me why all of this is happening, I'm going to find out who the rifleman is, and then I'm going to kill him."

He went to the adjoining room and closed the door behind him.

The door creaked open in the night.

Though Gabe was supposed to be sharing a room with Ben, the writer and his co-conspirator were still out there concocting their plots at two thirty in the morning. They were Rumpelstiltskins spinning straw into literary fool's gold. Gabe, staring at the ceiling and trying to trick sleep into ambushing him, barely heard their muffled manifesto through the thin wall. They were hip deep in something about terraforming. Apparently their characters were trying to build an atmosphere. Like would-be gods.

In the dark, Mira said, "Is this seat taken?"

Gabe heard her move the room's single chair across the carpet and position it near the bed. He wished he could rewind time and uninvolve her, just get her safely out of this wreck his life had become. He wanted to go home.

"I'm betting you're not asleep," Mira said.

"Does wishing count?"

"In this world? It doesn't seem to."

Gabe rolled over. In the dark, her face made more sense, simply because the heavy shadows gave him an excuse for not being able to recognize her. The curtains permitted only a vertical band of light to reach her, drawing a line along her cheek.

"You don't have to come tomorrow," he told her.

"And you don't have to try and talk me out of it. By the sound of things, I guess all four of us are going. Strength in numbers, you know."

"They won't let us all in. Prison policy says—"

"Only one visitor per inmate per week. Yeah, I heard what Ben said. But it doesn't matter. I'd rather be sitting in a prison parking lot than waiting here for him to find us."

Gabe didn't have to ask what *him* she meant. The rifleman. When talking with the first officers on the scene at the bookstore, Mira had referred to him as the man in the too-big coat. "There are two cops outside. I don't think he's getting in here."

"Sure. I've seen the movies. I know what happens to police officers who get assigned babysitting duty. They end up dead in their cars. I'll take my chances by staying on the move."

Gabe sat up, putting his back against the wall, as the bed had no headboard. "Fontecilla's been in contact with the embassy in Santiago. They're sending an attorney in the morning. He also said that he gave an interview to the paper about the fire in the desert, so this is officially getting out of hand."

"I think it was probably out of hand the moment you saw Alban Olivares running through the dark."

"Good point. You know . . ." A desire struck him with an abruptness that caused him to lose his train of thought. He suddenly wanted to be sitting across from this woman at dinner. Here he was, caught up in something that was liable to get him killed, when he could have been getting to know this person and, if he was lucky, saying something to make her laugh.

"I'm still here," she said.

A bolder man would've told her what he was thinking, but Gabe's bravery ended with chasing down malevolent murderers. "Maybe we should just get some sleep. Tomorrow could be . . . stressful. To say the least."

"Yeah, I know. I'll go disperse the great rainmakers of Mars and impose mandatory shut-eye. I just wanted to . . . say good night."

Gabe almost reached for her hand, thought better of it, then said to hell with that and reached for her anyway. "Thanks. For being here. For putting yourself at risk. For everything."

"I haven't done much but run for my life like a sissy, but you're welcome." She squeezed his fingers and left him alone in the dark.

Gabe lay there, thinking not about the rifleman or the morning's meeting with Micha Lepin, but instead about the warmth of her hand.

CHAPTER TWENTY-NINE

Razor wire screwed its way across the wall, catching red glimmers of dawn. Constructed in 1952 on the hardscrabble edge of the Atacama, the Región de Antofagasta penitentiary looked like something bolted to the desert floor, its towers fixing the cellblocks and grassless yard to the earth.

"Scary damn place," Ben observed.

With Gabe looking over his shoulder, Ben had conducted research on the Chilean correctional system through various Spanish-language Web sites. He now knew that the penitentiary was privatized in 2004 and had since dealt with two riots, a serious kitchen fire, and a government investigation into healthcare standards stemming from questionable living conditions. The facility was designed to house eight hundred inmates and currently boiled with four times as many, a gray cauldron over a constant fire. Ben and the others had ignored Fontecilla's counsel and left the relative safety of the motel to permit Gabe his rendezvous with the devil, one which they'd conspicuously failed to mention to the police.

"Maximum security," Luke said. "That's what this is, isn't it? Maximum security?"

Ben sat behind the wheel of the rental car. "Evil-looking, to be sure."

"Like something on Mars!"

"You think?"

"Maybe the bad guys built it there, next to one of the valleys."

"An awfully impressive structure for the likes of Martian architecture, and probably not very practical."

"Maybe the bad guys *didn't* build it. Maybe it's the *first prison* on Mars."

From the backseat, Mira said, "How long do you think this will take?"

"Oh, I reckon he'll be back fairly soon. Visitors who aren't immediate family or lawyers can stay only fifteen minutes. And when I was on the phone, I got the impression that Lepin hasn't received any guests in quite some time. Not surprising, seeing that his countrymen consider him reprehensible for what he did. They wanted to burn him at the stake."

"What did he do?" Luke asked.

"A lot of nasty things to a lot of good people."

"Like the Martian does?"

"Yeah, son. Just like." Ben stared at the prison compound. Two chain-link fences, each fifteen feet high, formed a double barrier around the wall. Between the fences lay a no-man's-land of concertina wire. He wondered how long it would take for the settlers on Mars to bring such concepts to their new world. At what point in his interplanetary travels would man move beyond the need for locks and keys?

" 'Stone walls do not a prison make,' " he said, mostly to himself, " 'nor iron bars a cage.' "

"What's that mean?" Luke asked.

"Something old Rich Lovelace once wrote, far more profound than anything I've ever pushed out of my pen."

"But *what's it mean*?"

Mira intervened. "It means that some people's imagination helps them to be free even when they can't go outside."

"Oh."

"*And* it means the opposite," Ben added, "that certain fools who shall remain nameless can get themselves all locked up tight in their minds, even when their bodies aren't locked up at all."

"Like who?"

"Formerly, yours truly. But like the man said, I am free at last." He smiled and patted the notebook on the seat beside him, though the smile itself was feigned. He was worried for Gabe inside the prison, for Jonah and Donner at the police safe house—they'd arrived from ACEF this morning—and for Mira and Luke right here in the car. None of them would see it coming if the rifleman fired at them from afar. None of them had the protection that bulletproofing provided.

"Lucky me," Ben said, and then waited for Gabe to emerge.

If he were to survive the coming fray, he would have to make his heart like this soil, the stuff of ancient iron.

Gabe recalled Luke's words as he sat on one side of a glass-divided booth. The ceiling was cracked and painted a pale green that made him think of Victorian-era sanitariums. There were no windows. Mounted on the partition wall was an outdated Bakelite handset, reminding him of the blocky phone that used to hang in his grandmother's parlor. Someone had used a black marker to write what appeared to be a poem on the little wall, though Gabe could make out only a few of the Spanish words. A pair of ceiling fans stirred the dull air.

Was his heart like ancient iron? Or at least close enough?

"Guess we'll see," he said, quietly enough that the guard behind him couldn't hear.

From deeper in the building came the subdued sounds of thousands of incarcerated men, seething in their discontent. Even from here, Gabe sensed the coiled energy of their words, as if they tipped toward critical mass and would soon lay siege from within. Somewhere in the orgy of their mounting pressure was the man Gabe had come to see, a fascist despised by his countrymen, as notorious as they came.

When Micha Lepin suddenly sat down on the opposite side of the ballistic glass, Gabe's first thought was *Speak of the devil, and the devil appears.*

The old man's shoulders were as broad as a wrestler's, but one arm ended in a withered hand, a claw that was curled and spotted like something subjected to radiation. He wore a blue denim shirt, open at the throat to reveal a cuneiform of partially seen tattoos. His white hair concealed his ears, the part down the center of his scalp so true that it appeared to be a seam along the center of his skull.

Lepin stared at him through the glass.

Gabe stared back, wondering what the man looked like. Was he as ugly as his crimes? Or defiantly handsome in his seventy-plus years? Was his face carved with the canals of age? Hardened by prison life? Or was he smooth and beguiling?

Gabe concentrated on keeping his hand from shaking and revealing his anxiety as he reached for the phone.

Lepin mirrored his movements, and the two men sat there with the black receivers pressed to their ears.

"Do you speak English?" Gabe asked. He already knew the answer to that, as Lepin's Wikipedia entry stated that he'd attended graduate school in chemistry at Berkeley.

The man breathed into the phone.

"Lepin?"

"Who are you?"

Gabe had been expecting a geriatric rasp but instead heard the throaty snarl of a man who might have been half Lepin's age. "My name's Gabriel Traylin."

"Yankee?"

"That's right." Though he'd been rehearsing this interview all morning, now that he was here in the trenches, facing the man through fingerprinted glass, his practiced lines eluded him. "I'm going to tell you something that you may or may not know, and then I'm going to ask you something in return."

"I don't know you. You some kind of reporter? Some kind of piss-ant snoop? I wasn't aware that anybody gave a rat's ass anymore."

"Actually, I'm an astronomer. Or at least I was, until your son-in-law's brother was murdered in front of me. They fired me after that."

This statement had its intended effect. Lepin turned his head gently to one side. Holding the receiver with his shoulder, he used his functioning hand to fish a pair of pince-nez glasses from his breast pocket. When he donned them, it gave his face a welcoming bit of dimension.

"I guess that means you're listening," Gabe said.

"I have two son-in-laws. They both despise me. I don't ever see either one."

"I'm talking about Sachin Olivares."

"And?"

"Sachin has a brother, Alban."

"So what?"

"He's dead."

Lepin lowered the phone. He tapped it on the plastic desktop, saying nothing, chewing on his thoughts. He might have been contemplating anything from Alban's death to what he'd eaten for breakfast that morning in the prison galley. Then, with snakelike suddenness, he leaned toward the glass partition and said seven words into the phone: *"Do you know what's happening to me?"*

Though Gabe gained no clues from the man's expression, he heard the shift in his voice, from belligerent to terrified. "Uh, I'm not sure . . ."

"For Christ's sake, make him stop."

The change in the man's demeanor was so extreme that Gabe lost his footing. Whatever he'd scripted for this was lost.

"*Please,*" Lepin said. "Please . . ."

Gabe pulled himself back to fighting form, at least as much as he could, considering his surprise at the pleading tone in the man's voice. "Who are you talking about? Tell me what's going on, and I'll . . . I'll do what I can."

Lepin was so close to the glass that his words formed as a fog. "You listen to me. You're with him, aren't you? You're here to pick the goddamn skin from my bones. Fine. You can have it. Tell him that. You want me dead? I'll pay somebody in here to open up my jugular with a fuckin' fork, but *you have to make him stop.*"

Gabe felt more helpless by the second. The game was being played with rules he didn't understand, by players with histories he didn't comprehend. Micha Lepin was a war criminal who'd aided a despot by torturing and eventually disposing of political dissidents and others who posed a threat to the regime. He used drugs and biological agents in his work, the stuff of nightmares, yet here he sat, begging Gabe for mercy.

"Tell him I'll do anything," Lepin said.

"I don't work for anyone. I'm here on my own."

"What?"

"I said I'm alone."

"Then what the hell do you want?"

"Is Nicky Lepin your grandson?"

"One of them, yes."

"I found him in the desert. Or what was left of him."

Lepin dropped the phone. He put his head in his hand and closed his eyes, screwing his forehead against his palm.

Gabe waited. Over Lepin's left shoulder, a black-clad guard stood erect and watching.

Lepin snatched up the phone. "He'll burn in hell for this. Just like me."

"There was also a woman."

Lepin gripped the receiver so tightly that his fingers turned the color of bone.

"Do you know who she was?" Gabe asked.

Lepin breathed in and out, in and out.

"Who was she?" Gabe demanded.

"My . . . my daughter."

The sympathy that swelled in Gabe's heart surprised him. By all accounts inhuman, Lepin was as wretched as Vlad the Impaler, but Gabe couldn't force himself to despise the man, not now, not after seeing the woman in the wagon and hearing the grief in her father's voice.

"He took them both," Lepin said. "He took them both, and . . . and he sends me letters."

Gabe bent closer to the glass, so that only centimeters separated him from the man who was rapidly dissolving on the other side. "If you want me to help you, you're going to have to tell me everything. Do you understand? I've been in touch with the police—"

"They can't do shit."

"What about these letters? The cops can use them to trace him."

Lepin shook his head violently. He dropped the receiver long enough to wipe his eyes with his working hand, then picked it up again. "The letters are codes. They mean nothing to anyone else. Listen to me. Paulina stole my notebook, and she must have given it to him. Everything was in there. And now he's using my own code to tell me about how he's hurt my family, what he's *done to them . . .* "

"Who? Who is he? Why is he doing this?"

"He read it in my notebook, my journal. He knows about *silencio.*"

"*Silencio?* Silence? You mean he's keeping quiet about something?"

"You have to make him stop, please, if he wants me dead, tell him I'll do it, but for the love of God, he's got to stop before my entire family's gone."

Lepin's reaction had not gone unnoticed by the guards. He and Gabe were being scrutinized by officers on both sides of the partition. No doubt they were also listening in. Everybody knew that prison phones were party lines.

Gabe did his best to stay in front of what was a rapidly disintegrating situation. There was no way to tell who could be trusted, which meant he had to walk the line between getting Lepin to talk and keeping his secrets from the guards. He chose the safest path he could find. "Why did he kidnap your daughter and grandson?"

"It's my fault. They're dead because of me . . ."

"Why?"

"Why the fuck do you think? Revenge."

"Revenge for what?"

Lepin hacked back a mouthful of snot, swallowed, and took several long breaths. He shifted even closer to the window. Then he revealed something that Gabe suspected he concealed from everyone else in the prison. He moved the fingers of his debilitated hand with perfect dexterity. He wasn't quite as handicapped as he let on. As Gabe watched, Lepin flashed a rapid series of numbers, using his body to shield his gestures from watchful eyes: 1-3-5-4-1.

He repeated the sequence, then said, "You've got to do something. I have one grandson left. He's my older daughter's boy, my little Nicky's cousin. He has a good life, a good father. The same thing will happen to him unless you make it stop."

"I don't know if I can . . ."

"He's all I've got." Lepin cried freely now. He sobbed so forcefully that his shoulders shook. "Please, mister, find him and keep him safe, and tell him I'm sorry—okay? *I'm so, so sorry . . .* "

The guard behind Lepin approached. Whatever he said was muffled by the glass, but Gabe figured it out. Time was up.

"Wait!" Gabe was about to lose the one lead he had. "Not yet! I need to know who he is, why he's doing this." Had he been able, he would've reached through the phone and grabbed the weeping old man by the throat, forcing the truth from him. He flattened his hand against the window. "Give me something to go on."

"I already have." He hung up.

Gabe sat there mutely while Lepin stood up. The guard glared. Lepin wiped his nose on his sleeve. Gabe had never wanted to see someone's face as badly as he did now.

It wasn't meant to be. Lepin, a sudden hunchback, turned and permitted himself to be led away. Gabe suspected he would never see him again.

Slowly he removed his hand from the glass. A ghostly impression of his fingers remained, as if mimicking the numbers Lepin had signed.

"One, three, five, four, one," Gabe said to himself so as not to forget. "One, three, five, four, one."

CHAPTER THIRTY

"What's dee-port *mean?" Luke asked.*

Mira produced what felt like a smile on its last leg. Running from murderers and visiting foreign prisons had rendered that expression nearly extinct. "When someone gets deported, it means the government asks them to leave the country."

"Why?"

"Because they don't belong. They're a citizen of some other place."

"So they have to go home?"

"Yep."

"Even if they don't want to?"

Mira and Ben had been talking about consequences. About the possibility of being forcibly returned to the States. Luke had missed a few of the finer details. "Most people who get deported don't have a choice. And before you ask, no, we're not getting booted out of Chile. At least not yet." As she said it, she glanced at Ben, who was looking over the top of his notebook at her. "Isn't that right, Ben? Nobody's deporting us, are they?"

"You asking for Luke's benefit or your own?"

"Most of the time," she told him, "those benefits are one and the same. Twins are like that."

"So I've heard." He lowered his notes and gazed for a time from the motel window.

They'd returned from the prison to find the attorney and his staff from the embassy waiting for them. Gabe had been gone for over an hour since then, whisked away by the lawyers, and the rest of them were strangely nervous without him. Or maybe it wasn't so strange. After all, he was the catalyst of this *Twilight Zone* that Mira's life had become, so it only stood to reason that his absence would leave her a little directionless. "Any luck on those numbers?"

Ben gave the notepad a shake. "One, three, five, four, one. Too short to be a phone number, too long to be a PIN. Could be the beginning of an address. Hell, maybe it's the number of a bank deposit box full of stolen diamonds, incriminating photos, and purloined letters."

"It's five digits long. Are there zip codes in Chile?"

"Maybe the number of people the Martian killed," Luke ventured. "That's a lot!"

"Let's hope not," Mira said. Her brother had spent the last half hour telling her of Tilanna and Vanchette, the grizzled astronaut who'd taught Dycar the dual arts of geophysics and gunplay. Apparently Vanchette had an idea how to infiltrate the base of the Kanyri insurgents . . . a base that now bore an understandable resemblance to the penitentiary they'd visited this morning.

"You guys keep writing," she said, getting up and heading for the bathroom. "Just remember me when it comes time for splitting up royalty checks. I play the part of the long-suffering sister."

"Sisters stink," Luke said with a laugh.

Just for grins, Mira flipped him off.

Luke's eyes widened so much they filled his face. He put a hand over his mouth. But behind his fingers, he was smiling.

"Haven't seen that in a while, have you?" She winked at him and closed the door.

Luke clapped, amused by it all. Through the door she heard him say, "Did you see what she did, Ben?"

"You mean the old one-fingered salute? I've seen that plenty of times in my day, and I'm usually on the receiving end . . ."

Mira turned on the water and stared downward as it plunged into the sink. If she was Tilanna, then she could only assume that Ben was playing the part of Vanchette. Subconsciously her brother was telling their tale as it happened, transposing it to the battlegrounds of Mars. But if that was true, then what character was Luke's?

And what of Gabe Traylin?

Mira bent down and cupped water to her face, enjoying its cold bite. She needed to powder her nose, as the old saying went. After the authorities had escorted them from ACEF, they'd been without their personal effects until a squad car finally delivered them. Since then, Mira couldn't get enough of her moisturizer and her twenty-four-hour, hypoallergenic deodorant. These small things grounded her, even when the rest of her was tracking the skies like a let-go balloon, a note tied to its string reading SAVE ME.

She grabbed her favorite face-wash without opening her eyes and pumped a generous dollop onto her palm. If anyone was going to save Tilanna, then it would be Tilanna herself.

And there she went, buying into her brother's word-association game. Without realizing it, Luke was helping Ben craft an allegory to what was happening around them. The man he called the Martian, aka the man in the too-big coat, was embodied in the despicable Kanyri, who were cutthroats and sadists, one and all. Everything was joined together, even if Luke didn't understand the joining himself. In fact, it wouldn't have surprised Mira if the real name of the man in the too-big coat turned out to be an anagram of *Kanyri*. It might have seemed preposterous, but in a world where a dyslexic nonreader could recite the passionate prose of a man who was reportedly impervious to bullets . . . well, damn near anything was possible.

A thought occurred to her, promising enlightenment, but it slipped away before revealing itself.

She lifted her head and looked at herself in the mirror, trying to tease the fragment closer. Her face was covered in creamy oatmeal-colored cleanser, only her eyes and nostrils visible. She was thinking about word association, but why did that matter? Why did it feel so significant?

Without bothering to rinse her face, she tugged open the bathroom door and asked, "What were those numbers again?"

Luke didn't even look up, just kept reading Ben's latest pages, his lips moving expertly as he sailed across the words. Ben glanced down at his hand. He'd written the numbers there as soon as Gabe had given his report in the car outside the prison grounds. "One, three, five, four, one. Why?"

"I'm not sure. It's like the tip-of-the-tongue thing, you know?"

"Usually happens to me with crossword puzzles. You think you have it figured out?"

"Not quite. But let me think about it and maybe I'll—"

Gabe let himself into the room, interrupting her. Mira was surprised by how glad she was to see him.

"I am officially unemployed," he announced. "My supervisor kindly told the university that I was no longer needed on the project."

Luke was the first to respond. "Are they going to dee-port you?"

"Not yet, but . . ." His eyes settled on Mira, and whatever he was saying trailed away. He looked at her in a way that made her wonder if she was living the real-life version of one of those dreams in which you forget to put your pants on before venturing to a crowded shopping mall, and everybody stares. Then she realized he was enraptured by her milky mask.

"What's the big deal?" she asked him. "Never see a woman exfoliate before?"

Very slowly, Gabe tilted his head to the side, like an animal in response to a strange sound.

"Gabe, you're freaking me out here."

"Sorry, it's just . . ."

"Just what?"

"I can . . . sort of *see* you."

She had no idea what he meant. Was she missing something? Why was he looking at her like that? "You have some kind of issue with pore-refining facial toner?"

He smiled weirdly. "No, it's just"—he shrugged—"it happens every now and then. It works with circus clowns, with all their makeup. And mimes. I can almost see them, too."

"Mimes? What the hell are you *talking* about?"

"Forget I said anything." Red circles appeared on his cheeks. "I'm gonna go hit the soda machine outside."

And he was gone.

Bewildered, Mira looked at Luke and Ben.

"I don't get it," Luke admitted.

"Nor do I," Ben said.

Mira returned to the bathroom and closed the door. Tilanna might be a rugged heroine who fought Martian outlaws with her dead lover's guns, but her life was no stranger than Mira's. In fact, with every passing hour, Mira figured she had Tilanna beat.

She turned on the water and rinsed her face, thinking about Gabe.

At least he was no longer a suspect.

Gabe considered that a feeble consolation. With the rifleman's appearance at the bookstore, he'd confirmed his existence in front of enough witnesses that the police no longer wondered if Gabe was making it all up; the boy was not crying wolf. But with every yin of good news came the yang of the bad. During his meeting with the State Department's attorney, they'd spoken to Rubat on a conference call that had ended with the paranoid observatory chief publicly firing his protégé. The project was already under too much scrutiny for economic reasons, and Rubat claimed he couldn't risk putting it in further jeopardy.

The soda machine spat out something that made sense: a Pepsi. At least there was one recognizable element in his life these days. Did he have enough cash for a plane ticket home? The lawyer from the embassy had made it clear that they wanted him gone as soon as the cops said he could leave.

He was cracking the top on the pop can when a gray sedan rolled to a stop at the curb. As a transit bus rumbled through the intersection and a low-riding pickup gunned its engine across the street, the driver's window scrolled down, revealing a mystery behind the wheel.

Gabe stopped with the can in front of his lips. He threw a glance at the motel door. Fifteen meters. Could he make it?

"Get in, Señor Traylin."

"Fontecilla?"

"I realize I am forgettable," Fontecilla said, "but by now I think you would know me."

"I'm not so good with faces." He got into the car and waited. He concentrated on his soda.

"And I am no Sherlock Holmes," Fontecilla said, looking at him.

"Your point?"

"Despite my shortcomings, I believe there is . . . something not right with you, if you will pardon the observation." He took his foot off the brake and drove.

Gabe had no rebuttal. Explaining his prosopagnosia wouldn't bring them any closer to locating the rifleman. Even if Fontecilla eventually accepted the story, he would likely only do as others had done; when they learned of Gabe's condition, they became unnaturally polite, as if he were some poor victim in *Invasion of the Body Snatchers.*

"Seat belt, please."

Gabe did as he was instructed.

"At first I thought you must be on the lam," Fontecilla said.

"On the what?"

"Is not that the correct expression? Like they say in the detective novels?"

"Sure, I guess."

"I contacted the U.S. authorities, and they have nothing to report about you, nothing whatsoever."

Nothing whatsoever. Story of my life.

"So this morning, when the four of you left your rooms, I followed you."

Gabe turned away and stared out the window at the passing storefronts. He found no refuge there. Amateur that he was, he'd permitted himself to be tailed all the way to the penitentiary.

"Do you really think my officers would have let you leave their protection without my permission? I followed you to the prison. After you left, I went in and flashed my badge. That's also something they say in the American detective novels, yes? I don't think I have ever said that until today. Either way, I found what I needed. The question is"—he signaled left and turned that way—"whether or not you found what *you* needed."

Gabe had no recourse but to confess what he knew, at least most of it. "The boy in your morgue or wherever he is, Nicky Lepin, he's the grandson of Micha Lepin."

"I realize this now. I also realize that you took it upon yourself to pretend to be a policeman, which is very flattering but not very wise."

Gabe saw no way out of it. Fontecilla had cut off his escape routes. "I didn't pretend to be anything. I never told anyone I was a cop. I just didn't know what else to do. I had to talk to him."

"I gave you my card. You could have called."

"I had to find out on my own."

"Why?"

"You wouldn't understand."

"You are probably right. I am not as empathic as the heroes of the detective stories. That is the proper word, isn't it? Empathic?" He guided the car from the main thoroughfare and onto a cobbled lane that ran between a color guard of Chilean firetrees. "I trust you learned things of great significance from Señor Lepin?"

"Only that somebody's after him."

"After him?"

"Paybacks, you know. Vengeance. For what, I don't know. But he's got an enemy. The remains of the woman you found under Mentiras . . . that was his daughter."

Fontecilla only nodded. Maybe he already knew the woman's identity or maybe he didn't. Everyone had a poker face as far as Gabe was concerned.

When a full minute passed and Fontecilla remained quiet, Gabe blundered ahead, further damning himself for obstruction of justice or withholding information or some other unintentional yet fully punishable crime. "I know you're going to ask me why I didn't let you in on any of this, and I don't really have a good reason other than I didn't want to get pushed onto the periphery. I wanted to see it through to the end. For whatever that's worth."

Fontecilla slowed the car. "I met the assistant warden. He was kind enough to permit me to listen to the recording of your conversation with Lepin. Perhaps you did not know that everything is recorded in those situations, in the event that such information is needed later."

Gabe sighed. There was an old joke in his profession. *Astronomers do it with long tubes.* This was only slightly less juvenile in its humor than *Astronomers do it with Uranus.* Gabe figured he'd screwed himself with about the longest tube around.

"You are quite the persistent investigator," Fontecilla said, without a trace of the sarcasm he was surely implying.

"The whole thing just . . . got out of control."

"Perhaps. But I must admit, though the recording I heard was enlightening, it really offered no further lead on the case."

One, three, five, four, one, Gabe thought. *How's that for a lead?*

"I am hoping you could be persuaded to let the police be privy to your plan, so that we might lend a hand as needed." He stopped the car and finally looked over. "Get out."

Only now did Gabe take account of his surroundings. Granite slabs lay on the ground. Headstones rose like obelisks from the grass, engraved with the names of the dead.

"A cemetery?"

"Follow me." Fontecilla struck off across the grass.

Gabe trailed him through the maze of markers, many of them more than a century old. Catholic iconography abounded, the crucifixes and cherubs recognizable even to a backsliding Protestant like Gabe. A replica of Michelangelo's *Pietà* cast an indigo shadow across the grounds, its depth surpassed only by the shadow of Mary's grief as she held her martyred son.

Fontecilla clasped his trilby in his hands as he stopped before a single marker made of rough-hewn marble.

Gabe read the name inscribed there—Beatriz Guajardo—but didn't recognize it. "Who was she?"

"Mother of three, former college athlete, law school graduate, practicing defense attorney."

"And?"

"They found her two years ago with her feet cut off, crawling along the road near the community's water-treatment facility. When they put her in the ambulance, she was . . . out of her head. What is the term? Delirious. She died en route."

Gabe's imagination, always rampant, served up every painful frame of that film, a woman he'd never met dragging herself forward, centimeters at a time. "Did he do it? The rifleman?"

"The case was never solved. Not a single viable clue. Even after seeing

Nicky Lepin's body, I did not make the connection until this morning when I realized who you were visiting at the prison."

"Was Beatriz related to Micha Lepin?"

"She was his lawyer many years ago. Though he was suspected of being responsible for the deaths of at least thirty-five people, the prosecution had solid evidence of only two. Only two, from all of those years and all of that suffering. During the proceedings, Señora Guajardo was almost able to counter the forensic facts with various tactics. She fought to keep Lepin a free man, but she failed. She argued that his trial was not fair, that the people were being vindictive and taking out their hatred of Pinochet's government on a man who was merely following orders. The appeal was denied."

"At least she helped him avoid the death penalty."

"No, Señor Traylin, we do not execute people in this country. We are not barbarians. What kind of point does it make to murder someone for murdering? No, we locked Lepin away for eternity."

"Okay, so America is a social backwater where we still permit state-sponsored killing. Whatever. But apparently your kind of justice wasn't enough, huh? The rifleman cut off her feet because she helped Lepin."

"He may have considered her an accomplice, yes."

"And he's been out there free for two years?"

"Yes."

"Maybe if you guys had just shoved Lepin in the gas chamber then, a lot of innocent people would still be alive, because that sick-o wouldn't have had reason to chop them up."

"As I told you before, I have no powers of fortune-telling. My grandmother was the clairvoyant. I can use only the gifts that God in His wisdom has given me." He knelt at the grave and trailed his fingertips through the grass. "If you are holding something back, Gabriel, then I will do what I can to convince you to tell me, even if it means arresting you. What this man is doing . . . it ends now."

Gabe admired the detective's resolve, but he wondered at his own reluctance to divulge the numbers Lepin had given him. Why was he so intent on making this his personal crusade? What debt did he owe the dead?

"I'm waiting. But I will not wait forever."

The hell with it. "One, three, five, four, one. That's it. All I have. Hopefully you'll be able to make more sense of it than I can."

Fontecilla finally looked up, his face meaningless. "Explain."

"Can't. He gave me those numbers. That's it. He left it up to me to figure them out."

"That is all he said to you?"

"He didn't say it, but yeah, that's it."

"It could mean anything."

Gabe had already given the numbers so much thought that they'd ceased to make sense. Their riddle remained impenetrable.

Fontecilla stood up, his knees popping softly. "I will see what the department can make of it. We are not an affluent organization, but we have a few resources that might help. Computers these days, you know . . ."

Gabe followed him back to the car. "Does this mean I'm not under arrest?"

"On what grounds? I have no probable cause." He put on his hat. "Besides, if you were in jail, how could I follow you when you inevitably disregard my warnings and set off after this man yourself?"

Gabe didn't bother looking at him to see if the wily cop was being facetious. It wouldn't have done any good.

CHAPTER THIRTY-ONE

The dust storm collapsed.

Tilanna lifted her head as the red cloud fell in on itself. Its infrastructure of wind suddenly stripped away, the cloud gave up its rage, settling in soft russet layers on the building Tilanna and Vanchette were about to infiltrate.

She wiped the powder from her faceshield.

Vanchette's voice, as hard as old oak, issued from the speaker near her ear. "Are you well?"

She wanted to tell him that she hadn't been well since Dycar, damn him, had abandoned her. "When have you ever known me not to be well?"

"That's my girl."

"What do you say we blow this Kanyri shithole to Andromeda?"

"I say lead the way . . ."

"Do we have to say 'shithole'?" Luke asked.

Ben raised his eyebrows. "Well, I reckon not. If they buy the movie rights, they can make it PG-13, but I guess we can lighten things up a bit. What word did you have in mind?"

"Dump."

"Dump?"

"Yep." He looked down at the notebook and read. " 'What do you say we blow this Kanyri dump to Andromeda?' " He looked up, frowning. "What's Andromeda?"

"A galaxy two and a half million light-years from here. Our next-door neighbor. It's got about one trillion stars in it, which is a shitload, unless you prefer *dump*load."

"Nah, that doesn't make any sense."

"I agree." Ben glanced across the room to where Gabe sat, poring through regional magazines, newspapers, and phone books. "Yo, astronomer. That's correct, isn't it? A trillion?"

"Give or take a few million." He ran both hands through his hair. "I'm starting to think this is pointless."

Ben wanted to say that pointless was okay. He knew the benefit of a good bout of pointlessness. It gave you time to live in your skin a while, get to know yourself, not get tangled up in the melee of smash-and-grab humanity. The trick was not letting your sabbatical of pointless living turn into a permanent vacation. He might have related his feelings on this and other, even more esoteric matters, but then he noticed Mira.

She sat in one of the motel's spiritless chairs, a map of Calama spread out on her lap. For the last half hour she'd been studying the damn thing for anything similar to 13541. But now she was looking at Gabe, though the dummy apparently didn't feel the substance of her stare. Fool. He was too caught up in the hunt to realize when an attractive woman was staring at him.

"What about word association?" she asked.

Gabe closed the telephone directory. "What about it?"

"It's something I thought of earlier. What's the first thing that comes to mind if I say those numbers to you?"

"A zip code."

"Okay, well, we've already established that zip codes aren't the right angle." She turned to Ben. "What about you? One, three, five, four, one."

"Certainly not the measurements of any woman *I've* ever met."

"I'm trying to be serious here."

"Fine. The number of angels who can dance on the head of a pin. I don't know *what* comes to mind because I've heard the damn thing far too many times. Why in blazes didn't that son of a bitch Lepin be more specific?"

"Because the walls have ears, I guess." Gabe grabbed his bottle of water, found it to be empty, and pitched it in the direction of the room's tiny trash can. "You never know how word's going to get around."

Mira was undeterred. "Luke, what do you think when I say one, three, five, four, one?"

"Nothing."

"Nothing at all?"

"Nope, nothing. Except for the keypad."

Everyone looked at him.

"Explain," Mira said.

"Remember when Dycar had to sneak into that room? The door was locked. Locked up tight. He had to steal the code to open the *keypad.*"

"Sure," Ben said, grabbing Luke's used-and-abused copy of *This Mayflower Mars.* "There's the scene in which Dycar first comes to blows with the rebel officer . . . he has to enter a certain code to unlock the door . . . but I'm fairly positive that his was a *four*-digit number rather than five."

"A code." Mira's forehead bunched up in what Ben thought was a look of classic consternation. "You know . . . it really *could* be a code, not one that opens up sealed doors on Mars, but . . . not word association but *number* association."

"I don't think that helps us," Gabe admitted. "We're still not any closer to deciphering it. And I don't know anything about encryption. I'm a doctor, Jim, not a code breaker."

"Huh?"

"Forget it. Geek humor."

Ben stared at the open book but didn't see the words. Number association? Maybe Mira was moving down the right highway but didn't know it. Ben drove that road a little farther, just to see where it led. He had to assume that the numbers were easier to solve than they seemed, because Lepin hadn't been expecting to pass whatever information they held to a random visitor; he'd figured out a way to communicate it on the spur of the moment, and thus he would've been forced to keep it simple. He probably used the first thing that came to mind. Say this was true, and Mira was right about the whole number-association thing. The easiest form of code was a simple substitution cipher. Take the letter *A* and turn it into a 1, while 2 becomes *B* and so on. He and Jonah had passed secret messages like that when they were boys, back in the Jurassic period.

"So what does that spell?" he asked aloud.

"Spelling is boring," Luke opined. "I'm glad you do all the spelling, Ben, and I do all the talking."

"Me, too. But play along with me for a second. If the number one is the letter *A,* and two is a *B,* then Lepin was trying to say—"

"That's not a word," Mira said. She performed a rapid count with her fingers. "*A-C-E-D-A.* That doesn't spell anything. Aceda?"

Gabe sat up straight.

"It may not be a word in English," Ben said, "but in *español,* it means—"

"Sour," Gabe said, nodding as if he knew more than he was divulging. "It's a verb that means to turn sour."

Luke looked from one face to the next. "Mr. Lepin was trying to tell you to turn sour?"

Gabe got slowly to his feet. "Aceda's a town, or it *was* a town, forty years ago. I saw it on a map. Now it's nothing, an empty stretch of sand in the middle of the desert . . ."

"Maybe he was talking about some other form of the word," Mira suggested.

"Probably. I've been out there. It was dark at the time, but if there'd been anything in the area, we would've run into it. The whole town's been wiped off the Earth."

"That may be," Ben allowed, "but if this used-to-be town is anywhere near the place where you and Luke found the rifleman and that poor woman, then I submit that it's no coincidence."

"Yeah, actually it's not far from there. Damn. But . . . there's not a thing to see out there."

"So it seemed at the time."

Mira stood up. "Personally, I think looking around sounds a lot more productive than what we've managed to accomplish here with phone books and street maps."

"We better call our dear friend Fontecilla," Ben suggested.

Gabe was already shaking his head. "The last thing I need is to lead the cops on a potentially pointless six-hour drive across the desert. If we left right now, we wouldn't even get there until sunrise. And then what? The police drive around and find me crying wolf again? No, thanks. I'm already on their semi-shit list. I take them all the way out there and they come up empty, they *will* deport me."

Ben put down the battered paperback, the poor scoliosis victim with its tortured spine. "Then what, do tell, are you proposing we do about the two fine constables sitting in the motel parking lot, wishing they were at home instead of playing nanny to four American fools?"

"The Ninja Turtles?" Gabe pointed to the bathroom. "We give 'em the old bathroom window treatment."

"Why did I know you were going to say that?"

"Didn't this Dycar character of yours ever climb through any windows?"

"Careful, now. It's dangerous to start thinking you're a literary hero."

Luke suddenly shot out of his chair. "That's why we wear our Danger Caps!"

Gabe pretended to don a hat. "Good enough for me."

"What if he's out there waiting for us?" Ben asked. "Then what, Mr. Protagonist?"

"He won't be. It's a wasteland."

"Humor me. What if he doesn't give a damn that it's a wasteland and he *is* there?"

"Guess we'll play it by ear." He headed for the bathroom. "If you guys are coming, you better pack your stuff. Fill up all the water bottles. Get some blankets. We can buy some food along the way. It's going to be a long drive."

Ben looked at Mira. "Tell me why we're doing this again."

"I don't think we have a choice."

"Sure we do."

Mira grabbed her bag. "Try telling that to Tilanna."

"What the devil's she got to do with anything?"

"Hey, you started this, not me. I'm just not sure if I'm following in her footsteps or if she's following in mine." She zipped her bag. "Why don't you guys skip ahead to the ending and let me know?"

Ben shook his head and glanced at Luke. "Damn the torpedoes, looks like we're taking this composition on the road."

Luke thrust his hand as high as it would go. "I call shotgun!"

As he drove toward the creeping dawn, Gabe glanced at himself in the rearview mirror.

Maybe he was a masochist. A punishment addict. Like one of those monks of yore who flailed themselves on the back until their skin peeled. He had no reason for trying, but still he looked himself in the eye and saw no one, the same damn no one he'd seen all his life.

Is that why you're doing all of this? A superhero born of frustration?

Yeah. That sounded about right. The Face-Blind Avenger. All he lacked was the spandex.

". . . but then Tilanna pulls him out of the way," Luke was saying, "so the ax misses and Vanchette gets to still be alive!"

"All right, all right, slow down a bit. This old fountain pen might be worth more than just about anything I own, but it ain't as fleet as your silver tongue, young master Luke." In the backseat, Ben wrote with the aid of a penlight. "Of course, it doesn't help when this highway is like the dented shores of Iwo Jima."

"It's the only road out here," Gabe told him.

"Then I blame our lackluster shock absorbers. Next time, my friend, we'll rent a Lincoln. No use chasing wild geese when you can't do it in style."

The Land Rover still sat in a police garage somewhere. It would remain there until the technicians were satisfied they'd extracted the last bit of ballistic information from its bullet-ridden steel. So Ben had suggested Calama's El Loa airport, where they'd rented an SUV whose claim to minefield fame was its ability to convince its passengers it was blowing to pieces each time it rolled through a pothole.

Gabe was still staring himself down when he caught Mira's eyes. Seated behind him, she met his gaze in the mirror. She didn't look away.

Interesting.

Stars made sense to him. Women remained dark matter. "You doing okay back there?"

"Don't I look okay?"

"Honestly? I can't tell."

"For now I'm fine. Ask me again after we get to Aceda." She scooted forward in her seat. "If we find something out there—"

"We probably won't."

"But if we *do,* then we're calling the police, right?"

"Your brother's the brave one, not me. So yes, I'm driving straight to the observatory and dialing the first satellite that can give me phone service."

"Good. And for what it's worth, you've been plenty brave enough so far. Anyone else would have boarded the first plane for home."

"The thought crossed my mind."

She leaned back. "I suppose that makes you Dycar."

"I'm sorry?"

"In the book. He's the reason Tilanna finds herself running pell-mell all over Mars, or at least I think that's the case."

"Indeed," Ben interjected, "you are correct. The man can drive a plot, to be sure."

"But isn't Dycar dead?" Gabe asked. He'd caught only small chunks of the story as it was written around him.

"Minor detail," Mira said.

"Yeah. Minor." On impulse Gabe winked at her, then looked back at the road.

He felt her eyes on him as the kilometers disappeared beneath their tires, but he resisted the temptation to look again.

An hour later he pulled off the road and headed into the Atacama's throat.

CHAPTER THIRTY-TWO

Mira stepped out of the car and into the nothing that was Aceda. The sun revealed a gray-yellow barren that reminded her of those places where daredevils tested their rocket cars.

"You're right about this place turning sour," Ben said, walking a wide circle around the vehicle. "It not only turned sour, it shriveled up and faded away."

Luke played games with his shadow, a westward-leaning ghost at his feet.

Mira hurried to catch up with Gabe, who was stalking the grounds, casting his eyes about for clues. But there was nothing out here. Bob Seger was up to his old tricks again. "Are you sure this is the right place?" she asked him.

Gabe slapped the decrepit map in his palm. "We traveled exactly twenty-two kilometers off the road to Calama. If we went due east that way"—he pointed—"we'd run into Mentiras in just a few minutes. You'll be able to see what's left of the buildings when it gets a bit brighter. According to the map, this is where Aceda used to be."

"So what happened to it?"

"Same thing that happened to a lot of towns in the American West. Boomtown shows up, resources go dry, people tear everything down or just move out, and Mother Nature lays claim to it."

Mira put up the hood on her Cornhuskers sweatshirt. The morning chill, combined with the lofty elevation, made her wish she'd brought along a heavier jacket. So much for the misconception that all deserts were hot. "It's hard to imagine that anyone was ever here at all. It's just so . . ."

"Vacuous!" Ben called from where he roamed fifty feet away.

"Yeah, that."

Luke made his arms into an airplane and raced his shadow across the flat ground.

Though Mira was thrilled by her brother's newly discovered creative streak, she also knew that she was no closer to solving the puzzle of his ability to read Ben's writing. Gabe had dramatically sidetracked her. Yet the most obvious question was why she'd permitted herself to be distracted. Asking her to chase down a murderer wasn't high on the list of Ways to Endear Yourself to Mira Westbrook's Heart, but nevertheless, here she was, working on mysteries with anorexic clues.

"I'll go this way," Gabe said. "Maybe if we fan out—"

"I gotcha." She struck out at a right angle from him, knowing there was nothing to find but happy to play her part. When in Rome.

"I don't see anything!" Luke yelled as his faux fighter plane banked into a sweeping left turn. "I. Don't. See. Anything."

Neither did Mira. So much for Lepin's secret numbers. Aceda might have once contained the riddle of the man in the too-big coat, but now there was only a blank slate of ground, an unhelpful tabula rasa that ran on forever in all directions.

Then again, maybe it wasn't so blank after all. She noticed a slight bulge on the desert floor, no more distinct than a pitcher's mound.

She checked on the others. Gabe and Ben had headed in opposite directions, already almost a hundred yards apart. Luke engaged in a dogfight with the F-16 that was his swooping shadow.

Mira went to the little hill.

The ground here was the same color as the rest of the range, a kind of gray-orange that offered up no vegetation. In the story, Dycar had been obsessed with the Martian soil, almost to the point of investing it with imaginary life. He talked to it when he was alone, which was his state more often than not. Luke was the same way, anthropomorphizing the objects around him, respecting their kinship as if they were his fellow men.

If Mira was Tilanna, did that mean that Luke, rather than Gabe, was Dycar?

It made sense. Wasn't Tilanna attached to Dycar on a spiritual level? And didn't she also wrestle with the by-products of that attachment?

Could be. But if that was true, then where did that leave Gabriel Traylin? Ben might have portrayed the role of Vanchette, but there were no characters left for Gabe.

Or were there?

Mira took two steps and stood upon the mound.

The sun levitated higher into the sky. The far shadows receded. The land revealed by the morning light lay flat all the way to the brightening horizon. Her position seemed suddenly tenuous. What if their rented car decided not to start the next time they turned the key? Unless they happened to be found by police spotter planes, they wouldn't survive. It was a world without trees to make a fire, without a water source, without anything.

There were no secrets here. Aceda had vanished.

She stepped off the hill and heard a hollow sound.

Looking down at her foot, she noticed nothing out of the ordinary. She tapped the ground with her heel. Was it just her imagination?

She knelt and brushed the dirt. But there was only more dirt.

Determined to wipe away a few layers, she applied both hands to the task, whisking the soil with her palms and splayed fingers. Half an inch down, something stung her.

"Ouch!" She examined her finger, fearing a spider bite. Were there spiders out here? Scorpions? She saw it was only a splinter. A quarter-inch barb had snagged her ring finger.

As she plucked the thing out, she realized that a splinter meant *wood,* and wood was something other than dust and sand.

She redoubled her efforts, and a few moments later she uncovered a section of . . . What was it? The lid of a buried treasure chest? A pine casket in a shallow grave?

"I found it," she said to herself, amazed.

She shot off the ground and threw her arms into the air. *"I found it!"*

The others ran toward her. While they came, Mira just stood there being proud of herself. Maybe it was silly to be joyful about such a thing, considering the circumstances, but she couldn't suppress the girlish glee at having *found something buried in the ground.* There was an excitement to it that almost made her forget the ineffable acts that the man in the too-big coat had committed.

Gabe arrived first. "What is it? Where?"

The other two converged. Luke looked fine, but it was apparent that Ben wasn't maintaining a healthy exercise routine. In her delight, Mira almost giggled at him.

She stepped back and pointed at the ground.

"What do we do now?" Luke asked.

Gabe dropped to his knees. "We dig."

The four of them went at it with their hands, until they were covered in the dust that was the Atacama's sloughed-off skin. Minutes later, they'd uncovered what Mira recognized as a cellar door.

"A fraidy hole!" Luke exclaimed.

Gabe wiped his face with his sleeve. "A what?"

"We have a lot of tornadoes back home," Mira explained. "If you're not fortunate enough to have a basement, then you have a cement-lined shelter in the backyard. The colloquial term is *fraidy hole.* The doors look like this."

"I can assure you," Ben said, "that there aren't any tornadoes on this little patch of God's earth. Though this could very well be some kind of root cellar."

"Stand back," Gabe said. "Let's see what Lepin was talking about when he sent us out here."

As the others looked on, Gabe found the handle, which was little more than an indentation in the wood. Just before he opened it, Luke said, "Stop!"

Gabe froze, bent over the door.

"This is Mars," Luke said. "Hey, Ben, maybe when Tilanna and Vanchette get inside the rebel place, they can open a hidden room. A room like this!"

Ben put his hands on his hips and improvised. "And at last they stood, trembling, before the vault of the Kanyri leadership. Around them was only the yawning mouth of silence, a silence pure enough that Tilanna imagined she could hear the transit of her blood and, more importantly, the stirring of new life in her belly. What would she find when she eased that portal wide?"

Ben swung his eyes at Mira. "What *will* you find?"

Mira stared into his dark eyes. The silence he mentioned was indeed complete.

She looked at Gabe. "May I?"

He seemed uncertain. "You sure? We don't know what's down there."

"That's why I'm sure."

Gabe nodded and then withdrew, giving her space to reach down and work her fingers under the shallow handle.

"And as the deities of Mars looked on," Ben said, "Tilanna entered the proper code, and from within the steel wall came the sound of piston-sized bolts retreating."

Mira opened the door.

The cave exhaled dead air.

Crouching at the head of the stairs, Gabe waved away the smell as decades of stale atmosphere drifted from the darkness. The steps were concrete and chipped with age, descending into the unknown.

"What is this?" Luke asked.

"All that's left of Aceda," Gabe said. "When a ghost town gets wiped off the map, the only things remaining are the basements."

"The fraidy holes?"

"Those, too." He slipped the silver lighter from the pocket of his button-flys. He'd been out of smokes and unofficially cold-turkey quitting for at least a full day now, but he was thankful he'd held on to what would now be his only torch in the underworld. "This is what Lepin wanted me to find. Whatever's down here . . . hopefully it'll help us stop the rifleman."

Ben cleared his throat. "I trust that you're going to lead the way."

"If Alban Olivares was here, I'd make him go first. And he would. But instead you're stuck with me." Yet saying this didn't make the actual *doing* any easier. He hesitated to take that first step, not because he thought someone was waiting for him below, but because he wasn't sure he wanted to see what Lepin had been hiding all this time. A man like that had secrets that would probably make Satan squeamish.

"Ancient iron," he said to himself, then struck the lighter's wheel and started down.

Had these ten stone steps been located anywhere else, Gabe imagined they'd be strewn with tapestries of cobwebs and puddled with limestone-tainted water. But in the vacuum that was the Atacama, a world without water or insects, the concrete bunker was devoid of both vermin and moisture damage. Gabe walked into a time capsule, a place likely unchanged since Lepin closed its door. "Everybody stay topside for a sec. Let me check it out."

He thrust the lighter into the chamber at the bottom of the stairs.

Shadows lurched and shifted as his tiny flame revealed an earthen cavity lined with shelves. Gabe glanced quickly around the cramped room, his imagination having already built moldering skeletons here, and bloody knives and corpses chewed up by experimental nerve gas. He saw nothing of the kind. But what rested on the shelves was even worse.

A doll with black button eyes sat next to a woman's purse, its contents arrayed beside it: lipstick, tampons, and a brush tangled with blond hair. Nearby were a man's wedding band and a carefully folded pair of white cotton underwear. A dozen necklaces dangled from screws inserted into the edge of the shelves.

"Everything kosher down there?" Ben asked.

Gabe moved the light, revealing more accoutrements of the dead. A pair of dentures. An open kit of diabetic syringes. Wristwatches. A single wrapped condom. A plastic bin of men's wallets. A prosthetic lower leg.

How many lives were represented here? How many people had been murdered, their private effects turned into trophies?

"Gabriel? Say something. You're spooking us spectators."

On yet another section of plank shelving, neatly displayed, were eight sets of eyeglasses, one of which was tortoiseshell, while another had a shattered left lens. A clump of credit cards and driver's licenses was rubber-banded together, sharing space with a small mechanical device that Gabe suspected was a pacemaker that had been removed from someone's chest.

"Jesus."

"Dammit, Gabe, if you don't say something—"

"They're all here." His mouth was as dry as the desert. "Everyone that Lepin experimented on, all their things . . ."

Ben led the others down the steps.

Photos stripped from billfolds and handbags revealed glimpses of loved ones left behind, smiling relatives with outdated hairstyles and snapshots of places never to be visited again. Two neckties dangled like snakeskins from a hook. A hatbox held a miscellany of passports, theater tickets, shopping lists, and receipts. On the floor beneath the shelves lay a single brunette wig.

Ben put both hands on his head. "Goddamn."

Mira whispered something Gabe couldn't quite make out.

He shifted the flame again. Standing in the corner was a pristine file cabinet, its three drawers alphabetically labeled. Next to it was a fifty-five-gallon blue plastic barrel, its lid held in place with a metal clamp.

"Are they all dead?" Luke asked.

Gabe wished he'd had the foresight to bring a bottle of water from the car. His throat ached. "Fontecilla told me that Lepin was convicted of torturing and killing two people. Only two. They didn't have evidence of anyone else."

"They sure have it now," Ben said.

Gabe considered the bundled stack of licenses and credit cards. With the exception of the children, who carried no such IDs, here was the complete roster of Lepin's experimental subjects. Here was a roll call of the *desaparecidos,* the ones who were taken away with blindfolds over their eyes and never brought back.

Luke shook his head several times. "I don't like it here. It's creepy."

Mira remained at his side. "It's okay. We're here together. Just like always."

"This ain't like always, Gretel. It's creepier than always."

Gabe thought about the rifleman. Somewhere in this museum of the murdered was a clue to the man's identity.

But where?

"This is the point at which we call the police," Ben suggested.

"No cell service out here," Gabe reminded him.

"Then we'll drive to ACEF. Or that observatory of yours. Or *anywhere* as long as they have a phone."

"In a minute."

"What do you mean, in a minute? Luke's right. This is creepy shit. And it's also a mountain of evidence that we risk contaminating the longer we stay here."

The light went out.

"Not good," Luke said. "Notgoodnotgoodnotgood."

Gabe thumbed the wheel and rekindled the flame. "Sorry." He took a step toward the back of the cellar, where the steel cabinet and barrel had been standing for the last twenty-plus years. The filing cabinet was still strapped to a two-wheeled dolly; whoever had deposited it here, presumably Lepin, hadn't bothered untying it.

Gabe swung the lighter toward the barrel.

"Don't open that," Mira said. "I don't want to see whatever's in there. Please, just leave it for the police."

Gabe didn't argue. He returned his attention to the cabinet.

"We start going through that stuff," Ben said from behind him, "and when the cops *do* arrive, they'll know. And if word gets out that we messed up a crime scene—"

"It won't matter," Gabe said. "Lepin is in prison until he's dead. None of this stuff changes that. There won't be another trial. All of these things"—he swept his hand around the cellar—"they're good only to finally bring some peace of mind to those who lost somebody. They get some closure, if there is such a thing. Either way, the fact that we open those file drawers doesn't change anything."

"Then why bother? Oh, wait, never mind. I remember. You're bothering because you think you're avenging this Olivares guy who you never actually met. Whatever."

Gabe turned on him, the anger surprisingly real behind his teeth. "You think you know me? Is that it? As it turns out, you may be right. When I look in the mirror, I don't even know myself. So you may be able to see me, but you *didn't* see Lepin's daughter with her tits cut off, no arms, no legs, and her *lips sewn shut.* Or her son who'd had three limbs amputated. No, Cable, this is no longer just about the Midnight Messenger. This is about the rifleman dying and me pissing on his fucking corpse."

He spun around and jerked open the top drawer.

The silence choked the little chamber as he set the burning lighter on the top of the cabinet and flicked his fingers through the row of manila folders. The tabs were labeled in a handwriting so precise it looked tooled by a machine.

It was a roll call of the victims. Cesar Barros, Alexia Duran, Luciano Encalada . . .

Gabe slipped one out at random and opened it. Ricardo Gamboa. The photo paper-clipped to the corner depicted a graying man in a blazer, standing in front of a wall of books. "I can't read most of this." He offered it to Ben. "Would you mind?"

"Why should I?"

"Because it's in Spanish."

"That's not what I mean, and you know it."

"Please. Just give me a few more minutes, and then we'll drive straight to the observatory and borrow the phone. I promise."

"I don't know you well enough to trust your promises."

"You want to see this guy stopped, don't you?"

"What I *want* is to stay out of jail for meddling in all this evidence. I have a book to finish, in case you haven't heard."

Luke tapped Ben on the arm. "People write books in jail."

"That's not what I want to hear." He looked at Mira and sighed. "I suppose you're party to this madness, being that you've taken on the headdress of our widowed Amazon."

Mira only stared at him.

"Yeah." He shook his head. "That's what I figured. Team up on the resident Negro." He took the folder, smiling faintly, and shook his head again. "I guess this beats growing old in the Santiago snooker halls." He returned to the stairs and advanced up the first few steps in order to take advantage of the rising sun. "Uh . . . looks like Gamboa here was a history professor at the Universidad de Chile." He spent a minute skimming the pages. "Judging by this, my guess is that some of the professor's publications and lectures ran contrary to the official government line. He was censored a handful of times, gave some speeches that were probably inflammatory . . . and then I suspect he didn't come home from work one night because he was stuffed in the trunk of a car en route to Lepin's lab."

"Does it say what they did to him?" Gabe asked.

"Unfortunately, yes. Here at the end . . . damn."

"What? What's it say?"

"That they put him in a glass booth and introduced small amounts of carbaryl into his air."

"Carbaryl?"

"Insecticide."

"Christ."

"It didn't kill him. Apparently his body was able to metabolize it. When he wouldn't tell them the names of possible dissidents on the university faculty, they peeled the skin from his left arm and dumped a kilo of table salt on the exposed meat."

"Enough!" Mira shouted. "We get the picture already."

"The man wanted to know what was in the file," Ben said.

"All we need to know is the name of the guy in the too-big coat. That's it. So I say we concentrate on finding *that* and let the police worry about the victims. Can we do that, please?"

Gabe needed no more encouragement. He loosened the dolly's strap and opened the second drawer. Working in such anemic light, he had trouble making out the writing on the folder tabs. "I think this is Lepin's personal information, his dossier. Here." He handed a thick folder to Ben. "See if there's anything worth knowing in here."

"Your wish is my command."

Gabe ignored the sarcasm and tried the third and final drawer. Like the two above it, this one sported crisp folders that had been arranged alphabetically and marked in the same exacting hand. The topics varied, from simple handwritten supply requisitions to dot-matrix printouts of obtuse demographical reports.

"Lepin was married twice," Ben reported from the stairs. "He did a short military stint, was right-handed, and was considered something of a polymath."

"A *what*?" Luke asked.

"He was good at a lot of things," Ben explained. "He had one son, Julian, but the child was apparently born out of wedlock while old Micha was still hitched to honey number two. Maybe that accounts for the divorce. He holds two master's degrees and had several boring jobs until Pinochet scooped him up in '71. Is any of this crap pertinent to what we're doing here?"

Gabe stopped with his fingers above a tab marked SILENCIO.

"Silence."

Mira knelt beside him. "Pardon?"

Gabe removed the folder and opened it. Mira held the lighter close.

The folder contained only a single sheet of paper. In a column on the left side were as many as two dozen names, printed in an outdated typeface. On the right was a hand-drawn map consisting of nothing more helpful than five lines that might have represented roads from any country on Earth. Printed below the map in Lepin's efficient penmanship was a set of coordinates, followed by the legend *El Lugar de Silencio*.

Gabe realized he was holding his breath. He let it out in a rush. "That's what Lepin meant, this is it, this is what he was saying when he told me that the rifleman knew about silence. He wasn't talking about being quiet. He was talking about *a place*."

"Where?"

"The Place of Silence. The burial site. Probably a cemetery or . . . or a mass grave." He tapped the coordinates. "That's where we'll find the victims."

Ben recited more details from the dossier. "In addition to the bastard son born in his later years, Lepin also had two daughters, Carella and Artemis. I assume that one of them was the woman you found below Mentiras."

"The wagon lady," Luke said.

Ben closed the folder. "There's nothing in here as important as a potential pit full of murder victims. If you think you found such a thing, then it's high time to mosey on over to the observatory and ring up the boys in Chilean blue."

Gabe agreed. The rifleman had used Lepin's stolen journal to locate a place by the code name of Silence, where Pinochet's stormtroopers had buried the tortured dead, probably covering their bodies in quicklime to conceal the stench. Though this failed to explain the impetus behind his quest for revenge, it was one more tile in the mosaic of his ultimate motive.

Lepin also had two daughters, Carella and Artemis.

Gabe looked up. Ben's words, delayed, sounded a note in his memory.

Mira saw the look on his face. "What is it?"

"Lepin's daughters."

"What about them?"

Gabe couldn't elude the image of the woman in the wagon. The moment the stitches were cut from her lips, she had told him to run. *Corra.*

"Her name must have been Carella."

"So?"

"The other one . . . where have I heard that before?"

And then he knew. He stood up. "Vicente."

"What?"

Gabe clenched the folder so tightly that he nearly folded it in half. "Lepin said he had one more grandson still alive, Nicky's cousin. He asked me to protect him, to keep him safe before the rifleman got him, but . . . Shit, my friend Vicente, the guy who was with me when we found Nicky and when I first met you. He works as maintenance chief at the observatory. Remember him?"

"What about him?" Mira asked.

"He told me that his wife is named Artemis, like the Greek goddess. *Lepin's other grandson is Vicente's boy.*"

He looked at their faces as he said it, these empty, black-hole faces. For once in his life he didn't wonder what expression he might see there. He knew it was the same as his own.

"We need to go," Ben said. "We need to go *now* and make sure that kid is safe."

"Keep that file," Gabe said. "We'll read it on the way."

"Got it."

"This won't be over until that bastard's dead."

Ben took the steps two at a time. "Agreed."

Luke's voice stopped them midway up the stairs. "What about the barrel?"

They turned as one and looked at Luke, then at the dark corner where the barrel stood.

"Hell," Gabe said, and hurried back down.

CHAPTER THIRTY-THREE

In order to distance himself from the sight of whatever that fifty-five-gallon drum might contain, Ben projected himself to the prisonlike headquarters of the Kanyri rebellion. There was Tilanna, guarding Vanchette as the old man placed the last few meters of det cord. There were her guns, one held in each hand, metal winking coldly in the dim light. There was the resolve etched on her cheeks, her skin as fair as a Botticelli Venus but her eyes like a comic-book heroine's, too large and too full of loss.

Gabe popped the steel ring loose and heaved up on the barrel's lid. He stepped aside as the lid clattered to the floor, hands over his nose and mouth.

Ben's first thought was, *It's not so bad . . . not so . . . fleshy.* He cringed, but a moment later he realized this wasn't the wrenching stink of rot he'd expected. Had a body been shoved into that blue container, all these years of decomposition surely would've made his eyes water when it was finally let loose in the air. The odor was bad, but it wasn't death. Instead, it was multilayered and . . . antique.

Gabe reached into the barrel and extracted a white cotton dress.

A few stray hairs clung to the soft fabric that still smelled of the woman who'd been wearing it the day she was abducted. Other scents marked other clothes, a pungent strata of perfumes and body odors.

Ben stepped closer. Gabe braved the pile and pulled out a rhinestone belt, a twill cap, and a pinstriped suit coat with blood on the collar.

"It smells bad," Luke said. "Smells like *people.*"

Ben agreed. Like people standing in a crowded bus. Like people in line for the toilet and some of them not able to hold it.

Gabe found a police uniform.

It was all there: badge, belt, radio with batteries long since dead. Pinochet's bagmen had kidnapped a cop. The man had probably refused to walk the regime's rigid line, or he'd spoken out one too many times against corruption. Whatever his crime, he'd been handed to Micha Lepin and used as a lab rat.

Gabe found a little girl's dress.

"That's enough," Mira said. "Please, I don't want to see any more. Besides, I thought we were in some kind of hurry."

Gabe returned the dress with a reverence that Ben found extraordinary. Then again, such respect was only appropriate. You never knew what you'd be wearing on the day when your life changed. When the girl's mother had chosen her outfit in the morning, she'd had no idea . . .

"Wait!" Ben stepped forward just before Gabe dropped the lid on the barrel.

He fished out the cop's gun. The service revolver had rested in its holster for well over twenty years. The leather was as stiff as wood, but the weapon itself appeared untouched by time. He glanced at Gabe. "What do you think?"

"About keeping it?"

"Yeah. Bad idea?"

"You assume it still works?"

"I don't know," Ben said. "Do bullets have a shelf life?" He cleared it from its holster. It was black, bulky, and not sexy at all like the sidearms in the movies. "Mira?"

"Either keep the damn thing or put it back, I don't care. We just need to get out of here and warn your friend while there's still time."

Ben waited for Gabe to make the call.

"We're keeping it." Gabe dropped the lid on the barrel and held out his hand.

Ben handed him the gun, glad to be rid of it, but at the same time worried about letting it out of his sight. He'd feel safer if he could keep an eye on it. "Just don't jam the thing down the waistband of your britches," he suggested as he headed for the stairs. "Because if you shoot anything off down there, I'm damn sure not carrying it to the hospital in hopes they can sew it back on."

"Ow," Luke said.

"To say the least, my young friend. To say the very least."

Mira braced herself half a second before Gabe drove his foot against the brake. The SUV's rear end slid to the right, rocking up a dust wave that was quickly dispersed by a sudden Atacama wind.

"Are we there yet?" Luke asked, just to annoy her.

Gabe swung open his door. "Close enough." He bounded out and ran, yelling his friend's name.

"We better follow him," Mira decided. "He may need our help." She slid from her seat and into the sun, shielding her eyes to get a look at the observatory.

It failed to impress her. She'd been expecting something grand, a monumental stone edifice with a telescope jutting from its domed roof. What she saw instead was a collection of plain rectangular buildings with white metal siding beside an array of what looked like enormous satellite dishes.

She hurried to catch up with Gabe, reaching him just as he collided with an elderly man in a doctor's coat.

"Where's Vicente?" Gabe demanded, clutching the man by the elbows.

"Gabriel? Why are you here? You have come back why? I believe I made it clear very perfectly on the phone that you—"

"I don't give a shit about this job, Rubat. It's irrelevant. I need to find Vicente. Do you hear me? Where is he?"

"You are meaning the maintenance man? Why?"

Gabe shook him. *"Where is he, goddammit?"*

"Not here! Not here! He was . . . called away or something last evening. I don't know the details. Some sort of . . ."

Mira guessed it. "Family emergency."

Rubat glared at her. "Yes, actually. Who are you?"

Gabe released him. "We're too late."

"Call him," Mira suggested. "Do you have his number?" When Gabe didn't immediately reply, she turned the question on the man called Rubat. "Do you know how we can get in touch with him?"

"Of course. He's an employee here."

"Then we need his number *and* we need your satellite phone. Please." She tacked this last bit on only as an afterthought; if this wrinkled little man didn't hop to posthaste, she was liable to karate-chop him.

Perhaps Tilanna was wearing off on her.

"This is serious," she told him. "More than you know."

"Fine. *Fine.*" Rubat left to do her bidding.

"This place is cool!" Luke announced. "What's that? And that? Do you talk to space with that thing?"

"Space talks to *us,*" Gabe said. "But we don't always understand what it's trying to say." He turned to Mira. "We're too late. If Vic's already been called away—"

"We'll see." Without thinking about it, she took his hand in hers. "Keep the faith, right?"

"Does that ever really do any good?"

"Sure beats standing around being scared. For now I'm choosing option A."

Ben joined them as Luke roamed between the huge parabolic antennas like a visitor in a museum of dinosaurs.

"He's gone?" Ben asked.

"He got a call," Mira explained. "Something about his family. He left last night. We're currently in don't-panic mode, but it may not last."

"The rifleman got him," Gabe said. "After he chased us, he went straight to Vicente's house . . ."

Mira hated to see him falling apart right in front of her. Wasn't he practically a stranger? What business did he have affecting her like this? She wished she could distract him with some clever bit of banter, but Catherine Westbrook's only daughter could think of nothing to give this man any peace. "Your friend lives in Calama and works all the way out here? That's one serious commute."

"He's only here two days a week. The place is pretty much self-sufficient. I hope we're wrong about this, I hope his aunt died or his son got in a fight at school or *something* . . . "

Rubat appeared with the phone and a look of undisguised contempt. "Place your call, please, and then be on your way."

Mira released Gabe's hand, surprised by her own reluctance to let go.

Gabe checked his wallet for Vicente's number and tapped it into the phone with such haste that he botched it and had to start over. The man in the too-big coat was one step in front of them. Though the authorities now had his description and were broadcasting it throughout the country, he was determined to complete the cycle he'd set in motion, systematically destroying everyone connected to Micha Lepin. It was no wonder that Gabe's fingers stumbled over the keys.

"It's ringing."

With that, there was nothing for Mira to do but wait. Not for the first time, she envied her brother, who could be aware of something without letting it disturb him. Though in many ways he was an adult, this childish insouciance armored him. Ben wasn't the only one who was bulletproof.

"Anything?" she asked.

Gabe shook his head.

Mira resisted the urge to pace. Her trip here to South America had been about getting answers, but all she'd produced so far was more open-ended questions. Why could Luke read Ben's writing? Would she ever find out? And did it really matter if she didn't? Her brother was composing a novel. If it was published, his name would appear on the cover. And if that didn't make her want to say *shit is holy,* then nothing did.

"Vic? Vic, it's me, Gabe Traylin. Is everything all right? Are you okay?"

Mira didn't want to hear the man on the other end of the line. She didn't have to. Gabe's face melted into his hand as he listened.

She looked at Ben. "He got him, didn't he? He took that man's son."

Ben said it all by saying nothing.

Gabe sank down on a knee. "I know, Vic, I know. I'm sorry, I'm so sorry, but listen to me, just for a second. Are you hearing me, Vic? Are you listening?"

Mira understood Vicente's panic, at least in one fundamental way. It was the helpless feeling of being unable to protect the one person who mattered most. Luke had put her through that a couple of times. And now he was a novelist. Damn.

"I'm going to find Sergio," Gabe said into the phone. "Do you hear me? I'm going to find him and bring him back."

Mira knew what this implied. When Gabe said *I* these days, he meant *we.*

"No, it doesn't matter how," Gabe said. "Vic, stop. Listen to me. I have to go now, okay? No, I—no, did you not hear what I said? I'm going to get him back. That's all I can say. I'm going to get him back, all right? I'll call you." He hung up and dropped the phone in the dirt.

Rubat stood silently, chewing on his lip. Luke returned from his inspection of the property. Ben crossed his arms and waited.

Mira was afraid to ask, but who else would speak up if she didn't? "Now what?"

Gabe got to his feet, dashing a hand over his eyes. "We find him. Like I said."

"Sure, but find him where? Oh, wait. I think I know."

"We'll call Fontecilla and have him meet us there, but Calama is at least six hours away. And Sergio may not have that much time. Even if they bring a chopper, we'll get there first."

Luke stepped between them. "Get where first?"

Mira knew but didn't want to say. El Lugar de Silencio.

Ben put a hand on Luke's shoulder. "I think they're talking about Mars."

"Like Tilanna and Vanchette?"

"Just like."

"But what about the Martian?"

"I think we're going to try and sneak up on him before he hurts somebody else."

Luke made a pistol of his fingers. "And then we'll *zap him with a ray gun.*"

"You bet we will, good Lord willing and the creek don't rise."

Luke laughed. "What does *that* mean?"

"I have no idea."

Listening to the two of them, Mira wished they'd completed more of their story. She wanted to know how it turned out. She wanted to know if she survived.

CHAPTER THIRTY-FOUR

When you were an astronomer, in the end it always came down to a lens.

Gabe was ten years old when he built his first refracting telescope, a lightweight affair made mostly of cardboard and tape. It sported a three-centimeter magnifying glass as an objective lens. Six years later he constructed a twenty-centimeter Dobsonian beauty that resembled a howitzer but revealed passions from which he never recovered. He fell in unrequited love with objects he would never be able to gaze upon with an unaided eye. Gabe had been staring through lenses his entire life, wishing that he had just one in which to see a human face.

"Looks expensive," Mira said.

Gabe glanced down at the binoculars on the front console. She was right. The Zeiss Victory boasted 10x magnification and ran about two grand. "I sort of hope to see him before he sees us."

"By the looks of them fancy specs there," Ben said from the backseat, "I'd say we'll get the best of him on that account unless he's using the Hubble."

"That's the plan."

"I guess it pays to have connections."

"I didn't exactly ask to borrow it. If Rubat knew, he'd probably have a—"

"Shit fit?" Ben suggested.

"And then some. I break it, I buy it. Same goes for the GPS unit." As he drove, Mira in the passenger's seat and Luke behind her, Gabe wrestled with the idea of the gun they'd found in the barrel at Aceda. He didn't intend to use it. In fact, his most ardent desire was to find the rifleman going about some kind of neutral business, with Sergio perfectly unharmed. Then Gabe could simply spy on him from afar until Fontecilla's rotor blades whisked the landscape into a fury. But if things were bad, if Sergio was being tortured . . .

Ben interrupted his darkening thoughts. "It says here that Lepin was reprimanded by his superiors during something called Operation Whisper." He turned the pages in the folder on his lap. "If I read between the lines, I'd say his conduct with a certain prisoner went a little too far."

Mira turned around in her seat. "You're kidding, right? This is a man who injected people with poison and experimented on them until they died. What could he possibly do that would be worse than that?"

"You sure you want to know?"

Luke covered his ears. "This is gonna be gross."

"He raped her."

Gabe's fingers tightened on the wheel.

"How do you know?" Mira asked. "Does it say that in the file?"

"Not in so many words. But it mentions 'non-objective-specific physical conduct' with a prisoner named Paulina Herboso. Looks like Lepin's commanding officer didn't mind what the hell happened to the victims so long as it was in the name of the objective, that being the safeguarding of the all-mighty state. Evidently they didn't think that having sex with the captive in any way advanced their cause. Even tyrants draw the line somewhere."

"I know that name," Gabe said. "Lepin told me that someone called Paulina stole his notes, and somehow those notes ended up with the rifleman. If Lepin recorded everything he did to those people, all the experiments, then his diary contains some stuff that I don't ever want to read."

Luke lowered his hands. "Are we there yet?"

"Just what I need," Gabe said, trying to inject a little levity in his voice. "A backseat driver."

"Easy to drive out here," Luke told him. "No roads! No white lines! Just . . . *ground*!"

"You want to give it a try, then?"

"I don't have a license."

"Don't need one. You see any highway patrolmen? All you need is a pair of eyes and a lead foot." *And the willingness to shoot a man who deserves it.*

Mira read his thoughts. "Is there no other way to do this?"

"Sergio's been missing for over twelve hours. I guess the rifleman probably took him shortly after we ran into him outside the hotel. Vic's wife is flying back from Rio right now, if she hasn't already landed. Sergio was supposed to be staying at a friend's house while Vic made the rounds at the observatory. Nobody knows if he was kidnapped or if he just wandered off and got lost."

"Maybe his disappearance is a coincidence."

"Yeah, sure. Lepin told me that he had one grandson left alive, now that Nicky's dead. But the rifleman got to him before we figured it out."

"Maybe he's holding him somewhere in Calama. Maybe they never left the city."

"I don't think so."

"What if you're wrong?"

"Wouldn't be the first time."

"Think about it." She twisted in her seat so that she was facing him. She hadn't bothered with a seat belt. Barring a sudden blown tire, a wreck out here was impossible. "We really have no way of knowing *anything* about this guy, so what makes you think he's anywhere out here? What if we're headed in totally the wrong direction?"

"This is his place. I'm sure of it. This is where he goes so no one can find him. The Atacama is like outer space, in case you haven't noticed."

"I *have* noticed, thank you very much, but I'm still not convinced we're doing the right thing."

"The right thing? Micha Lepin hid everything, all the clothes and mementoes, everything those people had. Before he got arrested, he hid them in a place where no one would've found them, *ever,* if he hadn't tipped us off. He thought he'd done the same with the bodies at Silencio, except the rifleman learned about it in the journal he got from the rape victim, Paulina Herboso. We never would have known about Aceda if Lepin hadn't told me about it. The *wrong* thing would be to do nothing. The *right* thing is calling the cops and then getting the hell out there before he amputates one of Sergio's arms. And I'm not letting that happen."

"Because you're his guardian angel."

"Yes, goddammit, I am, for lack of anyone more qualified. I didn't ask for any of this, by the way."

"You sure asked for the gun."

"What's that supposed to mean?"

"I don't want to kill anyone, Gabe. I don't want anyone to get hurt. And when you came into the motel room to tell us that they couldn't identify the woman's body, you said—"

"I know what I said."

"And?"

"What? You don't think he deserves to die?"

"I'm not sure if that's for me to decide."

In the backseat, Luke said quietly, "Why are they fighting?"

Ben replied, "Lovers' quarrel."

Gabe pretended not to hear them. He checked the GPS. Having programmed the unit with the coordinates found in Lepin's notes, he knew precisely how far he was from completing the circle the Midnight Messenger had begun. Eight-point-three kilometers. The distance seemed insignificant and momentous at the same time.

"Check out the hills!" Luke exclaimed.

Over the last few minutes, the landscape had changed. Sharp-edged mounds rose from a ground that had been relatively featureless since Calama. These hills were sudden and angular, like fists pushing themselves up through a film of orange earth. Swirls of dust crawled along the slopes, ghostly observers of the SUV's passing.

"We should stop," Mira suggested. "He might hear the engine."

"Another kilometer or so."

"The closer we get," she said, "the more chance we have of being seen."

"We'll be okay. Just a little farther."

"This isn't just your own life you're putting at risk. It's all of us, Gabe. All of us. Yes, I may be acting like the sissy girl of the group, but this is more than just a Lipstick Smear, and I'm not going to put any of us in any more danger than we're already in. Now stop the car."

"What do you mean by a lipstick smear?"

She stared from her window. "Skip it."

"Mom used to say that," Luke said.

Gabe eased off the accelerator. He had to keep Mira on his side, and if that meant hiking a bit farther than he'd intended, so be it. He supposed that he'd be willing to do a lot more than walk a few extra kilometers for her. Maybe if things were different, if she understood what it was like to see her through his eyes . . .

They rolled to a stop in the shadow beside a hill shaped like a boxcar.

"Do we get out now?" Luke asked.

Gabe shut off the engine. It ticked hotly in the silence.

Luke looked at each of them. "Hello?"

When it became apparent that no one else was going to go first, Gabe reluctantly threw open his door, binoculars and GPS in hand. While the others filed out, he spent a moment getting his bearings, summing up the land.

They gathered around him. Gabe the loner, Gabe the isolationist, suddenly surrounded by a tribe of his own creation. He knew them only by their shapes, their clothing, and their voices. He didn't have to see their faces to sense their faith in him, as misplaced as it might be. What he'd done to deserve it, he couldn't say.

Mira held the gun at her side.

"Let's go," Gabe said, and led them over the hill.

The youngest of the Cable boys, known to his older brother as Benjo, realized after a mile of walking through the desert that he was a damned fool.

The reasons were many. For one thing, he didn't own a decent pair of hiking boots. His scuffed oxfords were fine for the Santiago pool halls and for composing the second novel of his lapsed career, but they had no business matching wits with the Atacama. Every man needed at least one pair of postapocalyptic footwear. Secondly and rather bluntly, he'd wasted too many years of his life.

"Thirdly," he whispered, "I am now in the lead." At some point during their seesaw trek through the badlands, Ben's long strides had moved him naturally to the front of their little band, this fateful fraternity of do-gooders.

"Did you say something?" Gabe asked from ten feet behind him.

"Nothing worth repeating." He mounted the ridge and headed down the far side, feet turning up fairy clouds of dust. "Soil's getting redder," he observed, loudly enough that his voice carried down the slope.

"Not just redder," Luke said. "Marsier!"

"Marsier." Ben chewed on that. "I like it. Have to write that in somewhere."

And finally reason number four: He had revealed his oldest secret. By telling Mira he was immune to gunfire, and by honestly believing it, he had potentially put the jinx in play. In sports, you didn't talk about a winning streak while the streak was running.

"Hold up," Gabe said, stopping beside him. "I don't want us to get too close." He handed Ben the GPS while he peered through the binoculars.

Ben wiped a thin line of sweat from his forehead and gazed up at the sun. The day wasn't particularly hot, but there was something about the lack of moisture in the air that made everything feel dead. In the humidity you knew you were alive. Out here you might have been nothing but a column of salt.

"A little closer," Gabe said.

Ben was happy to relinquish the lead. "You okay, Hemingway?" he asked Luke.

"I'm thinking about the Martian."

"We all are."

"He cut those people, cut 'em *apart.*"

"I suppose he did. But that usually means that karma's about to pull a U-turn and do a little cutting of its own."

Mira frowned at this.

"Sorry," Ben said. "But reciprocity, if you'll pardon the pig Latin, is an itchbay."

They kept walking, angling through a cleft between a pair of saw-toothed mounds that had been scrubbed clean by an eternity of dry wind.

"This is close enough," Gabe finally said. He squatted and brought the binoculars to his face.

Ben looked askance at Mira. She'd said nothing for the last several minutes. The brim of her baseball cap was pulled low over her eyes, but he could tell she was watching Gabe. Every few moments, probably without even realizing it, she'd check to make sure Luke hadn't drifted off. Ben wondered if she'd admitted to herself that one day she would have to let him find true north on his own.

"Take a look."

Ben accepted the binoculars—he preferred the term *field glasses*—and zeroed in on a faint blur that might have been at least a thousand yards away, if not more.

Luke edged closer. "What do you see?"

The world seemed to rush in from a great distance, startling him with its sudden proximity. "Well, I'll be damned and denied parole."

The wooden fence might have been a century old. It stood about waist high and appeared nearly the same color as the dirt around it. Within its perimeter were three or four dozen upright slabs of rock, a microcosmic Stonehenge.

"Ben, what *is* it?"

"Graveyard."

"No foolin'?"

"Not a single ounce."

The plinths thrust up from the earth in remembrance of those who slumbered beneath it, their names likely recalled by no one. In the middle of the stones rose a wind-scarred crypt with an arch over the door and a flat roof. Affixed to one side of this ten-foot cubical bunker was a lean-to made from a gray tarpaulin and stacks of wooden crates.

A shadow shifted beneath the tarp.

Ben immediately lowered the field glasses and sank to his knees so as not to be seen. "Someone's over there, someone moved . . ."

"It's okay," Gabe assured him. "We're too far away. Unless he's using his rifle scope and intentionally looking this way, he doesn't have a chance of spotting us. We're a kilometer out."

"Is that like a mile?" Luke asked.

"About sixty percent of a mile. Either way, we're safe."

Ben wasn't convinced. "You sure about that?"

"No."

"What the hell kind of answer is that?"

"You want me to lie to you?"

"Yes, as a matter of fact, that would make me feel a lot better."

Gabe gestured to the bottom of what Ben was beginning to think of as an arroyo. "Take a seat down there, keep out of sight, and he'll never know we're in the area. I'll stay up here and see if I can get a better look at what he's doing. I want to make sure he's not hurting Sergio."

"And if you can't confirm anything one way or another?"

"Then I'll have to get closer. And before you ask me if that's safe, let me say no, it's not safe. But I'm not letting him do that to anyone else, not what he did to the others."

Ben acquiesced with a frustrated wave. He wasn't going to raise his voice and risk being overheard. Like Gabe, he wanted to do what he could to protect the boy, but he suspected that Gabe's desire had crossed over into the obsession category, the way a hurricane builds power as it nears landfall and moves up in the storm ratings. "Fine. Be the lone wolf and leave the rest of us to chew on our nails."

"I'm just keeping an eye on him," Gabe said. "At least until the cops get here."

"Then shut up and get on with it." Ben joined Mira and Luke in the hollow where the two hills met. He needed to distract himself from what was going on, find a getaway into the sanctum sanctorum of fiction. "Thank Apollo I brought my notebook."

"Who's Apollo?" Luke asked.

"God of poetry."

"Are we writing poetry?"

Ben wanted to laugh at that, but his heart wasn't in it. "It may not be Shakespeare, but I guess it has its moments, just the same." He sat on a rock that he suspected hadn't felt rain since the days of the Bard himself. "Now keep your voice down and tell me what happens next."

Luke gladly settled in to relate the next chapter of their tale.

Though Ben tried to pay attention, his eyes strayed to the crest of the hill, where Gabe was sprawled on his stomach, staring through his stolen field glasses, and waiting.

CHAPTER THIRTY-FIVE

Mira watched the shadows for half an hour, while part of her tumbled deeper into the drama evolving next to her. Her brother had again picked up Ben's divining rod, and together they unearthed more buried fragments of their story—her *story.*

" 'Tilanna advanced down the hallway like a spring uncoiling in zero gravity,' " Luke read, " 'silently and full of energy not yet fully realized. The butt of the gun was a bit big for her hand. She imagined she could feel Dycar's touch on its wood, as she'd once felt it on her skin.' "

Mira eased up from where she leaned against the hill. She was tired. Tired of waiting here. Tired of being nervous. Tired of wondering if she was living the life of a fictional heroine who would probably end up dead by the story's conclusion. At least she could climb up there and give Gabe some company during his vigil. And maybe get some company in return.

She bent down and used her hands to brace herself on the stone as she ascended toward his position.

" 'Tilanna had left Vanchette behind to deal with their escape route. These last few steps to the core of the Kanyri stronghold would be ones she took alone, not counting the secret passenger inside her. What amazed her most of all was her willingness to risk that fragile seed. She would put both parts of her in the fire zone in her last mad effort to erase these men from her adopted home of Mars.' "

Mira reached the short summit and flattened herself on her stomach next to Gabe.

"Hey," he said.

"I got bored."

"Not much better up here."

"It's not very comfortable, that's for sure."

The cemetery was so far away that she could see only a haze.

" 'If they killed her now,' " Luke said, his voice clear and calm, " 'then they would in effect be killing her twice. But if she somehow slipped through them still alive, she would be living for two.' "

"Mira?" Gabe said.

"Yes?"

"Maybe we can go to dinner."

"I'm sorry?"

"Dinner. Maybe we can get some."

"Are you . . . asking me out?"

"Assuming all of this turns out okay, I mean."

"You didn't answer the question."

"Neither did you."

Mira was glad he was staring through the binoculars so he couldn't see her smile. "The answer is yes." Amazing. She had no other word for it.

"How can your brother read like that?"

Mira was still processing the dinner invite and consequently experienced some lag time before responding. "Uh, I don't know. Ben says we'll never figure it out. I've stopped worrying about it. Have you ever seen those people who struggle with some kind of debilitating mental handicap but they can play Mozart after hearing it only once?"

"Savants, right?"

"Exactly."

"Like in *Rain Man.*"

"Same thing. Medically they have no explanation for it."

Gabe lowered the binoculars and looked at her. "Now *that* is something I can understand."

"Meaning what?"

"Long story. And not a subject for a first date." He resumed his watch.

Mira wanted to pinch him. This was no time to be cryptic, not when the next few minutes could . . . No, she wouldn't let herself go there. Like Tilanna, she had to believe it would all unfold according to some predestined plan. "Anyway, I think I've convinced myself that it doesn't matter how it happens between Luke and Ben. The doctors are never going to be able to explain it. I've realized that the important thing is this story they're writing. That changes everything somehow. Or at least it feels that way. Still, it's a little weird."

"Well, weird is something that happens to be near and dear to my—"

A scream carried across the desert, then faded.

Mira tensed and held her breath. Down below, Luke and Ben stopped composing.

Gabe paused only for a moment, then dropped the binoculars and got himself moving down the hill as if it were a playground slide.

"Gabe, wait."

"It's Sergio."

Luke and Ben turned to watch him as he picked up speed.

"Get your ass moving, Tilanna," Mira said to herself. She slid down the smooth stone.

"Gretel?"

"I'm going with him. You two stay here."

Ben snapped the notebook shut, his pen flying into the dirt. "No way, sister."

"I have to."

"The hell you do!"

She held up the gun in its brittle, decades-old holster. "He might need this." She looked at Luke and fell in love with him again, just as she always did, this other half of her, this babe who'd shared Cathy Westbrook's womb with her. "I'm off to fight the Martian, Hansel."

"Follow the breadcrumbs to find your way back."

"Will do." Tears stung her eyes, but she refused them purchase on her cheeks. Her only choice was outrunning those tears, and so she set off after Gabe at a sprint.

The angular hills that rose and fell on her left blocked her vision of the cemetery, but they wonderfully worked both ways. She and Gabe would be able to advance without being seen—or so she hoped. Sunlight blinked through the ridges and valleys as she ran, a strobe light that had the effect of turning her shadow off and on.

Hearing her footsteps, Gabe looked back.

Mira didn't call out to him, but she was glad when he slowed down. If she was racing to her death, she didn't want to do it alone.

She caught up with him and breathed as quietly as she could.

"You shouldn't have come," he whispered.

"No choice." She held out the gun.

Gabe considered the weapon for a moment, then took it, pulled it from the leather, and dropped the holster in the dust.

Mira realized, then, Gabe's role in her story. Luke was Lieutenant Dycar, always present in her thoughts, and Gabe was Dycar's gun.

"I'm coming with you," she told him. Though she was as scared as she'd ever been in her life, her voice was remarkably steady. "Let's just get it over with."

Gabe surprised her by touching her face.

Then he nodded and resumed his run.

Mira ran beside him.

Ben watched them go, his hand forming an awning over his eyes.

Luke picked up the fallen pen. “Are we really going to stay here?”

“Not a chance in hell.”

“Thought so.”

Ben pocketed the notebook, and they set off across the slumbering Martian soil.

CHAPTER THIRTY-SIX

The screaming stopped.

Gabe knelt and peered around a desert rock shaped like a shark's fin.

The rifleman's camp was defined by the dead. Weathered grave markers stood like sundials, casting rows of oblong shadows that provided shade for canteens and rubber-sealed packages of military rations. Christ rose from one of the slabs, and from His crucified arms dangled a leather satchel and a pair of goggles reminiscent of the kind Rommel had favored in the African sand. In the middle of it all, the crypt door stood open, the darkness inside complete.

Where are the damned helicopters?

Mira pressed close behind him, straining to see.

An array of shovels stood just inside the fence, their blades stabbed into the ground, their wooden shafts marking what appeared to be some kind of pit. Gabe didn't have the proper angle to confirm what this depression might have held.

The stench made him wince.

Whatever was in there, it had been rotting for a long time. But decay in the Atacama happened differently. Without the trusty industry of maggots and the universal solvent of rain, things left for dead out here didn't so much decompose as *crumble.* Had there been any moisture in the air, he supposed, the stink would've been worse.

Mira tugged his shirt.

Gabe turned so that his face was near hers—and then pulled back, startled.

"What's wrong?" she whispered.

Mira wore a baseball cap, bright blue with KC stitched in white letters. The bill cast a full shadow on her face, giving her cheeks and mouth meaningful dimension, making shapes from the shapeless. Very rarely and very briefly, when the conditions were right, the prosopagnosia seemed to fall away, and it fell away now.

"Gabe, say something."

He barely mouthed the words. "You're beautiful."

Despite everything, she smiled. "No one but my brother has ever said that to me before."

Gabe, rapt, had no intention of looking away, but Mira said, "There's something at the gate."

Though he might not ever be able to re-create the moment, he sighed, turned around, and swept his eyes over the fence until he found the wooden arch that served as the cemetery's point of entry. A four-wheeled ATV stood just beyond the gate, with canvas-wrapped bundles lashed to its cargo rack. From his current vantage point, Gabe couldn't make out any details, but if the rifleman had left his weapon there . . .

He again positioned himself close to Mira, speaking as softly as he could. "I'm going to circle around, see if I can find his gun."

She held up a hand in an obvious question: *What should I do?*

He didn't know what to say. She was too much for him. Who was he to give instructions to the wind? He settled for a bit of daring and kissed her forehead, bumping the brim of her cap along the way.

Then he edged around the perimeter defined by the fence, staying low, revolver in hand. If he could ensure that the rifleman was without his gun, the very one that had killed Eduardo and shot up Vicente's truck, then he'd rearrange the odds in his favor. Though he wanted to charge into the crypt and save Sergio before the boy sustained irreparable damage, he feared that rushing in blindly would only get him killed. If the rifle wasn't among the items stowed on the four-wheeler, then at least Gabe knew what he faced when he called the cocksucker out.

He rounded the pit.

The crater was eight feet deep and full of bodies. Arms reached up at nothing. Legs were cut away. Skulls sprouted brambles of black hair.

The rifleman had found Micha Lepin's deposited dead, using the journal he'd obtained from Paulina Herboso. Within the hole lay people who'd been burned, gassed, and torn apart in the name of the state, an exposed choir of corpses that propelled the rifleman with their song. Gabe came within touching distance of a greater explanation for it all, a bridge between the rifleman's hacksaws and the ghouls in the pit, but the answer eluded him.

He lowered himself so that his stomach almost brushed the sand, then crawled lizardlike to the gate. He expected another sound from the crypt, but there was nothing. Whatever was happening to Sergio was happening in silence.

He reached the four-wheeler and searched it quickly. The saddlebags bulged. A sleeping bag was strapped down with nylon bands. A long shape wrapped in burlap turned out to be not a rifle but a set of flexible tent poles.

So much for disarming the man. The last thing Gabe wanted was the OK Corral.

He was about to backtrack when he noticed the keychain.

The keys hung heavily from the ATV's ignition, at least thirty of them of various sizes forming a loose mass of metal. Instead of a key fob, the cluster was held together by a wallet with an eye-ring attached to one corner.

A moment passed. The sun glared down. A muffled sound escaped the crypt.

Wallet.

Gabe slid out of his stupor and made sense of what he was seeing. His hand, almost as if it were unattached from the rest of him, floated up and outward. Of their own accord, his fingers closed around the wallet and turned it over to reveal a plastic-covered window.

Printed there quite plainly was the rifleman's name: JULIAN HERBOSO.

Ben had read in the file that Micha Lepin had sired an illegitimate son named Julian. And later they'd found that Lepin had raped one of his victims, Paulina Herboso.

Julian Herboso, the rifleman, was Micha Lepin's son.

Ben didn't bother staying low. He walked upright, as evolution had intended. Beside him, Luke played things closer to his ape ancestry, bending at the waist and scampering between the rocks so as not to be seen.

Ben knew who was the smarter of the two. Some fools, they said, never learned. Especially *old* fools. He touched Luke on the shoulder, a gentle reminder not to get too far ahead or reveal their advance by kicking an errant stone. They had the benefit of numbers and the chance to attack from a position of surprise, and Ben didn't want to be responsible for giving away their advantage. Hopefully they'd catch the bastard out in the open, and Gabe could simply shoot him and be done with it.

Ben asked himself if he was okay with that, just killing the man, assassinating him.

The answer was *You bet your black ass.*

The graveyard appeared between a break in the hills. Ben got his first unobstructed look at the place. Whatever community it had once served had long since faded into the annals of busted boomtown mythology. Only the jagged teeth of the tombstones remained, some leaning one way, some the other. The fence looked ready to collapse. The only sturdy part of the whole enterprise was the white stone cube that probably contained the remains of the town's wealthiest nitrate baron.

Luke saw it, too. They were drawn to it and whatever it might hold.

Reading the expression on the young man's face, Ben nodded, and they made their way to the back side of the fence. He saw nothing of Gabe and Mira. They were either hunched behind the hills or on the far side of the white vault.

Not a vault, he decided. *A sepulcher.*

Yes, that was a much more *writerly* word. A sepulcher. It sounded like some damn place that old Edgar Poe would've appreciated. No doubt the killer had made it his HQ.

They reached the fence. The wood had once been painted white and still was, mostly. Without any rain to dilute the color, the paint hadn't been washed away but rather scoured by the granules of dust in the desert's erratic wind.

Ben swung his leg over it. Luke followed him.

Sounds issued from inside the sepulcher, but the thick walls rendered them unintelligible. Ben approached the structure from the back, watching his feet to make sure he didn't come down on anything that would snap and give him away. As he moved to the right, he knew how incongruous he looked, a part-time billiards hustler and mostly failed novelist playing stealth commando on a German pillbox with a maniac inside. This was what he got for answering the door when the Westbrook twins came a-knockin'.

A few steps behind him, walking on his toes as best he could, Luke went left.

Only briefly did Ben consider reining him in. He suspected that Luke already had too many folks in his life treating him like a child, despite his sangfroid in the face of danger. Ben opted to trust him, just as he opted to have faith that the kind policeman had been correct in '79 when he said that Ben's bones were built from Kevlar.

He rounded the corner and found a hanging mobile made of body parts.

His knees failed him. He staggered, caught himself on the wall, and slid into a breathless crouch.

A frame of scavenged fence posts supported human limbs that dried like chiles in the Atacama air. Feet that had been severed at the ankle hung from silver wires. One had toenails that were painted a dull red. Yet another had no nails at all; they appeared to have been ripped out.

Ben jammed a hand over his mouth and tried to swallow.

Three arms dangled from clothes hangers. On a hook nearby, thigh muscles had contracted like jerky to reveal the ivory gleam of bone.

Ben pinched his nose shut before the smell could force itself down his throat.

Here hung the body parts of Micha Lepin's family, carved up and left to cure. Ben managed to get himself turned around. His eyes watered. He stumbled around the corner and leaned his back against the wall, breathing through his mouth as quietly as he could. These were all that was left of the victims Gabe had described, the boy in the backpack and the woman from Mentiras, otherwise known as Nicky and Carella. And soon a piece of Sergio would join them.

Luke appeared from around the sepulcher's opposite side. Incredibly, he was grinning.

Ben couldn't find his voice. He wanted to say *be quiet* because he could tell that Luke was excited about something, but his throat had contracted to a pinhole.

Luke gave him two thumbs-ups. "I found the Martian's gun."

Inside the little building, Sergio screamed.

CHAPTER THIRTY-SEVEN

The man in the too-big coat stepped from the crypt.

The scream followed him and faded as he emerged in the sunlight. Mira watched him from her position behind the rock, hating him for forcing such sounds from an innocent boy. She saw his face, with its drooping eyes and blade-sharp cheekbones . . .

Her nails bit into her palms. She tried to force her fingers to relax, but anger fused them shut.

The man wore an overcoat of transparent plastic. It was the kind of thing a butcher might have worn when standing amid the upside-down slabs of skinned cattle, or the man in the funeral home who drains the blood from bodies. Mira understood, then, what Gabe had already realized. Had they waited for the police, Sergio would've been dismembered and driven mad . . . if he wasn't already.

Before she could stop herself, she relinquished her concealment, moving clear of the rock and daring him to see her.

He did.

For a moment they stood considering each other from a distance of sixty feet, the grave markers and wooden fence between them. He held something in his right hand, a surgical blade that reflected tiny butterflies of sunlight. Insanity rutted with intelligence in his eyes. Startled to find himself confronted at his special place, his face went through a series of slow transformations. He looked exactly like what he was: ambushed.

On the opposite side of the cemetery, near the gate, Gabe appeared. Mira saw him, but she was careful not to give him away with her eyes. He had a clear shot. Mira's lungs yearned for deeper breaths, but she couldn't find the power. It took all her strength just to stand there and face the man like this, as Tilanna might have done when she was feeling ballsy and looking for war.

Gabe lifted the pistol in both hands.

Mira watched him without looking directly at him.

The man from the crypt bent his head to one side like an animal, trying either to get her scent or to convince himself she was real and no desert mirage.

"Good-bye," Mira whispered to him.

Gabe fired.

The sound was so sudden and so loud that Mira jumped, even though she'd been anticipating it. The bullet cracked into the side of the crypt, dislodging dust as it ricocheted with a high keening sound. The man darted to the side of the building, his plastic coat fluttering around him. He made a noise of fear and rage as he disappeared from Mira's field of vision.

Ben's voice rang out. "Luke, get back!"

Luke.

Mira's lungs found their air, that sweet, thin air of Mars, and she hurdled the fence and ran for the crypt.

Gabe's hand buzzed from the recoil. He cursed himself for missing even as he sprinted through the gate and careened between the tombstones.

Too late.

He'd been too late, too slow, too damned shaky with the gun. The revolver had bucked in his hand, the big cylinder rolled, and the thirty-year-old bullet had bull-rushed down the barrel and gone terribly wide, slicing splinters from the tomb.

And now he ran.

He'd get close, close enough not to miss, and maybe there was a time in his life when killing would've chilled him, but that was before he found Nicky Lepin in a backpack. He leaped a fallen grave marker, tripped, caught himself with his free hand in time to get a glimpse of a plastic jacket whipping around the corner.

He heard Luke's voice and kept running. Moments later, he jumped around the little building and brought the gun up wildly, his arm shaking with adrenaline.

Luke was sitting on the ground, a tiny lizard of blood creeping down his chin. Gabe recognized him by his tennis shoes. Ben hovered over him, trying to inspect the injury while simultaneously checking over his shoulder.

Mira appeared from the other side, throwing herself at Luke. *"Baby, are you okay?"*

"He hit me, Gretel, hit me and took the rifle!"

Ben looked at Gabe. "He ran there, behind those hills."

Gabe almost bolted after him. He caught himself, biting his lip. He threw a glance at the pistol. The embossed lettering read RUGER .357. It trembled in his hand. He aimed at the nearest hill and shouted, "Julian Herboso!"

The moment he'd seen the name on the ATV's keychain, everything finally made sense. Micha Lepin had tortured and raped a woman named Paulina Herboso. She'd given birth to a son. That son had used the detailed notes in a stolen journal to learn of his mother's past and to taste the blood of it on his teeth. He suckled on it like curdled milk, and in his evolving madness he'd sought recompense for his mother's aguish.

Micha Lepin was his father as well as his obsession. Julian had set out to mutilate and murder everything his father loved.

"Julian Herboso!"

By naming this man, Gabe gained a power over him that he was unable to obtain by seeing his face. No longer was Herboso the rifleman, or Gigante, or a cipher seen only in shadows. He was built of bones and brain matter, and he could be killed.

Emboldened, Gabe doubled back, hoping to flank him.

CHAPTER THIRTY-EIGHT

Ben knew a dead man when he saw one. Gabe had that captain-goes-down-with-his-ship look when he galloped toward the cemetery gate, revolver held near his head. Bent on avenging those he never knew, he would get himself shot by a man much more skilled with a gun.

Ben had one hand on Luke's shoulder. He touched Mira with the other. "I'm going."

"But—"

"I can help."

"He'll kill you both."

Ben thought about that only for a moment. "Ma'am, I was there when they buried Mr. John Wayne, the finest cowboy who ever lived. I know how a hero goes down."

He also knew a good parting line. He turned and headed for the hills where the Martian had disappeared, wondering if Luke would ever read again without him.

From inside the crypt: a soft, fluttering moan.

Mira almost chased after Ben. She wanted to drag him back, keep him safe, and trust that Dycar's gun would finish the man Gabe had called Julian Herboso. But she couldn't send herself in two directions at once, no matter how strongly she wished for it, so she took her brother by the hand and tugged him behind her as she ran to the entrance of the crypt.

A yellow light burned from within. Mira had no time to give herself a pep talk or worry about what might be lurking in there. She had to ensure that Sergio would live. Only then could she join the battle with her friends.

She stepped through the low stone arch.

The room reeked of piss.

Fear had caused that smell. Terror had freed it to run down the boy's pantleg and drip to the floor. He lay on a stone catafalque where the body of the crypt's original resident had once rested. Thick bands of duct tape held him in place, rendering his limbs immobile. An aluminum rack supported an IV bag, the tube of which snaked around Sergio's arm. The needle at the end of the tube, however, had not yet been inserted into the boy's skin; it dangled from the table's edge, evidence that the surgeon had been interrupted before his work began. The boy looked physically unharmed.

Mira wanted to fall to her knees in relief, but she couldn't afford the rest. There would be time for nervous breakdowns later. To everything there was a season, and right now the season entailed getting this kid the hell out of here.

"He's okay?" Luke asked from behind her.

"I think so. There's no blood."

He put his hand on the center of her back. "We need to help."

"Working on it." She took two steps into the small chamber and realized there was someone else here.

It was a man, naked and thin, strapped to an army cot. His skin was the color of cheesecloth. A stained bandage covered most of his head.

"Who's that?" Luke wondered.

"I'm not sure."

"He don't look so good."

"Doesn't." She aimed her attention at the boy.

Mercifully he'd slipped into an unconscious state. The bier on which he lay was sprinkled with black hair. His head had been shaved, but Mira saw no other damage.

"What do we do?" Luke asked.

Sergio's body radiated heat. Mira resisted the urge to coddle him and say soft things. The best remedy for him was a dreamless sleep.

The man on the cot whispered, *"¿Quien es?"*

Luke, surprised, made a little barking sound and spun on the man. "Mira, he's—"

"Yeah, I see, he's awake." She crossed the room and bent over the man, realizing that he was one more injured soul assigned to her, one more charge to keep. As if she didn't have enough already. "Who are you?"

Only his eyes moved, blinking slowly as he stared up at her through bloodshot corneas.

"I said, who are you?"

He tried to wet his lips with his tongue. *"Me llamo Alban Olivares."*

CHAPTER THIRTY-NINE

Gun in hand, Gabe crawled through the rocks. He scanned the ground, the hollows, the crooks between the boulders. Julian Herboso waited somewhere in this cragged maze of stone. Gabe had little hope of tracking him; his training for such a hunt came only from video games, first-person shooters that glorified your ability to frag your friends online but came up terribly incomplete when simulating the real thing.

He pulled back between the columns and pressed his spine against one of them, gripping the revolver in both hands. If he kept up like this, he'd start to swoon from too much oxygen, but what choice did he have? Herboso captained this world, thrived in it, butchered people in it. Gabe had no advantage here.

Or did he?

What he realized as he huddled there was that every sound, no matter how small, came to him perfectly through the Atacama vacuum. After so many years of depending on nonvisual clues, he'd refined his sense of hearing to the point that, if he held his breath, everyone around him revealed themselves by the noises they made. People breathed differently, yawned differently, walked differently.

Ben's footsteps separated themselves from the other sounds. His strides were long, and he had a tendency to slide his feet when he moved. Gabe had spent the last several hours marching beside him and discerned the difference, even if no one else could. Farther away were dull echoes that others would have dismissed but Gabe realized were voices in the tomb.

And something else. It was faint as hell, fainter even than the occasional puff of breeze, so Gabe did what he knew he shouldn't do if he wanted to avoid being taken by surprise.

He closed his eyes.

Here was his environment; here were all the faces he'd ever tried to see. And into this place came the sound of someone moving but trying so very hard not to be heard: the lightest step, the faintest passing of boot over sand.

Gabe opened his eyes and moved toward where Herboso thought he was hiding.

The sharp angles of rocks and wind-carved totem poles offered him no clues, their shadows too skinny to conceal anyone. Gabe trusted only what he heard, just as he did when meeting a new friend or navigating the faces on a busy street. The gun now surer in his hand, he kept low and moved with a swiftness that felt like it belonged to someone else.

From somewhere behind him, Ben kept coming, slower, more cautiously, but still moving.

Gabe stepped carefully over loose pebbles, veering slightly left, following the sounds that few others could have heard. He understood the irony: His disability had given him an advantage. The last time it had worked that way, he'd been a kid winning every game of hide-and-seek.

When he knew he was close, he stopped and lowered himself behind a column of basalt that might have been a million years old. Two, perhaps three meters away, the rifleman shifted slightly behind his own piece of cover, unaware that he'd given himself away.

At least Mira had said yes when Gabe asked her out to dinner.

That was his final thought before leaning out from behind the slab, the gun leading the way.

A face stared back at him.

Startled to find himself staring into someone's eyes, Gabe lost a few moments, the revolver pointed nowhere in particular. Just as the deaf probably wondered what a laugh was like, so too did Gabe sometimes imagine the vibrancy of recognizing someone's smile. One of his doctors had gone so far as to call him blessed, remarking that Gabe never judged people by their appearance or the pigmentation in their skin. Whatever. Gabe just wanted one time to know what was so damn fine about Marilyn Monroe.

The stranger, little more than an arm's length away, peered around a shelf of stone, and the one thing preventing Gabe from shooting a hole in the center of that moon-face was the tiny chance that maybe he was wrong. Had his ears sent him false signals? Was this actually Mira, chasing after him like Jill after Jack? Or Luke, the most honest of them all, trying to do his part?

Julian Herboso lifted his rifle.

Too late Gabe realized the truth. He threw out his hand and deflected the long barrel, but by then Herboso was already well into his second move, lunging out with a scalpel he must have been holding when he'd first stepped from the tomb. Gabe wasn't fast enough to defend both attacks.

The blade disappeared entirely into the meat of his left arm, all the way to the scalpel's handle. His biceps became a hive. Within this bloody hollow dwelled things with wings and teeth, biting deeply and spinning him around in a half pirouette.

Gabe fell.

Though he tried to catch himself, his arm would not respond, a flailing thing connected to the rest of his body. His tailbone absorbed the shock, nearly rattling the gun from his hand. From a sitting position he sighted down the barrel—

The scalpel drew a silent red line across his knuckles.

He tried to jerk the trigger, but his finger didn't respond. The instrument was so sharp that the pain held back, delaying, and then it came on all at once, an aftershock that forced his hand open. The gun dropped to the sand.

Gabe started to cry out but realized in the far edge of his mind that sometimes you can't scream because you're too busy dying.

The blade glimmered again in the sun.

Gabe pulled back just enough that the scalpel unzipped the skin horizontally across his forehead but missed the bone beneath. This time the pain was automatic, and so was the blood, rushing warmly into his eyes. He lost sight of the gun that could save him.

He wanted to tell someone he was sorry, but he didn't know where to begin. There were too many people in need of an apology.

Turn your tears into water, and your rage into rain.

Maybe there was truth in that, even here where all the strings were unraveling. Gabe had one more chance to lunge and tackle this man, and that would be everything.

He threw himself up from the ground, yelling without meaning, arms reaching for whatever was in front of him.

Herboso kicked him in the face.

Just like that, Gabe was through. He landed on his back, bleeding everywhere, the stuff flowing down his face and into his mouth. Herboso struck again at the nearest target, which turned out to be Gabe's knee, slicing open his pantleg and the flesh beneath it. Despite the blood in his throat, Gabe managed to scream. Hopefully Mira would hear that and have the sense to run. *Take the damn four-wheeler, baby. Just run and be like me: don't ever look back.*

Herboso stood over him, his plastic overcoat smeared with the dried fluids of his victims. Apparently satisfied that Gabe had no more resistance left, he let his surgeon's blade fall to the ground, bent over, and picked up the same gun he'd used to kill Eduardo, the one with the soiled shoulder strap and telescopic sight. The rifle's bore was huge, the kind of thing used on safari. Gabe, blinking back the blood, understood the symmetry in going out the same way as the Midnight Messenger. He was trying to make himself think about something worthy here at the end, something profound, when he heard Ben say, incredibly, "I strongly suggest you drop that rifle, pilgrim."

Ben Cable came upon the bogeyman. He reckoned the distance at thirty paces.

Hell. This was it. He had no weapon, not even so much as a good-sized rock to throw. All he had was a myth. Having delivered his best line, the only thing he could do was wait and see how it played out.

Slowly, as if his bones were powered by gears rather than sinew, the man looked away from where Gabe lay cut up on the ground at his feet. He turned his head, and Ben finally got a look into the abyss of his eyes. After all this, Ben wanted to see something there, an animal cunning, a gamey glimmer that at the very least revealed an undercurrent of sentience, but instead he saw only a descent and a sudden, dark ending. Like a desert hermit on a self-imposed fast, the man's face had tightened around his cheeks and chin, his jawline too prominent to be healthy. It looked as if the desert had dried the moisture from his skin. Behind his thin lips, his teeth were even but discolored. Black hair hung without form on either side of his head. He wore some kind of see-through raincoat over a bedraggled military jacket. Breathing in and out of his mouth, he hooked his finger around the trigger.

Ben, in contrast, breathed easily. Sure, he would die here today, but when that son of a bitch took aim and laid him low, Gabe would have the chance to get up and attack. And so Ben found himself charmed, even in death, because he'd come to a place on Earth where nothing lived and still found a way to preserve life. In fact, now that he thought about it—

The man lifted his rifle and fired.

The echo of the shot carried across the desert floor, and Ben thought no more. Time did not slow down, as he might have written in his stories of Mars, but instead the impact against his forehead happened almost instantly, staggering him. He took a step backward and squeezed his eyes shut, aware of the pressure just above his eyebrow, waiting for it to become an explosion of pain.

It never did. Everything simply ended.

Ben fell.

The moment Gabe heard Ben's voice, he knew the cagey old novelist was trying to give him an opening and would probably die because of it. Which meant Gabe owed him the courtesy of getting off the ground and doing something, even though he wanted nothing more than to remain here and let it be over. But there was the boy with the goddamn pinwheel, telling him he had to go.

Wiping an arm across his eyes to clear the blood, he rolled onto his stomach just as the rifle thundered.

Ben's eyes closed. He stumbled backward and dropped. In that single instant, the grief arrived fully formed, forcing a ragged cry from Gabe's throat. He was sorry for everything at once, for leading them all to this place, for not fighting hard enough. With tears clouding his vision, he pawed for the revolver with his right hand, his fingers slippery with blood. The thing weighed sixty pounds. He didn't think he could lift it.

Herboso ejected the spent shell from his rifle. The brass casing flicked in the sunlight like a dragonfly.

Coughing on the blood that had drained into his mouth from the horizon line on his forehead, Gabe got to his knees. He supported one hand with the other, hoisted the gun point-blank at the man, and pulled the trigger.

The revolver's cylinder spun. The hammer fell.

When the bullet discharged, the gun snapped upward in his hands and sent shock waves into his elbows and injured arm. The shot went between Herboso's legs and lost itself as a reverberation in the distance.

Herboso, hissing through his teeth, rammed another round into the chamber.

Gabe fired again.

His quivering muscles, the blood on his palms and face, the fire burning from the scalpel's work, the tears—these things defeated him, despite his proximity to his target. The bullet clipped Herboso in the arm, knocking his hand from the rifle.

Gabe's body thrummed with recoil. Frantically he clenched the trigger a third time. The sound deafened him. The gun almost flew from his hand.

The bullet entered Herboso's face just left of his nose, forming a black hole that quickly turned red. Undaunted by bone, the lead slug bored a tunnel and exited in a spray through his ear.

Unable to stop himself, Gabe let loose another round. It missed by half a meter.

And another.

The fifth shot took Herboso in the ribs. He said something Gabe couldn't hear, saliva bubbling on his lips, then dropped the rifle and fluttered backward. One leg collapsed, then the other. He crumpled like something struck from above.

Gabe drew the trigger back again. Though the hammer lifted from its seat, he didn't have the strength to complete the move. His hand felt broken. Maybe it was. The pistol again slipped from his grasp.

He wanted to fall right along with the gun, but he saw Ben's body through the moisture in his eyes and forced himself forward on his hands and knees, spotting the earth with his blood as he moved. When he reached his friend, he toppled and hit the ground with his face, one arm across Ben's chest. Behind him, Herboso bled out. The desert drank deeply until the man's body offered nothing more.

Gabe lifted his head, sand clinging to his lips. Through the blood he stared at Ben's face. The man looked no different dead than he had when he was alive.

I did this to you, Gabe thought. He'd led them all out here, and one of them had given his life for a cause that Gabe had never fully explained. Could he live with that forever? Or even for a single day?

He folded in on himself and gave the desert one more drink, this time with his tears.

And then Ben Cable sat up.

Ben came awake, forced to his senses by the throbbing in his head. It was the most devastating headache he'd ever experienced. When his eyes flashed open, a part of him expected to see the indescribable vista of the Other Side, the answer to the great riddle. Instead he saw Gabe staring at him with a look that Ben thought no less awestruck than Hamlet's when he recognized the ghost of his dead father.

Ben touched his own forehead, felt a considerable knot, found no blood.

"Ben?"

He spent a moment processing what had happened. Why was he still alive? He'd been shot in the head and there was no blood. He'd been shot in the head *and the bullet had bounced off.*

He looked at the sky and laughed the laugh of the immortals.

Let the bullets come like the rain that would never fall on the Atacama. Let armies rush in waves bearing muskets and machine guns. They held no power over him.

He raised his arms. *"Shit is holy!"*

CHAPTER FORTY

"Tilanna emerged from the rubble of the Kanyri fortress," Mira said as she passed between the tall rocks on the far side of the cemetery fence. "She counted herself blessed to be alive."

"Not blessed," Luke said. "Ben says on Mars you're either lucky or your dead."

"We need to hurry." She took her brother's hand and jogged through the obstructions, looking for her friends, hoping that they'd gotten lucky, too.

Luke pointed. "There!"

Mira darted between the boulders and saw Gabe on his back, Ben hovering over him.

She might have shouted Gabe's name. She never knew for sure. But moments later she was on her knees beside him, and there was so much blood that he couldn't be alive. A few feet away, the man in the too-big coat lay facedown, a red crater in the back of his head.

"Easy, sugar," Ben said to her, wrapping strips of a torn shirt around Gabe's hand. A similar bandage was already tied around his head. "He's a little woozy, and he has a right to be, all things considered. But I reckon he's going to live."

This time Mira was sure of the sound she made, a startled gasp of relief. She bent down closer to Gabe's face, forcing him to focus on her. "Gabriel? Sergio's alive. He's unconscious, but he seems to be breathing okay."

Gabe nodded. "You all right?"

"Did we win?" Luke asked.

"I'm fine," she told him. "We're all fine."

Gabe looked at Ben. "You want to tell me how you survived that?"

"Survived what?" Mira asked.

Gabe pointed to the swollen ridge above Ben's eye. "He was shot."

Ben smiled without saying a word.

Frowning at him, Gabe looked back at Mira. "Sergio?"

"We got here in time. He's not hurt, at least not badly."

Gabe pushed himself onto his elbows. "I want to see him."

Ben lashed a knot behind Gabe's knee. "Let me get these cuts covered first."

"No. I'm all right. Just help me up."

They got him to his feet. His skin was pale and his face smeared with his own blood, but Mira had never seen anyone more determined to move. She delayed him with a hand on his chest. "There's something else."

"What? What's wrong?"

"There's a man in there. Someone I think you'll want to meet."

"What are you talking about?"

"Come on. I'll introduce you."

Luke stayed with Ben as Mira retraced her steps. She heard him ask again if they'd won or if the dead man would rise up like a zombie, and in a dreamy sort of voice Ben replied that he wouldn't be surprised if that happened, not surprised at all.

"So it's over?" she asked, echoing her brother's concern.

"Maybe." Gabe coughed without covering his mouth. He limped heavily. "There's a lot of bodies to be ID'd. And probably TV reporters. And cops."

"Doesn't seem so difficult, considering." A true sense that it was finished still inched its way into her, slowly untightening the wires and giving her a bit more room to breathe. "You're really okay? Your arm isn't—"

"It's fine."

"Nothing I can do?"

"Well . . . right now a cup of coffee would be nice."

"Personally I'm thinking more along the lines of tequila."

His grin was faint, but Mira appreciated the effort.

"How about a cigarette?" she asked.

"Never again."

"Okay, I've got another question."

He tried to wipe the dirt from his mouth but ended up just streaking it across his chin. "Yeah?"

"Would you mind terribly if Tilanna, Amazon queen of Mars, held hands with you?"

Apparently he didn't mind at all.

Mira laced her fingers in his and led him into the crypt to meet the man he'd saved.

Ben thrust his hands on his hips and looked at Luke. "Why are you grinning like that?"

"Like what?"

"Like the cat that ate the chocolate-covered canary."

"What does *that* mean?"

"It means your sister and Sir Galahad just walked off into the sunset, the dead antichrist is lying in the dirt ten feet away, and you're smiling like a Cheshire Cat who's just smoked a doobie. What gives?"

"You're alive."

"I damn sure am, my young friend."

"I did it."

Ben's eyebrows converged at the center of his forehead. "Say what?"

"You're alive and I did it."

"Did *what*?"

Luke spoke very slowly, as if addressing a simpleton, which Ben figured wasn't far from the truth. "I *told* you. I saw his gun. Right there." He pointed to the sepulcher, where, upon their arrival, he'd reported to Ben that he'd encountered the rifle.

"Yeah, I dig. Then old Lucifer there came to fetch his fire-stick, cold-cocked you, and took off running with it."

"But not before." He smiled with all his teeth.

"Not before *what,* goddammit?"

"I put the pen in it."

"Huh?"

"You dropped your pen back at the rocks. I picked it up. Then I put it in the gun."

"Down the barrel?"

He nodded hugely.

"*My* pen? You shoved my pen into the rifle barrel?"

"It didn't blow up like I thought it would. Like the Road Runner's coyote. *Boom.* It didn't do that. But it still worked."

Ben, blinking, touched the tender spot on his head where the bullet had struck. He searched the ground, his eyes flying across the featureless soil . . .

An aluminum fragment the size of a matchstick lay a few feet away. And there, not far from that, was a more substantial shard, perhaps the very one that had struck him in the forehead.

"You gotta be shitting me."

"I wouldn't shit on you."

Ben forgot about the corpse and the gunplay and everything else, seeking and finding a third piece, this one still bearing a bit of gold inlay. The heavy Montblanc had deflected the bullet. Son of a bitch.

He sank down on one knee.

"Ben? What's the matter?"

Ben shook his head. After all this time, all these years . . .

"We're still going to finish the story, right?" Luke asked.

The story. *The story.* Here he was, all juiced up about the thought of completing his bit of science fiction, when his life was turning out to be far more fantastical.

I put the pen in it. Incredible.

"I want to see what happens next," Luke said.

Ben laughed. "Me, too, my friend." He laughed again. When you thought about it, Mars was a damn funny place.

Cold, but damn funny.

EPILOGUE

Gabe stared at the man in the glass.

The face that looked back at him was that of John Kennedy, handsome, self-assured, haunted by the coarseness of the world. On second thought, the face belonged to James Brown, full of hard living, hard loving, and undeniable soul.

"Yo, dummy," Gabe said to himself. "No more hiding in airport bathrooms."

Luckily he was alone. He saw no puddles of pants beneath the stall doors. This gave him time for one more weird indulgence: he dug into his carry-on and brought out the mask.

Made of plastic and papier-mâché, the mask depicted a laughing Incan god, rainbows peeling back from his eyes and feathers sprouting from his chin. In an earlier age, shamans had worn accoutrements like this to honor their deities. Currently they were peddled for five U.S. dollars apiece by Santiago street merchants preying on sucker tourists.

Gabe held it before his face and gazed through the eyeholes at the mirror.

There.

The rare clarity of it nearly stole his breath. Every color sang. The curve of the cheeks, the radiance of the artificial smile—was this what it was like to see a face?

He lowered the mask, causing his reflection to retreat to anonymity.

"Good luck with the curse," he said, repeating the next-to-last thing Fontecilla had said to him before finally signing the paper that permitted him to leave the country. Three weeks of debriefings and interviews had worn everyone like sandpaper on skin. With the exception of the tabloids, all parties involved just wanted it to end.

Curse? Hell, maybe it was or maybe it wasn't. Gabe zipped the mask into his duffel, figuring it didn't matter either way.

He left the restroom and stood lost in a swarm of strangers.

None of it made sense, neither their Spanish nor their appearance. Though their bodies differed, they could have been allies or enemies and he never would've known. He'd gotten a ride to the airport and needed to say good-bye to his driver, but damned if he could tell one face from the rest.

He turned slowly, eyes crawling for the hint of clothing or the color of a certain hand. Over the course of the last few weeks, he'd spent several evenings explaining to his new friends a little something called prosopagnosia. Ben, the dreamer, had been suitably fascinated by everything from the word's etymology to the disorder's effects on social interaction. Mira seemed saddened by it. Luke had made a much-needed joke. Telling them had been a catharsis more powerful than Gabe had predicted.

Fingers closed over his arm.

His reflexes had not cooled. Whatever had welded itself to his nerves during his time in the desert had not yet lost its heat. When he pivoted on the ball of his foot, he brought up his hand, where stitches had recently been removed, ready to shove or strike without time for consideration.

"Gabriel!"

The voice made sense. He exhaled and let his fist dissolve.

"I did not mean to frighten you," the Midnight Messenger said.

Gabe waved it away, wondering if his tension was as evident as it felt. "Not your fault. Lately I'm sort of high-strung."

"It is to be expected."

"I guess so." Over the last few days, Gabe and Alban Olivares had finally been able to trade tales, after all of the hospital visits and police reports and television spots. This was the man he'd watched sail through the Atacama night. The man he thought was dead. The man who sent him chasing after ghosts.

"How's your head?" Gabe asked.

Alban touched the bandage, now much smaller than before. "They tell me that women will think the scar is sexy."

"Your vision?"

"We made it to the airport in one piece." He might have grinned, but Gabe wasn't sure. "I need glasses. And no more rifle range."

Alban had been a firearms instructor, but that life was likely now behind him. Rumor had it that he was going to be medically discharged after receiving a commendation for locating and attempting to rescue his kidnapped nephew, Nicky Lepin.

The boy had been missing for weeks and police interest was waning when Alban, the indefatigable uncle, had bloodhounded his way to Mentiras. The only available clue was a shaky eyewitness account of a van seen in the area of Nicky's disappearance. The van was pulling a trailer, on top of which was mounted an ATV. Though the authorities were unable to plumb this lead any further, Alban got lucky in his ever-widening circle of interviews. The owner of a gas station on the edge of the Atacama reported occasionally selling fuel to a man astride a four-wheeler, a man who always drove away not on the developed highway but rather straight into the desert. Alban used that as his staging point three weekends in a row, pushing farther across the great emptiness with each foray. One night he came upon Mentiras, dead city of lies. He emptied his supplies and bundled the dying boy on his back.

Gabe entered the story a few hours later. He'd falsely thought the man was dead, and when he ran for help, Herboso had spirited Alban away.

"Your lady is picking you up when you land?" Alban asked.

"She's not exactly my lady."

"But you hope?"

"We'll see. Right now she's more focused on the book her brother is writing with their current houseguest."

"In the future? After the book?"

"You never know. Maybe I've earned a few good vibes from the universe."

"Tell them all again thank you. Thank you from me."

Gabe didn't know what to say to that. Alban had already paid them sufficient *gracias.* Gabe wanted only his friendship. "Check in on Sergio every now and then, okay?"

"Of course. He's young. His health is strong. But what will you do after you leave here?"

"Haven't you heard? I'm an internationally renowned astronomer. I did an interview on CNN. I'm just waiting for the offers to start pouring in." He couldn't tell whether Alban recognized the sarcasm or not.

"And what then?"

"I don't know. Mind my own business, for starters."

"You're not very good at that."

Gabe laughed. "So it seems." He offered his hand. "I'll call you."

Alban shook. "You still have my number?"

"Hey, I'm sure not losing track of you now. It was too damn hard finding you the first time." He wanted to say something more, something that could put the last and perfect dab of paint on this portrait of himself that he was leaving behind in Chile, but as always, he had only this awkward pause and this gentle blindness.

He turned and walked to the boarding gate.

Gabe was someone who never looked back. What good would it have done him? And maybe that was another piece of the curse or blessing or whatever it was. It no longer mattered. He had killed a man in the deadest place on Earth. Everything else played out from there, a rope on which he could either climb or descend as he saw fit. For now he opted to climb.

He took the phone from his pocket, a little pay-as-you-play model to get him by until he returned to the States. He sent a quick text to Mira. *One favor when I get there.*

She replied seconds later. *Name it, hero.*

That hat you wore in the desert, can you wear it when we go out?

Why?

He smiled to himself. *If we find the right lighting, maybe I'll get lucky.* He put the phone away and, remembering how the shadows shaped her face, headed for the boarding gate.

Something at the window drew his attention.

He turned. The array of reinforced plate-glass windows looked out onto the tarmac and a sky that had been turning grainier all morning. Gabe's reflection was there, mimicking him.

The last thing Fontecilla had said to him was "I hear the weather's changing."

Rain suddenly splattered the window.

Gabe ignored the image of himself. His eyes jumped skyward and then out across the vast airport grounds, where the rain fell and fell and reminded him of things the desert had made him forget.

The rain became a cascade, smearing his reflection from the glass.